"Bondurant is a nimble writer.... [His] prose is lyrical when the whiskey floods in, but also when the blood flows out.... Who can deny the power of a narrative so deeply rooted in childhood imaginings, when a mild and quiet grandfather hung those brass knuckles on the wall?"

—*The New York Times Book Review*

"[An] utterly engaging fable of bootlegging, revenge and remorse . . . Bondurant will be compared to Cormac McCarthy. It's warranted: Both have a gift for describing brutality so clearly that we see beauty in the honesty."

—*Men's Journal*

"[An] engrossing novel . . . Part family history, part fiction . . . [Bondurant is] wonderful at evoking historical atmosphere—the elaborate stills camouflaged in the woods, the music, the drunken gatherings that explode into shattering violence."

—*Entertainment Weekly*

"There is blood. There is whiskey. There is the scent of gunpowder and gasoline hanging above the space through which the Bondurants pass, unrepentant, robed in their own greed. It's a dark, flinty reimagination of what a memoir—and your grandfather's stories—can be."

—*Esquire*

"Whether fiction or biography, it succeeds in delivering a pungent slice of Americana, a portrait of a place and an era and a way of life that is part romantic, part viscerally violent, part metaphorical, all wrapped in a kind of rural poetry."

—*The Boston Globe*

"You have to go back to William Faulkner's novels about the Snopes clan to find the kind of cold-blooded Southern amorality that drives Matt Bondurant's second novel.... Bondurant's prose is thick with the kind of blood-soaked descriptions that would do Cormac McCarthy proud."

—*Washington City Paper*

"A stunning literary amalgam of genres."

—*San Francisco Chronicle*

"Bondurant has earned comparisons to Cormac McCarthy. . . . *The Wettest County in the World* is as densely layered and brooding as a Faulkner story."

—*The Roanoke Times*

"A remarkable story."

—*Paste Magazine*

"A gripping, relentless tale."

—*Publishers Weekly* (starred review)

"His rich descriptions of the county landscapes and the hardscrabble lives of its inhabitants invoke the small-town streets and struggling characters of Anderson's best-known novel, *Winesburg, Ohio*. At the same time, the action builds with the tension of a good thriller."

—*BookPage*

"A riveting story. . . . A gritty, violent tale, often dark but lightened by love and music, told through a relentless, driving narrative in clear, vivid prose."

—*Creative Loafing*

"Gritty, gripping depiction of very wild lives."

—*Kirkus Reviews*

"Gripping, hauntingly told . . . a treasure."

—*Library Journal*

"A book for thirsty American readers to guzzle down, a book for all young American writers to admire."

—Alan Cheuse, author of *The Fires*

"The gritty, suspenseful narrative gripped me and wouldn't let me go. It also touched my heart in all the right ways. Matt Bondurant's writing is as full of beauty as it is of verve and grit. Thank God it's legal to write so well."

—Lee Martin, author of *River of Heaven*

"A remarkably compelling, highly intelligent, and deeply moving novel."

—Margot Livesey, author of *The House on Fortune Street*

ALSO BY MATT BONDURANT

The Third Translation

WETTEST COUNTY
IN THE WORLD

A Novel
Based on a True Story

MATT BONDURANT

SCRIBNER

New York   London   Toronto   Sydney

SCRIBNER

A Division of Simon & Schuster, Inc.
1230 Avenue of the Americas
New York, NY 10020

This book is a work of fiction. Any references to historical events, real people,
or real locales are used fictitiously. Other names, characters, places, and incidents are
the product of the author's imagination, and any resemblance to actual events or
locales or persons, living or dead, is entirely coincidental.

Copyright © 2008 by Matt Bondurant

All rights reserved, including the right to reproduce this book or portions thereof
in any form whatsoever. For information address Scribner Subsidiary Rights
Department, 1230 Avenue of the Americas, New York, NY 10020.

First Scribner trade paperback edition January 2010

SCRIBNER and design are trademarks of
The Gale Group, Inc., used under license
by Simon & Schuster, Inc., the publisher of this work.

For information about special discounts for bulk purchases,
please contact Simon & Schuster Special Sales:
1-866-506-1949 or business@simonandschuster.com.

The Simon & Schuster Speakers Bureau can bring authors
to your live event. For more information or to book an event,
contact the Simon & Schuster Speakers Bureau at
1-866-248-3049 or visit our website at www.simonspeakers.com.

Text set in Granjon

Manufactured in the United States of America

7   9   10   8

Library of Congress Control Number: 2008014172

ISBN 978-1-4165-6139-2
ISBN 978-1-4165-6140-8 (pbk)
ISBN 978-1-4165-6164-4 (ebook)

For my parents

PART 1

In one county (Franklin) it is claimed 99 people out of 100 are making, or have some connection with, illicit liquor.

Official Records of the National Commission on Law Observance and Enforcement 1935, Vol. 4, p. 1075

What is the wettest section in the U.S.A., the place where during prohibition and since, the most illicit liquor has been made? The extreme wet spot, per number of people, isn't New York or Chicago . . . the spot that fairly dripped illicit liquor, and kept right on dripping it after prohibition ended . . . is Franklin County, Virginia.

Sherwood Anderson, *Liberty* magazine, 1935

Cruelty, like breadfruit and pineapples, is a product, I believe, of the South.

Sherwood Anderson, *A Story Teller's Story*

Prelude

1918

THE BRINDLED SOW stood in the corner, glowering at the boy. Jack Bondurant hefted a bolt-action .22 rifle with a deep blue octagon barrel, the stock chewed and splintered from brush and river-stone. He chambered a round, walked over to the sow and put the end of the barrel about a foot from a pink eye and squeezed the trigger. Across the yard his father and brother were tamping damp earth in the tobacco pit under the barn.

There was a crack and a slanting spray of blood and the great bulk of the sow shivered, the rifle falling into the muck, Jack leaping over the rails of the pen as the sow charged, a smear of blood on her forehead and a patch of glistening bone. The sow trotted around the pen, then backed into the corner. Jack retrieved his rifle through the boards, scrubbing off the muck with his shirtsleeve. He spat and worked the bolt action and reentered the pen and kneeling down in front of the sow, sighted the barrel down the length of her snout. He hooked the trigger again, *crack,* and the sow reared up slightly on its stubby back legs. On her forehead there was another slice of chipped bone, the blood spreading darkly into the pink eye. The shoats in the next pen set up a braying squeal and horned their snouts between the boards, ears flattened. Jack chambered another round, placed the barrel against the sow's head and fired. The bullet burrowed under the skin of her skull like a tunneling rodent, pulling back rippled folds over her eye. Jack squatted, watching the old sow pick herself up and circle on unsteady legs. He gripped the hacked stock of the rifle and rocked slowly on his heels, his feet burning in his boots. He squeezed his eyes and stifled a sob that erupted from his stomach.

When Jack looked up his older brother Forrest was there in the pen. A lean teenager with a permanent smirk, his blond hair dusted with red dirt from the tobacco pit, Forrest straddled the sow and sat down on her back, pulling her snout high with his forearm. As the sow's back arched the white folded flesh of her neck stretched tight. Reaching around with the other hand Forrest brought a long boning knife across her throat in a short rip of skin and metal. The blood came in a hot gush on the muddy straw and the sow's whine bubbled, the jet of lung air spraying from the open neck. Her body quivered and then went limp in Forrest's hands, tiny front legs dangling, body bent like a dead fish.

The next moment their father was there with the heavy chain and they used the tackle to hoist the carcass up to drain, Jack's father setting a metal bucket under the swaying body. Hot blood smoked in the calcified winter air. Jack crouched on the ground like a muddy toad, cradling the rifle and watching the stream of crimson like liquid fire. He was eight years old.

THAT NEXT SUMMER the Spanish Lady Flu epidemic swept through the southeastern states, finding its way into the deepest hollows and mountain ridges of Franklin County. The county went into self-imposed quarantine. Generations of families had known the ancient periodical ravages of sweeping illness like diphtheria, influenza, smallpox, and the certain knowledge of death's deliberate visitation ground all activity to a standstill as families huddled together in their homes. Jack's father, Granville Bondurant, closed up his vacant general store, itinerant mendicants and blasted road-men his only occasional customers. Families relied on the saved stores of food stockpiled in root cellars, cool springhouses. The Brodies who lived across the broad hill stopped coming down the dirt road by the house, as did the Deshazos, a black family that lived a half mile off. The pews of Snow Creek Baptist Church stood cockeyed empty and hooded crows roosted in the crude lectern.

The Bondurant family was prepared with plenty of dry goods from the store and Jack's mother had enough canned vegetables and meat to last them through the fall and winter. The family stayed close to the farm. It was a glorious time for Jack because it meant his older sisters Belva May and Era and his brother Forrest were around all the time, hanging about the house in the mornings, spending the long afternoon and evening in the family room by the stove. In those days Jack's father was what men called a cut-up, a man who grinned brightly through his thick beard in the evenings when his children rode his bouncing knee like a bucking horse or when he stood by the hot stove with other men at the store, quick with a wisecrack, his short white apron clean and starched. He didn't drink liquor, went to church regular, and still laughed a dozen times a day.

Forrest had a secondhand bicycle and in the afternoons Jack chased his brother down the wide field in front of the house, along the crumbling banks of the creek, laughing in the golden afternoons, the fields of purple clover at sunset, a haze of velvet across the rolling hills. After dinner his sisters clustered on the coarse rug in front of the stove, knitting and talking, Belva May and Era tying Jack's hands and feet with yarn, conspiring as Jack struggled, the girls laughing and speaking their own private language. His younger sister Emmy, the closest to his own age, clung to their mother, shadowing her through the kitchen and sitting in her lap in the rocker by the window. Emmy had an innocent air, naïve and quick to bawl, and so Jack was often left to entertain himself alone in the barns, long fields, wooded stretches, and the muddy branch of Snow Creek that ran through his parents' farm. In the evening his father Granville grinning through his beard, feet on the stove, their mother rocking by the window endlessly smoking hand-rolled cigarettes, blowing long plumes of smoke and watching the road for the rare traveler and for her oldest son, Howard, who was due to return from the war in Europe.

Jack's oldest brother Howard spent most of 1919 on an army troop ship, first crossing the Atlantic from England and then anchored in Norfolk harbor in quarantine. Influenza, was rampant on the ship, nearly half the men consumed with it on the voyage across, the deck littered with gaunt men in stretchers hacking and moaning into the scraps of cloth laid over their faces. At night Howard slept on a high stack of onion crates in an attempt to get space on the crowded ship and away from the red-eyed coughing devils, weary officers wading through the crowds with flailing canes, the reeling sick that clung to the rails. As he tried to sleep, struggling through the massive stink of onions, Howard tried to think of the hills and valleys of home, the smell of deep clay, the foaming loam of a freshly plowed field, the hollyhocks and honeysuckle along Snow Creek. But in his dreams the black sickness spread through his body and across the water and across the hills and into everyone he knew, and when he opened his eyes in the morning there was the horror of men dying in their own filth.

A third of the men in his company died in the six weeks they sat floating there in the harbor in a line with dozens of other ships. Every night the harbor blazed with the ghostly fires made of the clothing and belongings of the deceased.

When finally released Howard wandered through the city like a blind man. He quickly got blistering drunk on rotgut liquor and the next morning burned his service uniform and papers in a trash-strewn lot behind a boardinghouse.

A few days later Howard came off the train in Roanoke like a specter, the flesh curved into the hollows of bone. Howard was a giant man, broadly built and more than six and a half feet tall and his massive frame was wrapped tight like a ghoulish nightbreed. Granville came by the depot to pick him up in early November, the first frost wilting the creeper along the roadside and Howard never spoke of what happened to him in France or aboard the ship, and no one ever asked. For Jack, his oldest brother Howard was a stranger, just some older boy he happened to be related to, a bulky shape he remembered from early mornings as a young child, now a man stomping through the house, an angular shadow that crouched at the table and quietly inhaled his food. Howard kept away from the house most of the time, staying out through the night, and when he returned he reeked of corn liquor and collapsed into his bed like a dead man.

One night in December, toward the end of the epidemic, George Brodie hammered on the Bondurants' front door in the middle of the night. Jack was tucked under his heavy quilt, swaying lightly on the rope bed he shared with Forrest, and when the noise started his brother shot up and was out the bedroom door before Jack pried his eyes open. Brodie kept pounding away on the door until Granville jerked it open and Jack heard his father curse *Goddammit, Brodie!* Jack slipped out of the warm bed, the air sharp with cold, and stepping into the hall he saw George Brodie on his knees, the moonlight shining over his shaking shoulders, hands covering his face.

Jack had never seen a grown man cry before, and for a moment it struck his sleep-addled mind that Brodie was sleepwalking like Forrest sometimes did. The Brodies lived a mile away if you came through the narrow wood trail, more than three if you took the road. *Had Brodie gone mad?* Brodie raised his head and said something Jack couldn't make out, but he saw the tear streaks on the man's dirty face; he heard the crack in his voice that was unmistakable to a child. Granville turned and said something to Forrest and Jack watched his brother turn and come back down the hall, shirtless, his skin milky in the hazy light. Forrest shoved Jack inside and told him to go back to bed and shut the door.

For the next few minutes there was a hurried discussion in the front room. Jack heard his mother in the kitchen, the bitter scent of brewing chicory coffee. He lay there, staring into the dark, listening as hard as he could. Then Forrest saying something and his mother's voice raising a bit, an edge to it: *I won't have it, Gran, I won't have it.* The sound of his sister Era crying out. The sound of more weeping that made Jack shudder in the swinging bed. The front door shut, the gleam of an oil lamp under the door winked out, and footsteps padded down the hall. Then silence.

Jack lay there for nearly an hour before he understood that Forrest wasn't coming back, that Brodie had borne him off into the night and his parents had let him do it, and he gripped his blankets and grimly fought tears until morning.

Granville and Forrest returned late the next afternoon. Jack rushed the door as they walked up the slope but his mother swept him back with her arm. She had set out a supper on a small end table out by the toolshed, chicken, biscuits, and greens covered with cloth napkins, a pitcher of water, along with buckets of water, towels, and soap. Jack watched from the window as Granville and Forrest ate their supper out in the cold, their breath steaming in the yard. After they ate they built a large fire and filled the hog-scalding trough with water and began to strip down. His mother kept his sisters in their room but let Jack stand there as his father and brother washed themselves with the hot water, dumping buckets of it over their heads, pouring it over their reddening skin. Jack was astonished at his father's hairy body, a large swatch covering his chest, the thickness of his middle, his narrow legs and knobby knees, how he tottered when he walked. His face was set like granite as he tossed their clothes into the fire. Next to his father, Forrest looked small and frail, hugging himself against the cold, but he turned and spying Jack gave him a grin that lit the young boy's heart on fire.

They toweled off, wrapped in blankets and sat by the fire, Forrest every once in a while glancing toward the house where Jack and his mother stood in the window. The afternoon began to fade into evening, sparks from the fire swirling in the wind. Jack's mother tensed up, raising her shoulders and rapped sharply on the window with her knuckles. His mother and father exchanged a long look from across the yard and Jack knew that some essential transaction was occurring. She nodded imperceptibly and Granville got up and came toward the house, Forrest following. His mother fumbled with the door, ran across the porch, and threw herself onto Granville, clutching at his back with both hands as the blanket slipped from his shoulders. Granville put his arms around her and rested his cheek on the top of her head, his beard frosted with breath.

Forrest walked by his clinched parents and stepping up on the porch, gave Jack a grin and a solid punch in the chest before striding back into the bedroom with the blankets trailing behind him, his pink shoulders shining.

That night when they lay in bed Jack asked him what had happened but Forrest said Jack was too young and that he'd tell him later when he was older. Jack persisted and Forrest told him that George Brodie panicked when his youngest daughter began to convulse in her bed, her pillow a smear of bloody spew. His wife was already comatose and near death. Granville said he would come, and would bring his oldest daughter Belva May to help. Jack's mother protested. Era was inconsolable; she threw herself around her sister's neck. Granville was going to insist until Forrest spoke up, saying that he would go instead of Belva May, and with the smoky oil lantern in hand the two men and the boy walked back through the woods and over the ridge to the farm, where Brodie's family lay dying.

Then Jack asked if Forrest had the Spanish Lady Flu and Forrest chuckled and said nothing.

Are we going to get sick too? Jack asked. Are we going to die?

Forrest was quiet for a moment before turning to Jack in the dark. The windows were tacked over with quilts for the cold and there was no light but Jack could tell he was looking at him.

You think anything can kill the old man? Forrest said.

Of course not, Jack thought, but didn't say anything. Their father? The world would stop turning first. He blinked in the darkness. Forrest's eyes glimmered like fading coals.

That's right, Forrest said, as if he heard his thoughts.

Nothing can kill us, Forrest said. We'll *never* die.

THE NEXT MORNING Howard returned to the house, rumpled and surly. He had spent the night sprawled under a pile of burlap sacks behind a filling station in Boone's Mill, sleeping off a half liter of white mule. He gulped a cold breakfast of biscuits and ham on the front porch, wiping his hands on his greasy overalls, Jack sitting quietly beside him, drinking in the sour smell of his older brother. Howard stood and gave Jack a good pop on the back of the neck before lumbering off to the barn to help Granville with feeding.

A few days later Jack's mother, Forrest, Belva May, and Era were all stricken with the flu. The following days passed quickly. Jack felt like he was still in the twilight between sleep and wakefulness. Emmy knelt by the water pump, wringing the laundry between her red fingers as she rocked back and forth. Granville stood quietly for hours in the dim hallway like a ghost. Howard sitting awkwardly on the front step, long legs angled in front of him, hat in his hands, his slablike face blank.

On the morning his mother died, Jack stood by his father's chair and Granville put his hand on his son's shoulder as he gazed out the window toward the long road. Howard leaned against the stove, arms crossed over his broad chest, frowning at the floor.

Oh boys, Granville said. It's all gone.

Howard raised his head and stared at his father.

All the goodness has gone out of the world, Granville said.

There were tears on his father's face and Jack's heart squeezed like a fist. Though he tried hard not to, he broke down and sobbed on his father's shoulder.

Jack's mother died first, then a day later Belva May, followed immediately by Era. Forrest lay in bed like a stone for a week, his face impassive and leaden, refusing to eat anything. His skin puckered and turned an impossible shade of blue for a few days, soft and hazy like a robin's egg. Then one morning he rose from his bed. Afterward Forrest always retained the knobby aspect of illness, and in certain types of light his skin still had a blue cast to it. When he emerged after that week, his body gaunt and wasted, his eyes sunken, to join Granville, Emmy, Howard, and Jack at the breakfast table, it was as if his strength had withered and focused itself like a leather strap. Jack remembers taking a biscuit from the plate, his shaking hand.

His mother and sisters laid out on the floor, covered with a quilt.

Nobody said anything.

Chapter 1

1934

SHERWOOD ANDERSON crossed the Franklin County line, threading his car over a one-lane bridge that lay in a gentle saddle in the road. A few hundred yards beyond the bridge Anderson passed a filling station: a simple clapboard square and a steeply angled roof with an upper story that jutted out from the front, providing a covered pull-in spot in front of the narrow porch. A pair of petrol pumps stood in front, with hand cranks and glass spheres on top filled with fuel. Several things about the place held Anderson's gaze: a porch, but unlike most rural filling stations this one had no chairs and no name on the building, or advertisements for anything. Four cars were in the lot, brand-new sedans with engines running, as if lined up for gas though nobody was pumping any. A group of men stood by the front door, men in long coats and hats who all turned and watched Anderson drive by. A storage shed was set slightly up the hill that rose behind the store, a squat cinder-block structure with an open door like a key slot and as Anderson passed a tall, gangly man in his shirtsleeves and hat emerged from the building with a wooden crate in his arms. It seemed like his eyes locked directly onto Anderson's face. Then a blur of green-gold trees and the tires humming on the road and Anderson hunched over the wheel, humming up the backside of Grassy Hill and into Rocky Mount, the seat of Franklin County. Have to remember that spot, Anderson thought to himself, will have to run by on the way back to Roanoke and see what it's all about. Though even at that moment he knew that the look on the faces of the men waiting at the station and the eyes of the tall man in the storage shed would make that difficult. Anderson had lived in rural Virginia long enough to know that look, the simple, insolent expression that said: *Mind your own goddamn business.*

Anderson picked up speed down the empty road, blasting through whirling vortexes of leaves. Route 33 bisected Franklin County north-south in a jagged stroke, winding through the steep hillsides and deep hollows. It was the longest paved road in the county: Most roads were still hard-packed gravel, a soil-sand-clay mix, or merely weedy ruts that disappeared into field or forest. Driving through the hills of southern Virginia was reminiscent of some favorable sensations for Anderson, and he thought of the old restlessness. It was a good feeling to be on the move again.

THE TWO MEN Sherwood Anderson came to see lay in a crowded public ward in the Rocky Mount Hospital, a long windowless room with a dozen beds. Men of middling age, lined faces, stubble, indeter-minate. The first of the two lay motionless, tucked into the sheets like a sewing needle. He stared up at the ceiling with open, swollen eyes, his skin blanched like boiled meat, the bedding stained with a yellow-ish fluid around his groin area. Next to him the other man had a deep crimson scar running between his eyes and across his forehead, as if he'd been branded with a hot iron. A puffed goiter like a weathered leather bag hung under his chin. He was drenched with sweat, moan-ing and jerking his upper body from side to side, delirious with fever, the lower half of his body encased in thick plaster. The doctors told Anderson that a good piece of his tongue was also missing, likely due to an earlier injury. Anderson introduced himself and pulled up a chair between their beds. The man with the injured groin ran his eyes over Anderson for a moment before returning his gaze to the ceiling. His skin was tight like a sausage and he stunk of rot.

The doctors told Anderson that neither man would say what happened to them, but it was clear that one man's legs had been meticulously shattered, from ankle to hip, and the second man had been badly mutilated in the groin area. The police didn't get a thing either; the two men hadn't said a word, and they'd had no visitors. *There wasn't anything else to it,* the doctor said, shrugging. The mutilated man was hanging on by a thread and the infection would take him soon. It was a miracle he survived this long. *The blood loss was extensive,* the doctor said. *Clearly left for dead. Somebody anonymously notified us. Otherwise they'd be dead, easy.* The man with the shattered legs might pull through, but it was sure he would never stand or walk again.

SHERWOOD ANDERSON originally came to Rocky Mount to write a story for *Liberty* magazine about a woman named Willie Carter Sharpe. *Moonshine,* said the editors, the snoops up north; these hill people were living off mountain whiskey, bootlegging; it was still the cash crop. The Volstead Act of 1919, the legal enforcement of the Eighteenth Amendment, had created a many-headed hydra of illicit manufacture and trade in these mountains. Production didn't end in 1933 with the repeal of Prohibition: To avoid the heavy taxes on legal distillation, people still made their own or brought it in on rumrunners off the coast, but now that Prohibition was over people wanted to hear more about that supposed frontier period. These people weaned their children on the stuff, they said. They cooked their eggs in it, put it in their morning coffee. Everyone wanted it to go on, Anderson thought, the swells making piles of money and the consumers who savored that rancid sip of illegal bathtub gin in some dirty hole in the Upper West Side of Manhattan. They wanted that added flavor of illegality, and they wanted the dangerous myth, the wild notion of gunplay and desperation. *Get close,* they said. *The people, the characters, their desires, the inner lives and passions: That's what you do best after all.*

There was a big trial gearing up in Franklin County, a trial that was going to clean up the remnants of a messy, long-running battle between bootlegging syndicates including the commonwealth's attorney, who it was rumored would be accused of racketeering and conspiracy. All the major bootleggers in the county, including Willie Carter Sharpe, if they could catch her, were being called in for grand-jury testimony. Sharpe had originally married a big-shot bootlegger and soon became the principal driver for the operation, driving pilot cars as the caravans of booze careened and smashed their way through the hills of rural towns and into the conduits of the major cities, becoming a celebrity in the process. They said Sharpe had movie-star looks and diamonds set in her teeth. New York City society women sent her passionate love letters, desperate to be with her. *Liberty* wanted Anderson to bring the story to a national audience.

Sherwood Anderson had been in the southwestern part of Virginia for most of nine years by 1934. He built a house in Marion, the seat of Smyth County, to the west of Franklin, higher up in the mountains. He purchased two local newspapers and set about life as a small-town editor. Anderson was aware that more than one literary wag had suggested he was reverting to his former life, trying to go back to some lost place of youth. But he knew he wasn't trying to revert to George Willard and the town of Winesburg: In fact it was the thing he hoped to distance himself from.

While his house was being built, Anderson squatted in a rude shack on the hillside above. He spent his days watching the score of mountain men crawling over the frame of his house, working in their methodical, efficient way. He had a deal with his publisher, Liverwright, who would send him one hundred dollars a week plus a percentage of his sales, including those for the Modern Library reprints of *Poor White* and *Winesburg, Ohio*. Liverwright would publish whatever Anderson sent him. In those days Anderson's writing desk was neat as a pin, and he eventually went up to New York and begged Liverwright to let him out of the deal. The house he built was called Ripshin.

• • •

ANDERSON CAME FROM Ripshin the day before and stayed over at a hotel in Roanoke, then met with the editor of *The Roanoke Times* in the morning. It was still early when he left, the sky moving from purple to lavender and the trees along the road dropped their leaves, and he was glad to be out on such a morning and away from his house. Anderson ground his teeth and gripped the wheel when he thought of his naïve hope that Ripshin would become a rustic literary salon. A place where the intelligentsia would gather about him in his bucolic paradise. Perhaps even his friend Gertrude Stein would come and pace the floor of his study with him, talking painters and semantics.

Instead the two newspapers were holding him hostage; he was at the offices nearly every week, working with the printers and writing nearly the entire thing himself. To let off steam Anderson developed a character named Buck Fever in a column that dispensed humor and folksy wisdom, a sort of Will Rogers meets Mark Twain.

By 1934 Ripshin was filled with noisy, bothersome people, people who overstayed their welcome, people whom Anderson once felt were true peers and comrades but now seemed more like chattering urbanites out for a turn in the country, and he was merely the innkeeper. His only solace was Eleanor, the young woman he met in Marion during the final years of his last marriage. They were married the year before, and during his travels he wrote her long, passionate letters that shocked himself and that seemed to contain the vitality that he usually was able to produce only in his fiction. In fact the letters, the words and phrases, the sentiments and ideas, seemed to come from some shadowy character, not fully formed, that lay deep inside him.

THE EDITOR OF *The Roanoke Times* said it was likely some kind of payback. Sitting in his office that morning before visiting the hospital, cheap cigars in the cluttered, paper-filled room; Anderson felt sleepy and despondent.

Likely the trade, the editor said.

He had eyes like holes in a meat pie and an annoying snarl to his speech, talking out of one side of his mouth.

Those boys did something to somebody, he said. And when nobody talks, you can bet there is liquor involved.

The editor confirmed the rumors of the coming trial. Closed grand jury.

Well, the editor said, you won't find much of a story down in Franklin County. Unless you manage to pry it out of a dead man's jaws.

Such wit, Anderson thought. What a clod.

Sir, Anderson said, I am no greenhorn. I know these people and their plight well. I know something about moonshine liquor.

Pieface nodded, giggling, his broad frame shivering.

You spend enough time in Franklin, the editor said, you'll start tripping over it.

The editor waved his cigar in the smoky air in front of him. Anderson's stomach let out a whine of discomfort and he wished he'd had breakfast.

There's a fella, the editor said, down at the Rocky Mount jail right now. A fella named Tom C. Cundiff. But you won't get spit from him. The man's crazy as a coon. Couple fellas in there with him, all steady shiners. I wouldn't talk to any of them unless they was behind bars and would be there for a while. Actually I ought to tell you who *not* to try and talk to.

That'd be fine, Anderson said.

The editor dug through a file drawer next to his desk, pulled out a thick sheaf of papers. He licked a thumb and selecting a few pages of proof copy tossed it onto Anderson's lap.

Maybe you seen this, he said, from a few years back.

December 20, 1930: DEPUTIES GUN DOWN BROTHERS
AT MAGGODEE CREEK
Bondurant Brothers Shot Trying to Run Blockade
Near Burnt Chimney

I wouldn't seek *those* boys out if I were you, the editor said.

I'm not planning on starting trouble, Anderson said.

The editor put his hands together on the desk and craned his pie-face closer to Anderson, who could not help but lean away.

I'll tell you what, the editor said. There's only *two* things up in them Franklin County hills for those who are looking: *stump whiskey* and *free ass whippin's.*

BEFORE GOING TO the hospital Anderson pulled into a filling station just outside Rocky Mount to get something to eat. Three men and a young boy sat, chairs leaning back, against the clapboard station wall that was peppered with metal signs advertising Granger Rough Cut Tobacco, Mineraltone Hogs, Harrod's Medicinal Powders. They stared at him brazenly as he came up: blank, open faces that disclosed nothing but slight contempt. Anderson said hello and received a nod from each in return, even the small boy, who, Anderson noticed, was shifting around a quid of tobacco in his tanned cheek. Inside a woman stood behind a counter in a calico-print dress. A potbellied stove stood in the middle of the store, surrounded by a moat of wood chips. Anderson walked through the few aisles of scant merchandise. Two dirty-faced young girls eyed him from where they squatted against boxes and played with dolls made of burlap. He bought a couple packs of crackers—*nabs,* they called them in this part of the state—and a bottle of birch beer. At the counter, receiving his change, Anderson could hear the faint wind singing against the metal roof, the creaking chairs on the porch.

Anderson pulled out of the lot and onto a muddy road that spooled out before him into the dark trees. He rubbed the steamed windshield with his bare hand and stamped the chill out of his boots on the floorboards. Sure, he thought, it's everywhere; the streams are running thick with alcohol, the sky raining whiskey. He beat the steering wheel with his fists and screamed at the road.

• • •

AT THE Rocky Mount Hospital Anderson produced a bottle of whiskey from his coat and offered it to the man with the mutilated groin. A foolish gesture perhaps but he didn't know what else to do. The man's eyes flickered on the bottle and his lip curled in a sneer of contempt.

Is it money? Anderson asked. Why don't you just tell me what happened?

He sat at their bedside for almost an hour. The moaning man with the broken legs lapsed into unconsciousness and slept fitfully, his hands twitching under the sheets. Nurses came into the ward to tend to other patients and Anderson watched them squeaking down the row of beds, their crisp uniforms crackling like paper. After a while Anderson unscrewed the bottle of Canadian and had a bolt himself, the hot whiskey catching him by surprise and he coughed sharply, drawing looks from others in the ward.

Later Anderson walked the corridors and asked some nurses and doctors about what was reported in the papers and got nothing but shrugs and nervous smiles. Nobody at the hospital wanted to say anything. He sat beside the two men for another hour and read *The Roanoke Times,* sipping a paper cup of whiskey. When he finished the paper Anderson stood in the door to the ward with a cigarette and watched the two men, both of them now unconscious, their sheets soaked with sweat. Anderson felt his own damp jacket, his mouth dry as ash. He had drunk nearly a third of the bottle and yet felt completely sober. His trouser cuffs were stained with red clay, and he could feel the grit of it on his hands.

———◆———

AS HE TRAVELED through Franklin County over the previous few months on his long, meandering drives, Sherwood Anderson habitually stopped at farms, pulling onto rutted roads wherever he spotted men working in the fields. He walked with lean farm boys through the wide rows of tobacco in the dead of July, the sharp green of the drooping leaves, waist high and spreading wide in the sun. The boys and men said little, unwrapping their dinner, sandwiches of cold pork and biscuit, gulping at their food as they sat in a shady spot under the withered elms. Their eyes flitted across Anderson from time to time but mostly they seemed to be staring at something far, far off, their faces, necks, and arms burned deep from the sun. The earth cracked like a puzzle, the fine dust of that clay getting into everything, and by the day's end, standing on the sloped floor of his rented room in Rocky Mount, or back at Ripshin, he invariably found the red grains inside his shoes, in his socks, his pockets, in the corners of his eyes. Along the roads large swaths of clay on road cuts exposed like open wounds. When families sat down to eat supper freshly scrubbed from the fields they still carried the grit in the fine lines of their eyes and wrists, and it clung to the vegetables, it was baked deep into the hoecakes and corn bread, it lived in the crispy skin of the chicken, the blood of the pork.

Anderson marveled at the stoic endurance of these people, their masterful silence and complete allegiance to utility in all things. Barns were constructed from castoffs, old signboards and discarded pulpwood. Ax handles were filled with half a dozen tightening wedges; rusted plows hammered back into shape until they snapped, then to be reheated at the makeshift forge and hammered again; the pump handle a length of copper pipe; vehicles cannibalized and rebuilt, each permutation carrying the original further from the initial purpose and appearance. The detritus of their efforts lay rotting in the hollow below the house, a ravine of rusted muck. Even then, in the evening the old farmer would peruse his personal junkyard and wonder if he could get that old tie-rod to fit his thresher hub. It was a never-ending battle to make do with what you already had, and when things gave out they literally exploded into red dust.

ANDERSON WAS LEAVING the hospital when an orderly in the hall motioned for him to follow. Now what? Anderson thought. He was tired and the slight tang of a daytime hangover was coming on. The orderly led Anderson down another hall and eventually stopped at a door, holding out his hand, his oily face impassive and dead-eyed, and when Anderson gave him the whiskey he swirled the bottle around, eyeing the level, shrugged, and tucked it into his back pocket and extended his hand again. Anderson laid a dollar on his horny palm, and the orderly led him into a dim storeroom filled floor to ceiling with shelves stacked with shimmering jars of various sizes. The orderly pulled a cord for the light.

This were delivered to those boys the day after they was admitted, the orderly said, pulling a cloth off a half-gallon mason jar.

Just in a paper sack, he said, no note or nothin'.

Anderson looked and tried to understand what he was seeing.

That there is what you call white lightnin', the orderly said. Mountain licka.

The jar full of clear liquid and a grayish mass with loose tendrils, bulbous, mottled, a slight tincture of blood like a phantasm. A pair of irregular spheres, suspended like dead eyes.

And that'd be that boy's tackle floatin' in there, the orderly said, the man's gonads.

Anderson blanched, the sour whiskey rising in his throat.

Chapter 2

1928

JACK AND HOWARD BONDURANT stood on the corner outside the Whitehead General Store in Rocky Mount. Nearly six o'clock and the streets were clearing out, everyone settling down to their supper. Howard's muddy boots stretched over the curb, a sack of meal over his shoulder steadied with one hand. In the other hand he had a burlap sack containing a side of salted bacon. Howard's face was reddened from the cold March wind blowing in from the mountain. After the war Howard quickly put on weight and now at twenty-eight years old had packed a dense layer of muscle and fat on his massive frame, his chest broad and arms like uncut hams.

A gut-rusted Ford truck gunned up the street and drew up at the curb, exhaust rattling like a machine gun. Danny Mitchell stuck his head out the window.

You comin'? Danny said.

What took so damn long? Howard said.

Danny grinned. He had a miraculous set of white teeth, evenly set with fresh pink gums.

Howard set the bacon and meal in the truck bed and climbed into the cab.

What 'bout the County Line? Jack said. You gonna be there tonight?

Yeah, Howard said, and you ain't.

Jack spit on the curb. He wore a wool driving cap and his trousers were tucked into his knee-high boots, laced up tight.

Howard rapped on the dashboard and Danny floored the engine and the Model A clattered down East Court Street. Jack watched the truck as it jolted down the hill, hands jammed in his pockets. No damn direction or vision, Jack thought. When the truck was out of sight Jack tucked his hat down tight and started jogging lightly up the sidewalk into town.

DANNY MITCHELL took the truck out of gear and let it coast down the hill. Between his legs he held a jar with a metal screw-top lid. He steered the shuddering truck with his knees and took a deep drink, his eyes watching the road through the glass jar. In a minute they were outside Rocky Mount and heading south on 33.

Have a taste, Danny said.

Danny offered the jar to Howard, who took it in his broad palm, holding it up to the light. The liquid was clear at the top, a viscous brown swirl at the bottom. Howard shook the jar and beads the size of birdshot rose wavering and lurching, a thick mushroom of disturbed murk, swelling like an eruption, dislodging small bits of twigs, bark, and dirt that rose and drifted like fog.

This here's made with tadpoles and swampwater, Howard said.

Danny bayed like a hound at the windshield.

That there is East Lake corn, he shouted. The best there is! Carolina mule.

Howard sniffed the murky liquid that slopped onto his hand as the truck left the hard road and the tires settled into the worn dirt ruts that ran through the hills toward Snow Creek. He took a mouthful and ran it over his tongue, his throat constricting and something almost solid lurched in his chest, like something alive, bringing salt to his eyes, and as he swallowed all the solids in his head cavities liquefied and snot ran freely from his nostrils.

This the worst damn whiskey that I ever put a lip on.

Hell, Danny said, you jus' be careful. It'll get *on* you. Wake up with your liver in yo' sock.

Howard settled back into the seat and jammed his legs into the cramped footwell. In his pocket Howard had four dollars and thirty-five cents, all the money he had in the world. The rest of his money was in the corn, malt, rye, and molasses at the still up on Turkeycock Mountain. In three days, after they ran all ten mash boxes, they'd have 120 gallons of good liquor. They should get at least two dollars a gallon, and after supplies and splitting with Danny and Cundiff, he'd have nearly a hundred dollars to take home to Lucy and the baby. Then there were his debts: He owed Forrest sixty dollars, his father at least forty from due bills at the store. The whiskey slowly melted in Howard's stomach and he felt it settle there in the base of his spine. The sunlight came across the windshield and the trees swam overhead in great funnels of spiny black, amber, and cornflower yellow. Beside him Danny spat and wrestled with the wheel, hands and elbows clamped to it. A miasma of odors filled the cab, the strongest being the reek of the driver, a foul combination of crotch rot, toe jam, tobacco, hog shit, and soured saliva.

A fool idea to make a run in winter, Howard thought. They'd have to keep the mash warm all night and through the next day, a tricky thing to do with simple pit fires and no device to measure temperature other than fingers. Then he'd have to borrow Danny's truck tonight to get back down to the County Line Restaurant to help Forrest. It was part of the arrangement for the new loan: Forrest needed backup for a big sale to some men from Shootin' Creek set to go off around midnight. It would take Howard at least an hour to get to the restaurant in the dark, so he figured he'd get the still hot, the mash boxes set, and head out and let Cundiff and Danny handle it through the night.

Danny looked over to him and grinned. Well damn, Howard thought, Danny ain't such a bad fella anyway. He took another slug from the jar and passed it back. Howard sneezed three times in quick succession.

I'll tell you what Danny-boy, Howard said. We gonna need to stop off somewheres and get a better pop o' whiskey. That shit ain't fit to slop hogs.

JACK RAN ALONG East Court Street, dodging the stray pedestrians who slouched off with their late-afternoon purchases. He stayed off the muddy streets, rutted with tire tracks and mule dung. Downtown Rocky Mount was lined with a few blocks of shops bordered by rooming houses and apartments, two hotels and a strip of agricultural-supply warehouses, and the streets were perpetually littered with animal refuse and farming scrap. As Jack neared the Little Hub Restaurant he slowed to a walk and pulling off his cap fluffed it and set it back on his blond head at the appropriate angle. He gave his weathered boots another look over, flicking away some street mud, smoothing his britches and coat. He had a fine sheen to him in the plate glass of the colored barbershop and he felt erect and indomitable. Jack paused in front of Slone's Haberdashery and inspected the burgundy calfskin boots with brass eyelets in the display. He scratched the top of his foot with the sole of his other boot. My first two dollars free and clear, Jack thought. The creamy yellow insides of the boots looked smooth and he imagined they felt like soft butter. Inside the store a man in a fur-trimmed ankle-length coat stood at the counter making a purchase. Jack eyed the brand-new Dual Cowl Duesenberg Phaeton angled at the curb. The two-tone paint job gleamed deep blue-black in the afternoon light, a fine spray of red mud on the running boards and whitewalls. He had never seen one in Franklin County before, only in advertisements. That car cost more than ten goddamn Fords, Jack thought, maybe more.

When Jack reached the restaurant he found his friend Cricket Pate at the counter, drinking a cup of coffee and eating a doughnut.

Hey Cricket, Jack said. You finished stuffin' your gullet?

Yeah, Cricket said. Let's get on.

Cricket crammed the doughnut into his mouth and the two young men set off down the street to Cricket's ramshackle Series 80 Pierce-Arrow coupe.

Lemee drive, Jack said.

Jack fired down the street in the rattling heap, Cricket shaking his head and holding on to the frayed ceiling.

C'mon, Jack, he said. Ain't no reason to bust us up.

Cricket Pate was an old classmate of Jack's from the Snow Creek school, though Cricket was three years older and didn't stay in past the third grade. A reedy kid with awkward bowed knees from childhood malnutrition—a case of the rickets that made him walk like he was straddling a fence. Cricket had been living on Smith Mountain since his mother died when he was fourteen; he never knew his father. He'd shoot squirrel and run trotlines for mud cats in the lake under the mountain, sometimes picking up slop work during harvesting season. He was married at seventeen to a red-haired strumpet from Sontag and divorced the next year. Cricket was famous around the county for his inventive on-the-spot fixes for farm equipment; it was said that with a bit of spit and twine he could get your tractor or thresher up and running in a slap. And since he was fourteen Cricket made liquor up on the mountain, small batches of rotgut and jimmylegs, whatever he could scrape up.

Relax, Jack said. I can drive anything.

As he drove out of town to the south Jack worked his boots off and scratched his feet, careful to set his boots on the seat and out of the crusty mix of mud and leaves in the footwells, working the clutch with his bare feet. The two young men had the remnants of a cracked old still lined with mud daub on Smith Mountain, but no worm or cap and no money to stake the ingredients. Jack was hoping to get Howard to take him and Cricket on but he couldn't get his oldest brother to even courtesy the subject. Jack thought for a moment about heading west over to the County Line Restaurant, to see if Forrest needed some help; perhaps Forrest would lend him the money. But he knew that his brother wouldn't take to it: He never did. Besides, Cricket had to get back across to Smith Mountain by dark and Jack promised him if he took him into town he would get Howard to take them on as partners for a run. He knew Cricket had spent his last nickel to get a cup of coffee and doughnut while Jack talked to his brother. They drove down the darkening road in silence, Jack slowing now as he took the turns, turning the wheel easy with his palms. Cricket hadn't asked how it went and Jack figured he didn't have to tell him.

NEARING DARK and trudging up Turkeycock Mountain, Danny working his way through the brush and jimsonweed with his hands, one holding the nearly empty jar, cursing the bluestone protrusions and roots and the cold. Howard a few paces behind, off to the side a dozen yards so as not to create the hint of a trail, shouldering the meal and bacon. The trees hung in stark relief against the dark blue sky, coal black like negative images, leafless and spindled. Howard found himself wishing for the warmth and cover of leaves.

After a short plateau the two men walked through a copse of birch trees, and then on the eastern side of the mountain again and into a dense thicket of pine and gum that stood against the side of an exposed rock face nearly forty feet high. Firelight flickered at the base of the rock and Howard grimaced at the thought of how it would look from down in the valley; the square rock face lit up like a rising planet on the side of the mountain. But nobody would come up here, even if they knew. *Especially* if they knew. One of the easiest ways to end up with a faceful of birdshot was to creep up on an active moonshine camp at night. Danny began to call out toward the light, a series of high repeated whoops.

Tom C. Cundiff sat on a log staring into the fire, a shotgun over his knees. He wore a scuffed bowler pulled low, a wool scarf tight around his neck. He was a wiry man with oversized facial features, his eyes broadly apart on his face and his limbs oddly stunted. The still sat in the shadows behind Cundiff, a hulking mass of dark metal. The camp was littered with firewood, splintered boards, cans of blackstrap molasses, and empty tins of potted meat and cracker wrappers. Howard walked over to the mash boxes they had hammered together the week before, four feet deep and three across, the outside seams sealed with clay mud. The blood pounded in his temples and he felt the liquor thrumming in his body. His nose ran freely and he wiped it on the sleeve of his coat.

They would need extra wood for the slow-burning furnaces to keep the mash warm through the night. Cundiff hadn't done this like he should, which meant there was something worrying his tragic, bent mind, but Howard also felt that rooted deep in the blue-eyed madness of Cundiff was a trickle of intelligence and compromise. Cundiff was the perfect partner in many ways: He could mix up a solid mash, determine the pressure by "whoppin' the cap" with his fingertips, measure the bead and proof at a glance. He had been up on the mountain for four days now and it looked like he hadn't slept in all that time. Most important, he kept his mouth shut.

Sure, Howard thought as he uncovered the mash boxes, he wants me there to back him up when he makes a big sale. Forrest wouldn't even give him a cut of the deal; he'd just say he'd take it off what Howard owed him already. Howard picked up a jar from their previous run and shook it in the firelight to check the bead. Heavy bubbles the size of marbles settled on the surface of the liquid; 150 proof at least. Cundiff could watch the cooking mash through the night, and when he finally succumbed to exhaustion and went down, Danny would take his turn through the next day until Howard got back.

Howard sent Danny off to gather more firewood and taking up a plank he stirred the mash boxes, checking under the cap of malt, dipping his finger and tasting the still beer. Before the light was gone completely they needed to get the first batch in the still, the mash already snowballing, the foaming, lumpy expression of fermentation that came to the surface and eventually overflowed the mash box. Cundiff rose from the fire and together they dragged the long half tube of beaten metal up to the run that they had diverted from a spring draining down the mountainside, and set up the flue that would carry a good stream of fresh water down to the cooling barrel that held the coil.

An hour later they got the first mash box of beer into the still and Howard opened a fresh jar of corn whiskey, sending the metal lid spinning off into the darkening woods with a flick of his fingers. The three men sat by the fire splitting off the jar, wordless, the first sip like swallowing hot ash and then the rest strangely cool, like a refreshing drink from a spring, the three of them staring into the glowing coals, their numb throats working convulsively. When Danny finished off the jar he dashed the dregs into the fire and they exploded in blue light.

Later as the evening grew dark and colder Howard fried up some bacon, sticking it under the still, and the men ate it with their fingers right out of the skillet.

Why should I care? Howard thought. I ought to just let Forrest handle his own damn business. He blinked at the fire and thought about just what all he owed his brother.

Cundiff was stirring the still and sealing the cap, tapping it down and crisscrossing the chains over the top to hold it down under the intense pressure. The thumper keg, connected by a length of copper pipe between the still and the condenser coil and filled with a slop of steaming mash, began to knock woodenly, a steady beat as the pressure built. Danny was sleeping, curled up near the side of the still, hands under his head, the hot bricks warming his skinny body, his pale ankles naked above his boots. There was a tinkle, a metallic music, a pattering of light, and for a moment Howard thought he was hearing music like bells ringing but then he breathed again and slouched lower on the log, the soles of his feet hot from the fire. The tall trees swam in conflicting arcs of light above him and he closed his eyes again.

Howard awoke to find himself sitting on the ground leaning against the log before the furnace, Cundiff kneeling by the condenser, watching the singling coming out of the cooling barrel and into the pail, the first run working its slow, singular way in a tiny puff of steam, the foreshot bubbling with small knots of material, a hot stream of liquor and sediment. Cundiff's face a flickering, cracked carapace like a beetle's wing. Howard's legs were splayed out before him like deadwood. He began to feel the mountain breathe with him; each time he expanded his chest the mountain swelled, bringing him hundreds of feet into the air, beyond the trees, into the darkness of the sky lit with stars that he dimly knew could not be there. Exhalation brought him back through the canopy to the ground, the fire shimmering crimson and gold through his eyelashes, then darkness.

Howard's body snapped like a greenstick, his feet flipped under him, hands on the ground. The thumper keg was rapping hard, echoing down the mountainside, and a jet of steam raced out of a hair-thin seam in the cap, making a high whistle.

Forrest. The County Line.

Howard crabbed over and rolled the unconscious Danny, dumping out his pockets in the dirt. Pocket watch open in the firelight: nearly midnight. He fumbled in the flickering dark, the ground cold and sticky with wet leaves and spiderwebs. Keys; Danny's truck parked down the mountain along the road.

Turning down the steep trail, Howard stumbled, kicking empty molasses cans. Glancing back he saw Cundiff in a circle of wavering light, patching the cap with a cup of clay, dabbing at the steam with his fingers, elbows held high, his hands jointed and fluttering. It wasn't midnight quite yet—he could make it. Howard let his weight pull him down the mountain, his upper body rolling forward, legs keeping up with the generated momentum, floundering in the leaves and brambles, hooking his shirt, tumbling down sections of shale, stumps barking his shins, cursing and swinging his forearms into branches, mashing down small trees with his boots. The slight ribbon of the creek at the bottom shone like a gray vein; that was the valley and the road and he had to get to that and then he would find the truck.

Howard's boots crunched the hard-packed dirt and gravel of the road. In either direction he saw nothing, just a faint chalk trace of road, no trees, no mountain, just low darkness closing in, no stars or moon and he knew he would have to run down the side of the road in each direction until he collided with the vehicle; there was no other way to do it. Howard began to run, one arm stretched out to feel the contact. He felt a cold dampness on his face, and the dark world turned and was suddenly dotted with light, like a plague of white fireflies, and he stumbled in fear, the flies thickening, incandescent, filling the dark. The air turned white; it was snowing. Howard lowered his outstretched hand and pumped both arms, feeling his gathering speed, running hard through the snow.

Chapter 3

MIDNIGHT AND THE MEN who sat in the County Line Restaurant had nowhere else to go. A group sat playing cards, piles of dusty nickels and dimes between their elbows. A few men sat at the bar, haggard and dog-eyed, cigarettes burning down to the knuckle, a loosely held mason jar with an inch of clear fluid at the bottom. A radio on the counter played a music broadcast from Wheeling, West Virginia: the Carter Family singing "Don't Forget This Song." A man in hobnail boots and a stained overcoat rapped his fingers on the bar to the beat. The windows rimed with hoarfrost and shadow, stained clumps of sawdust on the floor.

I courted a fair young lady her name I will not tell
Oh why should I disgrace her when I am doomed for hell
But now upon my scaffold my time's not very long
You may forget the singer but don't forget this song

In the kitchen Forrest Bondurant stood holding his hat in his hand, looking out the window into the back lot as it filled with snow. He wore a heavy shirt tucked into dungarees and his hair was greased and parted on the side. He stamped his boots on the floor a few times. He was a tall man like his brothers, with great bony knuckles and jutting ears, a thinner version of Howard. Forrest was annoyed because his boots were wet, his socks soggy and cold. He had just been in the storage room out back rearranging stock and in the back lot he stepped through a puddle of black ice, going ankle-deep in dark water. The dishwasher, a black man named Jefferson Deshazo, turned to watch Forrest stamp his feet, then looked back at the brown soapy mess in front of him, a cigarette streaming off his lip.

Two of the men drinking in the front room were waiting to purchase eighty gallons to take northwest across to Shootin' Creek in Floyd County. His brother Howard was late, and if he wasn't on the road already he wouldn't make it in time. He would have to ask his counterman Hal to back him up with the shotgun. Forrest thought of the stock in storage, more than two hundred gallons. A few convoys had come through that week and Forrest had over six hundred dollars locked in a cashbox hidden in the kitchen under an old stove. He fingered a small gnarled lump of wood in his pocket. Too much goddamn money on hand, he thought. A fool thing to do.

The weather was due to break open; all day the sky had been gathering and folding along the ridges, and Forrest had a good twenty miles to travel through the mountains to get home. The County Line Restaurant stood astride the Franklin County and Henry County line, just down off the western spur of Thornton Mountain, where routes 19 and 21 met and turned into the hard road that led on to Martinsville, west to Patrick County and Floyd, and on south into North Carolina. A simple place with a wooden counter and stools in front of a grill, a few tables, curtainless windows looking out onto a muddy lot. Most people in that part of the state knew that it was a place where a man could sit and get breakfast, a sandwich, a piece of ham, biscuits, and a drink or two of decent mountain liquor. On a regular night for a half dollar the counterman Hal Childress would set you up with a quart of corn whiskey or brandy, good stuff, not the heavily sugared rotgut they sold to the convoys taking it up north. A single snort would cost you a dime. You could sit close to the box stove and listen to the radio for the whole afternoon as long as you didn't make any trouble.

Evenings men would play a few hands of cards at the tables and Forrest held regular weekly games that ran late into the night in the closed restaurant. If you wanted a larger order of liquor Forrest Bondurant could handle that too; the real business at the County Line was late at night or early morning when small convoys of cars and trucks pulled into the lot and men swung crates of liquor, in half-gallon fruit jars and five-gallon aluminum cans, some heading south, others east to Richmond or west into Tennessee, some men with muddy boots and sleepy, sunburnt faces, mountain men bringing their still whiskey down out of the hills, and other men in long coats and crisp hats who spoke in clipped phrases, picking up booze and headed for points north, Washington, Baltimore, Philadelphia.

Or men came into the County Line Restaurant to watch Maggie, the woman behind the counter who fried eggs and bacon and made biscuits and sandwiches. Maggie was a tall, angular woman around thirty years old with long features and wide shoulders. She carried herself with a strange bearing, a wariness, aloof, as smooth in her movements as a housecat, and there wasn't much anything like her for miles around. She had long auburn hair that during work hours she often kept in a high bun, and Maggie wore new dresses and frocks, dresses with lace and machine-made patterns and exotic fabrics, all the latest fashions ordered from catalogs and delivered to Rocky Mount. Men sat at the counter and watched over their jars of apple brandy, her shoulder blades twitching under her fancy dresses as she worked the grill and when she turned they inspected her long neck, downy with dark hair, resisting the urge to finger the glistening fabric that slid like liquid over her hips. Maggie didn't seem to mind and men would sit and stare brazenly at her, a line of men's heads following her down the counter as she stooped for some butter or across to the cooler for a hunk of cold meat. When it was quiet Maggie would lean on the sink and smoke a cigarette, blowing plumes of smoke from her nose. Maggie always looked a bit over the shoulders of men as they gazed at her, like she was looking a long way off.

Forrest put two fingers in his mouth and whistled low and Hal stepped through the swinging door into the kitchen, wiping his hands on an apron. Hal was a slight man, hair combed carefully over his bulbous scalp, who uttered perhaps a dozen words a week.

Shut 'er down, Forrest said.

Hal nodded and returned to the front room.

As Forrest began to put on his coat to return to the storage shed he heard a shout from the front. He stood with one arm stretched out in his coat sleeve and listened. The pop of shattering glass; he could tell someone had thrown a jar into a wall. A clatter of wood and the heavy sound of struggling bodies; a man yelped in pain. Jefferson took his hands out of the soapy water and began to dry them on a rag.

A man was stretching a bloody hand across the bar trying to get hold of Maggie's waist, her back against the grill, hands behind her back. His hat was on the floor. Another man in dirty coveralls stood next to him; their stools lay on the ground. It was the two Shootin' Creek men who came to make the buy. The men at the card table were all standing now as well, still holding their cards. On the radio Jimmie Rodgers sang

Gonna buy me a pistol, just as long as I am tall

Hal stood at the end of the counter, holding the wooden club they kept under the bar in his hand, watching the two men. His hair hung in limp hanks by his ear and he was breathing heavily.

That's it! Forrest shouted. Everybody out!

The man leaning over the bar twisted around. His face was streaming with sweat. He tried to grin, his mouth shaky and wet-lipped.

I done paid for another and she won't give it, he said. Then the bitch done cut me!

He held up his bloody hand, a deep slice running across his knuckles, the skin peeling back.

Forrest looked at Maggie and she shook her head slightly. He looked back at the two men.

You didn't, Forrest said.

Buy me a pistol, just as long as I am tall

We gonna buy near a hunner' gallon, the man said. Now you ain't gonna throw in some extra?

You ain't buying a damn thing, Forrest said. Get out.

Hal bent down behind the counter and picked up a long-barreled Colt cavalry pistol, flecked with blood, and held it out to Forrest.

He pulled it on her when she wouldn't give him one, Hal murmured. She brought the knife around and caught him.

Forrest looked at the two men blankly.

Did you pull a gun on this woman? he said.

The man pounded the bar with his fist and seized another jar.

Throw that damn jar and you're gonna get yourself seriously hurt, Forrest said.

The cardplayers were putting on their hats and coats, sweeping change on the table into their palms, stuffing half-empty quart bottles into their pockets, and tumbling out into the night, the door slamming. Forrest glanced at Maggie who stared over the heads of the men, her right hand still behind her back gripping the carving knife she used for slicing cold ham, the blade smeared crimson.

Gonna shoot po' Thelma, just to see her jump and fall.

The man hocked a wad of mucus onto the bar and then heaved the jar just to the right of Maggie, into the large mirror. When the mirror exploded, raining glass into her hair, Forrest felt the flaring up inside. He could tell these men hadn't come to buy anything. Too much cash on hand, it was a foolish thing, as was coming out here to confront what he knew was trouble without the shotgun or his pistol. It was lucky these men only seemed to have the one gun and this pinned them as desperate fools. Howard's very presence would have made this whole thing a lot easier. They must have been waiting to see if he was going to show up; late enough now and they would take their chance. Didn't matter, Forrest thought. If it was punishment they sought then they would get it.

All right, the man said, and he squared up to Forrest and the man in the dirty coveralls stepped up behind him. This second man was medium height but thicker than most. He had a flaming goiter under his jaw that swelled out like a turkey's comb, and his face was set in a grim line. That ol' boy ain't drunk, Forrest thought to himself. That's the one to watch for. It was in the sizing up of a man, when you could tell how it would go—that foreknowledge was what made Forrest's ears crack and his knuckles go white. Forrest saw in his head the anger in a triangle of fire floating in a field of night sky. He focused on it and put a dark box around it, making it smaller until a cold blankness ran over him like water and he wanted to fling himself onto the back of the world with both fists crashing down. When he looked at these two men they were like animals standing on their hind legs.

Forrest stepped away from the bar to give himself some space. Hal stood behind him holding the cavalry pistol but Forrest knew they would charge and the old man wouldn't fire. The four of them stood there for a moment and then the sweaty-faced man came at Forrest with both fists, howling, and Forrest sidestepped him and pushed him into a table and the man crashed to the ground. Jefferson rushed out of the kitchen in his apron and sat on the man's kicking legs and Hal put the pistol to the man's temple and told him to lie still.

When Forrest turned around the man in the coveralls was driving at his face and Forrest twisted and caught the blow on the ear, moving with the momentum, covering up with his elbows, and then the man was on him. The man got both arms around Forrest's midsection and was trying to pick him up, grunting, his lips curled and his mouth open, his breath foul and hot and Forrest felt himself come off his feet and then he knew that this was real trouble. The man lifted him and staggered into the bar and when his grip loosened for a moment Forrest got a hand free and brought the heel of his hand up sharply under the man's chin, into the soft pouch of the goiter. The man's teeth clacked hard and he let go of Forrest and stumbled back, his eyes wild. A fleshy sliver of tongue dribbled over his bottom lip followed by a sheet of blood that ran down his chin and neck. He caught the piece of tongue in his palm and groaned. In a fluid motion Forrest slipped on the iron knuckles he had in his pocket, jerked him around by his collar and caught him with a crunching overhand right between the eyes, laying his forehead wide open to the bone and dropping him to the floor.

They dragged him out by his ankles and threw him into the ditch beside the road and when he hit the muddy snow he moaned and clutched at his bloody head. Then Forrest and Jefferson threw the sweaty-faced man out into the parking lot and he rolled about cursing and crying as Forrest kicked him with his heavy boots for a while. He waited for the man to turn or move his arms to get a kick in at his ribs or head, walking around his body and winding into him with a few steps for momentum, his boots slipping in the snow. It was a cold night, clouds building from the east range of mountains and the pines across the hard road standing tall in the darkness. When Forrest's boot found a soft part the man grunted and wheezed. Forrest felt tired and irritated by the whole thing, though he was not surprised. The word was out about the money and desperate men would always show up to take a chance. Forrest rubbed his split earlobe with his fingers as he aimed a short hard kick to the man's kidneys. Goddammit, Howard, he thought, why bother even say you're gonna do something?

Maggie was sweeping up the glass from the mirror and the jars when Forrest came back in. The radio was still playing and there wasn't another sound for miles. Forrest felt a bit ashamed suddenly and he thought of saying something or apologizing but instead turned away and went into the back with Hal and Jefferson to finish up in the kitchen. She's no child, Forrest thought, and she'd seen worse it was certain.

In the kitchen Jefferson was washing his hands in the sink again and Hal was smoking as he paced the floor, mumbling to himself, still keyed up. Forrest took out his money clip and peeled off two fives and stepping in front of Hal he placed one in the old man's trembling hand. Hal nodded, and Forrest clapped him on the back. Jefferson dried his hands and folded the other five neatly and placed it in his shirt pocket.

Much appreciated, Mister Forrest, Jefferson said.

Well, I appreciate your help, Forrest said. It won't happen again.

Jefferson scratched his head and looked at him thoughtfully.

I'd like that, Jefferson said.

That makes two of us, Forrest said.

LATER MAGGIE was standing in her coat and men's felt hat counting the money in the till. The restaurant was quiet and empty. Jefferson and Hal had both gone home, Hal driving south down the hill into Henry County, and Jefferson Deshazo striding off into the snowy darkness to his cabin that lay a few miles south. Maggie had her own car, a cut-down Model T truck that was her father's before he died, and she always insisted on driving herself wherever she wanted to go. She usually stayed late, counting out the till and collecting the receipts. Forrest had a place on Cook's Knob, to the north up in central Franklin County, but it was a long drive and it had been snowing hard in the mountains. On nights like these he would stoke the stove hot and have a few knocks of white mule and sleep in the back on a bedroll between the racks of canned goods. Forrest stood there watching for a moment but she didn't look up, her eyes intent on the small pieces of paper and stub of pencil.

Whata you doin'? Forrest asked.

Eatin' ice cream, Maggie said.

She took a cup down from the cupboard and poured herself coffee and tucking her long hair behind her ear she gave him a tight smile, her dark eyes smudged with weariness. Her coat hung open and Forrest could see a fine spray of dried blood across the waist of her dress.

You better get on, Forrest said. The roads are fillin' up.

I'll be out in a minute, she said.

Forrest stepped out into the parking lot to check on the snowfall. It fell slowly and in fat shapes, large torn pieces drifting so slow you could catch any one you wanted to, and this meant that it wouldn't last much longer. Still, there was far too much on the road for him to get up across Thornton Mountain. There was a splash of blood on the snow and Forrest pushed some fresh snow on top of the mark with his foot. Across the lot Maggie's truck stood next to his pine-green 1928 Ford. Something seemed wrong with the shape of it, the outline of it against the falling snow, and so Forrest walked across the lot to his car and as he neared he could see that there was a body slumped against the front fender. It was the man he had hit with the knuckles, the blood coagulating on his forehead in a dark smear. He must have dragged himself there. The other man he had kicked into unconsciousness was gone. The car lot was empty other than his car and Maggie's truck. There was no wind and Forrest could hear snow falling softly through the trees and the whine of a truck engine somewhere high up in the mountains.

Then he saw his hood slightly ajar and the hot anger returned and he figured he'd toss this man into the ditch and break his legs for it. He'd prop his ankles on a stone and stomp until his shinbones cracked. The thought of it made him tired and he sorely wished the man hadn't done it. He bent down to feel the man's neck for a pulse and felt the steady pull of blood. He was alive, and that meant he would suffer much more before the night was out. It amazed Forrest that so many men seemed to wake up in the morning needing some kind of beating or another, men saying and doing fantastic things for the sake of getting another man to smash his face. Perhaps it was the aftermath, the burning humiliation of it they sought, when the aching morning came and they rolled over in the dirt and felt their mouth for teeth or lightly touched the split ear, the face in the rearview mirror swollen and crusted with blood. Forrest figured if these men wanted it he might as well give it to them. Either way he would push him off into the ditch and break his legs and if the man died then it was his own fault.

He squatted down and grasped the man's lapels and was about to shift him off the running board of his car and drag him to the ditch when the man's eyes shot open and his cold hands gripped Forrest's wrists. His face curled into a snarl, blood still surging between his lips as Forrest twisted his hands to free himself.

Damn, son! Forrest said. You want more?

Suddenly he felt another man close at his back and hands around his collar. The man behind him leaned on his back and the weight kept Forrest from standing. The man holding his hands grinned, sticking out his stump tongue like a mottled piece of bloody sausage, his eyes wide, his swollen goiter flopping against his chin and collar. The man behind him hooked a forearm under Forrest's chin and pulled his face up to the sky. Low clouds rolled dusky gray and charcoal.

Forrest felt the razor being drawn across his neck, a cold sensation like the line made by a piece of ice on skin, a cool tracing of metal, and for a moment he marveled at how smooth and painless it was, watching the specks of stars through torn clouds, knees in the cold snow, feeling the dampness of his boots, the man behind holding him tight, the man in front holding the wrists of his outstretched arms and leaning his face in close, grinning. Their combined breath billowed around them. A weight drained out of him and a sudden weakness took its place. Then he felt the blood pouring down his chest and down his throat, swallowing the stuff in salty gulps—that was what got him: *Down my throat? My God, he is cutting through, he will cut my head clean off!* The man behind him was sawing roughly at his neck and Forrest lurched and bucked, pulled an arm free and stuck it into the face of the man behind him. He felt a cheekbone and an eye socket and pried his thumb into the soft part and the man cried out and was off him and Forrest got his feet under him and staggered a few steps back toward the restaurant, then fell heavily in the snow on his hands and knees. He marveled at the quantity of blood that poured from him like a watery bib onto the snow, making a steamy slush between his hands. He crawled across the lot to the wall of the restaurant. There was the splintering sound of a door kicked open and shouting from inside the restaurant and he knew they had gone inside.

Forrest leaned against the wall, searching for the edges of the cut with his numb fingers, the ground a world of white in front of him. He gripped the edges of his cut throat and thought to himself that this would be one of the times where one ought to consider the balance of his life; but all that came to mind was that these men had wanted a beating and he had given it to them and so what was all this about?

A part of me is missing, he thought. There was only one whole being in the universe and it was the one who rose in the morning, who stepped over the mountains and reaching down with massive, blunt fingers plucked men's souls like weeds in the furrow. When Forrest looked up the roof of the sky was gone, just a ragged hole, the stars gone out and light coming down in slow glistening streams. The hole in the sky rotated and he felt his weight shift and it seemed like the earth and all the people in it were in a box that was being tipped over, to be dumped out into the black. Not yet, he thought. More shouting and breaking glass from inside. A woman screaming, a strange, high, desperate scream that burrowed into Forrest's heart and twisted something in him, hard, but he couldn't focus on why it was happening or who it was. Forrest looked at his legs splayed out before him, trousers sticky with blood, and knew that they wouldn't respond.

Later it was quiet and Forrest watched the ragged wisps of snow, like falling clouds settling in a white layer on his legs and the lot and the trees beyond the road. He let his heartbeat settle; his breath coming regularly in short puffs. His muscles began to relax.

It wasn't so bad, he thought.

The soft pat of falling snow. Faint music from the radio coming through the window above him. He turned his mind to the music that slowly faded, then a voice saying:

This is for our sick and shut-ins.

Then a chorus of voices singing a hymn, slow and deliberate, the words unclear.

Forrest jerked his eyes open. Somewhere across the road and at the edge of the wood there was a smear of movement. He couldn't tell what it was. If it was God then he would have him. He would reach out and break his head and kick him to pieces in the road like a clod of dirt. It wasn't so bad, in fact it all made perfect sense. Then his face was down in the snow, the ice on his cheek, fingers still holding the edges of his throat as he fell into darkness.

HOWARD BONDURANT AWOKE lying on his side on the front seat, the steering wheel pressed against his bared teeth. He sat upright and stared out the windshield. A whiteness enveloped the world as if the ground were lit up from underneath. He lay back down on the seat for a while, pulling his legs up into a fetal position, kicking his toes against the dashboard to regain feeling, groping at his armpits with his burning fingers. His gut ached and he shuddered and wished desperately to slip back into unconsciousness.

Later Howard wrenched the truck door open, breaking a crust of ice and nearly a foot of snow from the roof that fell into the cab, covering his pants and shoulders as he swung his legs off the seat, some of the cold powder going down his neck. Sky and ground were the same, luminous white and rolling and for a moment he didn't understand if the truck was straight or crooked or floating in the air. To his left the snow undulated up a hill then across, evenly spaced bumps of white suggested a fence line. To the right a stand of pines stood in a line as far as he could see, their tops bent with weight, each drooping in different directions like a crowd of people sitting in chairs asleep. The truck lay half-buried at a steep angle and Howard figured he must have put it in a gulley. He watched the trees for a while until the thin breeze ruffled their bent tops, sending sprays of snow drifting off like banks of rolling mist. The mountains began to separate from the air, and putting a frozen elbow awkwardly against his knee he bent and retched into the snow.

Forrest.

Using the muffled fence line and the pines as a guide Howard started off down the road, heading east, toward the pale disk of the sun.

Chapter 4

THE NEXT MORNING Emmy Bondurant stood in the kitchen in her housecoat with a book of matches in her hand, the air in the house spiked with cold and the damp chill of morning. Jack watched his sister light the stove and make coffee for their father who was sleeping later now than he ever did during the first fifty years of his life. Emmy was tall and bird-stooped like Jack and his brothers, the narrow blades of her shoulders like fins as she craned over the stove. She cut off a hunk of fatback and tossed it into the skillet. She kept her hair short and pushed to the side with a nervous finger as she stirred the sizzling fat. Her hair was once blond-white, almost like glass, but had developed streaks of steely gray even though she was only sixteen, two years younger than Jack.

Jack stood by the window as he buttoned his shirt, watching the snow-covered road for signs of his brother. Forrest made a delivery on the first Friday of each month around the county and sometimes he took Jack along to run the cans. Jack had to watch the road because Forrest would never come up the drive to the house with a carful of liquor, and he would stop on the road only for a few minutes. If Jack wasn't sharp he would be left behind.

On these mornings Jack would spy Forrest's car nosing the end of the drive and he would gulp the rest of his coffee and bolt out the door and down the driveway with a cold greasy biscuit in his mouth and another in his pocket. Running toward his brother's car Jack felt the urge to whinny like a colt and he would bound down the dirt path past the livestock barn, passing through the long rows of peas, beans, and cabbage, summer vines rotting in their furrows. In the car the silhouette of Forrest's hooked nose and fedora lined down the road, the flared fenders of the car squatting over the tires, weighed low by sixty gallons of liquor. Making local deliveries with Forrest meant dollars in his pocket, and being seen in Rocky Mount with his brother always made Jack fill out his jacket a bit more.

Jack would hop into the back of the car, nestling tight in a niche left in the stacked five-gallon metal cans and crates of half-gallon jars, his forearms across the sloshing liquor, holding it steady as Forrest pushed the stocky four-cylinder Ford up the hard road. Along the way they stopped off at various farmhouses, Jack scooting up and around to the back of the house to drop the cans on the back porch. In Rocky Mount they hit nearly half of the houses and business locations, Jack running through spattered alleys to leave jars on the back windowsill of an office; stamping up flights of stairs and knocking on doors in cramped, slanted apartment buildings, the residents answering the door to find a jar sitting on the floor in the echoing hallway; deliveries around the courthouse, the police station; they delivered to church parsonages, to lawyers, to judges, to city-council members.

Then they would head north up Grassy Hill and go westward into Burnt Chimney and Boone's Mill, stopping at a little crossroads where a cross-eyed man at a filling station stood under the porch, a rifle leaning against the wall, a car idling in the lot, unloading thirty gallons without a word. Then east to Smith Mountain Lake and dropping off the rest at a filling station run by a man named Hatcher, a group of men waiting in cars and trucks, the squared Nash Victoria Six, long Studebakers, supercharged Packards, the ubiquitous Model A's, the hubs riding high over the wheels, the springs tuned tall and tight to handle the weight. Men standing quietly, some with pistols sticking out of their beltbands or casually thrust in pockets. In a car idling in the parking lot Sheriff Hodges and his son Henry, a deputy, sat sipping hot coffee out of a metal thermos.

Sometimes there would be a small paper packet on the back stoop when Jack dropped off a can and he would bring this to Forrest who would put it in his shirt pocket. In all the times he went out with Forrest he never saw anyone handling money. The open rush of it worked in Jack's blood; waiting at the corner in downtown Rocky Mount, men and women out on the morning streets and Jack in his brushed boots, cap at a sly angle, a five-gallon can in each hand, his long arms knotty and taut with the weight. He enjoyed the way people glanced over him without seeing him, how all kinds of people struggled unnaturally to avert their gaze. How young women's eyes widened for a moment just before they looked to their hands folded on cotton smocks and pleated shirtfronts. Jack could tell that they felt his presence like a dark field, an invisible weight moving through them like charged wind. He relished each moment and relived them in his dreams.

THAT MORNING Forrest never came. The road was a smooth white drift; no one had traveled down it since the snowfall and Jack figured his brother was unable to leave the restaurant. After standing by the window for an hour he gave up and sat down to a sullen breakfast. Emmy served Granville his biscuits and apple butter, then brought hot coffee, fried eggs, and a steaming bowl of hominy with cracklings. By the time she joined them, Granville and Jack were nearly finished bolting the grub. Jack saw Emmy smirking in her coffee and he wondered if she was glad that Forrest failed to show. Why the hell would she be so happy about Forrest leaving him out once again? Granville poured his coffee into a saucer and sipped like a whiskered penitent. When he finished he scratched his beard with both hands and looked out the window.

You goin' somewhere this morning?

I thought I was, Jack said.

Well, Granville said, then it looks like you can get that stack of pine out there. First break up the water in the barns and give them a bit of the silage.

Forrest might show any time now, Jack said.

Granville turned to Jack and squinted at him like he was looking at something far off. His father's forehead was a tangle of creases, starburst eyes, throat mottled with spots and hanging skin puckered in three parallel lines.

You don't have to go anywhere, Granville said. You help your sister with what she needs and then see to them cows and that wood. Emmy stood quickly and began to gather the dishes. Jack eyed her face, looking for some indication of amusement or accomplishment.

I'm supposed to be helping Forrest, Jack said.

Well, get him to put you up then, he said.

Granville got his hat and coat and went to open up the store. When he was outside Jack turned to Emmy at the sink.

What? Why you smilin'?

I didn't say nothing.

She bustled with the dishes and Jack figured there was little use trying to pry the source of amusement out of his sister. He stood and drank his coffee at the window and watched his father clearing the smooth cap of snow off the car and gingerly negotiating the driveway to the road, his snow chains tinkling as he passed up the hill.

JACK WAS SPLITTING wood when Hal Childress came up the drive in his car. The day had warmed considerably, remnants of snow clinging miserably in the trees, and Jack was stripped down to his undershirt, his body steaming like a workhorse. Hal picked his way through the snow and Jack could tell there was something wrong because the old man's face was drained of color and he held his clenched fists in front of him like a drunken boxer. Jack wondered why he was here instead of running the grill at the County Line.

I don't right know, Jack. Hal said. Think somethin' done happened to Forrest.

Jack looked back to the house. The windows were dark, the dim outline of curtains, his mother's rocking chair. Hal rocked in the snow.

Howard about?

No, Jack said. I ain't seen 'im.

A car chugged up the road, snow chains rattling, and both men turned to watch it pass. Jack's skin felt prickly and his feet itched in his wool socks.

What happened? Jack asked.

Don't rightly know, Hal said. A deal with some boys from Shootin' Creek went bad. Took care of it, but now this morning Forrest's car is there but he ain't.

Jack thought about his father at the store, probably standing with the usual group of gassy old men around the potbellied stove, shuffling their feet in the sawdust. He wished Howard was about as his brother wouldn't say a word but simply get in the car with Hal and Jack could then ride along and everything would be fine.

Hold it a second, Jack said, and he walked quickly into the house.

The heat in the house was stifling and Jack wiped a sleeve across his forehead. Emmy was sitting in their mother's old chair, holding a book and looking at him with large eyes.

I don't know, Jack said. He's sayin' something happened at the County Line.

Jack walked into the cold-storage room that was filled with shelves of canned goods and jars of vegetables and preserves that Emmy and Granville had put up that fall. Jack knew his father kept a rifle in the room, but he wasn't sure where. He pawed through the shelves, looking through an old bureau in the corner. When he realized he was opening drawers that couldn't fit a rifle he felt like a damn fool and cursed under his breath. He didn't want to find that gun, he didn't want to deal with this at all and this thought wedged under his organs like a sickle thorn.

Jack stopped in the living room and rubbed his hands together for a moment. He could tell his sister was pretending to read, watching him.

Look, he said, don't say nothing to Daddy about this.

Emmy nodded, wide-eyed.

Jack walked back out into the yard, slinging on his coat.

Well, he said, let's go see.

The air was clear and the snow melting fast. During the drive Hal explained to Jack the nature of the altercation they had at closing time with the men from Shootin' Creek, how Maggie had sliced the man's hand with the carving knife and how Forrest had finally subdued them. As they drove the snow chains made a racket on the hard road and Hal had to shout.

Forrest's car was still there in the restaurant lot, the hood ajar. Man makes a near hundred dollars in a week, Jack couldn't help but think, and he buys an eight-hundred-dollar cracker-box Ford. They pulled up to the restaurant door and cut the engine. The tire and foot tracks were clear and smoothed by another inch of snow, and it seemed clear to Jack that there was an awful lot of activity in the lot that night.

Look here, Hal said, and gestured to the restaurant door, which was closed but was splintered around the handle, kicked in. Jack was looking at a trail of stained snow that led from the side of the building to a large crusty maroon patch, melted down to the gravel next to Forrest's car.

We got that one fella good, Hal said. But all this here ain't his. Not unless he opened up a vein hisself.

Inside the restaurant was littered with broken glass and shattered furniture. The register lay smashed on the floor, drawer gaping, every shelf behind the counter cleared of its contents. The carving knife on the bar, its blade smeared with a dark crust.

Maggie? Jack asked.

She normally leaves just after us, Hal said. Car's gone, so I 'spect she made it home.

In the kitchen Jack kicked through the pans and utensils that littered the floor.

We done cleaned up, Hal said, Jefferson and me. It wudn't like this.

We better call Hodges, Jack said.

Better check in the shed first, Hal said. Forrest wouldn't want us to bring the sheriff around here with all that white mule on hand.

They went out the back door of the kitchen and found a clear set of tracks that led to the storage shed and then around to the front, and the ruts of car tires indicating a series of trips. The storage shed was open, the door in splinters, hacked apart with an ax that lay in the snow. The sun blazed on the back lot and Jack put his hands on his head and tried to think, his mind like a hive.

How much did he have in here, Jack asked.

Near two hundred I 'spect, Hal said.

In the dark shed there were some broken jars and a few empty five-gallon cans scattered on the floor and the air was fetid with hard corn liquor. After his eyes adjusted to the dark Jack could see the shed was otherwise empty. So many gallons; they must have had several vehicles, several men. Worth at least five hundred dollars. He stepped out of the shed. Hal clenched his hands in front of him. Jack felt like he had just woken up from a long sleep, slight traces coming off the points of things, the trees shaking even though there was no breeze and no sound except the two of them crunching through the slush. Jack knew that Forrest wouldn't have let that much liquor go without a fierce scrap, and the thought struck him that the men who had taken the liquor had also taken his brother out of this world.

JACK FIGURED the first thing would be to ring the hospital in Rocky Mount and see if they had admitted anyone matching Forrest's description. They used the phone at the County Line, Hal sweeping the debris as Jack was connected. The next call would be to the morgue. But Forrest was there, in the ICU ward, alive, and the two men drove in to Rocky Mount. Forrest was stretched out unconscious, his throat a swath of bandages. They stitched up the ragged line across his throat, starting just under one ear and passing under his chin just an inch above his Adam's apple and ending at his jaw on the other side. The blood loss was massive and the transfusions replaced every pint he had. The nurses said that he came into the hospital sometime in the night under his own power, staggering into the lobby, holding the edges of his throat together with his fingers. Before Forrest passed out he told the doctors that he'd had an accident. It was nearly twelve miles to Rocky Mount from the County Line Restaurant, most of that twisting through the mountains on rough roads. When asked how he arrived there, Forrest replied that he walked.

Chapter 5

1929

THE ONLY ROAD NORTH from Rocky Mount slashed back and forth
in a series of switchbacks across a steep mountain called Grassy Hill.
Over the summit the road continued north through Burnt Chimney,
running along the bottoms of the hollows, crisscrossing streams and
winding on into the rugged settlement of Boone's Mill. This small set
of hills separated Franklin and Roanoke counties, the county line running along a thin branch of Blackwater Creek. Thirty miles after
crossing the creek you would reach the city of Roanoke, the central
hub of southern Virginia.

This branch of Blackwater Creek was called Maggodee Creek, a
local term that once referred to the profusion of maggots that inhabited its waters. Like the main trunks of Blackwater Creek, the water
carried a dark, maroon tint caused by the many chestnut trees that
grew along the banks and dropped their spiny seed husks into the
water which bled out their color over time. The bridge over Maggodee
Creek was a simple four-post affair, planked boards laid crosswise, the
width of a single car. Deep woods of chestnut, gum, and pine spread
on either side.

About two hundred yards south of the bridge toward Rocky
Mount, a small filling station stood in a niche in the wood just off the

50

road. That winter when Forrest left the hospital he bought the station from Lou Webb and took up residence in the upstairs rooms. Forrest's suppliers and contacts followed and within days cars were lining up and he was running his operation out of the filling station. The block-aders could blaze through Rocky Mount, over Grassy Hill, stop at the station and pick up and drop off and make the run to Roanoke, cross-ing over the county line in mere minutes. The demand for liquor was steadily increasing and at night the still fires winked across the moun-tainsides like fireflies. In the winter the heat trails sent plumes of still vapor rising in thin strings from every hollow and hill.

There was no sign on the station, but from then on, even long after Forrest's eventual death, it was known as either the Blackwater Sta-tion, Burnt Chimney station, or the Bondurant station.

When he got out of the hospital Forrest removed his stake from the County Line, selling the restaurant cheap to Hal Childress. Forrest also bought a mobile sawmill setup: donkey-engine-powered band saw, a long portable cutting shed, blades, tools, and hand-cutting supplies. After hiring local hands he began to operate a contract sawmilling operation, moving around the county and processing stands of hard-wood and pine, his days and nights split between the sawmill camp and the Blackwater station. Behind the station the mountain swelled up and a dozen yards up this hill Forrest built a stone storage shed with a heavy chestnut door bound with iron with a large padlock on the han-dle. He kept the key on a short chain around his neck, the key hanging in the bony hollow just below his Adam's apple.

A few weeks after the incident at the County Line, Maggie appeared at the Blackwater station, manning the small grill there. The upstairs apartment had three rooms and a narrow water closet with plumbing. Forrest set it up with some old furniture, castoffs mostly. When Mag-gie arrived with her valise, wearing a scarlet dress with ribbons of gold, Forrest turned without a word and led her upstairs. He put the iron-framed single bed in one room with most of the decent furniture and put a straw tick for himself in the other room. Maggie's room had an oval gilt-edged mirror mounted on the back of a chest of drawers made of stained black walnut that Forrest's grandfather built. In the sitting room there was a lumpy old couch covered with a sheet that faced the front window looking out over the road and down toward Maggodee Creek, the cracked and chipped castoffs of his mother's old china stacked on the kitchen shelves.

Forrest hired a young man from Boone's Mill named Everett Dillon to run the petrol pumps. Everett was a quiet man in his twenties, dark-faced with a thick shock of black hair who kept his head down, worked hard, and never asked a question about anything. He had a girl up on the mountain having a baby and he needed the steady money. Maggie worked the counter grill like she did at the County Line, though no one bought food at the Blackwater station, so mostly she leaned against the grill, smoking and watching the road through the window. There were regular card games at the station, mostly after hours, and the fuel business was steady, but mostly men wandered in from all over the county and from areas to the north, seeking liquor.

In the mornings Forrest made breakfast and coffee downstairs while Maggie sat on the edge of the bed and brushed her long hair in front of the mirror. Forrest had the radio from the County Line and in the evenings they sat on the couch looking over the road and smoked cigarettes, listening to the broadcasts from Wheeling or Richmond. When Forrest was sleeping at the sawmill camp Maggie sat on the couch and listened to the radio by herself. Later she would sit in her bed smoking and flipping through the Sears catalog. Sometimes Forrest would come home late when she was already asleep, and when she woke in the morning to the smell of bacon and coffee she knew that he was there.

Maggie hadn't said a word to anyone about leaving the County Line, what happened that night, or anything about moving in with Forrest at the Blackwater station. Forrest never once mentioned her to anyone, and nobody ever brought it up, even his brothers.

Hal often thought of Maggie as he stood in the County Line Restaurant during business hours, pouring drinks and wiping down the bar, a new woman working the grill. The old man for many years afterward found himself wishing to see her out of the corner of his eye, her long form leaning against the grill. Sometimes at the restaurant Hal and other men would talk about the night when Forrest got cut. Hal told them how Forrest laid that man out with the iron knuckles and then nearly kicked the other man to death in the snow, and how Forrest gave him a five spot and told him to go on home, how Hal, Maggie, and Jefferson all left, and Forrest was alone when the men attacked him in the lot and left him for dead in the snow. Over time Hal began to embellish certain things, adding details that seemed to fit the conclusion: a flashed knife, Hal and Jefferson wading into a fray of struggling bodies, Forrest knocking men comatose with clubbing blows, more men waiting in the parking lot, long coats and fancy cars, Northerners perhaps. Forrest standing in the dark doorway, empty-handed and blood smeared on his face, daring them all to come on. The story grew and changed and after some time nobody believed the old man and the story remained shrouded in speculation.

Forrest also never told anyone about what happened to him that night. There was no police investigation. Men eventually got around to it in the presence of Jack and Howard: *How in the hell that man get twelve miles through the mountains, in a foot of snow, to the hospital in Rocky Mount, with his goddamn throat slit wide open?* The brothers merely shrugged as there was no way to know such a thing.

DID YOU GET 'EM? Jack asked his brother as he lay in the hospital.

No, Forrest said.

What you gonna do?

Forrest's facial expression was placidly neutral above the puckered wound on his neck, purple scabbed and heavily stitched with black thread. A glass of tepid water stood on the bedside table. In the hallway a patient was pleading hoarsely with a nurse for the use of a phone. Forrest's eyes gazed at some spot beyond the ceiling, and Jack felt moved by the sudden plaintive sight of his brother struck low. His visage reminded Jack of their grandfather, a haggard veteran of the Civil War. In his dim memories the old man sat stiffly on the edge of his bed and whittled small knots of wood.

I'll hold them down myself, Jack said. I want to be there.

Forrest smiled, lips parted over bare teeth, the corners of his bristling scar drawing up like some kind of second mouth, a ghastly double smile.

I'll call on you, Jack, Forrest said. And they'll wish they were dead before we're done.

Jack felt in a nauseous rush how his brother's life would be eventually hacked off at the root like an old stump, and how until then Forrest would live in violence and pain and never rise from it.

Nothing can kill us.

Chapter 6

1934

SHERWOOD ANDERSON sat in the Little Hub Restaurant in Rocky Mount in the late evening, nursing a cup of coffee and watching two bearded men wearing the plain dark clothes of the Dunkard Church eating ham steaks and buttered toast. The Little Hub seemed to Anderson a good spot to lurk and perhaps pick up a whiff of something as the sheriff and most of the deputies frequented the spot, as did the commonwealth's attorney, Carter Lee, whom Anderson had been unable to gain audience with. He'd been in Franklin County for three months and had accomplished little more than a few notes, his desk at the rooming house littered with scraps of paper, jottings about scenery or people. He had spread nickels and dimes all over the county, most to small boys lurking about the filling stations or lunch counters.

Willie Carter Sharpe? Yeah, I know of her. Never seen her though.

You don't know? Where you from anyhow?

Anderson did learn that no one around Franklin County called the thing "bootlegging." That might as well have been a foreign word. You mean *blockadin'*, sir? What blockades? Nobody ever said "moonshine" either. *White Lightning. White Mule. Moon. Stump Whiskey. Mountain Dew. Squirrel Whiskey. Fire Water.* He had seen plenty of it over the years in Marion. When building Ripshin his foreman, a seventy-year-old man named Ball, a bear of a man with an outsized belief in his abilities, would take a lark every month. He would hire a car and driver, fill the car with booze and drive around the county stopping off at friends' places and inviting them to join his roving bender. Once Anderson arrived at Ripshin to find all the workmen drunk, falling from the scaffolding, covered in the white muck of plaster. Most of his friends drank liberally; Faulkner in particular had a true penchant for the stuff and they drank plenty of whiskey together in New Orleans. So what was different about it here? Every other night lines of cars raced through Rocky Mount, the whine of engines working through the walls of his room at the boardinghouse.

Anderson's connection at *The Roanoke Times* got him a copy of the preliminary report, issued in July, submitted to the Acting Deputy Commissioner of the Alcohol Tax Unit, which provided the basis for the grand jury investigation "United States vs. Charles Carter Lee."

In the fall of 1928, Charles Carter Lee, The Commonwealth's Attorney for Franklin County, Virginia, and Sheriff Pete Hodges called the various deputy sheriffs of Franklin County into the office of Pete Hodges, singly and in pairs, making them a proposition to divide the County up into districts for the purpose of assessing illicit distillers and bootleggers a certain amount (from ten dollars to 25 dollars) per month for the privilege of operating with the protection of County officers.

The grand jury was set to convene in a few weeks, though the location had yet to be set; the papers proposed the trial would likely be outside the county to prevent jury tampering. Several key county law-enforcement officials would be indicted on charges of racketeering and conspiracy, though the coconspirators wouldn't be named until the actual indictment. In spite of this the blockade runs went on, seemingly unimpeded. Anderson had learned that if he came into certain filling stations and slipped a five on the counter without a word, then stepped outside and waited by his car, in a few minutes a dirty-necked boy would jog around from behind the store and hand him a half-gallon jar of corn whiskey in a paper sack. At one station he handed a slatternly teenage girl a fiver and she turned and scampered up a hill into the bramble and disappeared into the forest. Anderson waited an hour by the road until he figured he'd been hoodwinked in the simplest way, but soon enough a mule came ambling down a trail, a saddlebag bulging with fruit jars of booze. It wasn't exactly raining from the sky but they were right that the county was full of it. His mistake before was to actually *ask* for the damned stuff; he found that such transactions were done in the same manner as most in Franklin County, a wordless combination of timing, simple gesture, and mutual assumption. Anderson had six different half-gallon jars in his room at the boardinghouse, lined up along the dresser. It was research of a kind. He had sampled them all and determined that in fact there were some real differences, and he had to admit that some of the stuff was excellent, a layered, complex taste with several discernable characteristics.

Anderson watched the darkly clad figures in the Little Hub Restaurant. A few farmers sat drinking coffee. Temperance folk obviously, Anderson thought, as everyone else in the county surely must be out gallivanting around a bonfire somewhere in the mountains drinking illegal liquor. The counterman folded his arms over his bulbous midsection and smoked thoughtfully. Another man read the paper at a booth with a stub of pencil in hand, hair neatly parted and oiled. He was dressed in a tight suit and bow tie: a salesman passing through. Anderson looked at his own hands and knew that their delicate fineness would immediately indicate an outsider to anyone who bothered to look. The thought that he would need a translator, an introduction into the world of the working class, made him burn with shame and anger. And now the mythical Willie Carter Sharpe: *The only man or woman alive who could hold a Ford wide open down Grassy Hill!* as they said on the front porches and around the stove.

I could give it right back to them, Anderson thought, give them the character they wanted. Nights at the boardinghouse Anderson sat scribbling at a battered old sideboard table, trying to think of all the things he had seen that day, trying to remember the hands of the men in the fields, the boys in the curing shed, the grim farmwives in the cookhouse, the lines of their faces, the cut of their work shirts, the seams of their shoes. But in all these things he saw very little. It was as if the character of these people encouraged a sort of blank anonymity, so unlike the peoples of the Midwest and their quaint charms and frustrated lives, who seemed to open up like a flower for Anderson when they talked. He could read everything in their flashing eyes, their blurring hands. The wide-open spaces of the Midwest allowed a man's mind to stretch and think. But the strange confines of Franklin, its long skylines, rolling hills, left him with a feeling of enclosure and confinement, as if something dangerous was contained there and the minds of the citizens had to focus on not letting it out. The way the men slouched in their walk, hips forward, legs kicking out in front of them, slew-footed, shoulders rounded, hands buried deep in the pockets of their coveralls. The way they wore their hats low, eyes down on the red clay. Women who had apparently set their faces in a placid grimace for the rest of their lives, hollow-eyed, always in motion, working, fiddling, never sitting still. The straight, worn shifts and muddy boots, a simple cord around a wrist perhaps, a thin cross on the neck. And nobody *said anything*.

Then why didn't he go home? Eleanor? Nobody really knew exactly where Anderson was, including Eleanor, and he thought of this mysterious absence with grim pleasure. It reminded him of the time he walked away from his job in Elyria, Ohio. The Anderson Manufacturing Company, marketing an inexpensive roof coating. He was learning to play golf at the country club that year, 1912. One day he walked out of the office, with nothing but the clothes on his back.

What's the matter? his secretary had asked him, her face in rigid alarm. She was an intelligent woman, he thought, even more intelligent than himself. A rainstorm drummed on the windows.

My dear young woman, Anderson said, it is all very silly, but I have decided to no longer concern myself with this buying and selling.

You're sick? she said.

She was right in a sense, and Anderson knew he had to get out of there right away. He felt if he could just reach the door, then it would be okay. His feet would carry him to wherever he needed to go. Did she think he was crazy? Was he? Anderson looked at his feet.

My feet are cold, wet, and heavy from a long wading in a river, he had said. Now I shall go walk on dry land.

As Anderson left the office he knew that it was *the words* that had lifted him out, and he swore allegiance to them and he passed out of town along a railroad track.

When he reemerged days later, penniless, dirty, and miles away, people said he must have had some kind of breakdown. Temporary insanity, perhaps, related to stress. They concocted all kinds of reasons why he did it, and when he later became a writer, many others began to ascribe his disappearance to his "artistic temperament." He tried to explain it in *A Story Teller's Story,* the rambling autobiographical piece he was paid far too much for, but it too was a failure.

They were all wrong. That episode was about something else entirely, and something far more mundane. A hillside of freshly mown grass that overlooked a churchyard. A train platform where a man in a tuxedo stood with a bouquet of flowers, and a woman weeping in the vestibule. Shivering in the damp dirt of an apple orchard at dawn.

What stories now?

A FAINT HUM in the air of the restaurant, and the man with the paper looked up. The counterman flicked his eyes to the window, then the Dunkards, and Anderson heard it too; the low moan of motors accelerating. A run coming through town.

Anderson stumbled out of his seat and through the front doors. Might as well see the damn thing up close, he figured, and squaring his hat he positioned himself on the front steps, looking south down Main as the engines grew louder. He picked out sets of headlights flashing then disappearing around curves as they wound their way through the southern reaches of Rocky Mount.

The man with the bow tie stood next to him, paper tucked under his arm. Glancing back Anderson saw the Dunkard family standing by the window. Two sets of lights, then three. Then the light *pock pock pock* of gunfire, and Anderson and the salesman both ducked and raced back into the restaurant. Here they come, the counterman muttered, and Anderson saw through the window a long black Packard roaring up Main Street, swerving side to side, and behind it two cars, the first with a man leaning out the passenger window with his arm extended, pointing a pistol. The Packard thundered past the courthouse and through the intersection of Court and Main, then slowed suddenly, the back end rising up; the chasing cars swerved to avoid collision, one going through a short section of clapboard fence, the other going up on the sidewalk. Anderson could see the hunched forms of the drivers, gray flannel suits, all shoulders and elbows, as they threw their bodies into the frantic steering. At the intersection the Packard locked its brakes and the back end came around sharply in a cloud of smoke, overcorrected, and then the car shot back south on Main, the chase cars extricating themselves with clumsy three-point turns, then back in pursuit. As the Packard passed the restaurant Anderson caught a glimpse of a passenger wearing a small bowl hat, curly hair, a tight smile on dark lips. A woman.

Anderson was about to say something but the salesman was already out the door and running for a parked Dodge sedan, his neatly folded paper fluttering to the sidewalk. Anderson bolted after him, shambling in his greatcoat.

Hey, Anderson yelled. Hey!

Anderson sprinted over and pulled the passenger door open and slid onto the seat and was confronted by a revolver barrel poking into his cheek.

What the hell you doin'? the man demanded.

Anderson gestured weakly at the disappearing headlights, gasping for air.

I think I know that woman, Anderson said.

Seeing the cars dip around a corner the salesman dropped the revolver into his lap and punched the throttle and they lurched forward, the seat throbbing as the Dodge picked up speed. The salesman hunched up close to the wheel, peering out the windshield, saying nothing. Anderson steadied himself against the door as the curve threw its weight at them and the car lost traction for a moment, wheels hopping, then righted itself.

My name's Anderson.

Anderson held out his hand and realized the futility of a handshake when traveling nearly sixty.

Watch it! shouted Anderson.

The salesman jerked the wheel and they swung around a square metal can lying in the road. Turning on Seventh Street they came upon the three cars. The Packard was up a short grassy bank and over on its roof. The two chase cars flanked it and four men stood in the headlights pointing pistols at the overturned car. A telephone pole was snapped neatly off at the base, the wires sparking on the street, dancing and popping like bullwhips. More metal cans spilled out the open rear door of the steaming Packard, wheels spinning blindly.

Shit, the salesman hissed, and yanked the car to a halt. He jumped out and jogged toward the accident. Two of the men immediately turned around and covered him with their pistols, shouting at him to stop. Anderson climbed out of the car and stood waiting. The salesman pulled out a badge. Richards, he said, sheriff's deputy, and after looking it over the men turned their attention back to the Packard. Anderson sidled forward. There were a few houses and shops along Seventh Street, but the porch lights remained off; no one came to the doors. The front of the Packard was badly smashed, the grille folded neatly where it struck the pole, the windshield shattered.

Easy boys, Richards was saying. We can take care of this.

Elmore, one of the men yelled, go check the door.

Easy now, Richards said.

Elmore peered into the smashed window and then yanked open the passenger door. A body slumped out, loose and flaccid and bending in unnatural ways. Anderson quickly looked away, then back again. The face was badly crushed, but they could all see it was a woman. The driver's door was pulled open and then they were dragging out another body and laying it on the grass. It was also a woman; she had on stockings, and her crushed hat had a large daisy pinned to it. She appeared to be all right and she covered her face with her hands, her body heaving with sobs, her dress wadded up around her waist. Richards was bending over the dead woman and muttering to himself. Anderson stepped closer, trying to get a better look at her.

Who's this?

One of the four men, the one called Elmore, was gesturing with his pistol toward Anderson.

Well, Richards said, who are you?

Name's Anderson. I . . . thought I knew this woman. Is that Willie Carter Sharpe?

No, Elmore said. What's your business here?

Another man approached them.

We got to git this here lady to the hospital.

Okay, Elmore said, take Wilkins with you.

Elmore turned to Richards.

The damn woman was throwing full cans at us. Near smashed up several times. Sheriff, you gonna get your boys out here?

Yes, yes, Richards said, we'll get it taken care of.

I need to ask you to back up, sir, Elmore said to Anderson.

You are federal agents? Alcohol Tax Unit? Anderson asked, slowly backing up.

Richards pulled out his pistol and leveled it at Anderson's head.

You *better git* on back down that road. Ain't nothin' here for you to worry about.

ANDERSON WALKED BACK down the road to where a can lay half crushed in the gutter. A square five-gallon can with a simple twist cap. He could smell it before he got within ten feet: the rich, heady aroma of rotten corn mixed with a trace of burnt sugar. Anderson pushed it with the toe of his boot. It was the same kind of can he had seen scattered along the roadsides, piled in the gullies all through Franklin County. Once he saw a group of children playing with a pile of them, kicking the cans about an alley in Rocky Mount. Anderson stood on the sidewalk behind a tree and watched the men at the crime scene; it seemed that Richards just wanted the ATU agents to leave and let him handle it, but they were insisting on something.

A few minutes later the Dunkards from the diner came down the road in an old Ford Model T truck. They pulled up short by Anderson and the older man who sat in the front passenger seat leaned out.

Is they all right?

No, I'm afraid not, Anderson said. One of them's dead, the other is gone to the hospital.

Who is it?

Not sure, Anderson said. Two women.

The driver spoke up.

That's Pearl Hoover's car. I'd seen her in it yesterday.

The old man fixed Anderson with a steely gaze. His unshaven upper lip was full and wet, a trace of gravy in his beard.

White lightnin', he grunted.

What's that? Anderson asked.

Whiskey trade, the driver answered.

The old man stared hard at Anderson's face, his gray eyes milky with cataracts and Anderson figured he couldn't see him too well in the fading evening light.

My name's Sherwood Anderson.

Tazwell Minnix, the driver said. This is my father R. L. Minnix.

Be not conformed to this world, the old man mumbled, fingering his beard.

What's that, sir?

His vague pupils gazed up at Anderson.

Blackwater station, he hissed.

The driver put his hand out and placed it on the old man's shoulder. The old man spit the words at Anderson.

Them boys there. Them Bondurant boys. The worst bunch to ever hit Franklin!

Another car motored down the hill from downtown, swerving around the Dunkards and pulling up just behind the wreck. Three men got out, including a stocky middle-aged man in a gray suit who emerged from the back of the car and strode over to the ATU men with the others in his wake.

Who's that fellow? Anderson asked.

We better be gettin' on, the driver said. Have a good day, sir.

And with that Tazwell Minnix threw the old truck into gear and they pulled away.

The man in the gray suit had pulled Jefferson Richards aside and had him by one of his lapels. They argued in hushed tones, Richards gesturing down the road, the man in the gray suit close to his face. Liquor from the smashed car had seeped into the road and now ran down the gutter by Anderson's feet in a rippling stream. The ATU men were covering the dead woman's body with a coat.

ANDERSON WALKED BACK up the hill to the Little Hub Restaurant and paid his bill. Describing the man in the gray suit to the counterman he learned that it was likely Carter Lee, the commonwealth's attorney. He made a note that he must speak with Mr. Lee as well as with the sheriff, a man named Pete Hodges. And this Jefferson Richards fellow? Anderson also got directions to the Blackwater station in Burnt Chimney. The counterman, a small paper cap perched on his pointed head, eyed him warily. Then in a very sincere voice suggested that Anderson stay away from that place.

Ain't the kind of place for a city gentleman.

I grew up on a farm, sir, Anderson said. I'm no city slicker.

I'll tell you what, the counterman said, they ain't gonna ask you about your family history at the Blackwater station.

BACK IN HIS ROOM that night Anderson took a couple bolts of mountain whiskey and lay on his bed. The whiskey made him feel safely constrained, like he was curling into himself. I can understand how men might favor it, he thought. A bit hot on the throat, and it kept burning in the gut like a ball of coals. But the warmth and flush was immediate and his muscles relaxed for the first time in days. *White lightning.*

Anderson knew that many people in this part of the world still believed there were two kinds of lightning, one being blue-red and the other white. The difference was that a fire started by white lightning couldn't ever be put out: It would burn until it ran out of things to consume. This was the lightning of the great sweeping summer forest fires, the roaring demons that consumed everything. White lightning was the kind of drink that brought your hand to your pounding heart after each swallow, as if to hold it in your chest, because you knew that fire couldn't be put out.

As the liquor warmed his body and brain Anderson thought that the situation here was familiar: the rising tide of industrial greed that pushed men away from their workbenches and their craft to become part of the machine. Progress. It turned them into simple parts, expendable, replaceable, cheaply made as if their hearts were constructed of tin with shears and paste.

Hell, Anderson thought, that seems to be an appropriate thing to drink to, and he raised the glass to his lips and downed the last sip. When he closed his eyes for a moment he saw a great shape in a dark field, above him in the indeterminate emptiness. Its force and mass were terrifying, its slow, descending sway. By the time he got his shoes off and lay back down the whiskey crept up his brain stem and took him, dead asleep before he laid his head down.

Chapter 7

1929

IN THE SPRING Jack Bondurant saw Bertha Minnix playing the mandolin for the first time at a corn shucking at the Mitchell place in Snow Creek. She held her head cocked low, eyes concentrating on the frets of her mandolin, made in the old teardrop style, the rounded bell of the instrument like a wooden scoop nestled against her narrow waist, the tight lace Dunkard bonnet on her crown and the long black dress to the wrist and ankle. Jack stood against the wall, Howard at his side in his shirtsleeves, both men gazing at the players with half-lidded eyes.

It seemed the two men from Shootin' Creek who cut Forrest had melted away. Forrest put his energy into his sawmill operation and the Blackwater station. Jack was surprised that Forrest didn't seem too interested in finding the men who cut him; it was unlike his brother not to wreak vengeance, but then there was much about Forrest that Jack wasn't privy to, and this was the arrangement they'd had since birth.

Jack watched Bertha Minnix's fingers ply the strings, the fret hand moving in quick jumps, her plucking a blur of twitching knuckle strokes, working through "Billy in the New Ground" while people slapped their hands in time. The two men beside her played guitar and fiddle, local men from Burnt Chimney whom Jack had seen before. It seemed an odd thing to Jack, as Dunkards didn't usually allow instrumental music of any kind, instead relying only on their careful harmonic singing. But Howard said they were "new order" Dunkard, and therefore more lenient about such devilry. Strands of Bertha's dark hair fell in her face and at the end of each song she raised her head and cast her eyes over the crowd, a slight smile, a nod of embarrassment. After the second such movement of her head Jack felt a momentary breathlessness, surprised by beauty and split to his core.

JACK AND HOWARD arrived as the sun was going pink on the horizon and the shucking nearly complete. Men stood at a long table of sawhorses and planks and ripped through the corn, tossing it into the temporary cribs hammered together out of birch logs and old sheet metal. The afternoon was cool and the air sweet with the smell of this knobby fruit of the earth, and the men laughed and slapped bare arms as they shucked at top speed. The younger men in the group stamped their heavy boots in the dirt and sang "Old Phoebe," shouting the cadenced words in the direction of the house where the women were preparing supper.

Just a year ago Jack would have been among them, arm in arm, heaving their chests out, snorting like mules, fired with a little corn whiskey, singing in his rough voice. If there was dancing he'd dance every song with any girl that would, his thin lips curled and his dark eyes wet with excitement. Local girls used to call him Injun Jack or Chief because of his prominent nose and thin face, darkened like he was kin to a lost race. The younger girls rarely spoke to Jack anymore, and never kidded him in the lighthearted tone that used to make him smirk and cock his cap. Just a few years before he had watched his brothers Howard and Forrest and wished he could join that shady fraternity. They wore their hats low and *nobody* ever tried to make a fool of them; only the old men could hiss *no 'count* when they weren't around. Men like Talmedge Jamison, Tom C. Cundiff, his brothers; everyone respected them, even if that respect was steeped in fear and awe that at almost any time these men might have a pistol and a hundred dollars wadded in their pockets.

That spring Jack found himself busting his knuckles on pine boards along with Howard at Forrest's sawmill camp, leapfrogging around the county with a gang of roughnecks, itinerant laborers who drifted into the hills come payday and often didn't come back. Because Forrest included a bonus for camp minders and because he had nowhere else to go, Jack slept at the camp along with Howard during the seasonal months. It was in his estimation a temporary and unfortunate setback to his arch plans. Along with Cricket Pate and a few others he managed to brew up a batch of liquor occasionally, putting a few dollars in his pocket, but it seemed he was broke again before the week was out.

Forrest gave him work occasionally at the Blackwater station stacking cans or moving crates, or sometimes Jack and Howard merely stood to the side in the lot, pistols stuck in their waistbands, Howard's beefy arms crossed over his chest. Several times men in long coats from points north stood smoking cigarettes with rifles cradled, watching him and Howard load liquor and each time Jack turned his back he felt the frozen spike of terror. After hundreds of dollars changed hands, and the cars roared off toward Roanoke, Jack couldn't help panting with fear, sweating down the inseams of his dungarees, his tongue a swatch of cotton wool. Maybe he wasn't cut out for it, he thought, as he watched his brothers' placid faces. Once I get a ride of my own, Jack thought, a fine car to make runs, behind the wheel, that's where I belong. Not loading crates for some city swell with a fistful of gold rings.

Howard split his time between the sawmill camp and his wife Lucy in Penhook, though sometimes he was up on Turkeycock Mountain for days, nobody knew exactly where, working up batches of liquor. When the night grew cool at the sawmill camp Jack and Howard rolled up in blankets and lay like weary dogs around the fire. They had biscuits and pork with white beans over the embers in the morning and in the afternoon when the sawmill shut down for the day they'd have another bite and share a jar until it was dark as pitch.

Howard would add a good thick chestnut stump to the fire and stir the coals for the night and Jack would gaze up at the tree-mottled night sky, his face reddened by the sun and his eyes shining, and tell Howard what he was going to do once he got some money together, the new boots he would buy, the automobile, how he would blast out of the county and head west or maybe north, to the open country. When Jack drank he grew expansive and good-natured, continually convinced of the infinite possibility of the world. He told vivid tales of fantastic dreams, of the spaces beneath the mountains he visited in his sleep. He gazed at the faces of people around him and clumsily attempted to describe just what amazing creatures they all were. Afterward people would lie in their racks at night staring at the dusty timbers of a ceiling and wonder *just what that boy was all about anyway?*

Aw hell, Jack would say, there ain't no real way to say it.

Go on, Howard said.

Jack peeled off his boots and vigorously rubbed his blistered and raw feet.

Go on.

AT THE CORN SHUCKING Jack grit his teeth and passed the jar with Howard and kicked at stray corn husks in the barn while the others ate. Jack surveyed the greedy faces at the supper table, sopping their biscuits in souse-meat drippings, dirt farmers who would never have a spot of good clothing on them, and thought how sad and ridiculous and hypocritical their lives seemed and how unaware they were of it. It was a bitter sense of righteousness; standing now alongside those men against the wall, Jack felt strangely cold in their company. He some-how envisioned that the other side carried its own sun, its own source of heat. Instead it was as frozen and remote as the principles of machinery, as the first star of winter. And they were broke besides.

No 'count.

He looked at Howard's heavy, passive face, standing there in the barn, his throat working slowly. None of it mattered to him, Jack thought. Howard didn't give a fig and never would.

• • •

THE NEXT HURT is always coming, always close by, Forrest had said, lying in the hospital. Jack stood by the bed and stared at the ragged stitching under his brother's chin, the black, bristling threads against his white-blue neck. *The only way through is to bury it deep in your gut and let the hot juices work on it for a while. Soon enough you forget whatever it was that pained you to begin with.*

HE THOUGHT OF the old men clustered in general stores, on the front porches of the filling stations, the haggard old crabs at the quilting bee, the thin spittle of bitterness bubbling on their lips, their razor eyes, the angry shaking of their bobbing skulls; they relive an echoing path of past transgressions, careless insults, lost animals, a horse cart disappearing over the hill, crying in the tall corn of summer with a dress around their neck, desperate curses, starlight on an open wound. They only chew on the cud of their past. That'll never happen to me, Jack thought as he watched the shuckers. Not to me.

THERE WAS A VOLLEY of shouts and a man named Wingfield was holding up the sport, the red-colored ear that he'd shucked. It was the only one of the night, and it meant he could kiss any one of the young women he wanted. Wingfield was about Jack's age and they sometimes played together as kids down in Snow Creek. He had grown into a blustery young man who talked with his hands, sported starched collars and snap-brim hats. He had gone all the way through high school and on to the University of Virginia. Wingfield's family was originally from the Tidewater area, plantation owners who now had stately townhomes in the exclusive sections of Charlottesville, and despite the fact that his own father was mucking it out in Franklin County, Wingfield acted like he was merely visiting this backwater before assuming his rightful place among the first families of Virginia.

When the musicians took a break there was a shout and Wingfield held the sport aloft like a torch and marched about, a short troop of men following him. Jack's sister Emmy stood in a corner with some other girls, giggling and pushing back her hair and Jack saw his sister lit with some kind of momentary happiness, a rare sight. He realized that since the death of their mother and sisters, Emmy so often seemed merely a shadow that flitted across the walls of their father's home, a set of hands that set food in front of you. As Wingfield came toward Emmy, Jack felt a flare of rage, but the troop of singing men passed her by and Jack was relieved until he saw the small quiver in Emmy's cheeks, the way she took a breath and thrust out her chin for just a moment as Wingfield passed, the sight of something in her eyes that he hadn't ever seen before. He knew so little about her and her life. Oh Lord, Emmy, Jack thought, and the slender trunk of his heart buckled for the second time that night.

Jack started over toward her and there was a roar from Wingfield's group; he had chosen a girl to kiss and the young people crowded around in a circle to watch. Jack said hello but the girls were too interested in whom Wingfield was kissing, up on their toes to see, and Emmy just put her hand lightly on his shoulder. Jack, taller than anyone there, could see into the circle where Wingfield held the arms of the Dunkard girl.

Why that's Bertha Minnix, one of the girls said. That Dunkard girl from Burnt Chimney, the one playing the mandolin.

Jack watched as Wingfield made a great display of it, gripping the girl by her elbows and ducking in a few times, making feints, drawing shouts from the crowd. Bertha Minnix brought her chin nearly to her chest as Wingfield whooped and the crowd laughed. That damn fool, Jack thought. Then Bertha Minnix raised her face, a tight smile on her lips, tilted her chin up toward Wingfield, who paused, seemingly baffled by her sudden insolence. There was an awkward moment and the crowd grew quiet. Wingfield recovered and winking at the men standing next to him he tucked his head in and kissed her firmly. When he backed away Bertha's eyes blazed and Wingfield let go of her arms, stepping back, uncertain, Jack could tell, but determined to make a good show.

Then the men bore Wingfield away and the girls clapped loudly, briefly crowding around Bertha who ducked her head again before heading back to the other musicians who waited with their instruments. The back of her neck under her bonnet was mottled pink and she touched her ear lightly and Jack knew it must be burning.

Back by the wall Jack drank from the jar that Howard handed to him, then stretched himself to his full height to find her eyes but the guitar player plucked a string and Bertha Minnix set her mouth again, cradling the mandolin to her belly, picking out the chords for "Old Dan Tucker," and the younger men and women standing there swayed and sang along.

Get out'a th' way for old Dan Tucker
He's too late t' get his supper
Supper is over an' breakfast fry'n
Old Dan Tucker stand'n an' cry'n
Washed his face in the fry'n pan
Combed his head on a wagon wheel
An' died with a toothache in his heel

Jack arranged himself along the wall in her line of sight, his cap adroitly positioned, the brim pulled to his eyebrow, letting his cigarette dangle out of the corner of his mouth. Next to him Howard drained the last of the corn liquor, his throat knobbing twice, three times, the quart jar like a water glass in his massive fist. It was an astonishing feat, even for Howard. Sweet Jesus, Jack thought, the man can *drink*. Howard nudged him with the empty jar and Jack turned and went out into the night.

The barn lay in a sloping hollow of open pastures with a narrow creek running down the seam. Jack took another quart jar from the box on the floorboard of Cricket Pate's muddy Pierce-Arrow coupe that they had borrowed. Cars and trucks filled the western quarter of the pasture, with a few Dunkard horse carts. Women leaned against fenders with their arms crossed and looked at men who stood in front of them, hands in pockets, rocking in place slightly. Other men perched on the hoods of cars or the tailgates of horse carts and passed a jar and laughed and slapped at each other with dusty hats. The night was warm and no moon out but plenty of starlight to see.

Jack had an expansive sensation that comes with the onset of certain evenings; the feeling that, in the end, he would be as free and clear as the air over the mountains. He heard the song build to a crescendo and end abruptly, the harsh chord of the mandolin coming through the air in the field and somewhere in the dark a woman laughed.

Jack opened the jar and raising it to his lips he thought of that sound again, the picked strings, the quick movement of her hands. Standing there in the freshly mown grass, tasting the hot liquor on his lips he felt the sky open up and the world come pouring in on him.

JACK COULD NAME the exact moment when Forrest began to distance himself from the rest of the family: as soon as he recovered from the Spanish Lady Flu, the morning when his long blue face rejoined them at the breakfast table. Like all of the Bondurant boys Forrest was a quiet child, prone to long bouts of silence brought on by the apparent opposite of shyness; rather he seized each situation as his own and felt that there was really nothing to add. What is there to say? But after the passing of his mother and sisters Forrest withdrew even further into his own sphere.

That night Jack was roused by the rocking of the bed as Forrest climbed in at some late hour. Jack curled himself away from the burning presence in the bed, a wad of blankets in his hand. Forrest lay on his back, rigid and staring into the dark.

Forrest became a figure who passed silently through doors at night, consuming food as if it was just something to get over with. As he aged Forrest retained the stringy, wan look of influenza, his skin even when burned by the sun seeming a slight shade of blue. His eyes remained sunken, his nose more knifelike, his thin, colorless hair already receding as a teenager. But his knotted muscles lengthened, his hands knobby steeples of bone and tendon with iron strength and unflagging endurance, his fists like post mallets. At work Forrest would hammer the tool into submission, bludgeon the task into defeat; he began at a young age to force the world to bend to his will.

As a teenager Forrest would rise before dawn and top tobacco and pull suckers till dinner, then walk four miles through Snow Creek Hollow to a lumber camp and work a crosscut saw until supper. The next day he would get up and do it again, seven days a week, substituting cattle work, apples, chestnuts, hog butchering, haying, busting clods, harrowing, plowing, carpentry, depending on the season, need, and paying customers. With Howard he took loads of walnuts and apples to Roanoke in oxcarts, and tobacco to Harrisonburg, Martinsville, and Richmond, where he slept on pallets stacked high with pressed tobacco hands in the darkness of the warehouse. He began to drink occasionally, accepting the grimy jar as it was passed hand over hand, though Forrest never took any pleasure in it other than that it helped him put his head down and get his eyes screwed tight long after everyone else had gone to sleep. People moved around him as if he were a wild dog in the street.

Granville was heard to remark more than once that he was glad at least one of his boys had a solid work ethic. *Forrest will never be no 'count,* he murmured to the men standing around the stove at the store.

HIS BROTHER'S dynamism was mesmerizing, and Jack had sought his whole life to find that source of drive in himself. He was eighteen and had nothing to show for it. Jack stood and contemplated the open barn door, a square of light against the dark hills, the drifting music. The cicadas swelled in the trees along the edge of the pasture. He felt like he could stand out there in that field, the liquor humming in his head, and listen and watch all night. It seemed he was plagued with bouts of indolence and idle fancy; such were his gifts. He felt he knew what he wanted, but his industry amounted to little, a handful of change, a few good stories, the same old boots.

Forrest became increasingly thrifty and even miserly, never a characteristic of the Bondurant men; Howard and Jack never held a dollar for more than a day, and Granville, while conservative in his money dealings, never paid much attention to the accumulation of wealth and therefore had managed to spend a lifetime in mediocre economic conditions despite a decent business. Forrest was conspicuously accumulating and obsessing over the money he made. He ate little and wore the same outfit every day until the seams gave out. By the time he was eighteen Forrest had proven himself a man not to be trifled with; the tomfoolery of youth was clearly spent, what lay ahead was only the grinding labor of adulthood and death. Forrest met both with narrowed eyes, knotted fists, and silence.

JACK WALKED BACK to the barn and passing the jar to his older brother he stood again with his hands in his pockets and watched the mandolin player cut through "Fire in the Gum" with her white fingers.

Say, Jack said, how come Forrest ain't gone after those sons a bitches from the County Line?

Howard flipped the lid of the fresh jar into the straw and dirt and took a draw and swallowed, his eyes staying on the musicians, a slight tremor crossing his fleshy cheeks.

Women gave them wide berth and every man dropped his gaze a bit as he passed by, nodding his head in greeting and quickly eyeing the dusty leather of his boot tops, for the presence of Howard Bondurant, especially when he was drinking, was like a bonfire at your back.

When the band finished playing Jack left his brother and stood at the edge of the small circle of people that gathered around the musicians as they put their instruments away. He watched the mandolin player speaking with various people, laughing in an easy, relaxed way. Bertha Minnix's thin neck stretched from her shoulders when she grinned, brushing her cheek to her shoulder. She had a small, plump nose like a chestnut. Have to see her again, Jack thought, have to make sure of it.

Jack turned and walked back to Howard at the other end of the barn and without saying a word the two brothers seemed to agree that it was a fine night.

Chapter 8

1929

ONE MORNING IN early May, Forrest was in the storage shed when Everett Dillon came trotting around the corner of the station. Everett tugged at his shirt collar with his greasy hands, his face shining with sweat, motioning toward the front lot and the fuel pumps.

Someone says they here to see you, Everett said. Sheriff Hodges and some others.

It was early: barely light and a cool mist clung to the roadway as it wound through the valley to Maggodee Creek. Forrest was in his undershirt and hatless; he reached inside the storage-room door and took a long-barreled .38 off the shelf and crammed it into the back of his pants and followed Everett to the front of the station.

Two long Ford Tudor Sedans, brand-new, idled at the pumps. Four men stood by the car, and another sat in the backseat, profile barely visible, looking straight ahead. One of the men was Sheriff Pete Hodges, a man Forrest had known for years and who occasionally came to Forrest to buy brandy for lodge parties. The smaller, older man was Henry Abshire, one of the local deputies; next to him his partner, Charley Rakes, a big red-faced man wearing suspenders and a fat tie. The fourth man wore a tight, ill-fitting wool suit with a bow tie and Forrest did not know him. He had his hair parted down the middle and oiled, his shoes new-looking but already worn around the toe and flecked with mud. The stranger stood with one hand in his pocket and the other on the hood of the car and he had a smile on his face that Forrest did not like. Forrest stopped by the front door and wiped his hands on a rag and the men approached him as Everett ducked back inside the station.

Sheriff Hodges was a round fellow, jowly and generally pleasant. It was Hodges who came to Forrest some weeks back to tell him they had no leads on the men who cut him at the County Line and that the county would be officially dropping the investigation. Forrest had figured as much as soon as he woke stretched under hospital sheets. He felt unmoved by the news; he knew that they would come under his reach again. It wasn't vengeance he sought anyway, rather something more like a reckoning, a balance. It wasn't something you had to seek.

Hey Forrest, Hodges said. This here is Jeff Richards.

Pete Hodges forced a grin and pointed at the new man. Hodges and his deputies normally avoided the Blackwater station, not even acknowledging its existence, and Forrest knew this was because they did not want to disturb the dynamic machinery of illicit booze that kept Franklin County relatively solvent and livable. And because they were afraid.

Hey there, Pete, Forrest said. Jeff.

The men shook hands.

New special deputy, Hodges said.

Abshire kept his head down and kicked at the gravel. A car came winding down the hill from Roanoke, a Dodge coupe, moving very fast over Maggodee Creek and by the station to the south. All the men turned briefly to watch it pass.

Forrest idly scratched at the ragged scar that ran under his chin, now stippled white and crosshatched with raised scar tissue.

I ain't seen you around before, he said.

My father worked a piece down in Patrick County, Richards said. Woolwine.

Who's in the car, Pete? Forrest asked.

Hodges winced and looked at Richards. The mist was beginning to burn off the road and the faint smell of woodsmoke drifted across the lot. Forrest rubbed the small lump of wood in his pocket with his fingers. Charley Rakes made an exasperated sound and mopped at his sweaty face with his fat tie.

Goin' get something to drink, Rakes said, and walked inside the station.

Anyone around, Hodges asked, other than Everett and the counter-woman?

Nope.

Richards put his hands in his vest pockets and rocked back on his heels.

That there is the commonwealth's attorney, Richards said. You know Mr. Carter Lee?

I know of 'im.

Hodges cleared his throat.

Look here, Forrest, he said. Carter Lee wants to work it out so everyone can do a little business. We just wanted to make sure we had your cooperation.

There was a clacking of metal on glass. Carter Lee was rapping on the car window with his ring. All four men looked toward the car.

Henry, Hodges said, go see what Mr. Lee wants.

Henry Abshire walked to the car and bent to the window.

Look Forrest, Hodges said, this is the way it is. We want to help you build your business. No one will bother you across the county all the way to Roanoke. We got a place in Rocky Mount will sell you whatever you need. Grains, sugar, yeast. Worms and caps too. We got spares at the station.

Nobody bothers me now, Forrest said, and what would I need all that shit for?

Jeff Richards chuckled and slapped his leg. Forrest could smell the pomade on him, mixed with the smell of fried pork. He glanced back at the station window and saw Charley Rakes's bulky form standing at the counter, gesturing with his hands, Maggie shaking her head.

Richards cussed with a smile and spit in the dirt.

Hell, we ain't *stupid*. We *know* you movin' liquor! We *know* you got it stored up there in that shed an' you movin' it from the station here.

Easy, Jeff, Hodges said. Ain't no reason to—

We know 'bout all of it, Richards continued. And if you want to *keep* movin' licka then we are going to need to 'ave an arrangement.

Richards had his head cocked to the side and a smile on his face and Forrest watched his eyes and felt the heat drain to his hands. He began to build the box to hold the flickering flame in his mind.

Pete, Forrest said evenly, just who in the hell is this son of a bitch?

Jeff Richards's grin wavered.

Look here, he said, Carter Lee—

You ain't from around here, Forrest said, taking a step forward.

Richards shuffled back and Hodges took his hands out of his pockets. Forrest had seen this before; once in a while someone came by the station and tried to set up some kind of racket, usually some men from Roanoke or Richmond in suits and long coats and sometimes there was trouble but after a few incidents they stopped coming. But the local sheriffs never came by to bother, and certainly not Carter Lee, the commonwealth's attorney, the highest law-enforcement official in the county. The long-barreled .38 in his pants was pressed against his spine and Forrest thought about the motion required to bring it out, the angle of his hand on the handle, the flip over his shoulder and across Richards's nose in a clean semi-circle of wood and steel. He knew that Hodges would bring him in for it and he might spend some time in the joint, but it was clear that this man needed to be hit. He needed to be hit for openly stating what one didn't talk about in front of the law, total strangers, your family, anyone. He thought about Charley Rakes, still inside the station behind him. If he hit Richards, Rakes might likely shoot him in the back.

Hodges stepped between them, putting his hand up.

It's all settled already, Hodges said. Everybody is getting on board, the whole county. I need you to talk to Howard about this.

Why don't you do it yourself? Forrest said.

Hodges grimaced.

It would be best if you did it. You unnerstan' right? Your little brother too. He's been running stuff, him and Cricket Pate and some others.

Henry Abshire walked back to where the other men stood. He nodded to Hodges who turned back to Forrest. Hodges's pupils were pinpricks in a field of blue and Forrest saw that he was afraid.

Look, Hodges said, we'd have to cut Howard's still, and we'd have to take all your stock. We know where the Mitchell boys, Jamison, and Cundiff and the rest of them are makin' and they are all gonna get on board or their stills get cut too. The entire county. That's the way it works. We'll send a man around every few weeks. Start at twenty dollars a month and thirty dollars a load, and that's complete safe passage through the entire county. No one will touch you.

Henry Abshire stepped up and held out a five-dollar bill.

Mr. Lee would like to have a jar of yo' best apple brandy, Forrest, Henry Abshire said.

Look, Hodges said, it's in everyone's best interest. Everybody pays, everybody gets along, we all make money.

There was a crunch of gravel and Charley Rakes came striding out of the station with a bottle of orange pop in his fist. Forrest looked at the car, the silhouette of Carter Lee, the brim of his hat, the aquiline nose and bunched chin settled into the stiff collar. *He won't even look at me.*

Nobody touches me now, Forrest said. And I don't speak for my brothers.

Richards spat again and Hodges snapped the five out of Abshire's hand and held it out to Forrest.

Now take it Forrest, Hodges said. Let's do a little business, all right?

Charley Rakes leaned on the car and drank his pop. A short breeze freshened the air for a moment and brought the smell of honeysuckle and phlox that grew in the woods behind the station.

Don't have any damn brandy, Forrest said, so unless you buying fuel, why don't you get the hell outta my station.

He walked back into the station, the long pistol stock riding up his back. In the darkened room Maggie sat on the counter reading a catalog, a cigarette between her fingers trailing fibers of smoke, the grill cold and spotless, clean utensils hanging on the rack.

Chapter 9

THAT SAME MORNING Howard Bondurant was walking down a small ravine on Turkeycock Mountain carrying a length of copper pipe on his shoulder. The pipe was stoppered at both ends, packed tight with sand. There was a small dirt clearing with a chestnut stump in the center, shoulder-high, stripped of all bark, a steel rail spike hammered at a sharp angle about a foot from the base. Howard stepped from the woods into the white light of the clearing and stopped for a moment, blinked, snapped out three heavy sneezes. He could feel the last knots of last night's drink leaving him, the hard transpiration process. He wedged the end of the pipe under the rail spike and getting to his knees he began to bend it around the stump.

AS A BOY Howard had fought men older than himself and beat them soundly, once as a teenager taking on two Shively brothers, both hard, violent men in their thirties, and thrashing them both. He relished the spasmodic wrench of farm labor, and could toss hay bales from a loft like empty packing crates. Sometimes while in the barn moving hay or in his father's tobacco field he would stop listening to the world and just work, concentrating on the basic repetition of movements, the strain and crack of his muscles. Every so often the perfect cycle of motion and strength was found and it was better than effortless, and the sweetness of the moment rang in delicious ripples through his body. And when Howard stopped, his back muscles shaking, his hands bloody, someone shouting his name, he felt like he had moved through a hundred years of time.

Lately Howard watched the world move by with terrifying momentum. At the sawmill camp at night Howard's body ached with weariness. Whenever he closed his eyes he'd see the moving lights and the fast mountains, the blurred trees. Howard had the same feeling on the troop ship as he sailed between continents, from one horror to another. The vast spaces of slate-gray water, the ship like an island in a rushing stream. It now seemed to Howard as if he ought to take a big handful of something, like roots or mountain rock, to keep from spinning off into the sky.

Their first child didn't live a month. It seemed clear that something was wrong, since the first day Howard saw the baby and stroked his cheeks with his rough fingers. They named him Granville Thomas after Howard's father.

When the second baby came they silently decided they would not name the baby girl until it was clear she would survive. She was stricken the same as the first, barely strong enough to breathe, her tiny rib cage heaving with effort, the almost translucent skin of her fingers like a newt, the blood vessels visible and streaked blue, the eyes capped with crust and tears. The baby wouldn't stop crying for a week straight and the doctor said there was nothing to be done except continue the vitamin treatment and hope that she gained weight and strength. After this next run he would buy some good cloth for Lucy and a box of dry formula, some fresh laying hens, corn meal, and seed vegetables. Then there were the doctor's bills and the money he owed Forrest, and the note on the cabin.

Howard thought of the cabin in the valley of hollyhocks and sweetbriar, bordered by stands of oak and locust trees that ran down to the foot of Smith Mountain, Lucy holding the baby every hour of the day and most of the night, moving through the house like a sleepwalker, the baby at her chest. Howard would come into the kitchen at night and find her at the table with the baby in her arms, no light on, slumped over, exhausted and weeping. The baby had lived now three times as long as Granville Thomas Jr., but they would not name her. The ax they laid under the bed to ease childbirth, old mountain magic, remained there, now forgotten by them both, covered in a light frosting of red dust.

———◆·◆———

THAT MORNING Jack was coming through the deep ravines on the western edge of Smith Mountain, riding one of his father's draft horses, a beefy Suffolk Punch the color of blood. In front of him on the saddle he trundled sacks of sugar and corn. The sky through the trees was overcast and the humidity put a bluish haze over the mountains. The corn and sugar Jack carried was bought on credit against his wages from the sawmill camp. Howard was going to collect his wages and hold them for him until the load was sold. If everything went well, in a few nights Jack would make more money than working several months cutting boards at the sawmill.

Howard had spots deep in the folded face of the mountain, excellent access to fresh springwater, nearly impenetrable scrub brush and thick leaf cover to obscure the smoke, and he made excellent liquor, doubled and twisted carefully, enjoyed mostly by local people who asked for it specifically at the Blackwater station. The county was full of small-timers clustered around tiny stills, all working sporadically and for small stakes; Jack and Howard and maybe a few others could put together a massive set of stills on Turkeycock and flood the county with liquor. If Howard would let him organize his stills, Jack thought, with Forrest handling the distribution like he did for various other syndicates, we could settle this whole damn thing. Most of the distribution ran through Forrest, so why not the production? With Forrest's connections they could just make the long runs themselves, convoys of cars through Rocky Mount and up Grassy Hill and into Roanoke, up the Shenandoah to Harrisonburg, New Market, even Washington, D.C. His brothers seemed intent on excluding him from a full partnership, relegating him to an occasional hand. So Jack had to cobble together his budding industry from whatever was available.

Jack leaned off the saddle to wrestle with his burning feet, clawing at them through the dusty leather of his boots. They could all make enough to buy whatever land they wanted. Maybe pay off the note on his father's store and clear out if they wanted, head up to Roanoke or Richmond and live like gentlemen in a brick house on a street with gaslights. Ride around town in the new car that he deserved, a Duesenberg or Packard, something with real flash. At least a damn Model A roadster with a four-cylinder flat head. He saw himself striding down the street in Rocky Mount with his new boots and camel-hair coat, black gloves and pressed shirt, his new roadster at the curb, gleaming in the sun.

The cicadas screamed in the trees overhead as the horse lurched up the hill. He could hear the Mitchell twins arguing before he could see them. In the clearing the stench of cooking mash was strong, and light wisps of smoke were drifting out of the windows of the cabin, the door, and various chinks and cracks in the logs. Radio music drifted across the clearing.

The fools set the damn place on fire, Jack thought, looking at the cabin.

The twins passed a jar back and forth on the warped porch. Both were shirtless, round bellies hanging over their belt lines, their skin burned a deep rust color. Cal and Eddie were impossible to distinguish, and most people in the county gave up trying and the twins assumed a sort of plural existence. They had the same bright, flawless smile and blond hair as their older brother Danny. When Jack whistled they turned to him in surprise and bounded off the porch and across the clearing to clap him on the back and proffer the jar. Jack waved it away, wiping the sweat that poured off his face with his shirttail.

Hey there Jackie, one twin said, how's things?

Good to see you, said the other.

Where's Cricket? Jack said.

Up in the house.

Cal or Eddie gestured to the smoking cabin with the jar, sloshing a bit on the ground.

Gimme that, you big dummy, the other said. Can't be trusted with a damn thing.

Say Jackie, the first twin said, you know the singer Vernon Dalhart?

Ain't he a Negro? asked the other.

He ain't right? He's a white man who just sings like that, ain't he?

Jack stared at the white smoke drifting from every orifice of the cabin. The radio broadcast was playing a hard-driving fiddle reel. This house wasn't exactly in a remote location. At least a dozen other mountain homesteads were up on this side of the mountain.

What the hell is going on with the house? Jack said. Is it on fire?

Naw, that there is just the still.

Can't you smell it?

Yeah, Jack said, I can smell it all the way across the county. Has he got the still in the house?

Oh yeah, you gotta see it.

It ain't just *in* the house.

They tied the horse in a shady spot and left the sacks in the clearing and following the twins Jack went up the steps and into the smoke-filled doorway.

Damn, Jack said. Smoke's kinda thick, ain't it?

Naw, you get used to it.

So, is Dalhart a Negro or ain't he?

The house was modestly furnished with rough wood furniture, sanded floors. Jack crouched down to get out of the rising smoke and held his arm over his mouth. A steady knocking sound was coming through the floor. The pungent odor of hot mash was intense, the sickly-sweet smell of starches leeching sugar, the germinated corn festering, yeast enzymes taking hold. What was most surprising to Jack was that the house actually looked lived-in, as if someone was still there. There was a sideboard with a few dishes displayed, an open larder with canned goods on the shelves, a rocking chair draped with a quilt.

Whose house is this? Jack coughed.

Aunt Winnie.

Old family relation.

She's gone down to Carolina to visit family, won't be back till next month.

Half blind and crazy anyway.

The twins opened a trapdoor and a thick gust of moist white smoke billowed out. They groped their way down the stairs toward a flickering orange glow. A row of empty barrels, the insides covered with calcifying mash, stood at the foot of the stairs. Cricket Pate was squatting by a twenty-gallon teapot still, feeding the brick furnace lumps of coal. He had a way of squatting when he worked, his bony ass nearly touching the floor, thin knees up around his shoulders. Cricket squatted when he ate, when he worked, and the joke was he squatted even when he slept; he only stood when he was taking a shit. The floor was covered with grain sacks, sugar bags, spilled corn, extra wood scraps left over from the mash boxes. Cricket turned and grinned at Jack, a broad jack-o'-lantern smile, his face blackened with soot. The thumper keg pegged out a steady beat as the condenser steamed and the hot liquor hit the cold pipes. Cricket unfolded his beanpole body and shook Jack's hand enthusiastically.

You gonna like this, Jack, he said. This is something we got going here.

What? The goddamned still in the cellar?

That ain't the half of it. Just wait here a second till I get this run finished off.

Well, I'm waiting outside, whatever it is.

Sure, Cricket said. He turned to the twins.

Ain't you two supposed to be on lookout?

Well, yeah.

And we seen Jack coming.

Well, Cricket said, get back out there. Remember the sign?

Sure.

Cal or Eddie pulled out a rusty revolver from his pant pocket and waved it over his head, mimicking firing off a few rounds.

Two quick shots.

We got it.

Jesus, Jack said. I'm getting out in the air.

You got the sugar, Jack? Cricket called out to him.

Yeah, outside.

Toss 'em down in a minute, will ya?

Jack made his way up the stairs and out the door. The twins came tumbling out after.

Have a taste, Jack.

Yeah, you gotta sample the product.

This gonna make us a bundle.

Standing in the yard Jack took a grimacing sip from the jar.

Tastes like twigs and fly spit, he said, handing it back.

Jack sat on the pine needles a safe distance from the smoking house. The twins sat down Indian style and took out tobacco and rolling papers. Jack swirled the jar around and watched the bead. The bubbles formed iridescent balls that shimmered as they rose, then thinning out to tiny grains of light, at least 120 proof. Decent enough, Jack thought, even if it did taste like hell. They could water it down, put a bit of color in it, some charcoal, iodine, or a bit of bark, and sell it as blended whiskey. Cricket had a knack for making do without essential procedures or ingredients and more than once they made a run of corn whiskey from a muddy cattle creek, liquor that ran brown not because they put any tobacco or bark in it to provide the smoky whiskey color, but rather the heavy clay sediment in the water they made it with, distilled only once halfheartedly in a patched tin can, an old radiator for a cooling coil sitting in a tin bucket, the liquor strained through Cricket's filthy felt hat. Still the thirst for liquor was so great that men came and bought it. Sometimes they only got a small wad of bills, maybe ten dollars for the whole mess.

Ain't you boys supposed to be on watch duty? Jack said.

Hell, Jack, with you here?

What would old Pete Hodges do anyhow?

You think he's gonna arrest *you,* Jack?

Hell. I'd love to see that.

The other twin nodded in agreement and they both tugged thoughtfully on their cigarettes.

Jack looked at the smoldering house. He took a big slug from the jar and then lay back on the pine needles, his hands behind his head, and gazed at the arching trees and sluggish clouds.

HOWARD DECIDED he would stay away from the cabin in Penhook. He would go up on the mountain and make enough money and that would be it. He would work the lumber camp for another season, save his wages and his cut from the tobacco crop, stay away from the card games and drink, and in the winter he would be home again and perhaps the baby would be stronger then and the crying ended. They would get current on the house debt and get out from under it. It was easy to convince himself that it was the best thing to do.

That afternoon Talmedge Jamison would come down from Rocky Mount with the still cap, corn, and barley, the yeast in a packet already at the camp, the mash boxes built and waiting. They could get the mash started tomorrow and if the weather held and if they could get some sugar or molasses, in two days they could run it. Talmedge would take it up to Roanoke in his DeSoto in a caravan with some others he knew, men from Shootin' Creek and Burning Bag, men with big cars with powerful engines to climb the hills, drapes over the windows to hide the jars and cans, men with guns who drove hard and deadly fast.

Howard had never made a blockade run and didn't plan to. If the local sheriffs or Alcohol Tax Unit caught you at a still they cut it up and if you couldn't get away they brought you in and you might do a few weeks or more but that was it. Long-range transporting was a different issue: high-speed chases, accidents, and gunfire. It wasn't Franklin County that you had to worry about. Local law enforcement wouldn't pursue a convoy rolling hard through the county; most often they looked the other way, especially if you dropped a few dollars. But ATU men were known for their tenacity and resistance to bribes and if you got caught with a big load going out of the county or in Roanoke you were dealing with people you didn't know, unlike the local sheriffs, and then you had trouble. Then there were the roving bands of hijackers, desperate men from deep in the mountains or even gangs from up north looking to take a load of free liquor from country rubes. It was the world outside of Snow Creek and Franklin County that presented the unknown variable. Be dammed if I die in a car, Howard thought. Take my chances on my feet.

When Howard finished he had a tight worm coil with nearly ten turns, three feet high, just slightly smaller than the circumference of a barrel: a perfect condenser. Men had different theories about how many turns a coil needed to produce the best run, but generally more turns meant more surface area for condensation and cleaner liquor. Howard pulled out the stoppers and rotated the coil around to drain out the sand packed inside. When copper was hard to get men in the hills would use electrical tubing, radiators, lead pipes, iron, anything that would hold water. He'd seen men running liquor through an old rusted-out Model T radiator, using water from a bottomland creek that was regularly washed out with manure, straining the run through old sackcloth, using nothing but sugar and a bit of corn. A radiator actually made a superior coil, the delicate tubing wound like threads in the block, condensing the liquor off steam along a hundred turns and passageways rather than the dozen or so you could get from a good bent copper coil. But the insides of radiators leeched lead into the liquor. When the demand was high and the money available, men would make it out of sugar water and color it with tobacco juice. Quality liquor was too slow. Who cares if some Yankee went blind? There had been times when Howard had drank such liquor, often called popskull, sugarhead, or rotgut, but normally only when there was nothing else at hand.

Howard slipped the coil over his shoulder and started back through the woods. He licked his lips and thought of a drink. Howard had discovered what every drinking man knows: that quality liquor can make time stop. For a few hours the world comes rushing back, the fields roll under your feet, your hand locks steady around the handle, your back like a piston again, the mountains rise up and form a sparkling crown around you. Anyone could tell it was no way to live, this daily illusion, a phantasm of possibility, followed by blind retching, churning gut, bleary mornings, black heartsickness. But it was better than nothing.

He would pay his debts to his brothers and that would be it. Jack would understand and give him time. His younger brother always seemed to believe in him, always loyal. He thought then he ought to tell Jack about what he had seen during the war. He ought to tell Jack about the ocean and how it moved, how small it made you feel, how it shrank your world into a single droplet. Howard stood beside a tall elm and rested a moment, one hand on the mottled trunk. He closed his eyes and confronted his latest humiliation: that his little brother knew he was drunk in a ditch at the foot of Turkeycock Mountain when Forrest got his throat cut. Howard knew that this was something that hung inside his youngest brother's chest like a rusted knife.

THE RUN WAS finished overnight and the next morning when Jack rolled out of his bedroll he saw Cricket squatting on the porch and smoking a cigarette. A few wisps of smoke still drifted from the house as if it were lightly steaming, the way a sweaty man's head will steam in the winter. Cricket's face was still blackened, and when Jack approached he showed his rotted teeth and clasped Jack's hand.

Come see what we got here, he said, and led Jack into the house.

Cricket and the twins had run the liquor directly into an old water-heater tank they'd sealed up. Using some extra copper piping they hooked the tank into the house's well-water lines. Aunt Winnie had a gravity pump set up to bring in water from a cistern in the basement, piped in from a deep well just behind the house. Upstairs in the bathroom she had a water closet with a flush toilet and a water basin with hot and cold taps. The hot-water tank had a sixty-gallon capacity, and over the last few days they'd just about topped it off.

See, Cricket said, this here is how it'll work.

They were standing in the upstairs water closet. Outside the twins were still sleeping, lying together in the sun like barn cats. Jack's head pinged a bit from the whiskey he had consumed, just enough to knock him out, his last memories from the night before of the twins rolling around the small fire, wrestling and shouting, someone's pant leg catching fire followed by sobbing and then deep snores. The bathroom had a pull-chain toilet scarred with iron stains, and a shallow basin of tin nearly rusted through at the seams. On the wall hung a crudely painted landscape, a set of hills, a fence line, what might have been a cow or a horse.

Aunt Winnie did that, Cricket said, nodding to the picture.

You don't say.

What happens is, Cricket said, man comes in for some liquor, brings his own container.

Cricket brandished a glass pint bottle.

Everythin' seems normal, Cricket said, just a nice little mountain house here, us fellows here watching the place, whatever. Well, at some point, after sittin' a spell, the man asks if he may use the water closet, and we say yes, 'cause he already done paid. And we say, try the hot water, it's real nice, or something like that. So he comes in here.

Cricket held the open bottle under the hot-water tap, and turned the valve. A few squeaky turns, a dull rumble in the wall, and then some murky gray water followed by a thin stream of steaming whiskey. Cricket filled the pint bottle, turned the tap off, and corked the bottle triumphantly.

Man tucks his bottle away, Cricket said, and out he goes.

Hell, Cricket, Jack said, that is the stupidest thing I've ever seen.

Cricket looked at the stained sink. He swished the pint bottle around a bit, then stuck it in his back pocket. Jack walked back outside onto the porch. At the edge of the clearing one of the twins squatted with his pants down, straining like a dog, one hand on a tree trunk.

The other stood a few feet way, seemingly unsure of what to do with himself while his partner was so engaged. Jack knew that Cricket and the twins wanted his help particularly because his presence would keep the sheriffs away and keep the thing orderly as far as customers were concerned.

C'mon, Jackie, Cricket said from the doorway. It'll go. Just wait.

The twins watched him expectantly, one with his pants around his ankles.

Guess we'd better go get some customers, said Jack. Damn, Mitchell, pull up your pants. Nobody'll buy any liquor with your goddamn gonads hanging out.

IT WASN'T LONG before men started to show up. The Mitchells spent the morning driving Cricket's Pierce-Arrow and dropping the word at various filling stations in Sontag, Penhook, and Burnt Chimney. By four o'clock they had a dozen men shuffling around the dusty parlor, a few in the yard, talking in low tones, bottles sticking out of their pant pockets, each waiting their turn to use the washroom. Fifty cents a glass, a dollar a pint. A few men brought demijohns and Jack calculated the price accordingly as he sat in the rocking chair on the porch and collected money. Cricket squatted just outside the washroom door, grinning and sipping from a jar. Thin streams of smoke drifted between the floorboards and the smell of mash was overpowering in the house. The twins were posted down the road as lookouts. Jack didn't know what they were looking for, as many of the men who wandered up the road afoot or on horseback and in various jalopies could've been anyone.

They had collected nearly forty dollars when the old ladies showed up. It was getting darker, and men loitered about the clearing, drinking, a few card games going, and music from the radio was playing through the open door. Jack was sitting on the porch counting the small change when the wizened lady in beaten leather boots came up the steps. She had a couple of other ladies in tow, all of them appearing at least eighty years old.

The Mitchell twins came running through the yard up to the porch, both of them shirtless and sweaty, their faces twisted with fear, crowing in odd, boyish voices.

Aunt Winnie!

Aunt Winnie, what're you doing here?

Aunt Winnie paused to scrutinize the twins, her ancient face folding up on itself into an escalating fan of wrinkles. She was a statuesque woman with a high shelf of shoulders that bunched about her ears. Her dress looked rough-hewn from standing gingham, with stitches like staples roaming across the heavy fabric. Her hair was whittled down to a patch of thin strands that hung in a swatch, barely reaching her collar.

Who you? she said.

It's us, they chimed.

Uh-huh, Aunt Winnie said.

Your nephews, one said.

Cal and Eddie, the other said.

Men on the porch and in the yard began to sidle off, looking like they were idly wandering or they had seen something of remote interest out in the yard. The two women behind Aunt Winnie peered at the twins. They were clearly related to her. After glaring at the twins for a moment Aunt Winnie shrugged and stomped up the porch and into the house, the two ladies following.

Nattie's boys then, Aunt Winnie said. Woman was a crooked liar but that don't mind.

The twins looked at Jack.

Ain't *this* a damn fine mess, Jack said.

Men were now streaming out of the house. Jack was slightly drunk, and the euphoric feeling was quickly mutating into a cloudy annoyance. Aunt Winnie trooped directly into her bedroom without seeming to notice anything unusual. The two ladies in tow sat on the couch and after working their dresses around their legs properly took out knitting needles from large bags. Aunt Winnie came out and stood in the door to her room, her hands on her hips.

Aunt Winnie! the twins cried.

Someone ought to get out a bite to eat around here, Aunt Winnie said, for the company.

Jack went into the hallway to the bathroom, where Cricket crouched by the door, jar in hand.

What? Jack said.

Something ain't right with this liquor, Cricket said, shaking his head sadly.

You better come and see who's out here, Jack said.

Gotta old boy in there, Cricket said, gesturing with his shoulder.

Well, get him out.

Don't think I can, Cricket said, smiling weakly.

Jack opened the bathroom door and it swung in a few inches and hit something. Jack forced it with his shoulder until it gave and a man yelled. Two old-timers stood there by the sink, holding jars of whiskey. One of them was a scraggly fellow with a tobacco-stained beard and he had his pants down around his ankles. At least the tap wasn't running, Jack thought, and closed the door again.

You old fools get the hell out, he hissed through the door. We're closed!

When he came back into the kitchen Aunt Winnie was opening a giant can of government-surplus beans. The twins, still shirtless and running with sweat, stood there with their mouths open. The other two women knitted while Cricket squatted by the sofa. He was stone drunk. Smoke drifted through the floorboards around Cricket's feet like he was squatting in a smoldering campfire. Aunt Winnie shot Cricket a nasty look.

I know you, boy, Aunt Winnie said.

Yes'm, Cricket grunted.

His eyes were watery and he swayed in his low crouch.

Backslider, Aunt Winnie said. Why ain't you been to church like you should?

I done tried, Cricket said.

You ain't tried enough, Aunt Winnie said.

Cricket looked like he was about to cry. His arms were folded across the tops of his narrow knees. The house was quiet except for

Aunt Winnie's struggles with the can of beans and the creaking floor-boards under Cricket's rocking feet. The twins stood by the door and looked like they were ready to bolt.

You gotta find the Lord, Aunt Winnie said. Then your life'll straighten up.

I done tried, Cricket said softly.

Cricket's head hung between his knees. He was only twenty-one and had a bald spot developing in the greasy swirl of his hair.

Was working out fine, Cricket said. Until the damn preacher ran off with my wife.

Cricket began to cry. One of the other ladies stood up and walked into the bathroom.

Aww, that ain't gonna be good, one of the twins said.

What's that stink? Aunt Winnie said. Smells like skunk nailed to a dead man.

<hr>

THAT EVENING WAS payday at the lumber camp and the men lined up to receive their money. Forrest stood behind the large table saw with his metal cashbox and ledger, ticking off names with a pencil stub. Howard stood in line with the rest, his stomach knotted in spasms as he waited for Forrest to finish his tallies. He fingered a slip of paper in his pocket. *Milk, three quarts, thirty-five cents. Bread, three loaves, twenty cents. Round steak, two pound, ninety cents. Flour, one dollar. Shortening, eighty-five cents. Formula, two dollars fifty. Nine dollars for medicine and doctor bill.* Along with his own money Howard picked up Jack's wages to hold, twelve dollars and some change.

After the money was dispersed Howard broke down the heavy saws, wrapping the blades in the oiled canvas bags and locking them down in the heavy boxes. The other men milled around, joking and laughing, making plans for the night. Howard began to sweat, his skin prickling. He hadn't had a drink since yesterday and his calf muscles felt wound like taut wire.

Up the hill in the woods by the campsite, Howard standing by the remains of the campfire. His back ached slightly, the thick sap of labor running down his neck into his gut. He watched the spinning leaves of the poplar trees; they waved palm-up, the pale undersides shifting silently side to side in spots high in the tallest part of the canopy. There must be another layer of wind, Howard thought, that plays through the highest parts of trees, small streams of wind. As he watched the poplars begin to vibrate hard, accompanied by the rising whine of cicadas, or is it the remembered scream of the power saws echoing in his mind? His calf muscles felt ready to snap, his whole body straining. Howard bent his head to the ground, fingering the roll of bills in his pocket, shifting his jaw, grinding his teeth.

It grew cooler, the sun behind the mountain and the shadows long and Howard turns and strides down to the sawmill site and caught a ride up to Rocky Mount with some of the other men. The men called out with blurred voices; they moved before him like ants across a broad piece of asphalt. Sitting on the gate of a truck as it banged down the dirt road Howard felt like a statue in a storm.

Howard was quiet in the company of the sunburnt men as they rolled into a filling station, somebody's brother made up a fresh batch of apricot brandy, a free jar, and the men stood around a storeroom passing the jar till it was empty. Men slapped him on the back, poke his fat biceps, telling stories that he doesn't quite hear, their voices muffled as if through thick water. He glances at their shining faces but mostly watches the jar of copper liquid as it passes hand over hand. Then back in the truck and off to another man's house in a run-down neighborhood of Rocky Mount. Bathtub gin, crude stuff, but Howard takes his share. Like swallowing hot mud, men cough and spit, then rolling cigarettes on a dusty windowsill, cobwebs, wadded insects, someone tunes in a radio to WSM and Olaf the Swede crackles to life, singing barn-dance songs in his nasal accent though nobody laughs, while in the dirt yard outside a man wretches pitifully, then collapses, curling up against a fence post, face smeared with vomit. A coon hound twisting on a line, staked down, yelping in fury. Howard opens a fresh jar and sent the lid spinning off into the darkness. The burning knot in his back begins to fade, the words come when he wants them; he feels in step with the motion of the world.

A few hours later Howard found himself in another car, the driver Talmedge Jamison chewing long leaf and spitting in the footwells, the other men jostling each other as smoke fills the cab. Talmedge grinding the gears as he churns up Grassy Hill to the north of the town. When they pull into Forrest's filling station Howard barely registers. He is thinking of the cards, the way he can see them ahead of everyone else. His hands feel light and fast; he has overtaken the world and now is the primary element, the thing that drives the fuse, and he can win. He's got the wad of money in his fist deep in his pocket. These goddamn hayseeds, Howard thinks, they have got batter for brains. He strides into the station, nods to Maggie who stands smoking at the grill and taps a finger on the bar. Forrest comes out from the back with a plate of salami and apples and, seeing him, pauses and gives him a long stare. Howard stares back, grinning now, and taps the bar again with a blunt finger. Forrest nods and walks over to the table where the other men are already crowding around, eating hunks of the greasy meat with their fingers, scraping chairs, arranging themselves around the table, laughing, their eyes bright with the excitement of the game. The first jar is handed to Howard and he spins off the lid and flips it over his shoulder before taking a deep swig and the men all laugh.

Howard knows he will win. He stretches his broad back, his fingers locked over his head. He feels supple, clean, his mind quick. The perfect throw, the cards line up, the perfect line. He can feel it in the flashing rot of his bones.

———◆———

AUNT WINNIE WAS boiling greens on the stove when the three men came in. They kept their hats on, and Jack could tell right off they didn't have the look of men who wanted to buy liquor, mostly because two of them carried axes over their shoulders. The third man carried a shotgun and all three men wore pistols on their hips. Jack froze, sitting on the couch next to the two knitting ladies, the cigar box of cash between his feet. Cricket was in the bathroom and the twins had disappeared. He had just finished counting and was trying to figure if they had even made a profit, a task muddled by the occasional swigs from a jar. One of the men was a portly fellow wearing a fat tie and suspenders.

Who's in charge here? Charley Rakes said, swiveling around on his heels.

His egg-shaped face was flushed with heat and exertion. He shrugged the ax off his shoulder and let it fall, the blade thunking into the floor. Aunt Winnie turned from the stove, eyeing the new men for a moment, the quivering ax stuck in her floor, then returned to her greens. The other man with an ax, slight and tired-looking, was Henry Abshire. The third man who held the shotgun across his chest was wearing a full suit and bow tie, with moons of sweat under the arms and around his neck. Jefferson Richards tugged at his collar and motioned Rakes to check the rest of the house.

'Spect no biscuits coming outta air round here, Aunt Winnie mumbled.

The room became quiet, the only sound the scraping of Aunt Winnie's wooden spoon in her pan, the faint clicks of knitting needles. Charley Rakes walked into the back. The other two didn't seem to notice Jack sitting there on the couch with the knitting ladies, and Jack was thinking that it would be best if he just sat there quietly and didn't move. There was the wrenching of a door and a squawking sound and Charley Rakes came back into the room dragging Cricket by his ankle who flopped like a worm in sunshine. He sat up and rubbed his eyes and stared at the men and their axes.

Three things you gotta tell us, son, Charley Rakes said. Where's the still, where's the liquor, and where's the money?

Cricket looked at him uncomprehendingly. Jack knew this was bad and with the slightest movement of his feet he began to inch the cigar box under the couch.

Shit, Charley, Henry Abshire said. The still is clearly in the basement.

Abshire wiped the back of his neck with a rag and shifting the ax on his shoulder pointed to a snake of smoke that flowed through a knothole in the floor.

Look at the smoke there. Excuse me, ma'am?

Aunt Winnie ignored him, slopping her greens around.

You ladies mind stepping outside?

Forget it, Richards said. Let 'em stay.

Rakes hoisted Cricket to his feet by his collar. Cricket promptly collapsed again, sinking down on his haunches, his head hanging low.

Rakes started slapping Cricket on the face, back and forth.

The money, son, where's the money?

Jefferson Richards cursed under his breath and with a slow turn he lowered the barrel of his shotgun into Jack's face. The open barrel seemed abnormally large and Jack knew it was because he had never looked at the business end of a gun before.

You, he said. Where's the money?

Jack brought up his hands slowly and shrugged. Richards stared at him, moving the barrel of the gun in short circles around Jack's nose.

What's your name?

Jack.

Jack who?

Jack Bondurant.

Richards smiled and whistled slightly through his wet lips.

I'll be damned, Charley Rakes said. Hey, Henry, this dumb polecat is one of them Bondurant brothers!

Yeah, Abshire said, that's the youngest one there.

We were told we'd find you here, Rakes said. And look, here you are. You are some kind of stupid.

You show him, Richards said, show the deputy where the still is.

Jack got up slowly, his hands at his sides. Between his feet half of the cigar box was wedged under the couch. Abshire reached over and grabbed Jack's shirtfront.

C'mon, son, he said. Let's see it.

In the basement Abshire inspected the still, walking around it slowly, feeling the bead on the joints, rapping on the tubing, following the lines that went into the hot-water tank. The deputy looked tired and washed out, like he had just woken up from a long nap. Abshire knocked on the tank and the dull reverberations of liquid echoed through the basement.

Well . . . that's a first, Abshire said. Don't that beat all. Almost hate to stick an ax in it.

When they came upstairs Richards and Rakes were ushering Aunt Winnie and the knitting ladies into the bedroom. Just wait here, ladies, they said. Official police business. Won't be but a minute. Aunt Winnie carried her pan of greens and her forehead was drawn up in a vicious look of annoyance. Cricket was still folded in a heap on the floor. The cigar box lay on the kitchen table.

You gotta see this, Jeff, Abshire said. This is a new one.

Jeff Richards handed the shotgun to Rakes and picked up the cigar box and held it out to Jack in one hand like a Bible.

Thought you said you didn't know where the money was.

You didn't ask me, Jack said. You asked him.

He pointed to Cricket.

As he said this, Jack felt the swimming, airy feeling that comes with strong fear, the loosening of the bonds. Jeff Richards smirked and gave a slight nod before turning and going down the stairs with Abshire to see the still. Charley Rakes grinned at Jack, his bottom teeth stained from tobacco, like a row of acorns in his mouth. He poked the shotgun against Jack's chest.

You boys don't get it, do you? There's a new system, and you gotta play along.

Rakes brought the gun down and held it across his legs. He looked at Jack and shook his head.

You gotta weapon on you of any kind? he asked.

No.

Gun, knife, anything?

No.

You tellin' the truth?

Yes.

You *are* a damn fool.

There was a sharp clang from the basement, the sound of metal punching through metal, and the next moment Rakes shifted and brought the barrel of the gun up quickly in a short arc. Jack flinched and the barrel landed in a glancing blow across his cheek. He stumbled back but retained his footing, rubbing his jaw, checking his hand for blood. Rakes seemed upset that he didn't catch him cleanly and he pointed the shotgun at his face again.

Come here, he said. Step forward.

More shots of metal rang out from the basement as the men attacked the still with axes. Jack came forward slowly, and when he was a foot from the barrel pointed at his face Rakes lunged and jabbed the end of the shotgun into Jack's teeth. Jack managed to get his head turned slightly and he felt the edge of the barrel bite into his upper lip and crunch against his gums. He turned and went to his knees, cupping his hands at his mouth as the blood began to flow.

Get up, Rakes said.

Jack was afraid to look at him, to look at the end of the gun any longer. He didn't want Rakes to hit him in the face again. The clanging in the basement was increasing in tempo, each blow ringing through the floorboards. Jack got up, his body a quarter turn from Rakes, hands up around his mouth. The front door stood partly ajar and outside in the yard dark shapes moved about. Jack thought about calling out to them. He knew that Rakes meant to hurt him bad.

You ain't so damn tough, Rakes said. I thought they said you Bondurant boys was supposed to be a bunch of hard-boiled son of a bitches?

Then Rakes reared back and hooked Jack in the ribs, a haymaker that flung Jack against the door frame and gasping and stumbling Jack went out onto the porch. Rakes was right behind him and swinging the shotgun low he crunched the side of Jack's knee. Jack stumbled and fell, rolling off the porch and into the dark yard. Shapes scuttled in the black, the noise of footfalls, muttering voices. The aunts? The twins? Somebody please God help me, he thought, please God. A churning-stomach sensation made his mouth water. The light from the doorway shone across his face and he could see Rakes's bulky silhouette standing there on the porch, the gun swinging from his hand. The nausea swelled and Jack began to retch in the dirt. In the distance two gunshots rang out, echoing across the hills. Rakes stiffened and squinted into the dark.

This is terrible, Rakes said. This just won't do.

He stepped back and set the gun inside the door of the house, leaning it against the wall.

I'll give you at least one good shot, Rakes said. Get up.

Jack curled himself into a fetal position in the dirt. I can't stand, he thought. No way I can stand and if I could he'll hit me again. Was that the twins firing off two shots? Was someone else coming? Please let it be Forrest or Howard. Please God.

I said, get up!

Rakes seized him by the shoulders and yanked him to his feet. Jack kept his chin to his chest and his arms in front of his face. One side of Jack's mouth was numb and swelling, and the blood ran down his neck under his shirt. The cicadas took up their chorus in the dark trees.

Gonna get you, Jack slurred. They'll kill you.

S'at so? Rakes said. That ain't gonna help you right now, is it?

Rakes smacked him with an open hand across the face, a spray of blood like mist.

So much talk, Rakes said, about the goddamn Bondurant boys. Hell, you ain't shit. You tell those two brothers of yours we're coming for them next. You *tell* 'em.

Jack couldn't think about anything other than the next blow. Rakes had handfuls of Jack's shirt and jerked him back and forth like a child. For a brief second Jack glanced up and saw how his arms, doubled up, were inside Rakes's arms and he would just have to drive straight out with a fist or elbow and he would catch Rakes square in his fat face. This is it, *now now now,* Jack thought to himself. But his arms remained tight and his chin down and then Rakes held him with one hand and began clubbing him with his other, the blows landing on the side of Jack's head, his neck, smashing his ear, Jack twisting away struggling, Rakes shuffling with him, his arm working in an even cadence, until he landed one flush on the temple and Jack's spine went numb and he crumpled to the ground. Before he lost consciousness he heard himself sobbing, crying out *please no more, no more* and the final sensation of the world was this gush of blood-hot humiliation.

Chapter 10

FORREST WATCHED HOWARD come in with the sawmill crew, grinning like a fool, the group of them loud and faces askew with drink, men in mud-spattered coveralls, stained undershirts, crushed derby hats, a pork pie, chewed cigar ends, bloodshot eyes, Howard's bulk looming over them all, looking like the blasted freaks of a lonely road circus. When they reached into the pockets of their dungarees for their crumpled wads of money streams of sawdust spilled onto the floor.

Forrest deliberately avoided any interest in the games, particularly when his brother was playing, but he knew that Howard had Jack's wages on him. As Maggie emptied the ashtrays she looked at Howard's small pile of bills and coins that lay between his meaty forearms. As she passed Forrest at the counter she would scribble a number on the pad, an update on what his brother was losing, and as the game went on Howard appeared to pant with the effort of breathing. Forrest stood behind the bar and worked his figures at the register. The other men at the table watched Maggie as closely as they dared, her dress of pale cotton with golden flowers, her bare arms. She never gave them a direct eye or a smile, and when she left the room they swore under their breath. *Damn if she don't gotta face that belongs on a coin.*

The radio played the National Barn Dance from Chicago. "The Blind Newsboy," Andrew Jenkins sang "The Death of Floyd Collins" in a watery voice. As she passed Forrest, Maggie gave him a simple blank look that told him his brother wasn't going to quit until he lost everything.

It was almost morning when the men left Blackwater station, and after the card game Forrest fried up a quick omelet, eating it out of the pan standing at the sink. After washing up he shut off the lights and went upstairs. He paused in Maggie's doorway to watch the breathing straggle of dark hair on the pillow, the outlines of her long legs under the quilt. If Forrest had been drinking more than usual, after a while his hand would slip on the door frame or his knees would buckle and he would stagger back to his room and collapse on his cot for what was left of the morning. Sometimes he actually slept standing in that doorway, leaning on the frame, his eyes narrowed, hands hanging loosely or fingering the small lump of wood he carried in his pocket. Sometimes he stood there so long he forgot to sleep at all and the light through the curtains and the dog barking down the road made Maggie shift, and Forrest would go into his room for a fresh shirt and walking out back he would pump icy water from the well, strip down and scrub his body with fresh water and a lump of pumice. When Maggie combed her hair and came downstairs Forrest already had bacon and potatoes frying on the stove, his face impassive, his eyes clear. Whether he slept or not, it was impossible to tell by looking at him.

That night Maggie woke, stirred by something, and she saw Forrest standing in the doorway. She was folded into the shadows of the bedding so that Forrest could not see the expression on her face. She pulled back the covers but Forrest turned away and walked back into the sitting room. After a few moments Maggie got up and walked out to him and when he turned he saw her naked body glowing in the dark.

On the couch Forrest held her face in his rough hands and brushed his lips across her forehead, cheeks, and throat. He smelled of sour corn, dirt, and sweat and she put her chin and mouth into the crook of his neck and softly kissed the scar, from one end to the other.

In the dim starlight through the window he watched her eyes as he struggled to hold her tight to him. Forrest wanted to stay light on her body, to hold her softly like you might hold a bird in your hands, and on his chest he could feel the warm, thrilling beating of her heart. When she looked up at him it was like a question formed on the soft lines of her forehead.

They said nothing to each other and when it was over and he finally slept she covered him with a blanket. He slept like a small boy, twitching and kicking, and she waited with him until his breathing grew even and his body relaxed before returning to her room.

PART 2

I got a letter from Hemy. This after he had written and published the book called *The Torrents of Spring,* and I thought it the most completely patronizing letter I had ever received.

In the letter he spoke of what happened as something fatal to me. He had, he said, written the book on an impulse, having only six weeks to do it. It was intended to bring to an end, once and for all, the notion that there was any worth in my own work. This, he said, was a thing he had hated doing, because of his personal regard for me, etc., but that he had done it in the interest of literature. Literature, I was to understand, was bigger than both of us.

The Memoirs of Sherwood Anderson

Abshire, who asserted he did not have his own gun out of its holster, said he then walked toward the boys and told Jack that neither he nor Rakes was afraid and that although one car had gotten away the best thing for them to do was to surrender and "take their medicine." Rakes then drew his gun, Abshire continued, and told the boys they were under arrest, but Jack turned sideways as if to draw his gun and Rakes fired as Abshire failed in his effort to catch Jack's arm.

Forrest, hearing the shot, ran toward them and Rakes shot again, dropping him in the snow covered road.

"Deputy Abshire Gives Version of Shooting of Bondurant Boys," *The Roanoke Times,* June 11, 1935

Soon there will be no such thing as individuality left. Hear the soft purr of the new thousands of airplanes far up in the sky. The bees are swarming. New hives are being formed. Work fast, man.

The Memoirs of Sherwood Anderson

Chapter 11

1934

SHERWOOD ANDERSON stopped at the Blackwater station in the early afternoon. He had on his old farmhouse coat and mud boots and hadn't shaved in days. The three days previous he had spent sprawled in his room at the boardinghouse, reading letters and writing to Eleanor, picking his toes and daydreaming, putting off this clear lead. He didn't actually admit to himself he was afraid until he pulled into the lot. Of course you are, he thought, you old fool. The day had turned hot and he was sweating in his coat. Two cars were pulled up to the side of the building, one covered with a cloth tarp, but clearly some kind of sleek roadster. A young man with a thick shock of black hair stood on the shaded porch watching Anderson drive up. When he parked in front of the petrol tank the man jogged out to him.

Ya need fuel, mister?

Anderson slid out of the car and adjusted his hat in the sunlight. The inside of the station looked dark and empty. The young man cranked the pump energetically, filling the glass globe with gas.

Y'all got something cold to drink inside? Anderson asked.

Sure.

Inside the station was dark and cool, and Anderson took off his hat and stood in the doorway until his eyes focused and he could see where the counter was. The smell of bacon and tobacco; a radio on a shelf by the window played low music. Anderson took a seat at the counter and drummed his fingers until he realized there was a woman standing at the far end, reading a magazine and smoking.

Hello, Anderson said.

Hello.

You got something cold to drink?

Pop?

You got orange?

Sure.

She put her magazine down and walked over to the cooler. Her hair, straight and dark, was tied back behind her neck. The station was otherwise empty. She set the bottle of pop before him and Anderson put a quarter on the counter. Her dress was neatly pressed, scalloped at the neck, the color of October leaves. It worked agreeably around her legs, giving a long line to the shape of them. Anderson hadn't seen a dress like it in months. None of the old obsessive Puritanism of the American spirit around here, he thought.

She picked up his quarter and rang the register and when she put the change down Anderson shook his head and pushed it back to her. She tossed it in a can by the register and headed back to her magazine.

What's the name of this place?

What?

What do they call this place, this station?

Most call it the Blackwater station.

Blackwater is the creek? The one just down the road at the bridge?

That's Maggodee Creek. But it's part of Blackwater.

Anderson sipped his pop. It was flat and old and sickly sweet. This must have been sitting in the cooler for years, he thought. Nobody bought pop here, that was certain. Maggie picked up her magazine. It was a mail-order catalog—Montgomery Ward. He figured he might as well jump right in.

My name's Anderson.

She arched her eyebrows at him for a brief second. It was the first time she had actually looked directly at him.

Maggie, she said.

Say, Maggie, Anderson said, I'm not trying to be a bother but I was wondering if maybe you had something a little stronger to drink.

She gazed at him with a beautiful, blank expression. It reminded him of gypsies, or Indians. The long, thousand-mile stare that said nothing. A hell of a poker face, he thought.

You know, he said, if a fella wanted something a bit stronger to drink.

We got Cokes, coffee, or some ice water. That's about it.

Anderson drank his pop.

You from around here? Anderson asked.

She put the catalog down again and blew smoke toward the ceiling. Not really.

Where from?

Not too far.

Anderson drank more pop and looked about the room. There was grease shining on the grill. Perhaps they did a morning business, he thought. But I'll also bet the boys came around just to see Maggie, to watch her work. There was a hardness in her face, like she had lived a bit more than others her age, which Anderson put at about thirty, and this maturity lent a cold beauty to her features.

How long you worked here? he asked.

Been some time now.

You married?

No.

Look, I'm not some rounder, I'm a married man myself. I'm just trying to talk. I do a lot of travelin' and don't get to talk too much, you understand?

Sure.

What'd you do before this?

Lots of things.

Like what?

Farming. Mill work.

You worked in a textile mill?

Yeah.

Where?

Martinsville. And some in Carolina before that.

What was that like?

It was all right.

Tough work?

Not so bad. We was treated okay.

Union shop?

Yeah.

How were the other girls?

Fine. They was mostly real nice.

Why'd you leave?

My daddy died.

I'm sorry.

Weren't nothing.

Maggie's dark eyes remained on him, or just over his shoulder, he couldn't tell, and Anderson felt as if something was bearing down on him. His stool creaked. He heard voices, two men talking; it was the radio. This is like pulling teeth out of a dead mule, Anderson thought.

How'd you get up here?

Hitched a ride.

From Carolina?

Yeah.

You done a lot of hitchhiking?

Sure. Got my own car now, though.

Anderson glanced outside and noticed the young man had finished filling up his car. Some kind of operation, he thought. This was the center of the liquor trade in Franklin County? He sipped his sweet pop. Every woman he had met from Franklin County so far was this way. What about Willie Carter Sharpe? Sharpe was still out there on the loose, the whole state looking for her, ATU men combing the hills. If he didn't act quick the *Liberty* article would be shot; Anderson had seen other newspapermen around Rocky Mount, nosing around, ferreting out information on the trial.

So, Anderson said, trying to warm up the conversation again, who's the proprietor of this place?

Forrest Bondurant.

The same who was shot back in '30? With his brothers?

Yep.

That happened around here, right?

Just up the road on that bridge.

Anderson found himself listening, intently, for extra movement around the station. Through the window the young man stood by the pumps, gazing down the road. Maggie drew on her cigarette. Nothing else moved.

He around? Anderson asked.

Nope.

Know when he might be back?

Doesn't have regular hours.

If you had to guess.

I'd guess he'd be here any time now, she said.

Maybe I'll stick around then.

Maggie shrugged.

Anderson stepped outside and squinted down the dusty road. He gave Everett money for the gas and the young man disappeared around the corner of the building. A pair of boys in a rusty DeSoto pulled up and bought fifty cents' worth of gas and bounded inside. He leaned on the hood of his car and tried to figure whether to wait there for a man whom he was warned not to talk to by two different people. A man whose liquor trade seemed like a load of foolish talk. After a moment Anderson walked around the corner of the station and found Everett Dillon squatting on a tire, reading a newspaper.

Any news? Anderson asked.

Everett didn't look up, only rattled the paper a bit.

Says here that Roosevelt gots cuff links for every day of the month.

I've heard that, Anderson said. Whadya think that means?

Don't think it means anything, Everett said, 'cept maybe I'm sitting here on this old tire thinking about all them cuff links.

The boys came out with soda and nabs and piled into their car and as the sound of their engine disappeared around the bend it grew quiet again.

. . .

ANDERSON SAT in his room and thought about Willie Carter Sharpe, out there in the night, at that very moment plowing through the dark at the helm of an overpowered coupe, coming down the mountain like a bobsled on ice, the trunk jostling with liquor as she rounded a steep curve on two wheels, a furious woman with a head of fire that streamed out the windows, a funnel of brimstone in her wake. The road leading into a muddy pit where men with guns in black hats waited with suitcases of cash. It all seemed so absurd. Even if it was real, what was the point? A human-interest piece, of course, but not the kind that was most compelling here. These other people, Anderson thought, the common folk here who dragged themselves through the days in the face of such bleak prospects, that's the story that he was interested in. And Maggie. That was a woman to launch a story, Anderson thought, sketched into the void of her scant details and silence. This is what he had always been able to do, after all.

Bill Faulkner said the very thing to him, at his house in New Orleans, the two of them going down Chartres, Faulkner limping from his "war wound" that turned out to be a fake. Another lie. The two of them talking about writing, America, Negroes, women. Anderson had felt at the time that their talks were of great import, and when the smaller man limped beside him down Canal he had looked up at the older writer with unabashed love and respect, those dark eyes shining. Why he would lie to him, Anderson didn't know. Maybe it was the drink. But then in 1926 Faulkner did the preface of *Sherwood Anderson and Other Creoles,* a caricature of Anderson as a saggy old busker. When Faulkner moved out of his one-room apartment in New Orleans he left behind an old card table and a bunch of empty half-gallon corn liquor jars. He told Anderson he had to drink to get to sleep at night; it was impossible otherwise.

Anderson sat on the edge of the bed and took off his shoes. It hurt him to be not working; it channeled his mind into funny things. He was angry at the salesmen, all the goddamn silent locals, about his work. The groundwater was lowered and he was swinging a dusty bucket. *Dark Laughter* had done well, selling more than anything else he ever wrote. He thought of *Ulysses,* and how when he read it he felt the cadence of the sentences beat in his heart and how he felt, yes, this is the new place of fiction; it is in our hearts and minds at the same time. He had felt that he could work that kind of incantation into a distinctly American style, his style. Now that bastard Hemingway was running around Paris, Anderson thought, reeling into cafés with his arm around a tall, heavily painted woman (*not a woman at all,* some said) and reading aloud to the Americans there something he called *The Torrents of Spring.* Anderson knew it was a parody of *Dark Laughter,* and he felt that this was one of the more cruel things that had ever been done to him.

I'm the one who told that son of a bitch to move to Paris in the first place!

Gertrude Stein wrote to say that she had advised Hemingway not to publish it, and that it had sundered their friendship, but that was little comfort. Anderson thought of Hemingway barreling up the stairs of his New Orleans place, broad-shouldered and shouting, carrying a large paper sack of goat cheese, hard sausage, pickles, wine, fresh rolls for them to eat. It seemed he was always bursting into some room or another, his arms full of plenty, the spoils of his good fortune and charm. He changed every scene he entered. He brought Hemingway to meet Liverwright in New York and got him started in writing. Just a few years ago his words were on the back jacket of *In Our Time:* "Mr. Hemingway is young, strong, full of laughter, and he can write."

THE NEXT MORNING, October 13, 1934, Sherwood Anderson walked from his boardinghouse to the Little Hub for a late breakfast. A crisp, sunny fall day and the streets seemed a bit more lively than usual. The restaurant was fairly buzzing, clumps of men gathered in booths and standing in the aisles, talking excitedly in hushed tones. In one corner a man was thumping the Formica table: *You know damn well who done it!*

Anderson ordered coffee, eggs, and bacon from the counterman. The restaurant quieted as he came in, the talking men returning to their food.

Say, pal, Anderson said to the counterman. What's goin' on?

The counterman in his smeared apron and paper cap regarded Anderson for a moment, then reached over and grabbed a newspaper and slapped it down. *The Roanoke Times.* Headline: DEPUTY AND PRISONER GUNNED DOWN IN FRANKLIN.

Deputy Jefferson Richards was murdered last night around 9:30 P.M. on the road between Rocky Mount and Callaway, near the Antioch Brethren Church. Also killed was prisoner Jim Smith. Both men were found in the road with multiple gunshot wounds.

Is this the same Richards, Anderson said, that was here, that night, when that woman was killed up the street?

The counterman, working at the grill, nodded his pointy head.

Every part of the automobile in which the men were traveling, a 1931 model Ford roadster, was riddled with bullets, most of which, so far as can be told, were buckshot fired from a shotgun. There are 13 dents made by the shot in the rear part of the car body, 12 holes through the top, and 24 holes in the windshield. Richards had at least fifteen wounds, from shotgun and pistol slugs.

Anderson looked around the restaurant at the men forking eggs and hash into their faces. Killed in the night while transporting a prisoner. Somebody, Anderson thought, wanted to be sure Richards was dead. The counterman served up his food and topped off his coffee.

THAT EVENING back at the rooming house Anderson stood before the mirror. First the two men in the hospital get discharged and disappear. A miracle they lived. One would be in a wheelchair for the rest of his life, the other . . . well, Anderson had seen what he would go through the world without. In the evenings it seemed to Anderson that his face looked like a workingman's, the face of a man who had seen and done much. The pouches under his eyes, the grim line of his mouth, the darkened complexion. Though maybe that was just the drink, he thought. It wasn't fooling anybody here, that's for sure.

Anderson regarded the jar of whiskey on his night table, a few inches of clear shimmering liquid. Perhaps a bit of that was what he needed. The real strength, the true gift of the stuff was its ability to strip away healthy illusions: It allowed a man to consider the hard realities of necessity, the thing that hung from his neck like an iron collar. The true, clear, unfettered logic. *The White Logic.*

Anderson smoothed a blank piece of paper on the desk with his forearm.

Dearest Eleanor,

I hope you are well and I hope your friends and relatives in California are well and your trip restful. Work on Ripshin continues. Old Ball is ever confident. The local men continue to surprise me with their work.

Last month an old mountain man came down and asked to do some stonework. I was wanting someone to do an arched stone fireplace. It is a difficult thing to work stone like that. This old guy was closer to a hundred than he was seventy. He was bent nearly double with some kind of stomach cancer. Ball and I laughed at him and let him do his measurements. He measured with bits of dirty string that he tied off in different lengths, muttering to himself all the while. Then off he went back home to do the actual carving. We figured we'd seen the last of him. A week later another man told us the old fellow had died.

On a whim Ball says we should go out and see what the fool had done anyway, so we went to his house up on the mountain. In the back room he had all the stones laid out. The measurements were sure, the carving clean and smooth and exactly as I'd imagined them. They are now in the fireplace where they belong.

I long to get back to Ripshin but mostly to you. Though I feel that I can reach you, even from here. I write to you from surely one of the darkest pits on earth. It is a place of silence.

Chapter 12

WHEN JACK got back to his father's place in Snow Creek the next morning his face was spotted with yellow-black bruises, his left ear split and swollen and a tight stitch in his side. He had an angry welt on his upper lip, a thin half circle the rough circumference of a twelve-gauge barrel. When Granville came in from the barn Jack could tell that he had been up for most of the night. His father gazed at him solemnly from across the breakfast table, his thick beard flecked with chaff and dirt. Emmy served him hot biscuits and Jack gripped his knife and fork, chewing slowly, trying not to grimace from the pain.

I'll need you this morning, Granville said.

Jack nodded and spooned the buttery eggs into his aching face.

JACK WALKED the rutted clay road to the cattle barn. Smoke was rising from the fire pit outside and his father stood in the doorway. Jack was surprised how bent and awkward his father looked; just a few years ago he'd seen him clamber up the side of a tobacco barn and haul sheet metal up with his bare hands to patch the roof. Now his father looked frail and his shoulders slumped forward and his hair just a fringe over his ears, gone gray white and his neck was mottled and scarred from exposure. He looked more and more like the brief and dim memory Jack had of his grandfather.

A veteran of the War between the States, Jack's grandfather had married and become a widower at a relatively young age and never seemed interested in women or marrying again. He lived to be ninety-four years old, and until the last few months he regularly walked the fields in the dead of summer with his sons and took the lead in winter hog killings, muscling the great slabs of bristly pork into the scalding trough. He died when Jack was six years old, and Jack's memories of the old man consisted mostly of his grandfather sitting on the edge of his bed in the back room of the Snow Creek house whittling small figures out of hunks of chestnut that he turned round in his gnarled hands. Jack remembered that their grandfather sometimes held Forrest in his lap as he worked, the young boy enraptured by the flashing blade and the forms that took shape before his eyes.

In the end Jack's grandfather died riddled with age and the horrors of the Civil War. At the onset of fighting he had enlisted in the 57th Virginia, a company called the Franklin Fire Eaters, made up of men from the county who joined up together. The 57th Virginia was the only regiment to break the Union lines at Gettysburg during Pickett's charge, that ill-fated attempt across a half mile of open uphill ground to Grant's center dug in behind a stone wall. The Union soldiers poured grapeshot and canister down the slope as the Virginians came on and the torrent of lead cut men down in great swaths of blood and bone. It was pure slaughter in that field and still the 57th came screaming on like some Viking dream. The Franklin Fire Eaters breached the wall at the Union center, but reinforcements were slow and the moment was squandered, the vanguard butchered at close range, and as the few survivors withdrew the back of the Confederacy was broken for good.

One summer day soon after he passed, Forrest rooted around in the back room and found the rough box where the old man kept his finished wood figures. He brought the box out into the yard and began to play with them in the grass; when Jack approached Forrest sent him bruised and bawling back to the house.

It was a set of carved military figures, some with hats, with rifles, boots, and bedrolls tied around their chests. There were more than fifty of them and nearly all seemed to be in the initial throes of death or madness. Men running, empty-handed, some looking over their shoulders at unknown pursuers. Another man curled in a fetal position clutching his stomach; various men missing limbs grappled with their stumps. A man carried a headless torso in his arms, and two men locked together in a deadly embrace, unclear if they were helping one another or struggling. Other men merely standing, holding a rifle, looking at the ground. An officer leaning on his sword, legs buckling. A flag bearer stumbling, the flag pitching forward. A man standing with his legs wide apart, arms outstretched and head back as if he were waiting to be plucked from the earth and lifted into the sky. A man on his knees covering his face with his hands, hat and rifle missing. They all appeared to be on the same side.

When his mother found Forrest that afternoon in the yard with the figures she quickly gathered them up and later Granville gave him a silent, grim-faced whipping and told him that he wasn't to touch the figures again. But Forrest got something into his head and he stole them from the room soon after and hid them in the woods to play with when he wanted. After several whippings he still wouldn't divulge where they were hidden so finally his parents left him alone. At the edge of the wood when no one else was around he arranged the men in formation, silently enacting the battle and moving the pieces as the melee progressed.

IN THE CATTLE BARN a brindled Hereford stood leaning forward on spread legs, knees askew in the muddy straw. The cow snorted with each breath, her eyes closed, her back bowed up like a bridge and her hindquarters trembling. Jack couldn't help swearing at this plaintive sight of suffering.

How long? Jack said.

Yestiday evenin', some ten hours maybe.

Granville walked to the cow and stroked her head; the animal strained against his hand as he ran his fingers over her ears. A stream of blood ran down the backs of her legs and pooled in the straw next to a coil of rope that led to a block and tackle on the barn's center post. Granville's sleeves were rolled up and his arms were greased and smeared with blood to his biceps; Jack knew that his father had already been inside the cow and that this meant the calf was breech or head up or worse and what they were going to do now was save the cow if possible. Jack's guts began to churn and he coughed into the back of his hand. Ever since he was a boy he shied from the bloody work, castration, hog butchering, de-horning cattle, birthing. His father pressed it on him; it was necessary for a farm to work. As a boy Jack winced and cried as he stuffed his bloody hands into the carcass of a hog to pull out the ropy viscera. The blood wasn't so bad; it was the splitting, tearing, and reaching inside another animal's body that bothered him. And there were the sounds, the honking bray of a dying cow, a sow's scream changing into a bubbling moan, the barking whimper of a wounded rabbit dragging its back legs across a field while Jack watched from a stone fence.

What do you want me to do? Jack said.

Granville stood with his hands on his hips watching the cow arch her back with effort, snorting sprays of foam, her head turned and watching the two men. Jack gingerly felt his torn and scabbed ear. When he woke this morning a rusty stain covered half his pillow. I wish he would just say it, Jack thought. Just come out and say it.

Granville pulled a coil off the wall, a thin cable saw, and handed Jack the saw handles. He stepped to the back of the cow, making a loop in the end of the cable.

When I get this placed, he said, you work that saw, boy. Work it quick.

Granville cinched up his sleeve and then closing the saw loop in his fist drove it into the swollen opening, working it quickly up to the elbow. He put the tips of the fingers of his other hand together in a point and slid it in as well, the cow shuffling a step, her back shuddering as Granville worked his arms in up past his elbows. Jack drew the saw cable tight and crouched with the handles, watching the side of his father's face, his cheek pressed against the broad backside of the cow. Granville worked for a few moments, the cow shuffling, snorting, fresh blood streaming down her back legs in thin rivulets and covering the old man's shirtfront and pants. When he nodded to Jack the young man quickly plied the handles, sawing away with the cable until his father signaled again. After each time Granville would slowly retract his arms, covered in blood and thick gray mucilage, and gripping a bony leg topped with a tiny black hoof. He tossed the leg in the straw and put his hands back in.

After a half hour Granville worked in a rope and got it around the head. Jack put a boot against the center beam and pulled the rope through the pulley, his back to the cow and his father. At first it was immobile, then more shuffling of feet and a heartbreaking bellow from the cow and the rope began to move and he pulled it hand over hand, not wanting to look back. A heavy, wet sound, and Jack heard the body of the calf flop to the floor of the barn. He dropped the rope and panted with his hands on his knees, his palms and arms aching with effort. Small fingers of sunlight ran through board chinks and across the floor. He became aware of other sounds for the first time, the noise of the waking world outside the barn. He drew his arm across his forehead, wiping at the clammy sweat that beaded on his face and stung the swollen welt on his lip.

When Jack finally turned to the cow he saw that his father had covered the calf carcass with an old feed sack. Granville stood at the cow's head, stroking the face of the animal, her giant eyes, black with fear, blinking slowly, her body no longer humped and straining, and Jack thought with relief that the animal would live. Lined up next to the feed sack were the limbs of the calf, wet, knobby things that looked artificial, more like empty bones or old wood than any part of a living thing. Jack stared at them in disbelief, something deep inside him twisted and he let out an involuntary groan. There were six legs there, six legs laid neatly in a row. Outside the dogs began barking in the pen.

If that ain't something, Granville muttered, still stroking the nose of the animal gently with both hands. Damned if that ain't something.

Someone fired up a tractor far away, must be Barbour out to push under his bean field, and the air above their heads seemed suddenly alive with insects, the whine of flies. Never seen such a thing, Granville said.

The cow shivered, then began to vibrate violently, as if it was shaking off water, and a fresh run of crimson, the brightest blood Jack had ever seen, began to pour out of the animal in steaming gouts. Granville held the cow's face as its knees finally buckled and the creature sank to the floor, eyes languidly opening and closing, mouth slightly agape and the tip of its pink tongue showing, and kneeling down the man held it as it died.

———◆———

JACK JOINED Howard at the sawmill camp that week. When the two of them shared a jar around the campfire, Jack was often moved to tell the story of a day when he was a boy, twelve years old. A spring afternoon, the outhouse behind the school, the heat and sound of lightning, the strong sulfur in his nose, trying to explain the things he saw then under the earth and how the shadow of such visions had a way of inserting themselves into his life. This proved difficult for Jack, as his palette of experience was too limited, but like many young men he was convinced that his fortunes would be different from the fortunes of those who struggled around him. And like most young men, Jack's feelings about this were crystallized by several distinct events when he was a young boy. That day in the pen with the deathless sow, the night George Brodie knocked on their door at midnight, and the day lightning struck. The world as he knew it was formed by these events, and with them he felt he would shoulder his way to the green end that was his alone.

THE FIRST THING was the stillness in the air, the rocking outhouse at the bottom of the hill, the long line of dark trees, then a smoky whiff of sulfur burning Jack's nose as he walked the stiff-legged crab of a boy with the painful need to urinate. Dark clouds rolled over the treetops, flexing like muscle and sinew. The nest of pines shook and then Jack was blinded by a terrific shattering light and thrown forward into the grass. The air crackled like wood fire and blazed with heat. Then it was dark.

The wind rattled the shutters of the schoolhouse and pushed the rain, rattling on the tin roof like gunfire and then advancing in a dancing line toward Jack's inert body.

At the same time Mrs. Rufty in the schoolhouse was repeatedly slapping Cricket Pate with a leather strap for sleeping in class, the boy's eyes still drooping as the plaint leather cracked across his skinny neck.

Jack lay in the grass for several minutes. He could not see or move yet he knew that he was still alive, still holding on to life, thinly tethered to it like some kind of string tied to a cloud receding into the distance. It was a sweet, luxurious feeling and Jack wished that he could stay swinging on that string forever. But instead a vision yawned under his feet and he began to dream of an island in the ocean, a place he'd never seen filled with monstrous lizards and birds that walked heavily through dense forests, searching for grubs among the rotted logs and ferns. The island was ringed by rocks, massive boulders the size of small mountains, and on those rocks strange fishlike dogs barked and dove into the blue waters, the sky filled with wheeling birds, white with bands of orange and gray, screaming at the dark shapes of the leviathans under the surface, the huge shadows that made the water rise at the rocks' edge as they passed. Jack could see through the surface of the dark rock, forest, and water into the inner machinery that lay below. He could see the massive gears grinding out their rotations, the spinning flywheel, a muddy U joint burrowing into the coupling, the snaking belts, spitting pistons whacking in their chambers, great steel piles thumping, rising on a jointed hinge knobbed with bolts, then plunging again, discharging great gouts of sparks. Under this Jack saw the grinding plates of stone that tore channels through the earth, the viscous lava moving in underground rivers and emptying into oceans of fire.

When Jack awoke he was soaked through, lying in a wet grassy puddle a few steps from the outhouse. Someone was shouting from the back door of the schoolhouse, a square of light, the silhouette of a boy, one hand stretched out to catch the rain, the other holding on to the door frame.

Jackie!

Even though his eyes were open his mind was still plunged in the dark rock and gears and the sound of his name seemed to come through the echoing chambers of the earth machine. Jack looked at the steps of the outhouse, trying to determine what they were. He rolled over and sat up, the rain pouring off his face and looked at the schoolhouse dark on the hill. It was his older brother Forrest calling for him. Mrs. Rufty had sent him to find his brother—*What was he doin' out there in the rain?*

Jack's shoes were thrown off and his feet were mottled red and burned like they were on fire. As the rain hit him he felt like someone was pulling something through the back of his neck, as if strands of his innards were streaming upward into the rain. He rubbed the back of his neck, then scratched his inflamed feet. His shoes lay in the grass a few yards away, blackened, the leather smoking in the rain. Again Forrest called to him.

Jack gathered his shoes and ran up the hill. Because the rain had soaked him through he didn't notice that his bladder was no longer full, and that the cuffs of his pants were burned black.

A FEW EVENINGS LATER Jack left the sawmill camp, borrowed Cricket's Pierce-Arrow, and drove out to the Dunkard church in Burnt Chimney. Jack sat with a jar between his jigging knees and his hat pulled low, eyeing the stream of Dunkards drawing up their teams and tying up, tattered Model T's with somber children stuffed in the open backseats. At the front door a man in a long black coat and full beard clasped the hands of the men and women warmly and, taking the arms of the men, kissed them on the lips. The old church was built deep in the previous century, its unpainted boards warped slightly, the beams of the front bent with gravity, giving the building a sagging look. The sky over Smith Mountain to the east hung heavy with purple light.

In the dim light Jack was unable to pick out individuals; he knew several Dunkards from his school days. Most families in Franklin County were related to Dunkards in some way and everyone knew that on the last full moon of summer Dunkards gathered in the evening for their annual Feast of Love, where congregation members shared their expressions of affection and hope for the coming year. Jack drank deeply from the jar and wiped his mouth and sweating face on the sleeve of his jacket, his scabbed lip stinging, night flies spinning recklessly out of the stubbled fields coming across the windshield. Jack thought of his father and the way he held the face of the cow as she went down. A row of legs like kindling sticks. The rest of the week had been lost. Jack wandered about the lumber camp, distracted, almost losing a hand beneath a load of boards, tripping over stumpwood, oblivious. That afternoon he got a jar from Howard and without a word left his oldest brother poking the fire, making hoecakes with sliced tomatoes for supper.

The stream of Dunkards dwindled and the field grew quiet. The bearded man by the front door swung his gaze across the parking lot, resting on Jack, who slouched lower in the seat and waited. The man clapped his hands together once, the report echoing across the dark yard, and then stepped inside, an angle of light spilling out for a moment then shutting again, the darkness nearly complete. In a few moments the dull hum of singing drifted from the church. Jack stretched to check if anyone was coming down the road, then stepped out of the car.

Inside there was a narrow foyer, the walls unfinished pine boards lined with coats hanging on pegs, an oil lamp on a small table by two doors that led into the main room. The bearded man in the long coat stood between the doors, watching Jack as he came in, a wry smile on his lips. Like most Dunkards his upper lip was shaved clean. He strode over to Jack and held out both his hands.

Welcome, brother.

Jack stood frozen as the bearded man took his hands and leaned his

face in close. Jack drew his head back quickly, putting the back of his
hand up to his mouth.

Greet ye one another, the bearded man said, with a kiss of charity.

Sorry, Jack said.

Peace be with you, the bearded man said, all that are in Christ Jesus.

The bearded man gestured to the coat pegs but Jack shook his head.
The man put his hand on Jack's back and steered him through the left
door.

In the main hall nearly a hundred parishioners stood in long rows,
men on one side, women on the other, the pews facing each other,
everyone singing. A lattice of wire racks along the walls held wide-
brimmed hats and women's bonnets. In the center of the room seven
men stood by chairs, buckets and blankets stacked beside them. A
short lectern with an open Bible stood before them. A cross made of
railroad ties hung from the ceiling. The heat was incredible, and Jack
immediately regretted keeping his coat on. There was a pause and one
of the men in the middle of the room, an elderly man with a long,
unruly white beard, slowly intoned a series of lyrics. After another
pause, the man next to him repeated the line with a tune attached,
delivered in a flat tone. When he finished, the entire congregation
repeated the line in full with the melody. They sang slowly, working
over each word with patience until the lyrics were rendered almost
unintelligible, full-throated notes, each languidly etched out in the air.
Oil lamps along the wall cast flickering circles of light, the air thick
with oil smoke, pine, and sweat.

> *Why should I be affrighted*
> *At pestilence and war,*
> *The fiercer be the tempest,*
> *The sooner it is o'er*

A few heads turned as Jack entered, then directed their gaze back to
the center of the room. The men, in cleanly pressed and collared white
shirts, stood ramrod straight. Across the way the women wore long
print dresses of homespun and long black capes, heads covered with

small lace caps, pinned fabric, high collars, and long sleeves. Jack would rather have slipped into a back row but there was no choice; the only open spot he could see was in the end of the front-row pew, just inside the door. Nobody held a hymnal, and he didn't see any kind of songbook around, so he just faced the center with everyone else, the seven standing men, the chairs and buckets, the simple hanging cross, blinking through the sweat that ran down his face. He winced when he caught a whiff of rotten corn; he reeked of liquor.

> *The way is so delightful,*
> *I wish to travel on,*
> *Till I arrive at heaven,*
> *To receive a starry crown*

What seemed at first like a muddle of sound began to separate, compartmentalize, and slowly Jack felt as if he could discern individual voices: the men next to him, the women across the way, the throaty intonations of the preachers. He could pick out one voice to listen to, follow the moving notes, then drop back into the thick stream of the multitude, then choose another. He quickly locked onto a certain wavering, thin tone.

> *To receive a starry crown*
> *Till I arrive at heaven,*
> *To receive a starry crown*

The singing stopped and one of the men in the center of the room stepped up to the lectern and began to pray. Everyone bowed their heads. Jack looked at the rows of women and girls before him. Most had broad Germanic features, solidly built, widely spaced eyes, their necks rolled with an extra ripple of white flesh as they bent over their clasped hands. The church grew silent save for the gravelly drone of the preacher, and Jack, the only one with his head up and eyes open, scanned the rows of women intently until his gaze fell upon the small dark head of the mandolin player. The preacher raised his book:

Who hath believed our report? and to whom is the arm of the
LORD revealed?
For he shall grow up before him as a tender plant, and as a root
out of a dry ground: he hath no form nor comeliness; and
when we shall see him, there is no beauty that we should
desire him. He is despised and rejected of men; a man of sor-
rows, and acquainted with grief: and we hid as it were our
faces from him; he was despised, and we esteemed him not.

When the prayer ended Jack tried to catch the eye of Bertha Minnix. She was watching the seven preachers at the table as they con-
ferred, one of whom was her grandfather, R. L. Minnix. In low tones
they seemed to be offering and refusing the right to preach, holding
out their Bibles to one another.

Be free, brother.

No, not I . . . you, brother, will you take the text?

No, brother, please, you take the liberty.

Not I, brother. I will wait for the call.

Be free, brother, I extend the liberty to you. Will you take the
text?

Jack had never seen a batch of preachers so unwilling to preach. In
the Snow Creek Baptist Church growing up they couldn't get them to
stop sometimes, and if they had been so willing to pass off the obliga-
tion a dozen or so old sod farmers would have leaped at the opportunity. Finally the eldest preacher accepted the call, Bertha's grandfather,
and the congregation settled down for the sermon. Jack was grateful
to sit; when standing he was helplessly rocking in place. There was a
faint hum of something in the background, like a large bonfire crackling outside. He shifted closer to the man next to him to try and get a
better angle on Bertha as she was currently hidden by a slab-cheeked
woman in the front row. Jack could just catch a bit of her chin and the
tip of her nose as she angled her face to the preacher who stood in front
of the table, swaying slightly, the Bible held in one outstretched hand.
Jack didn't hear a bit of the sermon that droned on, the church
motionless, sweat trickling down his back and down the inside of his

legs, his feet in his boots a rash of fire. The liquor he gulped in the car boiled in his stomach.

After the sermon the preachers lined up seven chairs in the center of the room. Several men and women came forward, including Bertha Minnix, and sat in the chairs and began unlacing their boots. The preachers moved the metal buckets in front of each chair, rolled up their sleeves, and tied long cotton aprons around their waists. When the seated parishioners had their shoes and stockings fully removed the preachers took one knee and dipping a rag into the water began to wash their feet. The women kept their long skirts arranged straight, reaching nearly to their ankles, looking mildly over the heads of the bent ministers that pawed at their feet with a rag. There was a low mutter in the room and another slow, deliberate hymn began as if by some secret cue. The music seemed to float over him, and Jack could hear only the low insistent hum, building into a grinding sound coming from above.

Bertha wore lace-up boots like all the women there, a dozen small eyelets, black strings, short black socks. She held up one small, pale, pointed foot for the preacher to dab with the cloth. As the kneeling men shifted Jack caught slotted glimpses of her feet, the flash of an ivory heel. He focused on that bare piece of pure skin, the whiteness of it shocking and a shiver traveled up his spine. The grinding noise grew louder and Jack, glancing around, was amazed that no one else seemed to notice.

After the seven women had their feet washed, they exchanged places and took up the buckets and aprons and washed the men's feet. Bertha delicately took a gnarled foot and dipped it into the bucket of water. Then the men in the front row with Jack began unlacing their boots and rolling down socks. The first pair of women, their heads bowed low, kneeled at the other end of the row to Jack's left and began to wash feet. The women remaining in the pews took up another slow hymn. R. L. Minnix, his pointed beard wagging, began to intone a verse over the low singing.

Love not the world, neither the things that are in the world.

If any man love the world, the love of the Father is not in him.

Jack wiped his nose and fumbled awkwardly with his boots. The harsh sound of ripping metal shot through the room, hammering like a blacksmith's forge, and he felt the floor begin to vibrate. The thick, yeasty smell of feet filled the room. Jack's boots were spattered with mud and he wrestled with the laces stiff with clay. He wore no socks. He removed his boots and stared at his mud- and leather-stained feet, his yellow toenails, the scabbed sores and raw patches. The hymn rose, the sound swelling like the cicadas at dusk in the trees, fighting to overcome the building metallic clamor. There was a strange jerking quality to Jack's vision and he coughed dryly. Something's wrong here, he thought. He became aware only of the outlines of things, the rising and falling shapes that occurred at the periphery of his vision as he stared at his feet, the singing buzzing in his ears.

For all that is in the world, the lust of the flesh, and the lust of
    the eyes,
and the pride of life, is not of the Father, but is of the world.

Then Bertha was kneeling at his feet, the bucket set to the side, the cool water reflecting his face, the horrified look, the staring eyes, and Jack passed a hand in front of it to make sure it was real before looking at her face. Bertha looked up, her delicate chin tilted, her mouth in a firm line. Wisps of black hair across her forehead, tucked behind the fine curl of her ear. Her eyes were gray, soft and unlined. Jack clutched at the pew and arched himself like a squirming cat. The spinning saws opened up in the attic, the thunderous whirr of razors, the blades churning away in the sky.

And the world passeth away, and the lust thereof:
but he that doeth the will of God abideth for ever

The preachers standing in a row all gazed at him with puzzled faces. Jack felt the floor twist under his feet and he struggled for balance, gripping the edge of the pew. There was a sudden flash of light, and as Jack watched the men come toward him the long beard of R. L.

Minnix, triangular and silver, looked like a double-edged sword emerging from his mouth, a broad sword trailing streams of light. Jack gaped in horror at the advancing line of men in black, seven men, the sword emerging from the lips of the preacher like a tongue of steel.

There was a sudden heat, a warm touch, and looking down he saw Bertha's hands cradling his foot, her fingers wrapped around his heel and toes. The firm line of Bertha's mouth trembled and then a slight smirk curled in the corner.

Jack pulled his foot away and exploded out of the pew, stepping in the bucket and thrashing against the men next to him, water spilling on the floorboards, the hymn breaking and faltering, growing quiet. Jack could feel the eyes upon him and he took a few steps and crouched, putting up his hands to his ears to blot out the rending sound that blasted from the ceiling. It seemed to make no difference. R. L. Minnix was saying something, gesturing to him, and then Jack was running to the door, banging through it, the ground lurching underneath as he rushed through the anteroom and out into the night, running across the lot in his bare feet like a man running across the deck of a heaving, wave-battered ship.

Chapter 13

JACK WAS SITTING at the counter drinking coffee and eating a plate of biscuits with apple butter when Tazwell Minnix pulled up to the Blackwater station the next morning. Tazwell's father, R. L. Minnix, sat beside him in the car, dozing peacefully. The dew a faint trace on the grass, the air still slightly crisp before the dead heat of August set in. In the lot Tom C. Cundiff was in the process of beating a man senseless.

To Jack the scene at the filling station struck him momentarily as some kind of spiritual ceremony: a man in a dusty coat, bareheaded, was on his knees in the parking lot, hands bent in supplication to a man who stood before him, a queer figure in a dirty bowler hat, suspenders, and stained shirt. A small group of men stood on the low covered porch, watching with halfhearted interest. A few glanced toward the new car at the pumps. R.L.'s head was slumped to his chest, snoring lightly. Tazwell shut the engine down by the petrol pump and climbed down from his truck, watching the peculiar episode that was unfolding. The man on his knees was crying.

Please, Tom, the man begged, don't hit me no more. I swear I'll leave you be.

The side of the kneeling man's face was a crimson mask of running blood. He had rippled clumps of scalp and hair on his forehead, fresh wounds, and his hands shook as he pleaded.

Please, Tom, please. No more.

Tom C. Cundiff's arms hung loose at his sides. In one hand he held a pistol, the hand spattered with blood and his sleeve stained to the elbow. Tazwell froze in horror. Cundiff languidly looked over at him, eyes like dark pinholes, his face twisted with wrath.

Please, Tom.

There was a stir of motion among the watching men and they began to back away. Tazwell saw a man standing in the doorway of the station, a tall, wiry man with a jagged scar under his chin who looked upon the scene solemnly. Another young man with a dark shock of hair trotted across the lot to Tazwell's car.

Tom, Forrest said from the doorway, that's it.

Fuel, sir? Everett Dillon said.

John Horsely began to sob, his hands clenched in front of him. Cundiff let out a short sigh and rearing back quickly on his heels he dealt Horsely such a clout on the side of his head that it shattered the stock of the pistol. Horsely dropped to the side like a felled tree, his feet bouncing. Cundiff tossed a crumpled piece of paper on the fallen man's body and spat a thick stream of dark juice on his back.

There's your goddamn answer to that, Cundiff said. Tell Carter Lee to stick it straight up his ass!

The men standing around the front porch began to drift away. Cundiff snapped his suspenders and shifted his quid of tobacco before walking back inside the station. Forrest stood there looking at Horsely's inert form with a blank look. Tazwell rushed over to the body and knelt beside him and felt under his bloody collar. His scalp was a mess of blood and torn skin, but he was still breathing.

What is going *on* here? Tazwell said.

Someone ought to take him up to Rocky Mount, Forrest said.

Jack got out of his seat and cupped his hands on the window to see better.

Isn't this man a sheriff's deputy? Tazwell said. Isn't this John Horsely?

Yeah, Forrest said. That's him.

Tazwell looked around wildly. A few faces showed through the windows, shimmering in the morning sun, including the bewildered-looking face of Jack.

I came here, Tazwell said, to speak to your brother Jack.

The cicadas began their shrill chord of language in the trees across the road. Bluebottle flies were buzzing about Horsely's head, settling in the sticky clumps of hair, crawling down his collar and across his face.

Did you know your brother came to our service last night? At the Brethren church in Burnt Chimney. Our Love Feast ceremony.

The faintest smile cracked Forrest's face.

I know the place.

Well he was there, Tazwell said, and he was drunk or crazy.

Forrest just stared at him.

Tazwell picked up the crumpled paper that Tom C. Cundiff tossed and smoothed it out. It was a summons to appear in court.

That man assaulted an officer of the law, Tazwell said.

Yeah, Forrest said. Shoulda known better than to come around empty-handed and alone when Tom's been into the stump whiskey for a few days. You gonna take him in?

What?

I mean Horsely here.

Tazwell looked back toward his truck to see the staring, horrified face of his father through the windshield. Jack backed away from the window and sat at the counter.

THEY LOADED the deputy into the back of truck and when they left Forrest came in and leaned against the counter. Jack rubbed his scabbed ear and pushed the crumbs around his plate.

What happened to your face? Forrest asked him.

Ain't nothing.

That so?

Maggie scraped the grill with a spatula, a cigarette clenched in her teeth, her ivory dress worked through with pale roses. Jack knew she was listening. Cundiff shuffled out, mumbling to himself, fired up his car and tore out of the lot and the other men drifted off the porch. Forrest punched the till and lifted out a stack of bills and began counting.

I heard, Forrest said, about what happened over at Winnie Mitchell's place. You and Cricket Pate.

Who told you?

Doesn't matter now, does it?

Jack sipped at his coffee. Maggie strode over and filled his cup. He caught her giving him a slight grin, her lips bending around the cigarette. Oh, God, Jack thought, how many people know? The whole damn county?

The question is, Forrest said, what are you gonna do about it?

This question stunned Jack.

What am *I* gonna do?

As soon as he said it he wished he hadn't.

You expecting someone else to handle it? Forrest said.

Jack was thankful no one else besides Maggie was in the station. He shifted on his stool, scraping the top of his foot with his boot heel.

That ain't what I meant, Jack said.

Forrest set down the stack of bills and stepped around close to Jack. He balled one fist and set it on the counter next to the empty plate. Maggie came over and collected the plate and fork on her way into the kitchen and for a moment Jack thought she shot him a sympathetic look but he couldn't be sure. She strode into the back, her dress whispering against the swinging door.

Here it is, Forrest said. As long as you're my brother, you better never let it happen again. You understand me?

I get it.

I don't think you do.

What if I can't? Jack said. You know I ain't . . . like you and Howard like that. I *never* been like you.

Forrest reached and gripped Jack's arm with his other hand, bending down close to his face.

There is only one answer, Forrest said. People will know, and you will suffer for it for a long time, maybe the rest of your life. *Do* something about it. If those animals out there see for a moment you are afraid, then they'll be at the door and it'll be over.

They told me, Jack said, to tell you that they are coming for you next.

I know it, Forrest said.

Forrest slapped the stack of bills into the register drawer. After a moment, Jack saw a wave of something like weariness cross his brother's face.

You wanna be a part of this, Forrest said, you best be ready to do what's necessary.

I am, Jack said. I'm just saying.

You want the money, but don't want to work for it.

Forrest's throat worked hard, the white rope of scar tissue undulating as he spoke.

We control the fear, Forrest said. You unnerstand? Without that fear, we are all as good as dead.

Chapter 14

1929

A FEW WEEKS LATER in the early fall the three brothers drove to the Jamison place near Thorton Mountain for a meeting. An outbuilding perched on a stubby knob near a stand of woods on Jamison's back scrubland, ringed with cars and a half-dozen horses. Jack noticed more than a few new cars in the lineup, vehicles you didn't see around Franklin, a few Packards, an Auburn sedan, a new Dodge coupe, a two-tone Buick Series 121.

Somebody around here is making some money, Jack thought, and here the three of us crawl up in Forrest's busted-down Ford!

As they walked past the Buick he could smell the supple leather through the window, the ripples of the seams, the burnished shift knob. A straight-eight engine, cast-steel block, 150 horsepower. That sweet mother would do seventy, *easy*. That life under his feet, the smooth roll of power at his toe, the lurch of torque. Jack thought if he could get a new car nothing else would trouble him to the end of his days.

When the brothers came through the door Jack was surprised by how many men were there, and how many men he had never seen before. Forrest had said that men from all areas of the county would be there: Smith Mountain, Linville, Sontag, Boone's Mill, Penhook,

Ferrum, Calloway, even some men from the border areas of Patrick, Henry, Floyd, Pittsylvania, and Bedford counties. After shaking some hands and nodding in greeting to others, the brothers positioned themselves to one side against a wall. The others shifted around in the straw, cursing the cold, waiting for something to begin. A few jars of apple brandy made rounds but most weren't taking. Jack recognized a few men: Roosevelt Smith, J. O. Shively, Arthur Land, Irvin Goode, Gummy Coleman, Posey Webb, George Barbour, Homer Johnson, Tom C. Cundiff, C. T. Cooper, Jimmy Turner, Walter "Peg" Hatcher, Aubrie Kendrick, Talmedge Jamison, and G. T. Washburne. There were at least twenty more he didn't know or had only heard of, like the Duling brothers from West Virginia, whose territory stretched deep into Floyd County. These men were the major players in the business, not just guys with a teapot in the hollow brewing up small batches, people like Cricket and the Mitchells, and it struck Jack just how many large stills were operating in the county and how much liquor was being produced. Peg Hatcher was one of the biggest runners in the county, and Roosevelt Smith, J. O. Shively, and a few others had syndicates that stretched across a few counties. Jimmy Turner, a man in his forties who ran shine out of Penhook, stood on an overturned bucket. George Barbour and Homer Johnson stood next to him.

Boys, Turner said, I appreciate you comin'. As you know, there have been some changes goin' on and I figure we ought to get together and straighten it out. We've got folks from various organizations, including Tom Carter's group up in Roanoke.

Jimmy Turner had a thick bristly mustache and a squinting smile, and was known as a calculating man and one that did not suffer fools.

For a long time, Turner said, we was able to go about our business here in Franklin, and nobody paid no mind. Lately there's been some trouble. We know the Alcohol Tax Unit goin' to come in from time to time an' cut a still and get they pictures in the paper.

He got a small laugh, and some swore under their breath.

The sheriff's department, Turner said, on the other hand, has always let us be. Looked the other way, what have you. But the fact is the ATU has been coming around more regular and Hodges and his boys have been under more pressure. Like usual, everyone is keeping their mouth shut so we don't have too much problem, but the ATU is making it difficult to move out of the county, even using the way stations like Shively's place in Penhook, Hatcher's filling station to the east, and the Bondurant station up in Blackwater.

Turner nodded to each man as he named them. Forrest didn't seem to register the recognition, his eyes flat and calm.

Some of you, Turner went on, already know that there is an offer from the sheriff's office, to make things a bit easier on everybody—

You mean paying a granny fee! Tom C. Cundiff roared.

Cundiff held an open jar, hands shaking. He looked like he slept in the barn. A few men hooted and began to murmur.

Call it what you want, Turner shouted over them, but you get something for your money. For things to go smooth you gotta grease the tracks.

Why don't you just tell it like it is, Cundiff said. Tell these boys where this plan is really coming from. The *sheriff*. Hodges don't have a say over his own pecker. This here is Carter Lee's plan. Revenuers nosing around only where he says to!

Now Tom, George Barbour spoke up, there's no need to get ornery about this.

Men started calling out: Who's running this here show? Hey now!

Nobody is running anything, Turner shouted, we are still running our own show. What we have is an offer of a clear ride. From still to county line, guaranteed. Now that is something worth paying a little money for. The way stations will still get their cut. Hodges and his boys will ward any revenuers off or send 'em on ghost chases. Less risk for everybody, and everybody makes more money.

What's your cut, Jimmy? someone shouted.

Men in the crowd were murmuring and shifting their feet. George Barbour, a fat man with great jowls, spat a stream of tobacco juice in the straw.

Same as you, Barbour said. Same as anyone.

Horseshit, said Cundiff. That why you three calling this here meeting?

Cundiff turned to the crowd. His face was inflamed and his bowler hat tipped far back on his head.

This here is Carter Lee talking, Cundiff said. The damn commonwealth attorney. This here is about making the fat cats richer. Well I ain't ever paid no granny fee to no man and I ain't gonna do it now!

Cundiff pushed his way through the crowd, swearing, and the barn door slammed. A few men laughed. That's ol' Tom, they said, but Jack could tell that many in the crowd were of the same mind.

Let him go, Turner said. He's just gonna make it hard on himself. They'll be a depot of supplies in the old tobacco warehouse in Rocky Mount, anything you need. You may even find some of your old worms and caps there. Sugar, yeast, even copper sheeting can be had out of the warehouse and from Simpson's place in town. A deputy will be assigned to each district and you boys are responsible for getting the fees together from those in your district. So get the word around to anyone you know is making in your area. The deputy will come by each week to collect and keep the ledgers. Everything gets reported to Jeff Richards and he keeps the tabs. Simple as that.

What's the price? someone yelled.

We haven't worked out the exact figures yet, Turner said, but somewhere around ten dollars a carload, plus twenty dollars a month to make.

Men swore and whistled, slapped their hats, and Jack watched the ripple of disgust and displeasure on their faces. Occasionally they greased the palms of Hodges and other local deputies, a bit of cash or a few cans of booze to look the other way; it was expected. But this was something else. This was a system coordinated countywide, no exceptions. This meant a man couldn't even set his own price for his liquor.

Look, Barbour said, for that you get *no trouble*. No lost product, no jail time, no blockading troubles. We can all concentrate on what we do best and leave the rest to the sheriff's office. Let's not forget easy access to all the supplies we need. Look, you fellas know that Prohibition is near over, done any day now. Now they'll still be a trade for untaxed liquor in dry counties in Virginia, but we have a chance to make a good stack of money here while the gettin's good.

What if we don't pay? Forrest said.

The room quieted and all turned to the brothers standing against the wall. Jack straightened his chin and tried to remain still.

What's that? Turner said.

What's Carter Lee gonna do if we don't pay? Forrest said.

Forrest, Barbour began, we was hopin' you'd be in, seeing as your station is a central depot for moving north and into Roanoke.

You gonna report him? a man shouted from the back.

Hold on, fellas, Barbour said. It ain't like that. We just trying to explain how it works. People that don't want in will have to fend for themselves, like always. Now they ain't gonna have the protection, and so when the ATU comes round, they the ones gonna get their stills cut and liquor taken. If the feds want a still, then Hodges will give them one. But not one of ours. Nobody is reporting anybody. That much hasn't changed.

Everyone turned again to Forrest and the barn grew quiet. He shifted his jaw and the ragged scar across his neck rippled. Jack knew that many of these men would rather go along with Forrest and whatever he decided. The granny fee alone would limit the profit of the small-time makers to a minimum, barely covering costs. And what about a man's private stock? If he wanted to make a batch for himself and his friends, he'd still have to cough up the fee, and then what was the difference between that and the government taking a tax? Forrest stared at Turner and Barbour like he was trying to figure what sort of species they were.

So Hodges and his boys will come after me if I don't pay?

Now, Turner stammered, I ain't saying that. I'm just saying there won't be any protection. Now I know that some deputies roughed up Jack there. That's the kind of thing that won't happen in the new system.

The men in the barn inspected his face for injury and Jack set a fresh array of curses on the head of Charley Rakes for this new humiliation.

And of course, Turner said, we don't want the deputies or ATU coming round your station, nosing round there. That would affect everyone.

Nobody bothers me now, Forrest said. No federal man ever come round my station.

That 'cause they know better, someone shouted, and there was a smattering of nervous laughter.

Forrest turned and addressed the room.

Any of you, he said, want to move liquor through me instead of the government, then come on. We'll accommodate you. We will continue to operate free and clear, like always.

A few men whistled and cheered, but for most there was an indecisive mutter and shuffle, silence.

Times are changing, Forrest, Barbour said. You can't do it the old way anymore.

I guess we'll see about that, Forrest said.

He started up and Howard led the way through the crowd to the door, the men parting to create a neat avenue for Howard's bulk. As Jack followed his brothers he felt the intense gazes of these men upon his face. He knew that at that moment these men respected their defiance; they wished they had the gonads for such a move. He only wished they would stay and take charge of the thing, push Turner and Barbour aside and do some talking. If Forrest wanted to he could have the whole crew of them on his side and they could overturn the thing. Jack felt that he could do it; if Forrest would let him talk he would give these men some sense and show that they only needed to band together and push Carter Lee and his cronies out. Who could stop them? Turner was right that there was a lot more money to be made in organization, but why should Carter Lee be the top boss? Why not he and his brothers? But he also knew that Forrest wanted none of it. His organization stopped at himself, so Jack kept his shoulders straight as he ducked out the door and followed his brothers into the glare of the sun.

Chapter 15

1934

SHERIFF HODGES had an office in the courthouse next to the commonwealth's attorney's office, but he was never there. Whenever Anderson came by a revolving series of men—deputies they appeared to be—sat in the office reading the newspaper or smoking cigarettes and they all said the same thing: that Anderson would have to talk to Sheriff Hodges and that they didn't know anything about the pending trial. One of the deputies, a pink-faced boy who couldn't have been more than a teenager, introduced himself as Deputy Hodges, apparently the sheriff's son. None of these men wore any kind of uniform.

Hodges was in street clothes as well, but it was easy enough to pick him out as he was the only one wearing a .38 on his hip at the Little Hub Restaurant. The place brimming with the usual lunch crowd but Anderson worked himself onto a stool next to the sheriff, ordered coffee. Hodges wolfed down fried chicken and potatoes at the counter and barely even looked at him. Anderson began by asking about the wounded men in the Rocky Mount Hospital.

They's two boys from Shootin' Creek over in Floyd, Hodges said. 'Bout all we know.

No suspects?

Pretty hard to figure suspects, Hodges said, when you don't have any witnesses and the two victims won't talk. I should say *can't,* as that one castrated feller is due to die anytime now. No one's coming forward to claim them or claim relation.

Actually, they're gone.

You don't say?

They were discharged last week.

Gotta say I'm surprised. Didn't think they'd make it.

What about connections, Anderson said, to this trial coming up?

Hodges forked a fried potato into his mouth, his chin shining with grease.

Is Willie Carter Sharpe in custody? Anderson asked.

Wouldn't know.

You don't have her, then?

Nope. That's a federal issue. She ain't in Franklin County that we know of.

What about the murder of Jeff Richards?

What about it? Can't talk about pending 'vestigation, you know that.

Hodges shrugged. The grill sizzled with frying onions and the doorbell rang constantly as patrons crowded in and out. Anderson put a hand on the counter near Hodges's plate. The bastard isn't even giving me the time, he thought.

I saw a run, Anderson said, come right through here, just a few nights ago. There was an accident. I saw you there.

Yeah? Hodges said.

A woman was seriously hurt.

She wudn't hurt, Hodges said, she was *dead.*

Seemed like there was some confusion there, with the ATU men? Richards was there. I'm just trying to understand something here.

Nothin' to understand, Hodges said.

Business as usual?

Hodges snapped his head around. That got to him, Anderson thought.

Just seems like nobody, Anderson said, really cares. Like this is all normal. Like nothing unusual is happening.

Yep.

Well, it don't seem usual.

Hodges wiped his mouth and tossed his napkin on his plate. He signaled the counterman for more coffee.

Where you from?

Marion, Anderson said.

I mean originally. Where was you born and raised?

Anderson felt himself flush. Was it possible he knew of him? Was he going to be caught in such a ridiculous lie?

How do you know I wasn't raised in Marion?

If you have to ask me that, Hodges said, then clearly you ain't.

Well, Anderson said, where I come from we don't have cars full of liquor blasting through the town square every night with women at the wheel, men getting castrated and their testicles delivered to them in the hospital, and nobody seems to care or say anything about it.

Welcome to Franklin County, Hodges said, and got up from his stool, pulling out his wallet.

Let me get it, Anderson said, and slapped down a dollar.

Oh, no sir, Hodges said. That would be unethical.

Anderson followed him outside to his car.

Look, can I come in and talk to Carter Lee?

You have to ask him. I'm not his secretary.

Every time I go over there I'm turned away by a deputy. Your deputies. Your son even. I've been over there three times.

Hodges sat in his car and rolled down the window.

Look, those boys in the hospital, Hodges said, they would be dead now if someone hadn't called it in. There ain't no conspiracy going on around here. Now why don't you go on back to Ohio or Kansas or wherever you're from, and let us handle it.

SINCE THE DEATH of Jeff Richards the town began to quiet, a distinct hush, and the normally reticent stopped talking altogether. Anderson had sat in a dozen country stores for whole afternoons, warming by the stove, cooling under a fan, drinking coffee and eating fresh pecans with local men who sat slouched in their leaning chairs, battered boots on the stove, saying nothing. Whole families came in to purchase goods, the children wandering about languidly, cooing to themselves in their secret language. Perhaps that old mountain-family rumor was true, Anderson thought with a smile, perhaps they really *do* wean them on milk and moonshine. Almost nothing was exchanged among the adults except the business transaction at hand.

What everyone in the county *did* talk about was tobacco. It hung on the lips of men like salvation, it was as if they believed if they repeated the word enough, *'bacca,* the chanting, the incantation, the sound of it would bring a strong crop and suddenly Franklin County would flower into prosperity. That summer Anderson watched as men, young boys and girls walked the rows of tobacco for hours in the devastating heat, seemingly endless rows that stretched over the hills, stooping to pull tobacco worms off the stalks and leaves, fat white grubs several inches long that writhed in your palm when plucked, their tiny black heads waving, beaklike mouths seeking purchase. They pitched the worms into tin pails they carried, which they dumped together later and burned—a scene Anderson did not wish to witness. The boys had a habit of skipping that final process and just pulled the worms and bit the heads off as they walked along, stooping and spitting along the hours of the day. The worms could wipe out a crop and they had to be sure they were dead. The certainty of this was the most important thing.

Then the pulling of the tobacco leaves, done several times in the season. When the bottom leaves grew wide and broad from the summer sun, their tips beginning to curl, they had to be pulled off individually and put into a sack, more endless wandering through the rows in the heat and earth. Anderson sat on the hood of his car and watched the boys and men stepping and then stooping, pulling a few leaves that they carried together in stacked bundles called "hands." When the wind came up the large fronds of tobacco waved together like fields of people, rippling like marching crowds, and Anderson thought of his time in the Spanish war, the long lines of blue, tramping feet, wind-burned skin, thirst.

Then the putting up of the hands in the tobacco barns, hanging the thick clumps from rafters at varying lengths in tall log barns mud-plastered with cracks in the mortar for ventilation. The heat playing lightly over the leaves, drying them to a golden calfskin then mottled brown. Putting up and taking down the hands was an arduous process. The air in the barns was incredibly hot, dust choked and stifling, and the boys worked quickly.

A writer friend who briefly raised a crop in North Carolina told Anderson how he prepared the field by burning litter over it, covering the soil with netting, then caring for the tender shoots. He said he shuffled on his knees in the dirt for weeks, pruning the plants diligently and picking the leaves throughout the season with care, always vigilant for the worms and grubs. This man didn't have a vehicle at the time so he rented a truck to take his tobacco to auction. Hundreds of men had their tobacco laid out in bundled sheaves in the warehouse in Winston-Salem, and in the morning the buyers from the tobacco companies walked through with paper and pen and discussed the quality and made bids. The first group of buyers strolled up to his tobacco and said: "Well, look at *this* mess!" In the end he only made enough money to cover the truck rental. The whole season of labor was for nothing. Anderson decided that despite the tender waving of the fragrant leaves, pulling tobacco—the total process of caring for and harvesting—was the most awful, thankless, and debilitating agricultural work he ever witnessed.

AT THE END of October 1934, Anderson returned to Marion for the winter to survey the work on his house. While Ripshin was being built Anderson mostly stood in the freshly cleared yard smoking and watching the men work, nailing posts, planing beams, cutting local stone. It was a stone house, and nothing of its kind had been built in the area around Marion before. But the man he hired to supervise the building, the robust old mountain man named Ball, assured him they could do it and it appeared they could as the house was nearly finished. He spent a quiet holiday at Ripshin with Eleanor and her family.

In the early spring he found himself back in Franklin County, at the boardinghouse. The notice of indictment was due to be posted shortly, and word was that Willie Carter Sharpe was in custody and would testify.

The editors at *Liberty* sent telegrams asking about his progress. He left them unanswered, folded into a pocket of his coat. Let them deal with what they get, Anderson thought. I won't be hostage to this thing. I will go down there and see this damn woman and write this thing up and be done with it.

Willie Carter Sharpe, *the only man or woman alive who could hold a Ford wide open down Grassy Hill*—the famous mountain pass north of Rocky Mount into the Burnt Chimney section of Franklin County and on into Roanoke. The Bootleg Highway, some called it, though only up north; in all his time in Franklin County nobody ever called it that. Anderson was beginning to wonder if it was all a fabrication of the urbanites, a new dream of a Wild West here in the mountainous south, the fantasy of a frontier culture.

WHEN HE RETURNED to the boardinghouse Anderson learned that another deputy had died that past fall. Charley Rakes died in his own bed from pneumonia on October 14, 1934, two days after Jefferson Richards. He was dead the day that Anderson talked to Hodges at the Little Hub. Both deputies were due to testify before the grand jury just two weeks after they died. One after the other; efficient, thought Anderson. Charley Rakes apparently died quietly at home, and there was no pending investigation or evidence of foul play.

Business as usual. He booked his room at the boardinghouse for the next two months.

Chapter 16

1929

IT WAS NEAR two in the morning and Jack sat in his father's Model A, watching Howard's bulky form trudging up the pass with the wheelbarrow into the darkness. They were on a hidden feeder road deep in the base of Turkeycock Mountain. Jack was dressed in his father's dark serge suit that he had taken that night, along with his father's car. On the seat next to him he had a few maps of Franklin, Bedford, and Roanoke counties and an old cardboard suitcase with a few changes of clothes. The trunk of the car was packed full with forty gallons of Howard's doubled and twisted crazy apple in five-gallon cans and another four cans under a blanket in the backseat. Jack eased the choke out of the Model A and the engine settled from a shuddering chug to a smooth purr. Behind him Cricket Pate ground his ramshackle Pierce-Arrow into gear, loaded with another thirty gallons of mostly popskull, sugar-liquor he made with the remnants of a chopped still he reconstructed in a moldy ditch. A blackened .38 hung in Jack's coat pocket, borrowed from his oldest brother.

Howard disappeared into the dark woods. He didn't say a word and Jack knew it was because the arrangement didn't suit him; making and selling was fine but he didn't like Jack doing the driving. Jack didn't care as Howard blew his wages in a card game at the Blackwater station and Jack was owed. He just took it back in booze and a bit of labor. Cricket Pate knew a guy across the line in Burning Bag, an associate of John Carter's, the man who ran the Roanoke liquor trade, who would pay five dollars a gallon for the quality crazy apple and three for the sugar-liquor. The suit, briefcase, and sample bag were intended as a last-ditch option, the faint hope he might pass himself off as a salesman on a deadline. Cricket said he'd dress likewise but his moth-eaten suit and car weren't going to fool anyone and Jack knew it. As they hit Route 33 and headed north Jack began to feel like a damn fool and wished they hadn't bothered with the disguises and just did it straight like other blockaders. They would move fast but they wouldn't look much like runners, and they would be through and back before daylight and if they were lucky they may not be noticed at all.

The Model A smelled like his old man: whiskers and pipe tobacco, linty socks and licorice candy. Jack rolled the car down the drive soon after Granville went to sleep and started it on the fly. If he timed it right he would be back in Snow Creek before six with the fuel topped off and his father wouldn't be the wiser. Howard would take a quarter share, Cricket would take fifty dollars, and the rest was Jack's. He'd make near $250, more money than he'd ever had in his life. He wrestled the Model A around a corner, the tires whining with effort as he hammered along the hard road. A new suit of his own, the soft calfskin boots, brass buttons halfway to the knee, an ivory Dunlap felt cap, a new car: He'd have plenty to put down on his own car and after a half-dozen more runs he'd have it paid off. A roadster, something with some flash and muscle.

They looped around Cook's Knob on State Road 219, hard-packed clay and gravel, low mist coming off the fallow tobacco fields that lay humped in the dark like dry whales, stretches of pine and gum deepening as they wound westward toward Floyd County. They crossed the county line just after three, making good time, and they hadn't yet seen a soul on the road other than lolling raccoons in the ditch, the scent of skunk wafting out of the dark. No real moon out and the watery headlight lamps probed the blackness. Jack found himself almost disappointed; an uneventful trip and his shirt began to dry from the cool air.

A few miles over the county line Cricket flashed his lights and Jack pulled in at a filling station. Burning Bag, or alternately Running Bag, no one knew which for sure, was well known, like Shootin' Creek or Blackwater Creek, as a sort of frontier outpost, a linking point between the worlds of those who walked out of the trees on the mountain and those with cars and money. Burning Bag did a cracking business in the whiskey trade and had its share of knifings and indifferent shootings, bonfire beatings, station-yard thrashings by men without names who existed on no register. The station that Jack and Cricket pulled into had no name, the fuel pumps rusted heaps that glowered in the dark, a one-story shamble with evident fire damage along one wall. There were already three cars in the lot, flickering gaslights burning in the station window where shadows moved with purpose and Jack felt the fear in the pit of his stomach again. This was John Carter's territory, run mostly by his son, Floyd, the man who married and divorced Willie Carter Sharpe. They lined up behind the other cars and killed the engines.

Cricket said he knew a man here named M. O. Walsh, an itinerant railroad hack who negotiated booze trades and sales when he was sober. Three men stood smoking and leaning against the station wall, hats pulled low. Drivers. One man's jacket gapped open to reveal a pistol stabbed in his belt with a barrel at least a foot long. They did not acknowledge Jack and Cricket. Another man sat on the cement stoop, spitting.

Cricket, the sitting man called out, and stood, smacking his thighs. He had a four-day-bender beard and eyes that burned under his watchman's cap.

The two men exchanged greetings and Cricket introduced M. O. Walsh to Jack.

I know of ye, M.O. said, a slight Irish lilt to his voice. I've heard of you boys from Blackwater. Your brother's the one who got his head cut clear off, yeah? Heard he walked it off and drank white mule through ta' hole in his neck.

Let's get on, Jack said, we ain't got much time.

What you got?

We've got sixty, Jack said, of quality crazy apple, the best in Franklin County. And then we got another thirty of rotgut.

It ain't so bad, Cricket said.

Hang on, then, M.O. said, lemme go talk to Floyd.

M.O. went inside the station, disappearing into the murk behind the greasy windows half plastered with newspaper. Cricket and Jack lit cigarettes and stationed themselves by their cars. The other three drivers stood locked against the wall like dark totems, their faces momentarily lit by a drawn cigarette, a set of pursed lips. After a few minutes the station door banged open and a man in a three-piece suit and tight derby hat came striding out. Floyd Carter was as tall as Jack and hooked like a sickle. His suit was clearly quite new, tailored and pinstriped, though worn through at the seams and stained around the cuffs. His long horse face was clean shaven and fleshy. He stopped before Jack and Cricket and thrust his hands in his pockets with conviction, M.O. close behind.

You boys got something to unload, he said.

Yep, Jack said.

M.O. says you got sixty of crazy apple and thirty of rotgut.

Yep.

I hear the commonwealth's attorney got you boys' nuts in a vise over in Franklin.

Shadows flickered in the station and men shuffled in the mud behind him. Jack was sweating through his shirt again, and the hanging weight of the pistol in his jacket pocket was like a lead yoke.

Damn shame, Floyd Carter said. Sheriffs escorting loads out every week, driving the price down for everyone else. I give you four for the apple. Two for that other.

Jack looked at Cricket, who was idly picking at loose threads on his coat.

Thought we agreed, Jack said, on five for the apple and three for the other.

We agreed? Carter said. Who is *we*?

Jack gestured at M.O., lurking at Carter's elbow. M.O. licked his lips.

Mr. Carter, he said, I figured we could do them a sight better.

Now why in the hell, Carter said, would I want to do that?

Well . . .

Sorry boys, Carter said, that's the going rate. If you don't like it you can turn yourselves around and head on back to Franklin. I'm sure the sheriffs will give you the same price, without all the fuss.

My name is Jack Bondurant, Jack said. We come from the Blackwater station.

Without taking his eyes off Jack, Carter popped a backhand across M.O.'s chest that raised a cloud of dust. Carter's fleshy lips rippled into a grin, revealing a mixed array of yellowed teeth.

Shit, boy, why didn't you say so? C'mon inside, Jack.

Carter turned and led Jack into the station. Inside a gaslight wavered on one wall, a few candles puddled on a table. A few men sat around the table at the edge of the light, only their hands distinct in the gloom. An open jar sat on the table, a shaker of salt, and a plate of dried beef and hard eggs. Carter led Jack into a back room with another gaslight that revealed a rusty sink and a tall china cabinet with punched-tin panels. A fat man stood in a corner with a shotgun cradled in his arms.

Look, Carter said, drawing his arm around Jack, I figure we can work out something.

His breath stunk of eggs and the lank hair under his hat was peppered with hunks of dandruff. Jack didn't know what to make of it, other than he was worried to be separated from his booze and to have Cricket out there alone to watch it. This man had been married to Willie Sharpe, the mountain beauty and blockading queen? The pistol in Jack's pocket clunked against something similarly hard and metallic in Carter's coat but Carter didn't seem to notice. M. O. Walsh came in the room with a can in each hand, one of the crazy apple and the other rotgut. After setting both on the sink he opened the cans and slopped a bit of the liquor into jelly jars, then poured a bit of each onto a saucer.

Now git, Carter said.

Walsh bowed slightly to Jack and lumbered out the door. The man with the shotgun shifted slightly, stretching his neck.

Always got to check, Carter said. You unnerstan'.

Carter struck a match and tossed it into one of the saucers. A blue flame rippled, wavered, sparkling. The sugar in that rotgut, Jack thought. Carter popped another match into the second saucer. The crazy apple burned with a more orange flame, weaker, because the alcohol was lower, but a more pure burn. Carter then shook each jar and raised it to the oil lamp and appraised the bead with a practiced eye. He winked at Jack.

Just 'tween us, Carter whispered, square?

He bent to Jack's ear.

Them other boys, he said, ain't getting but four.

Carter opened the china cabinet, taking out a strongbox. He lit a tallow candle on the table and proceeded to count out some bills from a wad that could choke a mule. The man with the shotgun hung in the shadows like an old coat, the shotgun a frozen halberd across his form.

Here you go, Carter said, sixty gallons at five is three hundred, and thirty at three is ninety. He handed Jack the two stacks of bills.

Carter clapped his arm around Jack again.

Welcome to the Midnight Coal Company! Carter said. Let's get it unloaded, what say?

When they finished transferring the cans Carter stuck his head in Jack's window.

Say, you tell ol' Forrest that Floyd Carter says hello. They say the goddamn sheriff's running things in Franklin but I figured ol' Forrest and that big ox Howard wouldn't bend over for no fat cat! You tell 'em I said so!

JACK COASTED the Model A up the drive and drew it up to where his father had parked it the night before. It was still before five, and Emmy wouldn't be up, so he leaned on the hood for a moment and watched the stars wink out over the hills. The tobacco fields began to take shape, the withered stubs casting star-shadow and the night was so quiet that Jack could hear Snow Creek gurgling at the bottom of the hill. He had a cigarette and counted out the money again. Two hundred thirty dollars and change. One week's work. The future rose up like the coming dawn before him and he grinned and kicked his heels in the grass before turning to the house and shrugging off his father's suit.

THE NEXT AFTERNOON Jack was in Slone's Haberdashery, working his blistered feet into those burgundy calfskin boots. The creamy inside was as soft as he dreamed it would be and the two dollars seemed like a mere pittance. He also picked up a long camel-hair coat, a sharp Dunlap cap to match, leather driving gloves with pearl snaps, two shirts with collars, a paisley bow tie, and a wool three-piece suit made in England with pinstripes. He tried them on in back and came out with his old clothes in a bundle and handed it to Slone.

I'll wear it out, he says to Slone. You can burn those other things.

At the counter he picked up a handful of nickel cigars and slapped down the cash for his purchases. Slone never looked at him straight, not once, but Jack didn't care, admiring himself in the shop mirror as Slone rang out his change. A cluster of men in the back murmured around a newspaper, shaking their heads.

What's that about? Jack said, jerking his chin.

Slone reached over and tossed a copy of the Roanoke paper on the counter. The headline was in four-inch bold type: NEW WALL STREET PANIC!

Give me one of them Brownie cameras as well, Jack said. May want to get a picture of myself with my new car.

Slone got the camera and rang it up.

I'll be back soon, Jack said.

I hope so, sir, Slone said, bowing his oiled head.

JACK HEADED straight to the car lot and ended up plunking down two hundred dollars on a 1928 Model A Sport Business Coupe, midnight blue and with a cargo trunk rather than a rumble seat. The two-hundred-cubic-inch engine would do forty horsepower, with three-speed transmission and four-wheel brakes. The speedometer, a wheel rolling back and forth through a small window, topped out at eighty miles an hour. The trunk would hold sixty gallons easy; he would tighten the springs up to take the extra weight and Cricket claimed he could put on a downdraft carburetor to up the horsepower; maybe they could even bore out the cylinders to increase displacement if they could get the right tools. Either way, to Jack it was the first step in his new business, the start of an empire. He had every expectation that in a few months he would head to Martinsville for the V8 Lincoln, maybe the Packard 8 Phaeton or Club Sedan. He drove the Model A off the lot, puffing a cigarillo, cap pulled rakishly to one side, the top down even though the day was cool with the onset of autumn. Twenty bucks in his pocket making a nice knot against his thigh. Now Forrest would have to support his plan; it was too easy and he had practically a guarantee from Floyd Carter in Burning Bag.

He thought of the look on Bertha Minnix's face when he'd step off the running boards in his new pinstripes, camel-hair coat, boots gleaming. He would make a present of the Brownie camera; he realized now that he was planning that all along. She seemed like the type who would like to take pictures. He saw the light in her face, her thin lips smirking at the corners in embarrassment, fingering the downy hair around her neck. Jack pushed the four cylinder till the valves pinged, shifting into high gear and drifting through turns, the fresh tires biting gravel and spinning hunks of clay and dirt into the wayside. There weren't many roads in Franklin County that you could get up past thirty except the hard road 33 and a few other stretches, but Jack figured he'd get his chance soon enough.

Have to make a serious impression, he thought, after that mess at the Dunkard church. A completely different man. An upstanding man of promise, an entrepreneur, a man who made things happen and did it with his own wiles. The world was changing, evolving, and the man who didn't jump would be left behind in the muddy hole. Yes, Jack thought to himself, it's time I did some courting. It's high time I begin to separate myself from the rabble.

Chapter 17

1929

THE FORD BANGED down a gravel road just south of Penhook near the Pittsylvania County line. The car swung into a dirt drive that carried over a rise and into a small hollow, the temporary sawmill camp, a clearing between two stands of pitch pine and black spruce. In the clearing a long covered shed made of logs and discarded sheet metal stood in the sunshine, a few smaller outbuildings flanking it. At the rear of the shed, nearest the circle of trees, a tall double boiler sat rusting in the grass, its smokestacks nearly twenty feet high and blackened with creosote and canted to one side. A truck sat under one end of the shed near a tall stack of uncut pine logs, an old Model T without wheels up on blocks, coughing out great gouts of black smoke. A belt was hooked up to the rear axle that looped around a set of cogs to a large-toothed table saw. Wood in various states of milling stood about in stacks and piles, the ground ankle deep in rich-smelling sawdust. In the clearing pairs of men plied long crosscut saws to enormous logs propped on sawhorses, wrestling the saws back and forth with a ragged, desperate motion; others hitched teams of mules to the logs to drag them to the shed. Other men under the shed worked the belt saw and still more were engaged in planing the logs and stacking them into piles.

Forrest stood at one end of the table wrestling the end of a pine log into the table-saw chute. His dungarees were dusted with wood chips, the sleeves of his sweat-soaked undershirt rolled up high. He was hatless, his hair matted with sweat and sawdust. Jack worked at a table under the shed with a bulky wooden block planer, shaving the edges off planks in long strips. At the other end of the clearing at the edge of the forest Howard pulled a crosscut saw with another man. A team of mules hitched to a wagon stood in the sunlight, nosing at crabgrass and thistles that lay trampled in the dirt.

When the roadster pulled up to the shed Forrest flicked an eye in that direction and continued to manhandle the log on the table. The men plying crosscut saws paused, releasing their handles and standing up from their feral crouches, wiping their brows with their shirt-sleeves. Howard glanced at the car and then nodding to the man opposite tore into the log again, his heavy torso shuddering with each stroke. Jack dropped his block plane onto the table as two men climbed out of the car. Both wore short, fat ties, low hats, muddy boots, and belted slacks. Charley Rakes's sour, doughy face was scrunched in the sunshine. Abshire the smaller man, finely built with a delicate mouth. They walked past the pairs of crosscut men and continued on under the shed.

Here we go, Jack thought, this could be it so get your yellow ass ready. No way Forrest would let them get away with what they'd done to him, and with Howard there too it ought to be some fun. I'll be ready, Jack thought, and I'll get my shots in.

As the men approached, Forrest kicked a heavy switch on the floor and the big saw spun to life with a raspy whir. He pulled his hat low and pushed the log along the groove that led to the blade. Rakes and Abshire stepped back as the blade met the log with a scream, sending funnels of sawdust in several directions. For a few minutes they all watched the log inch down the chute into the blade that split it in a clean line, Forrest hunched over the far end, using an iron hook to pull the log along, leaning into it. Then Rakes pulled out a revolver from under his coat and pointed it at Forrest's head.

Jack took a step forward and then looked to Howard, still sawing at the edge of the clearing. The circular blade started to smoke as it churned into the log and a small boy sprang from behind a woodpile with an oilcan and lubricated the blade with a practiced eye, then turned and ran back to his spot in the woodpile, where he hunched over a small block of wood that he whittled earnestly with a jackknife, an eye on Charley Rakes's gun. Forrest leaned into the log again and Rakes swung his arm over to the Model T and put a round through the engine block, the *pock* sound barely coming through the whine of the saw. Without looking up Forrest backed the log off and kicked the kill switch. He watched the motor, oil sputtering from the bullet hole, beginning to burn off and smoke, then rattling to a stop. Then in the clearing it was just the sound of Howard's lone saw groaning for a few more strokes, and then that sound stopped too. A few of the mules shook in their harnesses, the quiet settling.

Forrest spat dryly into the sawdust.

Dammit Charley, Abshire said. He wiped his sweaty forehead with his shirtsleeve.

Other men working at the mill dropped their saws and wood planes and began walking away from the shed toward the shade of the trees. Jack could tell that the spectators worried Abshire. Charley Rakes walked over to the large boiler. He kicked the fire door open and rapped the pipe with his knuckles. Forrest touched a finger to the hot bullet hole in the engine.

Listen, Abshire said, we need your payment if you gonna run liquor. You and your brothers.

Rakes walked back to the two men, his thumbs hooked in his straining belt.

I'll tell you what, Rakes said, you boys get this boiler goin' and you could fire a dozen teakettles at once. Run the whole thing right here. Gotta be better than whatever you draggin' out o' the mountains at night.

Forrest looked out to the men standing in the shade. They all stood watching, hands on their hips, Howard wiping his hands on his overalls, his head hanging down. What the hell is the matter with him? Jack thought. Rakes was poking around the table saw, pushing a track of sawdust along the chute with a fat finger. He was only a few feet from the giant blade. Jack saw Forrest eyeing an old rebar pole they used to stoke the boiler. A stack of fresh-cut fence posts nearby. Then he turned and pointed at Rakes.

You gonna pay for that bullet, Forrest said evenly.

Abshire took his hand from his pockets. Howard put on his hat and began to stride across the clearing, his face set. Here we go, Jack thought. He started to sidle around the shed along the opposite side, to come at them from the back.

You threatenin' me, boy? Rakes said, coming around the table and putting his hand on his revolver.

Easy, Charley, Abshire said.

Rakes eased his gun halfway out, forefinger lying across the guard.

You think you a real hard-boiled son of a bitch, don't ya?

Real simple Forrest, Abshire said. Either we get our payment or we cut up the stills. All of them.

Hell, Rakes said, we'll dynamite the goddamn things. Then your station'll be next, unnerstand?

Charley Rakes stood in front of Forrest, lifted out his revolver, and lay it across his chest.

We ain't afraid of you and your brothers, Rakes said, like some is. Ask Jack what he did last time I caught him at a still. Ask him about how he blubbered like a little girl.

The cicadas sang high in the trees, and the men in the shade stood shoulder to shoulder watching. Howard had come quietly across the clearing and came up to the shed and stopped a few paces behind the two men, his hands hanging at his sides, his head still down so you couldn't see his face under his hat. Jack was now standing by the deputies' car, thirty feet behind them, coming slowly to their back. Abshire eyed the group of staring men.

Shit, Abshire said, c'mon, Charley. Bring it by the office, Forrest. We are willing to forget a few months, but we'll need at least sixty to start, as you got back pay.

The deputies turned and walked to their car. Jack stepped back to let them get in. Abshire glanced at Jack and shook his head and climbed in the car. Rakes stood there for a moment, looking at Jack like he couldn't place him.

Hey boy, he said. Your face healed up?

Jack said nothing. He stared at Rakes's fat, sweating face, trying to bore into his pig eyes.

You sure can squeal, boy, Rakes said. Ought to do some fine hog calling.

Rakes glanced back at Forrest, still standing under the shed. Howard's hulking shadow stood next to him.

Get in the car, Charley, Abshire said.

You gonna let your brothers get you into some things you can't handle, Rakes said.

I'll handle things fine, Jack said. Don't you worry.

Rakes chuckled again.

Lotta threats around here, he said. Lotta talk and nothin' doin'.

After their car drew off down the road the other men came back to their places on the saws, spat on their hands and took up the handles. Jack joined his brothers under the shed. One of the men was talking loudly, a skinny fellow with a drooping mustache named Whit Boitnott.

Don't need this foolishness, he said. All these guns and what the hell a man supposed to do about that?

He lit up a cigarette with shaking hands.

Goin' get us all kilt if he don't watch out. Man can't work in this kind of—

Forrest grimaced and stretched out and picked up the rebar pole and whipped it at him in one quick movement. Whit flinched, hunching down and bringing up his arms and screamed as the pole flipped just over his head. The pole sailed on out into the yard and stuck end up in the dirt, quivering, and the men began to laugh. Whit scrambled up and started running for the wood, clutching his neck.

Ed, Tyler, Forrest said, you boys get this boiler fitted out and ready and hook it to the saw.

The men set about setting up the old boiler, others moving to stack cordwood for fuel, emptying the ash pit. The brothers drew off apace.

Cundiff, Jamison, the rest of 'em, Jack said, they paying?

Not Cundiff, Howard said. He won't. Think we the only other ones left.

Look, Jack said, we gotta do something. We gotta get that piece of cowshit Rakes.

We don't gotta do anything at all, Forrest said.

Well damn, Jack said, I already done it. We run a hundred gallons to Burning Bag a few weeks ago. Floyd Carter up there told us to bring it anytime.

Forrest turned to Howard with a look of disbelief, genuinely surprised. Howard stared at a spot on his brother's chest, hands on his hips.

He's got places, Jack said, all over to drop, and we gon' do it again soon as Howard gets another batch up. I'm a part of his syndicate now, the Midnight Coal Company.

That so? Forrest said.

Yeah.

You don't know a thing about Carter or his Midnight Coal Company.

I know they'll take our liquor for a good price. I know they makin' money. Unlike us.

Forrest put his finger into Jack's collarbone.

You don't know a damn thing, Forrest said. Floyd Carter jus' as soon as plug you as shine his shoes. There ain't no kind of guarantee with them.

I can look out for myself, Jack said.

Can ye now? Forrest said.

Look, Jack said, you got that Sharpe woman running more through the county than anyone and they haven't caught her. I mean, goddamn, if we gotta pay to make it and then pay again per load for someone else to move it, it seems like we oughta cut them out. We cleared near four hundred between us. Me and Cricket did the driving. Easy as falling off a log backwards, 'specially now that I got my own car.

Forrest clapped the sawdust off his hat and seemed to measure a voice that came rising out of the trees.

Howard's got good stills, Jack said, and we've got some vehicles and we could get some more. I know you know where we can get our hands on some materials. We could put together a set of big submarine stills, do three, four hundred gallons at a time. Floyd Carter's people will take all we got. Once we get through a few times the others will quit paying and the whole thing will give. I'll drive the pilot car myself. And if Rakes and Abshire try to stop us I swear to God I'll shoot Rakes myself.

You'll shoot him? Forrest said.

I swear it, Jack said.

Once something like that gets started, Forrest said, something else will have to stop it.

Then we just keep it close, Jack said. We stop it ourselves.

Forrest fixed him with his eyes.

What makes you think, Forrest said, that after it gets going you will *want* it to end?

AS THEY BROKE DOWN the camp for the night Jack was working out the logistics of the plan in his mind. Forrest agreed to look for suppliers of heavy-gauge copper for some new, larger stills. If Jack and Howard could get it built they'd start making large runs in the early spring, when the weather thawed. Jack had no doubt that there was plenty of money to be made; his cut of it would be enough to put something down on a little place somewhere, maybe in Roanoke, and get out of the sawmill camp and his father's place for good. Forrest had done it before, Jack thought, that's how he got the money to buy into the County Line to begin with. A little stake to start something of my own, take my rightful place, fingers on the switch. To hell with breaking my back at the sawmill and picking tobacco for nothing but chips and whetstones.

That afternoon Howard came through the woods and into a large field. The sun was low over Fork Mountain to the west and shone over the matted grass and broom straw. A dozen red-and-white Herefords stood spaced over the hillside, down into the hollow and up the other side of the valley, broad swaths of green and exposed rock, the cows nosing for tufts of alfalfa and clover. The cattle turned to watch the man emerge from the forest.

Howard stepped over a three-strand barbed fence and strode down the hill toward a tobacco barn that stood up on a knob in the field like an island. The Herefords parted before him, some breaking into a heavy run, wild-eyed and snorting. The tobacco barn was built in the standard style of tobacco barns of the day and for fifty more years after, so common in that part of the county: tall and narrow, maybe thirty by twenty-five feet, chinked chestnut logs that would last forever, cross-tied and sealed with red-mud paste and a ribbed metal roof that quickly tarnished and took on a deep rust color. The barn was built upon a base of field rocks stacked tight with a fire pit in the back and two separate rock flues under the floor to circulate the smoke and heat to dry the hanging tobacco. The pine-board door was closed with a loop of wire and a stick, a broad fieldstone laid to provide a step. Inside the empty barn the smell of tobacco was penetrating, a keening, dry smell that went straight to your brain.

Howard stood for a moment in the dusty barn, letting his eyes adjust to the dark. The wind sang on the metal roof and a few cattle complained outside. His overalls were blasted with sawdust and his long boots muddy from crossing the creek. He was tired and his arms sore to the bone; he'd been chaining logs to the mule teams and working a crosscut saw all day. In another few weeks the camp would shut down for the winter and Howard knew he would be up on the mountain, with or without his brothers. He hadn't been home in over a week now. At quitting time he set down the heavy saw, wiped his hands on his overalls, and walked away from the camp while the rest of the men were having supper and came straight through the valley, walking the three miles along the creek and skirting the lake, to this field. Just beyond the next hill lay his house, his wife and daughter.

Holding his hands out in the dark Howard walked to the opposite wall of the tobacco barn. He found the pile of burlap bags and brittle piles of tobacco leaves and shifting around in them for a bit he found a two-quart jar with a metal lid. By the weight of it he could tell it was nearly full, and holding it up close to his face he could almost see the beads on the edge of the glass as he swirled it around, the clear liquid sloshing quietly. The pungent, sweet smell of rotten corn rose over his face. Howard stood there in the dark barn, holding the jar in his hand to his chest, breathing, listening to the wind against the roof, thinking about the pistol he had seen this morning pointed at his brother and the way the gunshot rang out in the clearing. The lurching panic in his throat and the familiar rage building in his arms. His youngest brother staring at him, waiting for him to do something. Standing in the open sunlight with a line of other men, watching the pointed gun barrel.

Howard opened the jar and took a deep swallow, then put his face in the crook of his arm and sobbed briefly.

Outside the cattle sighed, giving up the afternoon to the long grass field and the eye of the smooth lake.

LUCY SAT IN the kitchen holding the baby. An oil lamp flickered weakly on the table. A pot of collards simmered on the stove and filled the close room with the dull scent of cooking greens and fatback. Howard emptied his pockets with some things he pilfered from the lumber camp: a hunk of sausage, a butt of soft pork, a small bag of tough biscuits. Lucy watched him closely, holding the nuzzling baby to her breast, hoping to get her to nurse. Howard knew she was watching him for signs of drunkenness, but he felt so tired that he didn't much care.

I hear everything is closing up, Lucy said. The revenuers shuttin' Forrest down.

Where'd you hear that? Howard asked.

Around.

Lucy shifted the baby on her chest. Howard was annoyed that such a thing was being discussed, here in his home with his wife. The new system had made people bold: Wives and neighbors talked, everyone seemed to know everyone's business now. I guess it don't matter, Howard thought, if there's nothing to be afraid of in knowing. When the law is running the liquor, who's to arrest you?

It ain't always, Howard said, the way people say it is.

So they ain't shutting you down?

Howard took the folded dollar bills from his pocket and slapped them on the table.

This look like we shut down?

Lucy pulled the pile of money across the table and sorted through it, counting with one hand. The baby was quiet and looked almost pink, a good change from the dark-red-faced squawling creature that had inhabited their house. She seemed to sleep contentedly on Lucy's chest. His wife looked worse, Howard thought, peaked and washed-out, like she was draining color, like it was transferring to their daughter.

This ain't gonna do it, Lucy said.

I know it.

We need the money, Lucy said. You know it. We got a new set of due bills and the receipts from your father's store . . . if he means to make us pay up.

We'll pay up.

So you and your brothers got something going?

Don't you worry 'bout it.

Oh, I gotta worry 'bout it, Lucy said. Someone has to around here.

I'm going out for a bit, Howard said.

Howard, Lucy said. There's only so much liquor to drink.

She rocked the baby gently.

It'll never be enough, she said.

I've got plenty set aside, he said.

Lucy stared at him, her eyes saucers of limpid blue, the baby nestling at her neck. Howard looked out the front window. On the porch the luna moths clustered, throwing their furry bodies against the window glass.

One day, she said, that jar'll be empty and nothing you can do about it.

Not if I can help it.

Oh, Howard, Lucy said, how much liquor is there in this county? In the world?

Might try to find out, Howard said, and stepped out.

Later that night Howard would stand in a bar of pale light from the window outside of his home and watch his wife feeding his daughter. He would make some money and he would give it to her and then he would be on his way; that was the arrangement they had made. When Howard looked at the wispy blond head of his daughter lying against his wife, there rose up in him a long, low note that wasn't about tenderness or affection. He fingered the crumpled bills in the pocket of his overalls.

Plenty times, Howard thought to himself, I had a wad of money in my pocket to choke a mule but I'll be damned if it ever made a hint of difference anyhow.

Chapter 18

THAT WINTER FORREST arranged for a shipment of heavy-gauge copper and several hundred feet of copper tubing for the new submarine stills, an investment that took a significant chunk of his savings. Jack and Howard went to Rocky Mount to pick it up from the rail yard in the morning, the rails and gravel covered in a veneer of ice. After a packet of money changed hands a gritty trainman in coveralls led them to a boxcar and threw it open. Inside there were copper sheets stacked four feet high and dozens of bundles of copper tubing. Enough to build fifty stills with worms and caps.

All this here our load? Jack said.

The trainman wheezed into a soiled handkerchief.

Shit, son. You think you the only boys makin' in this county?

The trainman threw open another boxcar that was stacked eight feet high with sacks of sugar and boxes of cake yeast.

Seems to me, the trainman said, in a few months this here whole county'll be floatin' in it!

As they unloaded the materials raggedy men sifted out of open boxcars like smoke, disappearing into the woods. At one end of the yard a dozen men squatted around a small campfire warming themselves. The trainman spat angrily, shifting his quid.

Shit, he said. Y'all unload. Got business to attend to.

He slipped a fat teardrop-shaped leather sap off his belt loop and advanced on the men, who began to stand and gather their bundles.

HOWARD BROUGHT in Cundiff and Jack brought Cricket Pate, and through the months of January and February they hammered out four three-hundred-gallon stills and fashioned solid caps and worms. They worked in a shed near Howard's cabin with a makeshift forge and bellows, stripped to the waist, and at the end of the day the tin walls of the shed glowed with heat. Howard's spot on Turkeycock was clearly the best location and they set about readying the camp for expansion, clearing more brush and trees and setting up a thick blind on the open side of the mountain to block light and vapor. Cundiff rigged up a set of hollow steel rings that fed a mixture of gas and air through a tire pump that he claimed would give them a more even temperature and less heat trail.

In the late spring of 1930 Jack turned twenty years old and moved back to his father's house temporarily to help with the tobacco crop. Howard and Forrest came by the farm during the sucker pulling and worming, and they would help with the eventual leaf picking and curing. The project was slowed while the brothers worked the fields, though some afternoons when they had time Howard and Jack went up on Turkeycock and helped Cundiff and Cricket with the stills. There was nothing to be done and Jack knew it; though it was only three acres it was the best strip of bottomland their father had and the money was vital to their father's ability to continue to pay his notes and keep the store running. Business was down drastically this year, road traffic reduced to itinerants and the wandering jobless. Several of his suppliers of trade goods collapsed or disappeared altogether and the shelves at the store were sparsely furnished. Granville normally gave his sons a cut from the tobacco crop, enough to make up for the lost work or wages from the sawmill, but they all knew it wouldn't be coming this year.

Jack found it strange to lie in the old rope bed he used to share with his brother, the slow creaking of the hemp ropes, the way the wind sang on the roof, his sister Emmy cooking and cleaning and spending afternoons by the window in their mother's old chair. It seemed to Jack as if his sister was determined to forgo youth altogether and head straight into middle age. She misses Mother, sure enough, he thought, and her sisters too. Thinking of Emmy and her misery since that time made his eyes water as he pulled suckers through the long afternoons in the field. Jack suddenly felt guilty for his return to the world. How often had he thought of Belva May and Era in the last few years? His mother? How had he come to move along so easily while Emmy remained in mourning? He straightened up in his row of tobacco and wiped his face with his sleeve.

One morning in the hay barn across the road from the house, Jack dug around and found a large burlap sack and set about filling it with a mixture of dirt, straw, and clay. Granville was across the yard burning trash in a barrel, fanning the murky flames with his hat. The sun worked its way over Turkeycock Mountain and flooded the yard and the road beside with light. The spring had been dry and the summer looked to be even drier. On Sunday churches across Franklin County were packed with tobacco farmers. In the kitchen Emmy rinsed her hands and arms after doing the breakfast dishes in the sink, the cold well water splashing on her white skin.

When the bag was full enough Jack tied the end securely with some twine and tossing a length of rope over a rafter hung it level with his head, a swaying, lumpy mass of burlap, bits of straw sticking out, streaming dust. Jack assumed a boxing pose like he'd seen in pictures and poked at the bag as it swung at him. He began to hit harder, stopping the momentum of the swinging bag as it came at him. After one shot his knuckles popped and Jack swore and grabbed his hand, massaging his fingers.

There was a crunch of gravel on the road and Howard came into the barn. His shirtsleeves were rolled up and he carried a spool of baling twine under his arm. Jack stopped the swaying bag. Howard gave him a quizzical look for a moment, then stepped to the bag and poked it with his beefy fingers, prodding the worn burlap. He looked at his little brother and grinned.

Regular Jimmy Braddock, Howard said.

Hell.

Let's fix it up a bit.

Howard untied the rope and brought the bag down. Using the spade he broke up some hard clay and filled the bag deeper until it took a cylindrical shape, the dirt packed down hard. Then he took some spare burlap and tore it into strips.

Fellas in the army showed me this, Howard said.

He took Jack's hand and wrapped the strips of burlap around it and between his fingers, pulling it tight.

So's you don't bust your hands, Howard said.

When Jack's hands were well wrapped Howard stepped back and nodded and Jack pawed at the bag a bit, embarrassed to do it in front of his brother. He threw some jabs with his right.

Here, Howard said, quit foolin' with that stance. You gotta twist your body with it. And you gotta lead with the left first, save the right.

Howard shot a couple of straight left jabs into the bag.

Jack tried some left-right combinations. Howard grabbed the bag to stop it from swinging.

Other thing you need is a good hook, he said. Most fellas will throw everything real wide, which will leave them open.

He feigned a few wide, looping haymakers.

You gotta throw your hooks short and tight. Dip the shoulder.

Howard squared before the bag and dipped his left shoulder slightly.

Then hook it hard, he said.

He ripped a short hook into the midsection of the bag.

Now, he said, you do that after he's thrown something. It's gonna be a right hand, you see, 'cause most is right-handed. He throws the right hand . . .

Howard dipped slightly and moved his head to the side.

. . . and then when he misses he will be wide open for the hook.

Howard fired two quick hooks into the bag.

Jack set his feet and practiced his jabs, right cross, and left hook. Howard watched with his arms folded.

You plan on whippin' somebody?

Nah, Jack said. Just messin' around.

Howard picked up his spool of baling line. He wiped his forehead on his shirtsleeve and squinted in the sunlight.

Never does turn out like you think, Howard said. When the first swing happens everything is new an' nothin' is the way you thought.

All right, Jack said.

I'll tell you what, Howard said, you only need to know one thing. Something ol' Forrest knows. That's you gotta hit first, hit with everythin' you got, and then keep hittin' until the man is down, and then you hit him some *more*.

Jack nodded.

Many men, Howard said, like the *idea* of fightin' but very few likes to get hit. You can make a man wanna quit real quick with that first shot. A good straight left into the nose bone and most will let it be. A man who *likes* to get hit is the one to watch out for.

Looking at his brother then Jack realized that he never considered Howard much of a sentient being, never considered that he ever had a real thought or plan about anything. He had always thought of him as some kind of machine or animal, reacting to the world in an instinctual manner. This thought alarmed and embarrassed him.

Too damn dry, Howard said, kicking at the dirt.

Then Howard strode through the back of the barn and out into the field. The bag creaked as it swayed slightly. Jack tried to imagine the face of someone on the burlap, first the smirking, laughing face of Wingfield, and went after his nose with his right hand, stepping into his punches. Then he saw the face of Charley Rakes, his egg-shaped head, reaching out and holding Jack by the shoulders. Give me another shot like that, Jack thought. He tucked his fists to his chin and fired a series of tight jabs.

Chapter 19

1930

BY THE END of May the stills up on Turkeycock were steaming out two hundred gallons a week with Jack and Cricket making the night runs to Burning Bag without incident. Jack bought a few more suits, a watch fob, a brand-new Dodge Sport Coupe, and began to sock away money for a big Packard or some other chariot. He had four hundred dollars wrapped in a rag tucked under a loose board in his old bedroom and he perused the wares in town like a man without claim or notion of anything that was not himself. It was a splendid time and in between his father's tobacco fields, the stills, and the midnight drives, he began his courting machinations.

Jack managed to lurk at the ag-feed store when Tazwell Minnix made his regular run, and when the man had gone inside he strode by his truck in the lot, Bertha in the cab sucking on a bottle of pop or flipping the pages of a catalog, windows rolled down to feel the breeze. She would squint up through the speckled windshield to catch this swaying apparition coming down the planked walk, bow tied and suited, boots gleaming and strapped tight, a cigarillo streaming off his lip, face content as if there was nothing like a jaunt on a spring's day. Jack would turn and tip his cap to her as Bertha sat in the front seat, the catalog on her lap, wondering just what this fool was up to. After a few weeks he steeled his will and came to the car, knowing that he would have about six minutes before the old man came out with his sacks of feed.

Bertha regarded him with a disinterested eye and set mouth. She wore a dark shirt buttoned high. She instinctively moved her hands to her collar and then back to her lap. Jack propped a foot on the running board and flicked away his cigarillo.

Fine day, she said.

How'd you like to come for a ride with me sometime, Jack said, nodding toward his car parked across the street.

I'm waiting for my father, she said. But I guess you know that.

Huh. I wouldn't. I was just thinking you might want to take a ride.

Why would I want to do that? I don't need to go nowheres.

We wouldn't have to *go* anywhere, just for a ride.

Jack cranked his head around as the feed-store door slapped open. Some other old man shuffled out with a bulging sack over his shoulder and headed down the street.

You ought to be worried if my father catches you here. Talking to me.

Why's that?

You know. Coming to a meeting like that. Then busting out like a crazy person. Are you affected in the head?

This was not how Jack had pictured this thing going. He straightened his coat and checked his watch, squinting in the sunlight to read the hands.

It's all right if you are, Bertha said. I got a cousin who don't ever leave the house.

There's nothin' wrong with me, Jack said. Does a crazy person wear a suit like this? Does a crazy person have a car like this? This my second one besides. And me only twenty?

Bertha gazed over at Jack's car for a moment. Jack thought she seemed duly impressed. It was swinging back his way.

I suppose not, she said. But that don't explain why you acted like a crazy person. Daddy says you were drunk but I'd never seen a drunk like that.

I just didn't want my feet washed is all.

Bertha tsked and sucked in her cheeks.

Funny way of showin' it. I see you got some new boots.

All this is new, Jack said. This here is a tailored suit, from Richmond.

Hmmmm.

Jack dragged a toe in the dirt and eyed the feed-store window.

Look, I got nothin' to say about that, he said. 'Cept to say I wished I hadn't done it.

Well, that's something.

So how 'bout that ride.

You know I'm waiting for my father.

Later then.

Bertha seemed to consider this for a moment. She flipped through the catalog on her knees.

You ain't the kind of man a girl should be ridin' with, she said. I know who you are.

Oh yeah? Who's that?

Jack could not help but grin, and he put his hand up to feign scratching his lip.

One of them Bondurant boys, and that's enough. There aren't many that have a good word in for you.

That so.

Yep. My granddaddy says you boys the worst ever to hit Franklin.

Jack scanned the storefront for movement. Bertha draped her arm over the door and a short section of white skin scooted from under the cuffs, ending in her tapered hands like porcelain. Jack realized he was balling his fists and he jammed them in his pockets. A dampness spread across his lower back.

You know where my daddy's place is? Bertha said.

Yeah.

I get done with my chores around two, she said. Your watch will tell you when that is. If you came round to the end of the road I might take a ride.

Jack nearly choked, his mouth gone cotton.

Tomorrow then?

Bertha laughed, a bright musical laugh. It warmed them both and they suddenly felt silly in light of this charade. Jack was about to burst inside and run down the street like an inflamed preacher.

Sure is a funny way of courtin', Jack Bondurant, Bertha said. This is courtin', ain't it?

I'll see you tomorrow then, Jack said, and spun away and across the street just as Tazwell came out of the store, feed sacks in a wheelbarrow, his daughter in the truck idly picking at strands of her hair.

THE NEXT DAY Jack tried to concentrate on his driving. Bertha unwound her head scarf and placed it on the seat between them. The Dodge hummed up the hill, the frame screeching as it seesawed over ruts in the road. It hadn't rained in weeks, but when he picked her up it was drizzling lightly and she stood beneath a stooped elm at the end of her drive wearing a long black sweater and knickers with deep-red kneesocks. Jack was desperately working to come up with a way to entertain Bertha now that he had her in his car. As he made his way south he was well aware that he had no plan as to where they were going, and what they were going to do when they got there, but he couldn't concentrate on anything else at the moment other than the road and the scent of the girl sitting next to him. It struck him as something he knew well: On summer afternoons by the creek, an overgrown fence line, or sometimes inside the house by an open window, after a rain and when the wind was right, there would suddenly be a gentle wave of flowering honeysuckle in the air, the smell of deep summer, honey mixed with earth and water and sky. Jack couldn't be sure if this was her natural scent or if it was some kind of perfume, but on this raw day in May it seemed like a glimpse of summer, a moment in the sun.

I'll be leaving soon, Jack said. Getting out of this county.

Oh yeah?

Maybe Texas, out west or somethin'. Or maybe some city.

What'll you do? Bertha asked.

Shoot. Anything. Everything. Get myself set up.

The cab warmed as they talked, condensation forming on the windshield. Jack could now smell mostly the damp must of her sweater drying out.

What about you? Jack said.

Oh, I'm fine right here.

Really?

Yeah. I'd like to finish up at school. Didja hear they might close up the Co-Cola plant?

Yeah? What for?

Don't you read the papers? The country's in real trouble.

Not me.

Well, people are out of work all over. Daddy says Hoover's to blame. Cursed him up one side of the street and down the other.

That so?

I reckon I'll stick around, Bertha said. Stay close to my family.

Can't see why ya wanna do that.

Bertha furrowed her brow, and Jack knew that he had stepped in it. There was no way out but forward. He gave the coupe a bit more gas.

Well, Jack said, I mean, they always trying to . . . keep you from doing things. I know plenty a Dunkards.

Bertha lowered her head and Jack was afraid that he had gone too far.

It may seem like that, Bertha said, but it ain't. We like to be around each other. We have a lot of fun together.

Can't right imagine that, Jack said.

He wrestled the wheel around a particularly gaping pothole and then overcorrected, making the car slide in the mud for a moment. Bertha was staring at him with a bemused look on her face.

What do you know? she said. You show up at our church and then run out like a lunatic, and you think somehow you know my family? You don't see what we do, what it's like at home.

Yeah, Jack said, I know it.

So don't say things like that.

Okay. Jack said. Sorry I said it.

Oh, never mind, Bertha said.

But don't you want, Jack said, just to . . . get out on your own?

Sure, but that don't mean I've got to go far away. On your own has nothing to do with distance.

Damn, Jack thought to himself, she's making me look right foolish. She don't believe any of it.

Well, then, he said, when I go maybe I'll take you with me.

Bertha gazed out the window, looking at the withered tobacco fields, a stretch of puny alfalfa that ran over the hill. The dread thought hit his heart: The woman was bored to tears already and they had only been driving for five minutes. At least the rain had tapered off and the sun struck through the clouds. He steadied the wheel with one hand and reached inside his coat pocket.

Got you a li'l somethin'.

She looked over at him askance like he'd just claimed he could make the car fly. He extended the Brownie camera to her between his thumb and forefinger, his eyes on the road. He was afraid to see her expression. She took it from his fingers and turned it over in her hands, examining each side of it.

I can't take this.

It ain't nothin'.

This is one of them cameras.

Yep.

I ain't never had a camera before.

Well now you do.

I don't know how to operate it.

Shoot, Jack said. All you do is look through the little window and push the button. Ain't nothin' to it.

What will I take a picture of?

Jack turned down a side road near the foot of Fork Mountain, not too far from his father's place in Snow Creek. He realized that he had been heading steadily in that direction for unknown reasons. Perhaps it was familiar territory he sought.

Here, he said. I'll take a picture of you and then you can take one of me. How's that?

He jerked the Dodge to a halt at a small side cut off the road near a field of limp fescue flattened by the brief rain. The ground was already drinking the moisture deep, the road ruts hardening. They clambered out of the car and into the sunshine.

You got your car all muddy, she said.

Here, Jack said, stand up there by that crab-apple tree and I'll take your picture.

Wait a second, Bertha said, and she shucked off her long sweater to reveal a short-sleeved white blouse, tied at the neck with a blood-colored kerchief. Jack thought that in her knickers and blouse she cut a prim and divine figure as she stood in a shallow ditch of bramble, one foot cocked on the slope and clutching a sprig of the tree. She preened and mocked for a few moments, smiling and rounding her eyes.

Hold on, Jack said, let me get it, now hold it so's I can get it.

Bertha settled into a stony stare off to the side, away from the camera, looking out over the road and the fields beyond, her mouth in a grim line. Jack snapped the photo.

Why'd you quit cuttin' up?

That's how you take a picture, Jack, she said, you gotta set your face straight. That's how the movie stars do it in California.

She snatched the camera from his hand.

Now you.

Jack set about arranging himself on the car, sitting on the hood, his feet on the bumper. The thought occurred to him that this was in fact what he was really hoping for when he bought the camera. He had had his picture taken only a handful of times before, mostly as a small chap in family gatherings and a few others, and none in his new regalia, posed on his new car.

That's a good one, Bertha said.

Hold it, Jack said.

He fished out a fresh cigar and stuck it between his teeth, and set his hat back at a rakish angle. The sun fell directly onto his face and he squinted mightily but he figured it gave him a tough look, his boots crossed nonchalantly before him. He was going for his watch when she snapped the picture, and because she laughed and held her hand over her mouth he decided not to mention it.

Chapter 20

1930

EMMY DROPPED a dishrag that morning, so she knew that a visitor was due before sundown. She told Jack that this visitor would bring them bad news or worse. In the kitchen Jack watched his sister standing at the sink, her eyes shut, her hands clasped over her thin chest, considering the possible turning of fate.

Well, Jack said, then we'll be expectin' them.

The three brothers gathered for dinner after spending the morning pulling suckers in their father's field. It was July, and the withered tobacco struggled out of the parched earth and the suckers were thin and yellow. His father and brothers seemed intent on continuing the charade of harvesting. The drought had dried out the land till it broke apart and Jack thought they should be focusing on the stills.

Granville's store was nearly vacant and he only opened for paying customers, too tired of fending off the wretched looking for handouts. He kept the springhouse open across the street so that all could have a drink of cool water, but he couldn't give away any more goods. The jobs for Forrest's sawmill also began to wane as men tightened up around the county, unable to pay for his services, and the community began to revert to the old communal farming methods, relying on the available free labor. Many in the county went back to straight subsistence farming, others sending their boys out west to find work picking produce in California. The city council in Rocky Mount hired yard bulls at the train yard to keep wandering men from hopping out of boxcars, driving the flapping scarecrows back into the empty flats with clubs and locking the doors so they would be carried on to the next town.

That afternoon the three brothers watched the girl coming from a long way off, walking through the field of sorghum and red clover that ran to the north away from the house, up to the foot of Fork Mountain. She emerged from the trees a quarter mile away, a thin cloud of red dust at her feet. Sissy Deshazo walked with her head back, bobbing in a strange motion, like she was watching the sky. The day was heavy with humidity and low clouds filled every inch of the sky. She was wearing her Sunday dress, fringed with a streak of red clay on the bottom. Sissy Deshazo was crying, her chestnut-colored face, ashy from the summer sun, streaked with tears. Her grandfather had died, old Little Bean Deshazo, who had worked alongside Granville and his father in the tobacco fields. He had passed away sometime in the night, and Sissy was sent to tell the neighbors and invite them to the wake that was being held that afternoon. The Deshazos had lived in the county as long as the Bondurants, just over the first set of hills, one of a handful of black families in the Snow Creek area of Franklin County. Jefferson Deshazo, Sissy's older brother, had worked for Forrest out at the County Line Restaurant and Sissy herself had spent ten years cooking and cleaning in the Bondurant house after their mother had died. Little Bean, his sons Willy, Benjamin, and Horace, and all their children had been to the Bondurant house for hog killings or wood choppings, and their children often played with Jack and his brothers.

So after Emmy served them dinner the brothers cleaned up, washing their faces and changing their pants out of a cedar chest in Jack's old room as Sissy Deshazo went trudging back over the field to her grandfather's house. Forrest walked to his car and brought out a box of half-gallon jars of peach brandy to take along, and then fired up the car and went to the store to notify their father. Jack and Howard sat on the porch and waited for Forrest to return with Granville.

Jack was feeling uneasy with the idea of going to a wake; the last funeral he remembered was his own mother's, and because his brothers were all here there was something oddly reminiscent of that occasion. Jack knew that Little Bean was nearing ninety years old, an old man made of sticks who had lived a brutal life at times and by all accounts should have been dead long ago, but it still seemed to him as if some kind of injustice was done. Perhaps it was the streaked face of Sissy, normally a sullen girl whom Jack never really liked much. It upset him because he knew that Little Bean never had more than a few dollars in his pocket his whole life, and he died as poor as the day he was born, and the world seemed to be conspiring to make it so for so many others as well.

Howard lifted a jar out of the box and looking at Jack tapped the side of his nose. Jack smiled and Howard shook the jar, packed full of sliced peaches, before unscrewing the cap and flipping it off into the yard. They sipped from the jar, the brandy sweet and heady, a truly pleasurable drink, and watched the horizon soften before them. Jack had eaten two large bowls of crumbled corn bread with cracklings soaked in buttermilk, and the brandy seemed to warm the contents of his innards and relax his bobbing knees. Howard sat silently, his mouth set, lips narrowed, as they both reddened with drink.

We'll have to step it up, Howard said. This 'bacca ain't gonna come up.

I know it.

Howard pursed his lips and gazed at the horizon.

You hear about that fool Wingfield? Howard said.

What?

Since they were busy pulling tobacco, Howard told him, their father had hired Marshall Wingfield, home from UVA, to do some plowing with a mule and colter to set the bottomland for winter rye. Jack's father put a bell on the mule so he could hear from the house when Wingfield was working and he could pay him accordingly. Wingfield came by first thing in the morning and ate heartily of the breakfast Emmy prepared and trotted down the hill with the colter over his shoulder, the mule in tow. The bell commenced to ring steadily. A few hours later Granville was down at the spring and he'd thought he'd check and see how Wingfield was doing; this was a fresh stretch of bottomland that hadn't been planted in a few seasons and he'd run the harrow over it and burnt the turf the spring before. It was hard, stony ground, and Granville knew that Wingfield spent more time with his books than he did in a plow harness, so he walked across the narrow creek to the other side of the thin stretch of woods that rolled like a scarf through the valley, following the sound of the ringing bell. He found Wingfield stretched out under a fat pokeberry bush, hat pulled over his eyes, the bell in his hand in the dirt, which he twitched listlessly from side to side. The mule stood blinking in the sunlit field.

When other men kidded Wingfield about it, he denied that it ever happened and suggested that Granville Bondurant was getting senile and must have dreamed it up.

Jack was incensed, but Howard didn't seem to mind much.

Look, Howard said, everyone around here know Wingfield is a pointy-headed fool.

Still, Jack thought, thinking of the last time he'd seen Wingfield, preening with the sport ear at the Mitchell corn shucking the year before. Kissing Bertha Minnix. The way her eyes flashed as she bent her face to him. Jack had the urge to take ahold of that fleshy white neck of Wingfield's and squeeze it like a fryer. But liquor worked differently on Jack's mind than most and soon that image eased. The two brothers sat quietly for a while, passing the jar and watching the sky over the field. Jack enjoyed the silence between them and concentrated on the delicious transport of midday into the afternoon. It was quality brandy and soon enough what had just an hour before seemed like a pitiable situation for the Deshazos and himself now seemed like an opportunity for Jack to experience the great movements of life and this earth together in fellowship with other people. He ruminated on his life and experiences with the Deshazos and determined they were a solid people and that he would pay his respects with the honor and humility befitting a man who had lived so long. We should all be so lucky, Jack thought. And he was glad that his brother was here with him, and Emmy, his little sister, in his mother's old rocking chair by the window, watching the road.

I need the money, Jack, Howard said after a while. I gotta make more than what we got.

Just soon, Jack said, as this foolishness is done we will get all the stills hot and the money will flow like a goddamn river. You just wait.

Howard broke into a genuine smile.

Yeah, Howard said. That's what we'll do.

Forrest returned alone. Granville had some business at the store and it would be foolish to turn away good money. He would pay his respects later. Emmy didn't want to go, and the brothers knew that the presence of death would be difficult for their sister to bear again even if it wasn't family, so the three brothers had a good drink on the porch and then set off.

When they pulled up to the Deshazo house, a stocky, mud-wattled cabin built on a low rise with added bits plied about by various members of the clan over the years, it was undoubtedly clear that this was not a solemn affair. A half dozen motley cars stood in the dirt yard with several clapboard hacks and a score of knobby horses and mules. Despite the fact that it was still early afternoon and over eighty degrees, smoke poured from the chimney and a large bonfire roared in the front yard, children running in circles around it, chasing one another with sticks. All the windows and doors stood wide open and streamed with light. As they stepped out of the car they could hear the unmistakable sound of wailing women, lamentations in a seemingly unintelligible tongue, mixed with shouting, singing, a screeching fiddle, and braying laughter.

Ain't gonna need that brandy, Howard said.

As the children ran screaming around the fire Jack saw a man in torn pants lying facedown in the dirt yard, a dog nosing at his crotch.

Guess I'll bring it along anyhow, Forrest said.

As the three men stood in the doorway, hats in their hands, Forrest holding the boxful of liquor, an immense coal-black woman in a scarlet head scarf came to greet them. She nodded solemnly and gestured them inside the crowded front parlor.

I'm Ida Belle, she said. I'm Little Bean's second daughter.

Pleased to meet you, Forrest said.

We are sorry to hear 'bout Little Bean, Jack said.

Jack had never heard of Ida Belle, and it occurred to him then that Little Bean had probably sired some people who did not live in Snow Creek or maybe even in Franklin County. The house was packed with people swaying along to a fiddle player who hacked out a tune, thumping time with his foot on the floorboards, a song Jack had never heard before. People stood against the wall around the room, swaying lightly, and a second circle of people inside that one moved with some serious intent, stamping their feet in time and singing. Smoke hung like curtains in the room, the heavy smell of feet and yeasty crotch, incense, tobacco, wood smoke. A series of jars were being passed hand over hand and everyone drank liberally. Ida Belle set Forrest's box down in the center of the circle next to some other things, a few jars of liquor, bags of smoking tobacco, boxed candy, whole joints of pork in paper sacks, eggs, plates of biscuits, a hand mirror, snuffboxes, beaded necklaces, a pair of obviously used boots. The brothers were the only white people there.

I'll be damned, Forrest muttered, and when Jack followed his gaze he saw the guest of honor in the corner, surrounded by mourners, arms around his shoulders and singing: The corpse of Little Bean was propped up in a tattered suit, his body stiff with rigor mortis, yellow staring eyes, and the skin of his face beginning to swell and bulge so it barely looked like him at all. A burning cigarette was placed between his bloated fingers and different people took turns pouring cups of corn liquor into his open mouth, dribbling down his chin and onto his shirtfront.

Several of the Deshazo men came forward to shake hands with the brothers and thank them for coming. They were plied repeatedly with alcohol of various types and an hour or so later Jack stood in the

kitchen in the back to catch his breath. Howard sat at a table, idly picking at a lump of pig knuckles from a bowl and drinking from a fresh
jar, Forrest leaning against the drain board with his arms crossed,
frowning. The fiddle player was winding up some kind of a reel, the
pitch and meter going higher and most of the people in the front room
stomping their feet, raising a layer of dust that drifted into the kitchen
like fog. Men and women leaned against the walls of the small kitchen,
swaying with the music, some with their eyes closed as if they might
already be asleep. As Jack stood there the sounds began to separate in
his mind; he felt that he could pick out and listen to each individual
mote of sound—the voices calling out a cadence, the whining violin,
the creaking floorboards—he was able to listen to each thing individually and it seemed to him that this was the second time he had heard
such a thing, the first coming at the Dunkard Love Feast. Jack felt that
what he was experiencing was somehow part of something hidden,
the spare realm of musicians; is this what Bertha heard when she
played her mandolin? Rather than a catalog of sounds it sounded to
him like the very construction of music, a powerful and beautiful feeling, like manipulating the basic elements of the world.

Then the music seemed to increase significantly in volume and for a
few moments Jack looked at his brothers for some sign that they heard
it as well but they seemed not to notice. There was a cigarette in his
hand, an ash three inches long, and Jack threw it to the floor. When
did I light a cigarette? he thought. A noise like crackling tin, then a
harsh, tearing sound began to build from above him, and Jack looked
up at the stained and warped ceiling, wondering what was possibly
going on up there. It was like some kind of hellish carnival in the attic
made up of metal-rending machines plied by devils. Howard's broad
back was heaving at the table, and he held his face in his hands; he had
drunk a quart of straight corn liquor and half a jar of brandy, enough
liquor to kill a bull. The ripping sound in the ceiling built into a roar,
blocking out the screeching violin. It sounded like something was
tearing the building in half. Some of these fools get into the attic? Jack
thought. They'll bust through the ceiling. He saw Forrest giving him

an inquiring look, so he pointed to the ceiling and raised his shoulders. Forrest glanced up and shook his head, shrugging.

Do you hear it? Jack shouted above the din.

What? Forrest said.

The ripping sound built into something methodical, mechanical, and the ground began to vibrate. Not again, Jack thought.

Howard tipped up his jar and drained the last few inches, his throat working hard, two, three gulps. Jesus, Jack thought, no man can do that!

Howard's hat lay on the table beside his heavy forearms. The crown of his head a thinning swirl of muddy hair glistening with oil and sweat. Howard held the glass in front of him for a moment, then smashed it on the table, his palm coming down flat. Forrest blinked languidly and Jack felt the floor lurch under his feet and he wanted to flee, he wanted out of that house. Howard raised his hand and appeared to contemplate the bloody shards of glass that peppered his palm.

A bearded man leaning against the wall with heavy-lidded eyes nodded his head in time to the grinding music and when Jack caught his eye he gave an almost imperceptible nod of recognition.

Yes, there it is. You hear it, son.

There was a pause, when everything seemed to hold still, then Howard pushed out his chair, gained an unsteady crouch, gave Jack a tight smile, then went face-first through the table, splitting it cleanly into two parts. Howard floundered there on the floor in the detritus of broken glass, splintered wood, and cigarette butts. People standing near the table jumped back, cursing, and gave him wide berth as he rolled on the floor. Forrest picked up Howard's hat and stepping to his back clapped it onto his square head, grabbed two handfuls of Howard's shirt, and helped him to his knees. The kitchen was clearing out, people all busting for the door, cursing loudly, tripping on the debris, crunching through broken glass. Forrest kept his grip on Howard and pushed him through the back door, screen slamming against the side of the house with a crack.

Outside it was pitch-dark beyond the shaft of light that came from the kitchen door and Jack felt with his hands till he found Forrest's shirt and followed his brothers into the yard. The ripping noise was still above him, falling from the sky and the ground seemed to lurch like an earthquake under his feet. A large oak rose up out of the black, the silver-flaked bark glowing, and Howard leaned against the tree and began to retch. Inside the house people were shouting and as his eyes adjusted Jack saw the color of the sky had gone deep blue and clear and a single star showed just above the stubbled fields that spread from the yard.

A group of men came spilling out of the kitchen and they boiled around the brothers. Jack stood with his hand on Howard's back and Forrest stood in front of them both as the men gathered. Light from the window fell on Howard's face and Jack saw the crimson strings that hung from his mouth. Then Howard's body rippled and he vomited a gush of blood that seemed to come straight from his enormous horse heart. A man with no shirt on was screaming obscenities at them, his oiled torso gleaming. The other men gathered behind him. Jack's feet were on fire and when he looked down he saw his shoes were covered with Howard's blood.

You got no damn respect!

The crowd surged toward them; the men were incensed, incoherent, ravenously drunk, and Jack could tell the crowd wanted some action and would push the shirtless man into it. They urged him on and the shirtless man grinned and pulled out a short straight razor from his boot.

Cut that got damn cracker!

He crouched low and half circled Forrest. The straight razor was flipped open and the rounded blade flashed as the shirtless man waved it back and forth in almost feminine flicking motions of his wrist. Forrest stood straight, his hands at his sides, and Jack could see his shoulders settle and relax.

Then Forrest brought up his left hand very slowly, reaching for the brim of his hat. When he got his fingers around the brim he carefully took it off, then with a casual flick he sent it tumbling off into the darkness. A beat after the hat left his hand, Forrest's shoulders dipped slightly and his right hand shot out straight from the shoulder, his body torquing like a coiled spring, catching the shirtless man square in the teeth and making a *tink* sound that Jack would never forget.

The shirtless man's hands flew up in surprise and he went back sprawling into the crowd that parted as he fell. The set of iron knuckles hung loosely from Forrest's fingers, a fine spray of blood covering his hand and forearm. The men shouted as one with the blow but then seemed struck with silence, backing away. Jack felt a presence at his back and it was Howard, upright, his face a gruesome horror of blood and bile, his eyes mere slits. He was grinning.

Howard stepped next to Forrest and the crowd of men melted back into the dark, some running back into the house. Jefferson Deshazo stood there, his chest heaving. He exchanged a look with Forrest, who still stood in the same spot, the knuckles dangling, and in those seconds some transaction was made between them. Forrest nodded and Jefferson turned and went back to the house, corralling the women and children who gathered at the door, peering into the dark. To Jack it seemed the roaring sound coming from above was building into something like a scream. The shirtless man lay quietly in the grass, his arms stretched out, still holding the razor, his mouth a gory hole. Jack could see bits of shattered teeth flecking his red lips. Kneeling in the soft grass next to the unconscious man, Jack closed his eyes and put his hands over his ears to blot out the sound.

Chapter 21

1930

THE BANKS OF Blackwater Creek lay bare like a skirt lifted over old bones; thickened, sprawling root systems desperate for water snaked out of the bank and ran back into the flaking earth. The high walls of the narrow valley were shot through with blanched trees, nearly half of the leaves turning already, blotches of red and yellow amongst the green. Jack and Bertha stood watching the dark waters, now a trickle choked with birch leaves, their broad palms mottled orange and gold. Bertha stirred the leaves with a stick.

It's like autumn in August, she said. Seems out of place.

'Bacca won't come up in this heat, Jack said.

Bertha nodded. Jack could tell that unlike most people he knew she did not share the nearly unconscious association of weather with what was in the field, the progress of the season with the cash crop. This was something they had in common.

The last of the rain, in early April, gave way to the long waste of drought, blazing blue skies, cloudless, sparkling with dust. The early shoots withered in a matter of weeks, the bony cattle following the thin licks up the creek beds, planting their muzzles deep in any soft patch of mud. Fish crowded in the deep eddies and boys waded in to grab mud cats and carp with their hands. Headlights sweeping over a field at night found them alive with glowing eyes as packs of deer came down from the mountains desperate for water, parched and defiant. The old superstitions raised their hoary heads and traveling through stands of woods in Franklin County that summer you would occasionally find a snake hanging from a tree, nailed by the head, an ancient appeal to the wood gods to bring the rains back. Fields of yellow, stunted tobacco with untopped blooms covered the county. Red clay surged to the surface through the scattered weeds, the powder rising into the air on no wind at all, like transpiration, the dry sucking up the dry, and so a fine silt of clay was worn in every crease, in the eyes of dogs, in the skillets of fatback and pintos. A matter of minutes after you swept the floor clean you could draw in it with your finger. Men stood with their hands in their pockets, heads low, scuffing their boots, dreaming of sudden, angry cloudbursts. They knew when the tobacco died the shooting would begin. By August even the children grew quiet, beyond listless, and wandered down to the dry creeks in small groups, daydreaming of ice. In the summer of 1930 women all over the southern part of the state of Virginia stood in their dusty kitchens and wept.

Jack and Bertha sat under a stand of chestnut trees that leaned far out over the water. Mud turtles lay in a row along the roots. Bertha gazed at the water and Jack was relieved that she seemed content to sit quietly with him, watching the leaves fall into the water and the sky over the mountain grow purple with the coming evening. Jack's car sat in the field of red clover and fescue behind them, the engine ticking in the heat. Jack wanted to take them someplace in Rocky Mount or Roanoke but Bertha suggested they sit by the branch of Blackwater Creek that ran through a stretch of the Minnix farm.

Right about where you parked the car? Bertha said. When I was a girl my sister and I once planted twenty pounds of corn in that spot. Daddy said we could go swimming when we were done planting the corn. So we planted it.

Guess you didn't get away with it, Jack said.

Until fall we did. Anyway, we got to go swimming. A day a lot like this.

Jack eyed her calves, ensconced in her knee-high socks, tucked into her riding britches, a slightly rumpled white blouse damp with sweat. Her low brown shoes were soft and worn through with creases.

You want to go swimmin' now? he asked.

I don't think so.

He'd hoped he'd make her blush. Instead she regarded the water thoughtfully.

You go to church regular, Jack?

Wouldn't say regular.

What sort?

My mother used to take us to Snow Creek Baptist when I was young. I guess I haven't been back in a while.

Jack pulled at the tufts of johnson grass that bordered the creek, making a small pile by his knee.

That must have been hard on you, Bertha said.

What?

Your mother.

Oh, Jack said. Yeah.

Along with your sisters.

Jack eyed the notch cut into the mountain for the new power lines that stretched through the northern part of the county. Fireflies blinking in the woods along the creek bank and above a keyhole in the dark-blue sky. Jack had a brief memory of his sisters, their bodies stretched out on the floor side by side. His mother, her face covered with a quilt. Emmy sitting on the floor in the kitchen crying, her face slick with tears, her mouth stretched into a gaping howl.

What other kinds of instruments can you play? Jack asked

Oh, I can play just about anything with strings. Mostly mandolin, fiddle, banjolin. Played on a piano a few times too, at the Ruritan club in Roanoke.

Thought Dunkards believed you shouldn't play music, Jack said.

Bertha smiled to herself.

Not everyone. Some folks don't like it. But Daddy lets us play. Most in my family play something. When we were growing up my grandfather gave us all instruments. After a while my sisters stopped playin', so I just started playing all their instruments too. You like music?

Shoot. Yeah, I do.

When Bertha laughed Jack saw a flash and realized then that she rarely showed her teeth. Her eyeteeth top and bottom bore down into sharp points, cantilevered slightly toward the center.

Play anything? Bertha asked.

Naw, Jack said, we never had anything like that. I probably wouldn't have played them if we had. I prefer listening, dancing. My brother Forrest has a radio and he can pick up the shows out of Wheeling and other places. I'm goin' to get myself one soon.

You like our church service? Bertha said.

Sure.

Didn't seem like it.

Well, it's a funny thing, Jack said. It was the music. It sounded nice at first. Not like regular Baptist church singing, but still nice, the way the voices . . . well, you know. Then it kinda changed up on me. I could hear each person there singing, one at a time. Like I could separate them.

I think I know what you mean, Bertha said. I hear that sometimes too. When I'm playing, usually. I can pick out what everyone is playing.

I was drunk, you know, Jack said.

I know it, she said. It don't change nothin'. You still heard what you heard. I hear music in my head even when there isn't any. Do you?

I guess so, Jack said.

They were quiet for a while as the night came on; the low moan of the creek on the bank, the rising swell of crickets building from the thickets of chigger weed. He started to think of his brothers, the dying crop in the field. While his father could absorb the loss with his income from the store, Howard could not. Forrest would have to agree to make larger runs, but now Jack found himself thinking he would rather things remained the way they were. The images of that night at the Deshazo house rose up in his mind, the gruesome spectacle of Howard, the shattered man's face, the way Forrest moved with such languid ease. That sound from the attic like the movement of rusty stars.

I quit drinking, Jack said. I won't touch another drop.

Really?

At your church that night, Jack said. Like I was saying, the music was sounding . . . real good. Like nothing I heard before. But then it changed again. It seemed like—like the roof was coming off, like the air above my head was being . . . torn. Like thunder there in the church. Just kept getting louder.

Must have been that liquor, don't you think?

Maybe, Jack said. But I don't know. I'd been drunk before plenty and never had that problem. But the worst was when I started seeing things. Like your grandfather? When the preachers came toward me? He had . . . a sword coming outta his mouth. That's when I ran.

A sword?

After a few moments Bertha let out a weary laugh.

That's like . . . some kind of vision.

Maybe I was crazy, Jack said. Maybe I *am* crazy. Wait a second, I got something for you.

Jack hustled over to the car and returned with a large wrapped package.

I didn't know exactly what size an' all, Jack said, but they said they'd alter 'em however you want.

The package was covered with gold tissue paper. Bertha picked at the string around the package.

Jack, she said, I don't think this is a good thing.

Jus' open it.

Inside there were three dresses made of silk and satin, one with a fur trim, a purse covered with beaded scrollwork, two long embroidered scarves, and a set of silk handkerchiefs. She held each up and then placed them back on the tissue paper. The dresses were brilliant splashes of color against the parched ground, long and finely made. Her eyes brimmed with tears.

Don't you like them?

It don't matter if I like them, she said. I can't take these things.

The money don't matter, Jack said. I got plenty and these didn't make a dent in what I got.

Bertha sat back and crossed her arms.

Put them away, she said. Please wrap them back up. Please!

Jack clumsily gathered the things and balled them in the paper and retied the string.

Just wanted to give you something nice, he said. What's the problem?

Bertha wiped her face with fingers, composing herself.

Just where do you think, she said, I would wear something like that?

I dunno.

You think I could go back *home* wearing all that . . . those things?

Don't you like them?

It don't matter if I *like* them, Jack, I got no place to *wear* them, okay?

The creek water was now black, stretching around the bend and into a dark tunnel of trees like an open mouth. Jack felt the wide space of the field at his back. He looked at his grass-stained fingers.

I'll take you somewhere, Jack said. I'll take you somewhere that clothes like that are what you wear every day.

What makes you think, Bertha said, that I *want* that?

Bertha gazed up at the darkening sky. A milky band of stars stretched over the creek and the mountain. Hell, Jack thought, now what?

They were quiet for some time. Jack could feel the presence of the woman lying next to him in the johnson grass like a giant star in the ground. He felt suddenly naked and he shivered despite the evening heat. No taking it back now, he thought.

You hear some music right now? Bertha asked.

Sure.

How's it sound?

Oh, it sounds all right, Jack said.

Chapter 22

1935

THE BONDURANT GENERAL STORE in Snow Creek sat in a deep valley along Route 22, the road rising on either side several hundred feet up Turkeycock Mountain. The small gathering of old men around the stove directed Sherwood Anderson to the springhouse across the road to find Granville Bondurant. It was April, and the stove empty, but Anderson had noticed that regardless of the season the stove always served as the focal point, the fulcrum around which men gathered and levered their talk. The whitewashed shack was shaded with a leaning stand of black willows and sugar maples with fresh spring buds coming to full leaf. A cloud of ladybugs swarmed around the side eaves of the springhouse and the air cooled noticeably as Anderson approached the door. Inside, the floor and lower walls were mossy and glistening like a subterranean grotto, and Granville was filling a metal pail with springwater that shot from the tap with great velocity. Before Anderson could say anything Granville seemed to sense him and turned.

Help yo'self to some if you like.

He cinched down the valve, his bucket nearly full, and setting it down took up a dipper and had himself a drink.

Thanks, I will.

Anderson drank from the dipper, first surprised at how cold, then how sweet it was. It was unlike any water he had ever tasted, crisp, almost tart, with a slight citrus aftertaste, and he drank off the rest of the dipper. Granville eyed him as he handed the dipper back.

That's amazing water, Anderson said.

Never had Snow Creek water before, have ye?

I've never had anything like *that*. The name's Sherwood Anderson.

Granville Bondurant. Please to meet ye.

Granville leisurely drew him another dipperful.

Where you headed?

Nowhere, really, Anderson said. All the water in Snow Creek like this?

Some better than others. This one is particular.

Lot of pressure in that aquifer, Anderson said.

Going now for more than sixty years.

Granville shuffled to the doorway as Anderson relished another drink.

You see them mountains? Granville said. Almost pure limestone. Like this rock here.

He gestured to a shelf of blue limestone that protruded from the earth under a willow.

That's what does it. Filtered through all that limestone. This one here is free and open to all.

Anderson figured he would take his chances.

That's why, Anderson said, they grow them big around here, huh?

Yep. Good horses, strong cattle.

Tastes like some water I had in Kentucky a few times. Suppose that's why it's so popular with shiners, eh?

Granville squinted at him.

Suppose. Where you from?

Marion.

Huh. Long way to travel. Well, come on to th' store an' sit a spell.

They left the springhouse, Granville toting the pail of silvery water.

Mr. Bondurant, I was wondering if I could ask you a couple questions 'bout your boys?

Granville stopped walking and the two men stood by the side of the road and Anderson figured this was a sign of some kind of consent.

About December of 1930, Anderson said. When your boys were shot out by Maggodee Creek.

I caint tell you nothin', Granville said, that you don't already know.

Maybe, Anderson said. I'm just curious about the events that led up to that incident. The papers aren't clear. And what happened after. It seems like the charges against the deputy who did the shooting, Charley Rakes, they were dropped pretty quick.

Yep.

Can you tell me why that is? Just trying to understand the story.

Granville set the pail of water down. Out of the cool shade of the springhouse the sun was punishing. A car crested the hill from the north and came coasting down, rattling by the two men. Granville raised a hand in greeting, the driver lifting his fingers off the wheel. They watched the car whine up the hill.

Look, Mr. Anderson, Granville said, why don't you get to it.

Sorry?

Yer point of conversation.

I'm not trying to stir up trouble, sir, Anderson said, I'm just interested in the story.

You a federal?

No.

Granville digested this information without the slightest glimmer of a reaction.

People round here, he said, tend to mind their own.

I've noticed that, Anderson said. I'm just trying to understand how a couple of boys end up on a bridge in the dead of winter with three cars of liquor, and why a deputy would shoot them down in cold blood.

Times were hard, Granville said. Most folks didn't have much.

I know.

My boys' lives is they own.

I understand that.

Granville's face seemed to indicate the matter closed, but he remained there by the side of the road, the pail of water at his feet. Was the fact that his sons were infamous, bootleggers, criminals a source of sorrow for him? People didn't seem to have much problem with illegal liquor in Franklin, and many seemed to associate it with almost a civic duty; it made one a good citizen, a "real" Franklin County resident.

Some folks, Granville said, they say that making whiskey gets in your blood. It gets its hooks in you and won't let go.

He shrugged his shoulders and dusted his hands off on his dungarees.

My boys was raised right, as best as I was able. They lost their mother and two sisters in the epidemic back in '19.

I'm sorry to hear that, Anderson said.

Went hard on them, 'specially my youngest boy.

That'd be Jack?

Granville turned to him and gave him the gypsy stare, searching Anderson's face.

You have a good day, Mr. Anderson. Come by for a drink anytime.

WHEN HE RETURNED from Snow Creek that afternoon Anderson wandered through the streets of Rocky Mount, letting the pad and scrape of his feet lull him into insensibility. A flyer in a shop window along Orchard Avenue caught his eye: *Rally Tonight: The Virginia Anti-Communist League.* It reminded him, for the first time in some months, of the Bonus Marches, the crackdowns, the Union Square Riot of 1930. He wondered if the people of Franklin, the Bondurant boys and all the denizens of Snow Creek, had known or cared of such things. Did he give a damn himself? Years back in New York the leaders of the Communist Party asked to meet with Anderson, and he went. They admonished him for the open letter he wrote to President Hoover, published in *The Nation.* In the letter he said that they both came from the same background and that he understood Hoover's plight. The corruption of power, the influence of the yes-men and the

minions who steered noble inclinations astray. The Communists said
it would only arouse sympathy for Hoover.

Why yes, Anderson said, that was my very intention, to illustrate
the destructive influences that surrounded the president, the forces
that were growing in America.

Only money, they said. That is the scourge and he is part of the
problem. They tried to scold him but by then Anderson didn't care. I
was expressing my point of view, he said, not yours.

He was done with the Communists and their talk. Anderson
thought of his days in Harlem with Bertrand Russell, the great pacifist
living the life of reason, the elegant spokesman for the oppressed. One
evening in a club two Negresses had been placed at their table by their
hosts. They were both quite handsome and clearly had money and an
elevated social upbringing. Anderson talked with one through most of
dinner and later he danced with both of them. He remembered the
musical laugh and the soft, dark eyes, their languid way of handling a
remark. It was a pleasant evening and Anderson felt refreshed and
youthful. Afterward Russell accosted him in the street, gripping him
by the elbow, his shaggy eyebrows wagging. He was upset about the
dancing with the Negro women.

It isn't done, old chap, he said, *it just isn't done.*

This from a man who thought that children ought to be raised by
the state.

Old Lord Russell.

Anderson awoke from his plodding reverie to find the sidewalks
full of people. He was working up Orchard Avenue against a tide of
people that surged forward, dozens of men and women of varying
ages. The density was shocking, as it seemed that most of Franklin
County remained sparsely populated. Was there a gathering? There
was nothing hard in the glances of the crowd, and they acknowledged
Anderson as he edged past, their grinning faces, the hang of their
shoulders. No, the faces of these people were lit with the light of happiness. They were just enjoying the afternoon. Where were they going?
Where was he going? In the crowd Anderson felt as though everyone

else was enjoying the day, feeling a part of life, while he was merely trying to navigate through it. Why did it always seem this way?

When Anderson reached East Court Street he saw the source: the Coca-Cola bottling plant. The afternoon whistle had blown and the shift was departing, happy to be done with their day of work, Anderson thought, returning to their homes. Were they dulled with work, with the strain and repetition, their minds milled down to the nub? *Poor White* was a failure in the end, but watching the people Anderson felt that he had said something in that book that was as true as anything he had ever written. If they could just turn their minds to study, to intellectual application . . . but why? Why, when such a glorious afternoon lay spread before you, your work done and forgotten?

The American Worker trudges on.

At his boardinghouse there was a note for him slipped under his door.

> *Mr. Anderson—*
> *You wish to speak with me. Tomorrow afternoon at three o'clock.*
> *Respectfully—*
> *C. Lee*
> *C.A. Franklin County*

HIS OFFICE was dominated by a trophy buck, eight points, mounted on the wall behind his massive desk. Carter Lee wore a light linen suit of faint blue; his gray fedora sat on the corner of the desk.

This is solid butternut hickory, Carter Lee said, rapping his knuckles on the desk. Nice, ain't it?

Anderson nodded and smiled.

Did you shoot that deer?

Sure did.

Carter Lee beamed, his cheeks ruddy with pleasure.

Out in the valley, near Staunton? My brother has some land out there with some nice game.

Ever do any hunting around here?

Shoot, Carter Lee said, there ain't been a deer in Franklin County for forty years. Other than drought years. The need to drink is stronger than the fear of death.

Why's that?

No real way of knowing, Carter Lee said. This has always been tobacco land around here. Not like they was hunted out. I read your book *Dark Laughter,* you know. Interesting piece of work. You working on a new book?

Anderson was taken aback by the first mention of his work by anyone in Franklin.

No, Anderson said. I'm just here for the story. I have some papers over in Marion and—

I know all about your papers, Carter Lee said, waving his hand. That Buck Fever bit is a real stitch. You ought to put that in a book.

I might, Anderson said. But I'm here to talk about other things.

Carter Lee seemed genuinely saddened by this, his brows dropping in concern.

We sure got some stories in these parts.

That is true, Anderson said. Particularly this conspiracy trial, eh?

Carter Lee scowled and leaned back in his chair. Anderson took a cigarette from the pack that lay on the table and shook one out. Steady, he thought, this fella wants to strong-arm this thing with smiles and cheer. Direct action will kill that. He lit the cigarette and Carter Lee pushed the heavy glass ashtray toward him.

There is an *alleged* conspiracy, Carter Lee said, if that's what you mean. But you *know* I can't talk about that.

I understand, Anderson said.

Ain't nothin' to be done about that. I'd hate to think we just wasting our time?

You have Willie Carter Sharpe here in custody?

Carter Lee smiled good-naturedly.

Yep. Though not much doin' of ours. They caught up with her in Saint Louis, hiding out in the garage apartment of a blockader's mansion. We hauled her back here to Rocky Mount a few days ago.

Can I talk to her?

Nope. You have to wait for the trial like everyone else.

What about the murder of Jeff Richards?

We have some leads, the investigation is under way.

That's it? He was shot twenty times.

Yep.

Charley Rakes?

Well, poor Charlie was just unlucky. Pneumonia is no way to die.

I see. Then I wonder if we could talk about the shooting of the Bondurant boys at Maggodee Creek.

Carter Lee nodded his head and rifled through a drawer.

That was near five years ago.

I know, Anderson said.

It's been all over the papers, Carter Lee said. You can read all about it there.

But there was never an official investigation, Anderson said, from your office.

Wasn't no need for it, Carter Lee said. It was a clear situation. An agreement was reached.

What kind of agreement?

Carter Lee fished out some papers and flipped through them. He's not really looking at those things, Anderson thought.

You need to understand somethin', Carter Lee said, about those boys. They ain't the churchgoing type, you know what I'm sayin'? Ain't exactly choirboys. They been up to their eyeballs in it since they was in short pants.

Seemed like that deputy wanted them dead, Anderson said.

Carter Lee leaned over the desk, his eyes creasing to slits. His skin was smooth and unblemished, as if he used expensive creams or salves. His nails were shining, the crescent moons of the cuticles stark white. Two heavy gold rings, a wedding band. Clearly there was more money to be made in enforcement than in actually making illicit liquor, Anderson thought. The law came out ahead in the end.

Those boys, Carter Lee said, woke up that morning with guns in their hands. They directly threatened officers of the law.

How was it that Jack Bondurant was shot with his hands up?

Well, Carter Lee chuckled, sometimes people do funny things when they got a gun pointed at them.

He leaned back in his chair and knotted his hands behind his head.

Some folks, he said, seem to want to seek out the things that destroy them. Called an achimist, a fancy word, but a true one. Seems like they's plenty around here in Franklin like that. Those boys seem to seek out the worst, that's all there is to it.

Carter Lee droned on for a bit about the history of Franklin County and other matters and Anderson found his attention wandering. He examined the deer head and smoked another cigarette. He wouldn't get anything from this man. A spinner of half truths. If you are a born liar, a man of the fancy, why not be what you are?

He shook hands with Carter Lee and walked back across the court square to his boardinghouse. The fresh breeze on the streets brought the scent of the surrounding countryside and Anderson thought again of his time among the corn. Many hours he walked through the stalks, lying between the rows at night, watching the fronds wipe away the stars, the hum of insects in his ears, the deep smell of growth. The smell of life. He realized this when he wrote *Tar,* the story of his youth, in that narrow room in the farmhouse in Troutdale, surrounded by a sea of corn. In those days Anderson felt he was a mystic of the corn, at once its acolyte and priest. He read most of *Tar* aloud in that cornfield, to the insects and crows, and had declared that year to his wife that a book should be written so that it could be read aloud in a cornfield; *only* then would it be American and true. Hell, Anderson thought, I couldn't get a thing down until I created Tar in my mind and allowed myself to live through him. The same with George Willard. A man of fancy who tries to keep his toes in reality, the world of work, of real men with quiet minds. Could *Dark Laughter* be read aloud in a cornfield? *Perhaps Women?* How had he strayed from that essential feeling?

In his room at the rooming house Anderson tried to compose a letter to Eleanor. He sipped a short glass of some peach brandy he picked up at a station in Sontag and tried to conjure up the image of Eleanor that he could cast his love to. Instead he thought of the angular form of

Maggie in her flashy dresses, smoking behind the counter at the Black-water station. Something like his first wife, Tennessee, in her carriage. The brandy was sweet but tasty. Anderson smoothed a piece of paper on his desk.

Eleanor,

In many ways this place is like any other. The old love of craft has been strangled by the hands of industry here, too, and everyone here walks about the hot night like it is their last.

Yet the land here seems to rise up in formations. There is so much complication in such a simple land. I feel old and lonely. It is what makes beauty possible, of course, all this complexity and texture to the landscape. If the land were featureless, the world smooth and all the people in it, then we would see it all in an instant. Its flat, hideous, blankness.

In the hills of Franklin and on the streets here I know there remains the features of beauty. So why is it then that when I close my eyes I see the smooth blankness, this horrifying sameness that engulfs all?

In my bed at night I swear something is swinging out in the dark, some vast shape that looms and comes ever closer. It presses upon me like a deep weight.

The story will come along, I suppose, but I have another idea for something working here, perhaps a new book. I think it will be my final work and my best. If I can just move before the great swinging thing comes all will be well. I just don't know if I can.

Was the promise of Winesburg, that cursed little book, ever realized?

Chapter 23

1930

BERTHA MINNIX stood at the end of the drive wearing a set of men's overalls with a dark wool cardigan, her hair tucked under a floppy engineer's cap. Jack swung the car around and she was in before the car stopped moving. A raw November day, the sky slate gray, the wind relentless and the trees gone from broad rushes of scarlet and gold to spindled wire. Bertha was flushed with excitement and Jack couldn't help but grin as he hammered the Dodge down the hard-rutted washboard roads toward Snow Creek and Turkeycock Mountain.

So Daddy did the milking this morning, Bertha said, and Mother watchin' him bringing the cows up the hill to the house, and he milks them right there outside the back door, four pails' worth, then leads them back down.

Jack stuck a cigarillo in his teeth and popped a match on the dashboard. He was wearing a knee-length camel-hair coat and leather driving gloves embossed with his initials.

Anyway, Bertha said, so Mother says to him: Why'd you walk them cows all the way up the hill here to milk? Why don't you just milk them down there? And Daddy says: Well, I figure them cows can get the milk up the hill easier than I can!

That father of yours is a real cutup, Jack said.

Watch it, Bertha said, and aimed a sharp elbow at his ribs.

THEY STOPPED the car along an old lumber road a few miles along the western base of the mountain. Jack pulled the car into a shadowy thicket of birch and maples. They set out at an angle to the mountain slope, and as they walked through the carpet of dry leaves Bertha reached out and took Jack's hand.

When I was a girl, Bertha said, we used to kick through leaves like this and pretend the sound was our silk petticoats.

She shuffled a bit and smiled sideways at Jack.

On the way to parties, she said, a trail of us girls, we'd shuffle our feet and pretend we were wearing gowns and on our way to a party. Crossing a stream over a log was a sidewalk in the city. More than anything I wanted to go to a big fancy ball. And here I am.

She pulled at her oversized overalls.

You just wait, Jack said.

After a while they split up, Jack pointing out their guidepost and telling her to meander through the trees, not in a straight line, and at least fifty feet from him.

Walk lightly, he said, stop kickin' up leaves and don't break limbs if you can help it. Remember, the sign is a single shout: *Somebody!* Don't go back to the car.

She popped him an exaggerated salute.

I'm serious, he said.

I know it.

Bertha stayed far off to Jack's left on the downhill side, slightly behind. He led them around the bend of the mountain and across a plateau of high grass, then back into heavy woods studded with limestone that erupted from the earth.

Bertha had been hearing about the exploits of Willie Carter Sharpe and started peppering Jack with questions.

She's got diamonds set in her teeth, Bertha said. Ain't that somethin'? They say she has cars all over the state, hidden in various places, just for her to use, and nobody can catch her.

I wouldn't believe all that, Jack said.

You're just sore, Bertha said. She's the richest and most famous blockader around and you don't like it.

It ain't that.

I read she's a real beauty too. You ever meet her?

I've seen her around, Jack said.

Yeah?

I'm just saying it ain't like they say in the papers.

Jack had never clapped eyes on Willie Carter Sharpe himself, though others, including Forrest, had seen her. The Mitchell twins said they saw her at a station in Shootin' Creek, heading up a caravan of big cars. They told Jack she looked like a film star in a long men's coat, smoking cigars and laughing with the boys. They said she was as tall as any man there, with long dark hair, high-heel shoes, and diamond jewelry dangling from her wrists. Talmedge Jamison told Jack that he had seen her in Roanoke. He described her as short and built like a mash barrel, a crooked mouth and tiny pig eyes: *She had a face that could pull a stump,* Jamison said. She had picked up caravans at the Blackwater station to pilot out of the county, but all Forrest said was that you couldn't believe what you read in the papers. Jack had read some of the stories and grimaced at the sensationalism. He had learned too well in recent months the grinding boredom, stomach-fear, exhaustion, and panic of blockading. Bertha didn't believe him when he tried to describe it. Well, he thought, I'll show her a bit of the real thing. It won't harm nothin' and maybe she'll see that he was the real deal; Sharpe was just a fantasy of the newspapers. Jack wished he could tell her the truth, that *he* thought it would be like that too, that he bought the same story, and how ashamed he was that he still believed that it might materialize, that romantic vision, his life transformed.

We done some business with Floyd Carter, Jack said.

Really? Her ex-husband?

Yep. Up in Burning Bag. Just lately.

People say that place is like rum alley, Bertha said, men shooting each other every day.

Well, it ain't all like that.

Jack longed for some new way to impress the woman who now held his heart in the crook of her elbow like a package from the grocery. He had some sense that the larger spaces that he intended to inhabit would require her assured hand. As he walked through the trees Jack removed his hat and smoothed his thin hair, slick with lemon-scented pomade, smiling to himself.

The final leg after the clearing was up a steep section and through a spiny hedge of black huckleberry and ragweed. Jack began to whistle about a hundred yards out, and when they stepped in the clearing Cricket Pate was squatting by a still furnace with a pail of cement. The six copper submarine stills were already charred coal black after just one season of use. Mash boxes stood lined up in rows of ten, and in several the contents roiled and scented the air with the heady smell of fermentation. Cricket blinked a few times and stared at the apparition of Bertha Minnix.

Cricket, Jack said. This here is Miss Minnix.

Jack showed Bertha the mash boxes and explained the process. She dipped her fingers into the bubbling brew, pushing aside the snowballs, but wouldn't taste the still beer. Cricket stirred the mash with a plank while Bertha poked around the still, kicking around in the piles of debris that littered the site: sugar bags, scraps of lumber, crates of five-gallon cans. Jack showed her their water source, a gurgling aquifer coming from a cracked wall of limestone just up the hill, channeled with rocks into small collecting pools, then run through pipes into the camp.

We can put out a thousand gallons a week, Jack said. Hard in the cold weather without a whole team of still hands, but Cricket here manages all right. When it warms up we'll get 'em all hot an' flood the damn valley with Snow Creek white!

Bertha seemed wholly focused on the workings of the stills and watched closely as Cricket and Jack charged one with fresh mash from the boxes as the sun set behind the mountain. Once the correct temperature was reached the doubler keg began knocking woodenly, and Bertha bent to the condenser pipe to watch the first singling emerge, smoking from the barrel. In her baggy outfit she looked like a narrow-shouldered hobo, but when she turned she smashed Jack with her grin and slate-colored eyes. Oh my, he thought, I'm gonna feel this for a long, long time.

Say, Jack said, you got your camera?

She dug intently in her pockets for a moment, fishing out the Brownie.

Here, Jack said, let me get one of you. Cricket, get on away from that.

Cricket crouched by the cooling barrel.

Don't, Bertha said. Your brothers will get mad.

Don't worry 'bout that, Jack said. Look, just stand there for a moment. It'll be fine.

Ain't it too dark? Bertha said. It sure is getting dark quick.

Umm, Cricket said, storm rolling in I'd say.

He fingered the dirt.

Maybe we oughta clear out, he said. Jack, what say?

Bertha was standing by one corner of the hot still and when she looked at Cricket, hunched down in his overalls and crusty jacket, his knees above his ears like some kind of vagabond grasshopper, she shook her head and laughed and took a step forward, intending to step away from the still when Jack snapped the picture.

Got it.

A high-pitched whistle broke from the woods, once, twice, three times. Jack froze, holding the camera out. Cricket stood and began searching frantically through piles of burlap bags. Jack cocked an ear; there was a faint, steady rustle. Bertha clutched at Jack's arm.

What? What is it?

A voice bellowed from above them, high among the rocks: *Somebody!*

Who else is here? Jack said. Who's up the hill?

Jack heard the echoing snap of underbrush coming from down the mountain, the same way they had come. The brambles provided excellent cover but provided almost no lookout down the mountain. He would have to get higher to get a decent view. Jack leaped onto the still and, stepping on the cap, made the short jump into the branches of a nearby elm. He went just high enough to see down to the widely spaced section of the hillside to the grassy plateau. The tall grass rippled and four men emerged from the trees on the far side dressed in suits and ties, two of them carrying axes on their shoulders, the other two cradling shotguns. He scrambled down the tree and dropped to the ground.

Sheriffs, Jack said. Which way?

Cricket motioned up the hill.

Break up till you hit the hollow, Cricket said, then east along the stream.

Oh God, Jack, what d'we do? Bertha said.

She was bouncing from side to side like an animal ready to bolt. Jack grabbed her hand.

We run, he said. Stay with me.

He pushed Cricket in the back, into the woods.

Go, dammit!

Cricket took off and Jack and Bertha sprinted after.

ON A ROCKY outcropping about forty yards above the still site Howard Bondurant crouched like some kind of ruined gargoyle, watching the sheriffs coming up the mountain. He had his collar turned up against the chill wind and a wool cap pulled down to his eyes. An empty quart jar balanced on a small thrust of limestone. He had watched his brother come up with the girl, seen them traipse about the camp, Bertha exploring the elements with the acute eye of a woman who wanted a piece of a world that was not her own. He felt oddly unconcerned about the approaching danger, the sheriffs who would be in the camp in a few minutes and who would destroy the stills before his eyes. Howard was thinking about how his little brother had led a pack of revenuers right to the still, practically blazing a trail.

The sheriffs came jogging into the clearing, guns out and calling to one another. Howard watched Charley Rakes dip a hand into the still beer. He thought about Jack getting beat at the hands of this man and winced. Abshire leaning thoughtfully on his ax, lighting a cigarette. Jefferson Richards laughing and tapping the blackened still with his knuckles. The spread of the valley rippled before Howard like water, the knobs of the neighboring mountains bobbing like ships on the sea. Howard stood and lacing his fingers together stretched his arms over his head, the vertebrae cracking up his spine as he arched. He sighed and picked up the jar and dangled it over his open mouth, catching the last few strands of syrupy liquid. He weighed the heavy glass in hand for a moment, looking out over the valley, resplendent with faint tracings of golden fire, the small snake of Snow Creek, the hills of Rocky Mount. A thick bank of clouds was rolling in from the east. It would storm.

Too bad about the tobacco, he thought. Might have changed things. Maybe none of this would have happened.

Then Howard hurled the jar at the oval head of Charley Rakes.

THEY MADE A LINE across the face of the mountain, following the stream. They could hear the sheriffs in the camp as they scrambled through heavy brush, the ground littered with windfall and deadwood, Bertha working her way like a seasoned mountain girl, and Jack had to marvel at her athletic grace as they galloped along, high-footing it over logs and brambles. They were a few hundred yards away, working around the bend of the mountain, and Jack was feeling they were safe; there was no pursuit and they couldn't be caught with that head start, not by any man.

Cricket, Jack hissed.

Cricket slowed and crouched in the leaves, waiting for Jack and Bertha to catch up. When they reached him Bertha leaned her arms against a tree, breathing hard, and Jack put his hands on his knees and spit dryly several times.

Was that Howard? That yell?

Cricket nodded, blinking.

Hold on, Bertha said, what happened back there?

We better move on, Jack, Cricket said. They'll be on our trail here shortly.

Bertha pushed the sweaty strands of hair out of her face, her white blouse streaked with bark and bush grease. She wiped her palms on the legs of her overalls. Thick clouds were rolling over the mountain and under the trees the darkness settled heavy and close. Jack was about to reply when the distinct *thum . . . thum . . . pock . . . pock pock* of gunfire came echoing across the face of the mountain, coming from the camp. Two shotgun blasts, then pistol fire.

Oh glory, Bertha said.

Jack and Cricket looked at each other, Cricket's face a strange working of anguish that Jack hadn't seen before.

Ah Jack, I'm sorry, he said. I'm so sorry.

They were shooting Howard, Jack thought. The bastards were shooting his brother. Or he was shooting them.

The shotgun, Jack said. Where is it?

In a poke by the mash barrels, Cricket said.

Go, Cricket, take her. I'll meet you back at the station tonight.

What? Bertha said. Don't leave me!

Distant shouts from the camp, indistinguishable. Howard was alone, outnumbered.

I gotta go back, Jack said.

He took Cricket's hand and put it on her arm.

Go, dammit!

Jack turned and sprinted back as still more gunshots floated out across the dark valley.

CHARLEY RAKES was shouldering his ax, preparing to unload on the still when a jar whistled over his shoulder and exploded on the still cap.

What tha?

Charley Rakes dropped the ax and grabbed the shotgun out of Jeff Richards's hands.

What the hell happened, Charley?

Rakes raised his gun up the hill, and the other men saw the silhouette of Howard on a rocky outcrop above them, standing spread legged with his arms hanging loosely at his sides, a blot against the violet sky.

Who the hell is that?

Howard watched the men assemble, pointing their guns at him, their barrels like small black insects in their hands. When Rakes fired, Howard saw the charge of sparks and light and felt the shot whistle by, rippling his pant legs, the shot chattering on the rocks. Rakes fired his second barrel, again low, and Richards let go with his pistol, his bullets whining by Howard's head, one slug somersaulting by his ear, the sound like a tumbling bee. The valley echoed with the reports as Howard stood there, watching the men trying to kill him. They seemed like tiny feral creatures scrabbling in the dirt.

You, come down from there!

I swear I'll shoot you if you don't get down here!

Howard turned and walked off into the brush. To the men below it was as if someone had shut off a light; the darkness of the wood sprang at them.

Where'd he go?

Shut up and listen!

It's that big son of a bitch Howard.

You sure?

Then Howard was descending, the men could hear his footfalls, the crunching of undergrowth and they huddled together, their guns outstretched in a defensive perimeter.

Get a light goin'!

Howard's mind was quite clear as he approached the men. His eyes were nearly closed, mere slits, and he walked down the hill leaning far back on his heels. He felt relaxed and quick. The darkness did not seem to affect him; he stepped nimbly around log and stump, the glowing image of the four men like a beacon in the rapidly darkening wood. He would wade into them and explode in their midst, cut them all down.

JACK REACHED the shotgun as Abshire got a stick of pitch pine blazing. Jack crouched behind the mash barrels, a mere fifty feet from the four men who looked wildly up the hill, pointing their guns into the black. He could hear Howard coming down the hill toward them, crashing through brush like a wounded deer. Thunder shook the trees. Abshire got the torch going and held it aloft, illuminating the group, and Jack ducked back down behind the mash barrels, clutching the shotgun. He didn't know if it was loaded or not. There were no shells in the bag, and he was afraid to break it open to check. I'll just have to hope it is, he thought.

When you see 'im, pop him one, Jeff Richards said.

It seemed to Jack like Howard was going to walk right out into the clearing, walk right out into their guns. What the hell is he doing? Jack scrunched up behind the barrels and shut his eyes.

Hey! Jack yelled.

Dammit, there's another!

Who's there?

Watch him coming down the hill here!

You better run, Jack said. You better get out now.

He was answered with a few pistol rounds in his general direction. One round punctured the mash box he was hiding behind, the mash glugging out the opening, pooling at Jack's feet. The torchlight flickered over him. He couldn't tell if they were coming toward him or not. He poked the shotgun out with one hand and aimed it in their general direction, but high, and pulled the trigger. Both barrels let go, jerking the heavy gun out of Jack's hand. The torchlight immediately winked out and a man screamed.

Sweet Jesus! someone yelled.

Shit! Get that light, Henry!

Jack heard Richards scream.

He's here!

A pistol shot, a heavy grunt and thud, shoes shuffling in the leaves.

Jack peeked around the box and in the low light from the torch that lay on the ground he saw his brother springing from the woods like a coiled demon. The men quailed and shrank back, one man already on the ground holding his head. Using the force of his leap into their midst Howard drove a fist into the body of a man trying to twist away, striking him square on the shoulder, and Jack could see the arm fold up, the unnatural angles of bone coming through his shirt. Charley Rakes was on his hands and knees, searching for his gun, Jefferson Richards flashing out of the light, running fast down the hill. Abshire staggered to his feet, the side of his face a slick of blood. He grabbed the man on the ground, moaning and clutching his shoulder, trying to help him up. Howard stood there calmly in the flickering light, watching the three men struggle on the ground. Rakes looked up at him, pawing at the leaves, looking for a gun.

I'm gonna kill you goddammit!

Jack stood and leveled the shotgun at Rakes. He knew that he wanted the man to grovel for his life. He would put the barrel in his face and make him beg for it. The darkness seemed to separate him from the men and the gun in his hands. He charged toward Rakes, aiming the shotgun from the hip.

Hey Rakes, Jack yelled. Remember me?

Rakes cranked his head around, his face shifting, his eyes widening. Before Jack took three steps he had cocked both hammers and pulled the trigger. It surprised him; it was like the fingers acted on their own. Howard was looking at him too, his face blank as water. The hammers fell on the empty chambers with a solid *thunk*. Then Howard stepped on the torch, plunging them all into darkness.

Let's go, Charley! Abshire yelled. Richards is gone!

Jack froze, blinking in the dark. There was the sound of more struggle, the pitiful groans from the man with the broken shoulder. A faint glimmer of movement, arms around bodies, thumping footfalls. Another gunshot, the flash illuminating only the spidery limbs of trees and the outstretched arm that held the pistol. The crack and whine of a ricochet close to Jack's ear, the bullet cracking through the woods. Jack dropped into a crouch, arms protecting his head. He didn't want Rakes anymore; it was over when the hammers fell on empty chambers. He wanted to run. The patter of rain in the trees, then a sudden downpour, roaring. Then Howard's voice in the dark, close to him and clear and calm:

Go, Jack. Now.

Jack sprinted down the hill to the west, working toward the faint slice of horizon through the trees.

———————◆◆———————

JACK MADE his father's house by daybreak. He was mud-spattered and bone-tired, running in a black haze most of the night across the mountain and then along Snow Creek. The thunderstorm was brief and the ground already dry. As he came up the drive his father was heading out to the store and he passed Jack without a word or glance. Jack staggered into his room and collapsed on the bed and slept until noon, finally awakened by the shifting sunlight and the sound of voices outside. In the kitchen he ate a few biscuits washed down with several glasses of cold water. As he gulped the water the enormity of last night came crashing down; the deputies would be back in daylight and the stills would be destroyed. They would come back with more men and guns and dynamite the site. Thousands of dollars of supplies and materials, a whole season of work and the potential income, all lost. They couldn't have followed him, he was careful, and there was no solid trail. He winced and set the glass down hard on the counter, cracking the base and slicing his palm. *Dammit dammit dammit.* He shouldn't have brought Bertha; it was so damn obvious. Howard knew. Forrest would blame him.

He watched the trickle of blood running down the side of his hand. The voices outside the house continued, two people talking on the front porch. One of them was his sister, Emmy, the other a man he didn't recognize. The way she was talking was strange, soft and lilting, like she was talking to a child.

Marshall Wingfield was leaning on the porch post, legs crossed, dressed in a pale suit with a kerchief around his neck. He held a straw boater in his hand.

Hey there, Jack, Wingfield said.

Wingfield's cheeks were ruddy and he beamed at Jack, straightening up and offering up his hand. Emmy sat demurely, looking at her folded forearms in her lap. She had a small cluster of wildflowers on her dress, tied with a bit of ribbon. Emmy's glassy hair fell on both sides of her face and she did not lift her head.

Wingfield snatched Jack's hand, wringing it hard, grinning.

How are you, old sport? Wingfield said.

Emmy would not raise her head. Wingfield's car, a new Dodge coupe, sat shining on the lawn. The leaves of the stunted dogwood tree in the yard went belly-up, waving their undersides, and the clouds gathered. Gonna rain again, Jack thought. I'll be damned.

Think you done cut yourself, Wingfield said.

Wingfield held up his hand, smeared with blood. Jack looked down at the rivulets of blood going down his forearm, spattering on his pants. Wingfield was holding his hand up and away from his clothes, doing his best to maintain a pleasant smile. His suit seemed to pulse with a soft, glowing light.

That's a nice suit, Jack said. Real nice.

Jack struck hard with his bloody right hand, a straight punch that seemed to come from inside his chest and caught Wingfield flush on one rosy cheek with a loud *smack*.

Jack!

Jack's hands felt fast and as Wingfield bent at the waist, hands at his face, Jack cut loose with a series of left hooks into the side of his head until Wingfield went sprawling into the yard.

What th' hell's s'matter with you? Wingfield shouted.

Jack squared up to him. Lead with the left, he thought, use the left and set up the right cross. He put his left foot out and stepped to Wingfield who was in a low crouch, hands up in a defensive position. He reached out and tapped him on the forehead with the left, once, twice, three times, snapping Wingfield's head back, his hands going higher until he was trying to cover up with his elbows. There was a rush of wind and the ripping sound began again, low at first and building into a high scream. Just as Jack saw the opening for the right, Wingfield folded and sat down heavily on the grass, a sleepy look on his face. The sound from the sky poured forth into his ears, the earth ripping open. I got it this time, Jack thought, stepping up to Wingfield.

Get up, you son of a bitch!

He wanted to finish the combination; Wingfield was ruining it. The ripping sound wavered and cut and Jack paused, confused by the sudden silence. Wingfield crawled away, gasping for air, the rump of his suit grass stained, groping for his hat. Jack turned and saw the contorted face of his sister staring at him in horror, her face agape in a twisted shape of sorrow. Emmy took a deep breath and began to scream again.

Chapter 24

1930

GRANVILLE CLOSED DOWN his store early and picked up Jack at the house in Snow Creek. They drove west to Haw Patch Hill and the Jamison farm for a wood chopping. With the stills dynamited into a blackened hole of copper shards on the mountainside, Jack stayed on living with his father, helping out around the farm and generally avoiding his brothers.

Get out of here, Forrest told him when he turned up at the Black-water station a few days later.

It wasn't my fault, Jack said. No one followed us, I swear.

Get the hell *out*.

Jack hadn't seen Howard in weeks, but Jack got word that his brother was apparently unhurt and back at Forrest's sawmill. He hadn't seen or heard anything about Cricket, his hut on the mountain empty, his scant possessions scattered on the dirt floor as usual. Bertha, whom Jack saw only in passing in town, said he dropped her home and that was it, but he wasn't arrested so Jack figured his friend was okay. The tobacco crop was gone, and Jack had about forty dollars tucked into a soap can in his trunk. Forrest would get by, though soon the sawmill would shut for the winter and the Blackwater station was losing business; Carter Lee had put the word out that no one was to do business with the Bondurants, legitimate or otherwise. Everything Howard had and then some was in the stills.

The Jamison farm lay at the foot of Thornton Mountain in the western part of Franklin County, a rough, mostly wooded stretch with hard clay to well depth. Granville followed the dirt track that wound by the frame house and into the back fields dotted with cattle. Thin plumes of smoke rose from the fields abutting the mountain slope. The felling was finished, and the men were pulling stumps with teams of mules and rolling and carrying the heavy logs to the wagons for transport down the hillside, others burning piles of brush. Most of the able-bodied men from the southern part of the county were there.

Jack joined Howard cutting out stumps while their father helped the older men driving the mules and workhorse teams and cutting small limbs. Forrest was absent. Howard was stripped down to his undershirt and suspenders, his body smoking in the brisk fall air. Jack looked at his brother's face for some indication of his mood but Howard merely bent to the task. It was difficult and slippery work, the damp roots like rubber and the footing crumbled and shifted. Several times Jack bounced his ax off a bent root like black rubber and narrowly missed cutting his legs or feet. The roots had to be struck at the right angle to bite and eventually they swung into an easy rhythm of Jack setting the cut in a root and then Howard using his heavy broadax to chop it clean.

Lucy here? asked Jack.

Yep.

Working on supper?

Suppose so.

The two brothers worked in silence for the next hour, and Jack figured Howard felt there was nothing to talk about. But where was Cricket? They had been in spots before, plenty, and Cricket's usual response was a morose sort of defeatism and a period of hibernation. Bertha said he was in tears, apologizing profusely to her as they walked the three miles back to where he'd hidden his car. This was odd; he had seemed sober enough that night, Jack thought. He must be scared and laying low. Jack figured he would run over to his cabin again just to make sure he was okay. He would tell him that Jack and his brothers would protect him.

Jack and Howard worked on a black-chestnut stump that had put roots almost straight down, winding around hunks of limestone and clay, the taproot like a shaft of black muscle as big around as Jack's waist. They finally got chains under it and G. T. Washburne drove his team of Suffolk punch horses while Howard and Jack sliced at the taproot with axes.

Whadja tell Forrest? Jack asked.

Howard wrestled his ax from the taproot.

Told 'im what happened.

Water ran from each wound in the fibrous flesh, the roots covered in tiny hairs. Jack thought about how the combined effort of all these tiny hairs brought life to the tree, delicately sipping drops of moisture, eventually hauling thousands of gallons of water up the trunk and out to the leaves.

Didja say anything 'bout Bertha being there?

Yep.

Jack stopped chopping and leaned on his ax.

Well goddammit, Howard, whadja do that for?

'Cause it was a damn fool thing to do.

They didn't follow us. No way.

A damn fool thing to do, Howard said.

Well, Jack said, we all done made mistakes.

Howard paused, just a hitch in the stroke of his ax, then made a final, heavy cut. He stepped back from the hole, tossed his ax aside. Ah hell, Jack thought, now I've done it. Howard looked at him for a moment, the same blank look, then turned and gestured to Washburne, who drove the horses and with a crunching roar the stump was ripped from the ground. Howard put his hands on his hips and looked at the dark hole in the earth, the twisted ends of roots, rocks, red clay, and seemed to consider something for a moment. He took off his gloves and slapped them on his thigh. He glanced around for a minute, then turned to Jack with a slight grin.

What say we go find ourselves a snort?

The brothers joined the group of men around a small pile of pine knots. Aubrie Kendrick brought a jar from his truck and the men passed it around slowly and discussed the progress of the work. Jack pulled the Mitchell twins aside for a moment.

Y'all seen Cricket?

Naw.

Haven't seen hide nor hair.

Jack passed the corn whiskey when it reached him, and Howard grinned and took the jar and punched him hard in the arm, pointing across the broad valley. Three cars were slowly making their way from the house, the women with the food, and men began to put their coats on and after a few more quick drinks Aubrie Kendrick put the jar back on the floorboard of his truck before the women got close enough to see it.

When the women arrived they spread blankets on a patch of level grass and laid out bowls of sweet corn, greens with ham hocks, pork cracklings, hash gravy, plates of biscuits covered with napkins, and skillets of corn bread. Dick Jamison came over to the circle of men who remained clustered off to the side.

Well, set to it, he said.

Jack filled his plate and sat on a stump next to his father who was eating a hunk of corn bread. Women joined their husbands and the younger unmarried women present, mostly friends of Wilma Jamison and her daughters, made their own circle on a blanket, their soft voices carrying over to where the men sat. The light began to fade and pine-knot torches were lit and women wrapped wool shawls around their shoulders. Howard stood off a bit, speaking in low tones with Lucy. Jack hadn't seen her in some months and was surprised how fair-haired, slight, and freckled she was, like a young girl rather than a woman in her upper twenties. Jack had spoken to her only a few times, the first at the simple wedding they had at the Snow Creek Baptist Church. Her family was from Smith Mountain, dirt-poor hog farmers, a dozen straggling kids in a muddy patch of unworkable mountainside land, and Lucy seemed glad to be rid of them and to move into the little cabin in Penhook. Lucy's second pregnancy only seemed to waste her already-slight form even further, and as she stood in her calico-print dress and boots holding a plate Jack could see the heavy rings under her eyes as she looked up at Howard. It was clear that their second child wasn't doing well either. They needed money and Jack knew this wore on Lucy like a sore. Lucy turned and caught his eye and Jack turned away embarrassed.

Howard walked over with his plate piled high with corn, cracklings, and biscuits, the whole thing covered with white gravy. He sat at his father's feet and dug in with a large spoon and the three men ate together, glancing about occasionally and remarking upon the coming weather or the quality of the food. The sweat dried on Jack and his hands and feet grew cold and he wished he had worn an extra pair of socks.

How's Lucy? Jack asked.

She's fine, Howard said as he sopped a biscuit.

How's the baby? Granville murmured from his stump.

Up at her mother's place, Howard said. Same as ever I guess.

Howard chewed, his heavy-lidded eyes gazing out over the field and into the dark tree line. Women were gathering up dishes and folding blankets, and two young boys chased each other through the stubbled fields. Jack stretched out his legs, crossing his new boots in front of him. His father ducked his face back to his plate, a bit too quickly. Hell, Jack thought, the old man doesn't miss that much. The car, the clothes, the hours up on the mountain. Jack felt like a fool for this pathetic attempt at concealment, this conspiracy to keep his father in the dark. Night was coming on and the wind picked up, scattering sparks from the pine-knot torches.

You comin'? Howard asked Jack.

Jack looked at his father who continued to study his empty plate.

I suppose so, Jack said.

Howard nodded and then wrenched his body upright and brought his plate over to Lucy who stood in a small group of women. When she took it from his hands she touched his arm and looking up into his face said something that Jack couldn't catch. Howard nodded and then Lucy turned and gathered more dishes and bowls from the blanket.

She climbed into a car with several other women, laughing and waving to the men, some of whom called out to them to stay on, to come back. Jack stood next to his father and they watched as the cars of women made their way down the hill and across the valley to the house. Jack thought about the picture of Bertha standing under the crab-apple tree, holding a sprig with one hand, her mouth set in a prim line. Hell, Jack thought, I got to get my damn self together and do this properly.

Men gathered around Howard, joking and slapping his arms. He grinned, hands jammed in his pockets.

Sitting next to Jack, Granville grunted as he chewed the stub of a biscuit.

I'll tell you what, son, Granville said, if that boy had a mansion, he'd burn it to the ground.

He shook his head, gazing at his oldest son.

Well, Granville said, I guess I'll leave you boys to it.

He slapped the crumbs off his dungarees and walked off to his car.

The remaining men built a bonfire and were quickly flushed with liquor, sweating again in the firelight, passing jars freely and laughing loudly. Howard sat on a fat stump, putting away twice as much liquor as any man there, his face going slack, eyes narrowing on some faint spot a few feet in front of his nose. Dick Jamison came into the circle of firelight bearing a six-foot staff of seasoned dogwood about four inches in diameter. Men cheered as he held it aloft and everyone stood, taking pine-knot torches, and followed him up the hill to where the large trees lay felled. When the right log was chosen, a sizable oak three feet across, Dick Jamison laid the staff on the ground and the log was rolled onto it to the middle point. Then the money came out and the first two men spat on their hands, hitched up their trousers, and squatted down on either side of the log, worked their fingers under the staff ends and established their grip. Money bet on the contest was placed on the log in a pile and then pinned there in a rawhide bag with a knife. Belcher Whitehead pulled out a revolver and fired it into the sky and the two men lurched and heaved upward, straining against the bulk of the log, the other men shouting encouragement. There was a slight shift, a collective shout, and the log began to move slightly, one man pulling up on his end and forcing the other man's knuckles into the dirt, the shifting of the log putting more weight on his end until his hands were driven into the ground and he yelped and pulled away, stumbling on his backside. Men laughed and clapped the winner on the shoulder, the loser kneeling in the dirt, a jar proffered and a sheepish grin, crumpled bills changing hands.

Then Dink Amdams called out Howard for a contest and there were howls and whistles of disbelief. Jack looked over to Howard, who swayed in the torchlight, his eyes mere slits, his brow furrowed. Dink was a robust fellow with a barrel chest and legs like stumps, short, blunt-fingered hands, a broad back and thick neck. Near forty years old, he had been the acknowledged strongest man in the county till Howard came along. Dink hadn't had much to drink and he stripped off his coat and focused his gaze on the dogwood staff. Jack feared that Howard was completely insensible with booze and wouldn't be up to the challenge. He'd been watching Howard drink, Jack thought, and ol' Dink figured this was his chance. But then Howard's body swayed forward and he took a stumbling step to the log and the men erupted into cheers. Jack helped Howard off with his coat, his arms hanging limp, tugging at the sleeves as money began to pile up. Howard put his arm around his brother's shoulder, drawing him close, and put his lips right up against Jack's ear. He smelled of sweat and rotten corn, his breath foul with whiskey.

Did I ever tell you 'bout the ocean? Howard whispered.

Then he drew back and for a moment Jack saw a glint of something in his eyes, the slits widening slightly.

It's a hell of a thing, Howard said. I wish I knew how to tell it.

He clapped his hand around his younger brother's shoulder and gave him a squeeze that crunched Jack's rib cage. Jack fumbled in his pockets; he had two dollars and some change. The other men stood around them watching.

I'll match all of it, Jack shouted. I'll take all bets against my brother.

Money piled on the log until Dick Jamison put an end to it by stuffing the dollars and coins in the bag and pinning it to the log with the knife. Dink paced around his side of the log. Howard stretched his arms over his head, his feet unsteady; then slipping off his suspenders he reached down and pulled his work-stained shirt over his head. Jack stood behind him and was presented with the broad expanse of Howard's back, his shoulders pillows of flesh. Howard bent to the staff and Dink followed on his side.

The gun went off and both men heaved, their faces turned up, necks corded with strain. Howard's arms were rigid in the torchlight, thick veins in his forearms, the upper arms twisted masses of muscle as he squatted deeply and drove with his legs, eyes shut with effort. Dink grunted and began to jerk, heaving in regular lurches, his eyes pinched and his mouth in a snarl. Rivulets of sweat sprouted from Howard's face and neck and ran down his back and chest. Dink's jerking motion began to take effect, and the log began to shift, rolling side to side with each motion. The men on Dink's side cheered louder at this development, and Jack struggled to stay behind his brother in the throng, shouting in his ear. There was nearly thirty dollars on the log.

C'mon, Howard! Goddammit, Howard! C'mon!

The waving torches sent streams of sparks spinning through the cluster of men on the dark hillside, leaping and howling.

Then Howard grunted and his legs began to move, knees straightening, his face raging crimson; like some kind of ancient devil rising from the earth, Howard raised the staff and the log rolled down onto Dink's hands and forearms.

Dink screamed and men threw themselves against the log to keep it from rolling farther, and still Howard drove upward with his legs. Men dropped their torches and leaped over the log to stop it, Howard bringing the staff nearly up to his waist. Dink's screams choked off and his eyes rolled back in his head as the log crushed both his hands and arms. As if waking from a dream, Jack finally sprang forward and grabbed his brother's arms and tried to pull him off. *Howard! Howard! Let it go!* He shouted into his brother's face, grappling with Howard's arms that were slippery with oily sweat.

Howard! For God's sake, let it go!

Still Howard kept straining, eyes closed to the night, until finally the dogwood staff splintered and shattered, and Jack was thrown to the ground.

Looking up into the dizzy light from the spinning torches, Jack saw Howard standing with the broken staff in his hand, his face a terrible twisted mask of anguish. With a strange, cracking moan, Howard reared back and flung the broken staff off over the heads of the men out of the circle of light and into the darkness beyond.

Chapter 25

1930

EVERYONE IN FRANKLIN knew that Tazwell Minnix ran a clean, orderly farm in the Boone's Mill section of the county. In early December as the sun rolled over Smith Mountain, spilling light on the frosted hills and fields, Jack Bondurant parked his car at the edge of Minnix's lawn. The grass crunched under his wheels, the blades frozen hard. Jack shut down the vehicle and blew into his hands.

Tom C. Cundiff had been picked up for the assault on Deputy John Horsely. In the courtroom he lunged at Carter Lee and had to be chained to the floor. He was sentenced to two years and as he was dragged out he swore violent retribution.

Cricket Pate was dead. A few weeks after the destruction of the stills he was found lying on a shallow sandbar in Maggodee Creek, his open mouth packed full of red clay. He had forty cents and a few cigar stubs in his pockets. The stretch of creek ran about twelve inches deep in a mountain downpour. The sheriff's department ruled it an accidental drowning, which everyone knew was a complete farce. There was no funeral but Forrest paid for a plot and stone, and Jack went through the burial with a stony feeling in his heart.

When Jack got out of the car Minnix's dogs set to a chorus of yelps from their compound behind the house. Tazwell Minnix had a dozen hounds that he had bred and trained himself, excellent hunting dogs without equal in the county. Jack straightened himself and took off his hat, smoothing his hair, wiping the excess pomade on his handkerchief. That morning he elected to go with a simple gray three-piece suit, cuffed trousers with his black brogans buffed to a high sheen, an outfit that he felt bespoke his seriousness.

Before he could knock the front door was flung open, Bertha, her face stricken with anguish.

Oh, Jack, she cried.

R. L. Minnix sat at a table stirring his coffee. He craned his neck around and squinted at the door.

Who's there?

They wouldn't let him in, Bertha said. Why would they do that?

And she flung herself into his surprised arms.

When they came around the side of the house everything seemed to be normal, the dogs leaping and barking, Tazwell in the pen sifting through the wriggling animals. He had built a wooden shelter for his dogs to lie in at night, the floor covered with discarded blankets. Tazwell made his way to a lone dog standing near the back of the pen. It was tan and white and small, a runt that was prone to taking a beating in the yard. The dog didn't move as Tazwell approached, and coming closer Jack could see the light, sparkling sheen on the animal, the ice in its nostrils, the eyes filmed over with gray frost. The dog had frozen to death overnight, standing outside the pen. Tazwell knelt before the dog and regarded it like an icon. R.L. tottered up beside him, squinting.

Well, I'll be . . . , the old man muttered, letting the curse hang in the air unsaid.

I ain't never seen anything like it in the world, Tazwell said.

Bertha clutched at Jack's shoulder.

Why'd they do that? Bertha said. They didn't let him in the house!

When they returned to the house Bertha relaxed, her grief turning to exhaustion. R.L. squinted at Jack and growled to himself.

I'm sorry for what happened here, sir, Jack said. If I woulda known . . .

Tazwell sat at the table with his arms cast out on the table.

What possible business you have here, son? What?

I've come to make my intentions known, Jack said. Concernin' Bertha.

Jack opened his coat and buttoned it again.

Things are changin', Jack said. I know'd that I caused you trouble before, and I want to say that I'm sorry for it. Things are going to be different.

Tazwell seemed to be listening but his face was incredulous and furrowed, inspecting Jack as if he were some kind of apparition.

We know, R.L. said, where your money comes from.

I want to make my intentions known, Jack said. We . . . we've seen a bit of each other now and then. I just want to put it in the clear. I'm giving you my word. I'm giving up all the other soon as I get my packet together and get a good patch of land.

R.L.'s face was inflamed with ire. Jack steadied his breathing, watching Bertha as she stared wide-eyed at the floor, blinking slowly, her face slick with tears.

That dog didn't have a name, Tazwell murmured. Without a name the poor thing had no soul.

OUT FRONT Bertha leaned into Jack.

It isn't right, Bertha said.

Jack put his arm around her. Their breath steamed around them.

Those dogs didn't know better. Just plain bad luck.

No, Bertha said. Something awful is going to happen, I can feel it.

———— ✦ ————

LEAVE IT, Lucy said from the doorway.

She stood nursing the baby, the light from the kitchen framing her silhouette, hips canted to the side, the baby's head cradled in her palm. Howard was on his hands and knees by the bed. He could see the layer of dust on the ax that lay under the bed, put there before Lucy went into labor.

We ain't out of it yet, Lucy said.

She turned and went back to the kitchen. A pan of corn bread was cooling on the counter next to a small bowl of stewed tomatoes. She slung a dish towel over her other shoulder and while the baby nursed she placed a pitcher of buttermilk on the table, two bowls, two spoons, and sprinkled some salt on the tomatoes. A pot of wild ramps boiled on the stove. The baby was asleep when they sat down but was startled awake when Howard turned away and sneezed three times, quickly. The baby blinked and gurgled before relaxing her cheek on Lucy's shoulder. Howard spooned some tomatoes into his bowl while Lucy broke up the corn bread.

He was thinking of the old still, one he'd run with Jamison and some others years before, tucked into another fold up on Turkeycock. The mash was already working up a good steam, all the supplies paid for by Forrest, including another car.

I could head up to my mother's, Lucy said. They'd take me and her in.

No, Howard said. Ain't gonna do that.

If the weather held, in a few days they would run four cars up to Roanoke County and to Floyd Carter's gang, who guaranteed them five a gallon. His cut would see them through the winter. The thought of it exhausted Howard as he bent to his bowl of tomatoes, though at the same time he knew that he would go on. He would finish this meal, sleep like a dead man, and the next morning he would go out and do it all again. Lucy slid a plate of ramps to him on the table. Howard eyed the onions steaming on the plate, their strong odor burning in his sinuses.

You need to eat 'em, Lucy said. Purify the blood.

Howard grunted and turned back to his tomatoes.

Lord knows, Lucy said, you sure need some purifying. The stuff you put in you. It's a miracle you alive.

Howard forked the ramps into his mouth, contemplating the fine hairs on Lucy's forearms, the way she smoothed them with her hand.

He thought of the wood chopping, the deep taproots they hacked off, roots that tunneled deep into the interior of things. The locust larvae clinging to the roots, fat and white like grubs, sucking the moisture from the pulpy flesh. They stayed under there for a dozen years and more, waiting for the right moment. To cling to a root in the moist darkness, no sound but the beating of your own heart, waiting for that silent signal to rise. True enough, he thought, I oughta be dead.

Maybe that's the problem, Lucy said.

She fiddled with the mad stone that hung on a cord around her neck, a smooth flat stone that Howard found in the belly of a deer. It would protect her from poison and dog bites and Howard liked the pearly opalescence of it, the way it lay flat against her collarbone. The baby gurgled contentedly.

Maybe, Lucy said, all that stuff you puttin' in youself is the reason why our children is born the way they is.

Here it is, Howard thought, she finally said it. He had a flare of rage and his fingers gripped the table. He could shatter it with his hands or flip it like a coin across the room. He began to play it out in his mind, the way it would go. Lucy saw the look on his face and quickly got up, backing away, holding the baby with both hands. Howard looked at his hands, his knuckles torn and scabbed from wood cutting and the log-rolling game.

Hell, he thought, what is the goddamn point, anyway?

I can't break myself. No matter how hard I try.

———◆———

FORREST SET the valise on the counter between them.

What's that? Maggie said.

The money. I want you to take it.

Maggie lit a cigarette.

What am I gonna do with it?

Don't know. Whatever you want.

She seemed to consider this for a moment, then reached over and unbuckled the valise. Forrest wanted to reach out and take hold of her wrists but he didn't. She looked at the stacked bills inside for a moment, then closed the valise.

Let me ask you something first, Forrest said. All right? And I'll need an answer.

Maggie stared at him for a moment, her eyes narrowing, a tight smile on her lips.

I ain't for sale. You might just get it for free.

It ain't that. Somethin' else.

Her face hardened and she turned to walk back into the kitchen. Forrest reached for her elbow, brushing her with his fingers. When he touched her she froze.

Please, he said. I got to know what happened.

Nothing, she said.

Maggie stood at the kitchen door, arms folded, her back to him.

What? Look at me.

Forrest suddenly wanted forgiveness from this woman for everything he had done in his life.

I'm sorry, he said. I was the one that brought that trouble in here.

No, she said. That don't matter none. It weren't you.

Either way. Look at me.

She turned to face him.

I just gotta know.

Not a damn thing, she said, her voice low and measured. Now you know. Not a goddamn one of 'em, she said, *ever* did a damn thing to me.

He heard her footsteps clomping up the stairs, across the floor, and the groan of the bedsprings. Forrest walked over to the radio by the front window and turned the knob. It crackled to life and he scanned the static as he gazed out the window down the road that led across Maggodee Creek.

THE NEXT MORNING Forrest eyed the snow through the upstairs window as he slipped on his heavy socks, dungarees, wool shirt. The woods across the road from the filling station were dead still, the sifting snow falling straight down and piling neatly along the crooked fingers of birch and oak trees. Small drifts gathered on the windowsill. The weather would make things more difficult, Forrest thought, particularly the driving. They would need snow chains and shovels.

Downstairs the kitchen was black and cold and smelled of bacon grease and smoke. He lit the grill and started coffee before shrugging on his heavy car coat and stepping outside to clear off the fuel pumps and check the gauges. He thought of the storage shed behind the station, bare now save for empty five-gallon cans and crates of jars. Everett Dillon's face, blank as a clear sky when Forrest handed him the money. He accepted the deal immediately. He must believe that I can protect him, Forrest thought.

During the winter nearly anyone in the southern reaches of Virginia and northwest Carolina who was making cold-weather booze came through Franklin County to unload their wares. They were mostly scrawny, desperate mountain men, blue in the face, an unruly, stinking lot of spitting fools. Most came by Forrest's Blackwater station because they knew they would get a good price without trouble. Forrest was a known, stable quantity, a poor man's only real lasting wish. But it had been weeks since he'd had a run through, dropping off or picking up. He knew it was Carter Lee. They had destroyed the stills and locked him down, and now, Forrest thought, they would simply wait him out.

The cold intermittent touch of snow on his face reminded him of that night at the County Line, which for some reason always brought him a comforting feeling. He had been afraid as he knelt there in the parking lot, he was afraid of dying, and this thought made him want to go back to his bedroom and lie on the narrow cot with his blankets pulled up to his chin. They would have to go through with it. Once disorder was introduced to the world it could not be undone.

Walking back into the station he searched himself for a possible change, something that was different. Shouldn't something like that change a man? Forrest sliced some bread and cracked eggs on the steaming grill and worked the spatula around the bubbling edges. He had the same wants and needs, the world as a whole looked the same.

His feet still got cold in his boots, his eyes ached when he did the books in low light, he still stood in dark rooms for hours while others slept, his mind refusing to rest.

There was a rustle of cloth and bare feet on the floor and then Maggie appeared beside him. She took a cup down from the cupboard and poured herself coffee. She gave him a thin smile, her dark eyes smudged with sleeplessness. Forrest slid an egg and some buttered toast onto a chipped plate and handed it to her. Maggie stood by the window overlooking the road, chewing on her toast. Forrest watched her face as she took in the snowfall and felt his heart seize in his chest.

What're you doing? Forrest asked.

Eatin' ice cream, Maggie said.

She took a bite of toast and smiled.

Forrest had the sudden urge to take her in his arms and bury his face in her hair. It was unlike anything he had felt before. He drank his coffee and watched her some more and wondered to himself just how foolish he really was. He wondered if this was the end of it, or if there was more, and just what it would take for him to learn.

PART 3

The reader should bear in mind that Kit Brandon was and is a real person, a living American woman. How much of her real story can be told? You, sitting and reading this book, have also a story, a history. How much of that could be told? How much do we writers dare let ourselves go in the making of portraits? How close can we keep to truth? How much do we dare try to be true historians?

Sherwood Anderson, *Kit Brandon*

Neither of us—Hemingway or I—could have touched, ridiculed, his work itself. But we had made his style look ridiculous; and by that time, after *Dark Laughter,* when he had reached the point where he should have stopped writing, he had to defend that style at all costs because he too must have known by then in his heart that there was nothing else left.

William Faulkner, "Sherwood Anderson: An Appreciation"

Courtroom exchange during grand-jury investigation between Forrest Bondurant and defense attorney Timberlake:

Defense attorney Timberlake: You and your brother Jack Bondurant were both armed, weren't you?
Bondurant: Yes, sir.
Timberlake: And you covered the officers with your pistols while Everett Dillon made off with one of the liquor cars, didn't you?
Bondurant: No, sir. We never touched our pistols.

Timberlake: You told [deputies] Rakes and Abshire that "somebody is going to die" unless they let you go across the bridge, didn't you?

T. Keister Greer, *The Great Moonshine Conspiracy Trial of 1935*

There is a great black bell without a tongue, swinging silently in the darkness. It swings and swings, making a great arch and I await silent and frightened. Now it stops and descends slowly. I am terrified. Can nothing stop the great descending iron bell?

Sherwood Anderson, *A Story Teller's Story*

Chapter 26

1935

AS THE SUMMER wore into June, Sherwood Anderson could see the wear on the faces of the farmers kicking at the red clay that gathered along the sides of buildings like snowdrifts. Walking uptown on Main Street in Rocky Mount, the stools at the drugstore, the lunch counters, the dry-goods store, all empty.

Be chewin' on shoe leather before it's out, an old-timer said standing by the statue of a Confederate soldier in front of the city hall, chewing on his pipe, *just like we did back in '30, the worst in a decade or I'm a dead man standin' here.* Before him in the sunlight, a couple of middle-aged men with hands in pockets, dusty shoes. *Won't be the last time, neither.* The sky clear blue and the sun relentless. Driving along the road Anderson saw men standing in withered fields, hands on their hips.

The salesmen around the table at the boardinghouse occasionally talked of the drought but they didn't seem to mind too much. The optimism of the salesmen was annoying and seemed to Anderson an egregious display of false hope. The fat-necked men still smoked their cigars and laughed hard, faces going purple, *Slide that pie back down here please, don't mind if I do!* They had business plenty up the road. They discussed the drought with a speculative optimism that made Anderson's face burn. *Be a boon for one trade,* a round man in a porkpie declaimed one night after dinner, *them shiners doin' a serious trade, I'll tell you what!* Made sense enough, Anderson thought. For a couple of dollars you could stay blind for a week; a few dollars more, maybe even just sit the whole thing out altogether.

The newspaper clippings indicated that the drought of 1930 was similarly punishing, and it was clear that those who lived by tobacco would turn to other means. *The Roanoke Times* printed several reports on the incident at Maggodee Creek Bridge and the shooting of the Bondurant brothers, though no mention was made of the motives of the brothers or how they ended so obviously at odds with the local law enforcement. If the conspiracy rumors were true, the brothers must have been trying to skirt the racket. So what would lead them to take such a heavily laden caravan, four cars full of booze, through the snow in December? Why did the local sheriffs seem so willing to gun them all down?

At night in his bed Anderson listened to the caravans of cars blasting down Main Street to East Church and the hard road 33 heading north up Grassy Hill. The roaring of engines, first the pilot car, then the line of sedans going sixty, seventy miles an hour right past the courthouse. Occasionally a sheriff's car was in pursuit, but not often. Anderson got used to the sound and nobody seemed to pay much mind. When he closed his eyes he could see the distinct shift in the darkness. Some great thing, swaying, descending. It would not be stopped. The nameless terror rolled up and Anderson groped for the water glass of whiskey beside his bed.

AT THE ROCKY MOUNT jail Tom C. Cundiff glowered in his cell, hunkered over his bunk, fingering his ears. Anderson brought him some tobacco and put a few questions to him. In the next cell a thin black man sat on the floor with his back to the bars, his woolly head flecked with dust and leaves and he seemed not to notice Anderson or care. Cundiff met his queries with grunts and the grind of his jaws working the tobacco quid. The only reaction Anderson could get was when Carter Lee's name was introduced; Cundiff spat hard and glared at him, his small, close-set eyes burning.

Man's a goddamn crook and a liar, he said. You put that in your papers.

Are you saying that he is guilty?

Hell yeah, he's guilty.

Of what?

More things than I can count. Puttin' me in here for one. Takin' granny fees.

Bribes?

Yep. He ran the whole scheme from day one. The whole county payin' out to 'im.

And you wouldn't pay?

Nope, never did, Cundiff said. Around here it's Carter Lee's way and if you don't like it, you end up here, or worse.

Or worse? What do you mean?

Cundiff chuckled and shook his head.

What do you think?

Are you sayin' Carter Lee is guilty of murder?

He never done it himself, got others for that. But he pulls the strings.

What about the Bondurant brothers, Anderson said, you work with those men?

Cundiff's face went wooden, the old gypsy stare.

They also refuse to pay? Anderson asked.

Cundiff hocked the whole quid of tobacco against the wall and stretched out on his back on the bunk.

That why they were shot down at Maggodee Creek? Anderson asked.

Cundiff appeared to settle in for a nap. Anderson lit a cigarette and loosened his collar.

What's the problem? Anderson asked.

Cundiff closed his eyes again, relaxing on the cot.

Is it the Bondurants? Are you afraid of them?

Cundiff came off the cot like some kind of jungle cat, springing at the bars. Anderson was standing with his hands in his pockets, relaxing on his heels, and the move caught him completely unawares and his mind skipped a beat, his body a few moments behind the thoughts in his brain. Cundiff shot an arm through the bars; his stubby fingers jerked and clawed just a few inches from Anderson's face, knocking the cigarette out of his mouth.

You afraid, mister? Whadya think?

Cundiff was grinning his gap-toothed smile. Anderson took an awkward step back, looking down the hall to the anteroom where the deputy sat, his feet up on a desk just visible through the half-open door. The black prisoner in the next cell was giving him a sympathetic look. Anderson shook another cigarette from his pack with deliberate slowness, trying to look Cundiff in the eye. He lit it and inhaled deeply.

Something you want to tell me? Anderson said.

Can't think of anything directly, Cundiff said.

Why is everyone afraid of talking about the Bondurants? Just tell me that.

Tell you what, Cundiff said. Man got his head cut off with a razor. Left for dead, not a spoonful of blood left in 'im, you unnerstan'? And what if I told you this man got up, walked ten miles through a blizzard? What would you say to that?

I'd say that was quite a story?

Would you believe it?

No. I'd say that was a fable. A lie.

Well, then, Cundiff said, you got nothin' to be scared of, do you?

IN THE ANTEROOM the deputy said they were shipping Cundiff off to the county asylum the next afternoon. He was to be committed, against his will, on the orders of the commonwealth's attorney. Anderson took a seat on a bench; his knees felt loose and his mouth parched and he dimly wished for a glass of something strong.

Whadya think, the deputy said, of old Tom C. Cundiff?

He was grinning and Anderson knew that they thought Cundiff was insane and some kind of big joke.

He mentioned, Anderson said, something about one of the Bondurant boys getting his throat cut?

The deputy frowned and took his feet off the desk and examined his nails. There wasn't much that was clear about that case, he told Anderson. The only witness the surviving victim, who was attacked from behind, and what little information he had, he refused to give. No statements to the police at all.

Did they ever catch who did it? Anderson asked.

Nope, the deputy said. You don't catch men who do those sorts of things. At least *the law* don't catch 'em.

Anderson left the jail block to the echoing sound of Cundiff's braying laughter.

Crazy as a bat, I'll tell you what! the deputy called after him.

ANDERSON SPENT the next day in the file room of *The Roanoke Times* filing through reams of articles, searching for anything about names he had: Willie Carter Sharpe, Tom C. Cundiff, the Bondurant boys. The articles about Sharpe flourished through 1930–1931, then faded, then increased in the last few months. She had been caught before on May 12, 1931, in Rocky Mount, and spent three years in the federal prison in Alderson, Virginia. It was said she was seen piloting a convoy a week after she was out of jail. Now that the search was on, the public appetite was whetted for more exploits, and the papers rehashed the stories and speculated on her role in the conspiracy in Franklin County.

Then Anderson came across an article from December of 1928 concerning the assault at the County Line. *Attacked by unknown individuals at closing . . . a serious neck wound . . . Forrest Bondurant, who is expected to survive his injuries, made it to the Rocky Mount Hospital under his own power . . . no leads at this time.* Maybe he could come at this from another side.

Anderson got directions to the County Line Restaurant and headed out after supper. As he piloted his car through the rolling hills of Franklin County he felt the old indignation rising up like sap in his chest. The crumbling barns, muddy yards of children, decaying fences, and battered houses. At the filling stations glassy-eyed men sat on warped porches. He knew that inside, a few older farmers held their cracked palms toward the cold, empty stove, the woman behind the counter, her jaw set in a hard line.

The lot was nearly empty, the building dark, and Anderson was afraid it was already closed. A convenient location, Anderson thought, sitting astride the county line, easy access out of the jurisdiction of pursuing deputies. Just like the Blackwater station. He sat in his car for a few minutes. I can put that Sharpe story away in my sleep, Anderson thought, so I might as well pursue what seems to have the most potential.

Man got his head cut off with a razor.

His hands on the steering wheel tingled and he felt the draft down his spine. What are you doing, man? Work fast.

A black man stepped out the door carrying two bags of trash in his hands, a white apron around his midsection, a cigarette hanging on his lip. He tossed the trash into a burn barrel at the edge of the lot and splashed some kerosene on top. Jefferson Deshazo stood with his hands on his hips, staring into the barrel, then flipped his cigarette in. When the flames rose he turned and fixed Anderson with a deliberate stare. Anderson got out of the car and Jefferson turned to watch the golden flames licking the rim of the barrel.

Anderson introduced himself to the man who worked the counter. Hal Childress still kept his thin hair combed over his round pate, but in the intervening years he had aged, tottered over some kind of zenith of his life. When Anderson brought up that night Hal rolled out the tale he had repeated many nights to various men. It was a story he never seemed to tire of telling, and he went into it for Anderson with great relish. Throughout Anderson nodded in what he figured was a polite manner and pieced together the images in his mind. It was quite a story, he thought, but he wasn't sure if he believed it.

So, Anderson said, most folks think he walked all the way to Rocky Mount?

Yep.

When did Maggie leave?

Don't know. Sometime before.

After some prodding Hal told Anderson that he had known Maggie since she was a kid in Henry County. She was a teenager when she was shipped off to Carolina to work in the textile mills. A few years later her father got drunk and hitched up his plow team on a rainy night and when the team slipped into a deep hollow the back-band strap hooked around his legs and he was dragged down into the gully with the kicking mules. They found him in the morning, tangled in the harness, crushed under his broken and dying animals. Maggie needed work to pay the note on her father's house, and Hal fixed her up at the County Line. Forrest came along later and bought the restaurant and just kept them all on.

That's a tough-luck story, Anderson said.

None too tough around here, Hal said.

Hal frowned and scrubbed an errant spot on the counter with a towel.

She's a special girl, Maggie.

Hal worked the spot with the towel, working in circular patterns. Anderson waited for him to continue but the man just kept scrubbing.

How's that?

Hal sighed and turned away, slinging the towel over his shoulder.

Well, let's just say she was a good woman and nice to work with.

You see her around?

Ain't seen her in years, Hal said.

Hal kept his back to Anderson and wiped his face with his shirtsleeve. This man is affected, Anderson thought. Well, I'll be.

If you ain't buying, mister, Hal said, then I got work to do.

AT THE BLACKWATER STATION the next day Anderson ordered a cheese sandwich from Maggie and sat at the counter as she fried up some bread. She wore a shimmering violet dress, tailored at the waist, pearl buttons down the back. The place was empty save for Everett Dillon out front working the pumps, disappearing around the side of the building and reappearing whenever someone drove up. Anderson pulled on his orange soda and watched the window. The white light of midday was barely cut by the thin curtains and the room was warm. Footsteps creaked across the ceiling. Someone else is here, Anderson thought. He rolled up his sleeves and smoked a cigarette as his sandwich bubbled, Maggie absentmindedly patting it with a spatula.

How's business?

Maggie flipped his sandwich onto a blue plate, dug into a pot of stewed greens with a spoon, dropped a hunk next to the sandwich, and slid the plate in front of him. He bit into his sandwich. It was hot and the cheese buttery and crisp.

Maggie stepped off to the side and leaned on the grill. Anderson noticed that she had a towel draped so it wouldn't stain her dress. She lit a cigarette and eyed the window.

Is Forrest around? he asked.

Nope.

Coming back anytime soon?

Couldn't tell you.

Anderson polished off the sandwich in four bites.

You ever talk to Hal, Anderson said, over there at the County Line?

She turned and eyed him coolly, smoke billowing from her nostrils. That got her attention, Anderson thought.

I was just over there yesterday, Anderson said. Mentioned you used to work there.

She cocked her head at him, a slight line of concern in her brow. He found himself immediately confessing.

I want to know about that night, he said, what happened there. When Forrest was cut.

Why?

Because I'm a writer, he said.

Newspaper?

Yes and no. I write books. Look, I'm just interested in what happened.

Maggie stubbed out her cigarette. The footsteps upstairs seemed to be pacing back and forth, covering the width of the room in an even pattern.

What kind of car do you drive? Maggie asked.

What?

She nodded toward the window.

What kind of *car*. Do you *drive*.

I got a '33 Dodge.

She shrugged and folded her arms.

What? he said. What does that have to do with it?

I like to drive, Maggie said. I like to drive nice cars. I thought maybe you had a car I wanted to drive.

If I did, you would tell me about that night at the County Line?

Maybe.

Are you serious?

She looked at him with such a condescending look that Anderson felt humiliated. He stood up, his stool scraping and falling to the floor.

Say, what's the deal here? he demanded.

The footsteps overhead suddenly stopped. They all stood quietly for a few moments. Anderson reached for his hat. As he dropped a dollar on the counter Maggie smirked and turned away in a swirl of violet and lace.

He found himself standing out in the lot by the petrol pumps, holding his empty pop bottle, his hand on the car door. The heat was intense and his car hot to the touch.

What am I doing? *He's there.*

Anderson heard a low sound, an undercurrent of something happening down in the hollow next to the station, a tumbled mess of creeper vine and strangled oaks, some kind of dull reverberations coming from the deep gully. He left his empty pop bottle on the hood of the car and walked over and stepped down into the hollow. After his eyes adjusted to the shade he saw that the hollow was half full of discarded five-gallon cans, piles of them, hundreds, thousands perhaps, warping and thumping in the heat.

THE NEXT EVENING at Sunday supper Sherwood Anderson stood tensely in the yard, hat in his hand, watching his fellow boarders gathering on the back porch for a before-meal smoke. Through the windows Anderson could see the matron piling the sideboard with large cuts of pork shoulder and heaps of hot corn. She moved rapidly, drawing in and out of the lighted window, returning with steaming platters and then leaving again without an upward glance. The black maid placed a ceramic pitcher of milk on the table, wiping her hands on her starched apron, pausing in the lit frame to admire the set table. The men on the porch smoking and stretching, salesmen with yellowed collars, hard-sided cases of samples. They were ready to talk well enough. He clenched his fists as he thought of these rocking, yawning fools, buffing the toes of their shoes with a jacket cuff, joking with the matron and quietly cursing the country yokels who ignored their goods of sale. The ambassadors of the new America, the captains of capitalism. Peddling their cheaply manufactured wares while the craftsman stands alone in his garret, up to his knees in wood chips and no understudy, all the young men moving out of the towns and into the urban meat grinder. The love of the trade, the value of the craft: all going, all gone.

It was a fine summer night, almost cool, the clouds blue-black, rolling from the east. *Death in the Woods,* the dogs feeding on the body of the old woman. The animal hunger of man; this is something D. H. Lawrence knew well and captured artfully and without mercy. Dreiser, the master. At what cost are our ordinary, everlasting animal hungers fed?

In his room Anderson sat on the edge of the bed, eyeing his desk and the stack of notes there. He finished his drink and lay back, suddenly bone-tired.

Something loomed far above him, a sense of great weight, and he quickly opened his eyes. He put his hands to his face and felt his lined cheeks, the sagging jowl of his neck. There was a time I cut quite the figure, he thought. When he closed his eyes it came again, this shape looming above him; it's dark mass like the end of light.

Chapter 27

1930

FORREST WATCHED his younger brother step out of the white farm-house. As he walked toward the car Jack pulled on a wool cap, yanking the brim low, his soft leather boots laced high, the brass eyelets buffed. Forrest turned from his brother and stared out over the fields pocked with brittle clover and cut cornstalks. In the valleys a sodden affair; the plants dried out by drought now lay floating in puddles of muddy ice.

Forrest's legs were jackknifed in the wheel well, his knees cradling the steering wheel. In the afternoon light the ragged white scar across his neck glowed. Jack climbed in the car, moving aside a heavy revolver wrapped in an oil-stained cloth and a paper sack of canned beans, salt pork wrapped in wax paper, a hunk of baloney, a few large onions, potatoes, and two loaves of bread. Forrest gunned the engine and the car lurched down the drive.

TIGHT IN A NOTCH on the western ridge of Turkeycock Mountain a thin wisp of smoke rose through the still-dense tree cover. Above the ridge a stream ran fast down a series of exposed granite steps and into a small pool. The clear water was channeled through copper pipes down a small rise through a dense patch of trees into a small clearing bordered with heavy bramble and thick rolls of blackberry and poke-weed bushes, draining into the tops of oak barrels sitting on founda-tions of stacked brick.

Howard stood watching the water filling the condenser barrel. He stuck a couple thick fingers into the water and lightly tapped the coiled loop of copper tubing that spiraled into the darkness at the bot-tom of the barrel. The trees shook in the cold breeze that came down the mountain and Howard swayed with the wind, the soles of his muddy boots leaving the ground just slightly at the toes. A short silo-shaped cap daubed with a crust of baked mud sat on a squat blackened whiskey still, a contraption of ancient vintage, the ground around it blasted with soot and ash like some half-emerged knob of the earth's burning core. The still bore the distinct V-shaped notches of revenuer ax blows, patched over several times. Behind the still a dozen mash boxes stood in two rows, half of them containing a roiling mixture of corn mash, rye, and malt. Piles of firewood, spare boards, shovels, grain bags, sugar bags, and empty cans littered the ground with patches of snow clumped in muddy waddles.

A man's voice sang out in the distance and Howard stopped tapping the worm with his finger. He stepped lightly over to a wheelbarrow covered with burlap and retrieved an over-under shotgun and broke it open to check the load. A faint chilling mist from the waterfall drifted through the camp. Howard saw two men coming across the side of the mountain from the east, along a faint path that wound along the cliff face. Howard's large features slid into a grin and he stood up and walked across the hill toward his brothers.

———◆———

EARLIER THAT AFTERNOON Forrest stood in a tobacco barn in Snow Creek and handed Henry Abshire a small packet of bills. Abshire looked exhausted, his face worn and eyes heavy.

I'll do what I can, Abshire said.

I'm not paying for try.

Hell, Forrest, Abshire said. You owe us back pay ... if people found out I was even here with you? Well, it just ain't that easy. You know they gunnin' for you now.

Don't give a damn, Forrest said. Just doin' same as always.

Well, then why you comin' to me now?

This is different, Forrest said. This ain't for me.

Forrest patted Abshire's shirt pocket where he tucked the money. You just take care of your end and we'll handle the rest.

I can't promise you anything, Abshire said.

I can promise you, Forrest said, if anyone tries to stop us, somebody will be hurt.

———◆◆◆———

JACK FOLLOWED the finger of car lights coming along the switchbacks of Chestnut Mountain across the valley. Howard squatted on his haunches, poking the fire with a branch. Forrest stood with his arms folded over his chest, his chin low.

You think, Jack asked him, that Cricket really drowned like they say?

Nope.

Then you think Rakes and his crew did it?

Forrest shook his head.

Think the man died by his own hand.

But why?

Maybe he was afraid.

Jack thought of his friend, his nervous smile, the crouching figure in the corner, his brutal loyalty.

Just can't understand, Jack said, why he would go and do somethin' like that.

Guessin' he had a reason, Forrest said.

A breeze shifted low to the ground, the brambles and chokecherry bushes rustling, the cool air swirling around his ankles.

We got no way of understandin' this world, Forrest said. We got about as much sense of it as that bird there.

He pointed up at a grackle in the spindled canopy. Forrest regarded the bird, his scar turning pink in the fading light.

There's a lot that there bird don't know, Forrest said. But it don't change the fact that the world is happening to 'im all the same.

Jack shivered; his feet were cold. Goddamn brand-new boots, he thought.

Hell, Howard said, the only difference between Cricket and the rest of us is that he had the guts to do it. We're just takin' the long way round.

After a moment Forrest walked a few yards alongside the diverted stream, looking closely into the water. He fished a length of rope out of the water and following it upstream pulled up a half-gallon jar of clear liquid. Forrest poured the three of them a measure in some tin cups. Jack's hand shook as he held his cup, and he cursed quietly and spat on the gnarled roots of a maple that bowed out over the hillside.

Weather stackin' up, Forrest said. We gotta run it through the night.

The night stilled and they each stood next to a tree, placing one hand on the bark and lifted the cups of white lightning to their lips. It was well known you wouldn't ever want to drink straight doubled and twisted corn whiskey without having a hand on something sturdy unless you happened to be standing in the middle of a flat, empty field, in which case you'd better sit down.

For a moment the three men felt like the mountain was shrinking under their feet. To Jack it seemed the deep intake of breath from the mountain, filling its cavernous lungs buried deep under miles of limestone and basaltic rock, the dripping caves and endless chambers of shimmering ice, fire, and movement, like he had seen in his dreams. Howard turned his head aside and sneezed three times.

Pure corn whiskey comes at you like a knifing, Cricket Pate had told Jack once: point first, sharp and hot all the way down. This wasn't rotgut, the heavily sugared brew that mountain stillers produced for delivery to the bootlegger who would disperse it to the unsuspecting.

A shiner's private stock was made from the purest ingredients, the finest alcohol you could make, its taste and resulting effect unlike anything else in the world. A few ounces and even the hardest backwoods drinker, men who drank a pint or more a day for forty years, even giant men like Howard, felt it deep in their bones, as if something sucked the marrow out and blew in white fire. You opened your eyes again and the angles sharpened on things, the trees and sunlight coming together, the thunderheads to the north rolling with impotent fury; a man curled his hand and felt the steely power in his fingers, the dynamic strength in his legs, the hills shrinking before him, and he was filled with what can only be described as the infinitely possible.

The three men stood, waiting for the mountain's gentle exhalation that would drive the wind down the valley and through the night. Jack raised his cup and opened his mouth to say something, but nothing came out.

Chapter 28

DECEMBER 19, 1930

THE SNOW LET UP sometime after dawn and the brothers set out from the base of Turkeycock Mountain in a convoy of four cars. They had Jack's Dodge roadster, his '28 Ford, Forrest's Business Coupe, plus another Chevrolet coach that Forrest had purchased the day before, each car packed tight with between fifty and seventy gallons of white lightning. Howard would drive the '28 Ford and Everett Dillon the Chevrolet, and they would hit the hard road 33 quickly and blast through Rocky Mount and over Grassy Hill and cross at Maggodee Creek. Most intersections and habitual routes were being watched, and they figured they would take their chances on speed rather than stealth. Floyd Carter and his Midnight Coal Company would pick up the load in a barn outside Roanoke.

They loaded up without incident and crept along the feeder roads at the base of the mountain. The air was crisp and still, the sun vague behind a haze of clouds, the roads untracked. They had to use snow chains until they reached the hard road, and to Jack the crackling, tinkling noise of the chains was unbearable. They crawled around Fork Mountain and got on the hard road near Sydnorsville. The road was lightly tracked, the macadam visible through the ruts, and the four men quickly got out and took off their snow chains, a difficult process with numb, wet fingers that required them to unhook the chains, then roll the cars off them, then stop to pick up the chains again. A few minutes later they set off, Jack in the lead. He pushed the Dodge up to forty, the tires spinning in the slushy ruts.

In another ten minutes they were on the gentle slope into Rocky Mount, Grassy Hill looming. Forrest directly behind, then Everett Dillon, then Howard in the rear. Jack noticed Howard had a jar in his lap when they left but he seemed solid. They were staying in a tight bunch and Jack pushed the speed up to fifty as they hit the cleared roads of downtown. They hammered down Main Street, passing the tobacco warehouse, its doors open and dark, a smokestack steaming. Two men in the doorway, a pair of idling cars in the lot, and as Jack passed he saw the two men quickly chuck away their cigarettes.

Here we go, Jack said to himself, and pressed the gas.

They were going sixty, the convoy stretching out a bit as Everett and Howard struggled to keep up, flashing by the courthouse, men standing on the steps, a few people struggling through the drifts along the sidewalks, turning to watch them pass, and Jack had the urge to hold his hat out the window in a grand gesture, perhaps shout something. On the north edge of town the roads were not cleared and Jack was soon up to his hubs and slowing as he lost traction. He stopped the Dodge and stepped out into the middle of the road and squinted down 33 back into town. The hazy morning sunlight and the contrasting snow glare made two indeterminate swaths of white-gray, and he shaded his eyes and squinted. Nothing seemed to be moving.

Chains, Forrest shouted, make it quick!

All four men set to putting on their snow chains. Kneeling in the snow Jack struggled with the chains, laying them out flat, then scrambling into the car to drive onto them. Howard was the last to finish, and as Jack watched his brother through the back window he saw a vibrating smudge coming from town, separating itself from the gray buildings and snowdrifts.

C'mon, Howard, c'mon!

Then Howard was up and in the car and Jack pulled out, the chains biting through the snow and the convoy lurched forward into the stands of pine that surrounded Grassy Hill. Before the first switch-back, when they would bend into the pines, Jack craned his head out the window and looked back. Two cars had stopped at the same spot, and the drivers were kneeling at their tires, putting on chains. Jack brought the convoy up to thirty and after ten minutes they crested the hill without incident. The road down the northeastern slope was straight and nearly clear, the morning sunlight working on the snow, and Jack stopped again and leaped out of the car.

Mostly clear, he called to Forrest. Get the chains off and we'll be faster down the hill.

Forrest nodded and relayed the message to Everett and Howard who stopped behind him.

Who is that comin' on? Jack shouted.

Hodges, Forrest said. Some others.

Jack struggled to loose the chains, his blood pounding in his ears. They must have been expecting them to come through. His coat was constricting him so he shucked it off and threw it on top of the stacked five-gallon cans. There was a growing whine and groan of cars coming up the switchbacks and Jack scrabbled, his brogans slipping on the road, and jumped into his car to pull it forward. When he got out again he saw that he hadn't pulled forward far enough and part of the chain was still pinned under the wheel, the hooks wrapped around the axle. He sat in the slush and pulled at the chain with both hands, hoping to jerk it out from under the wheel. There was a roar of engines and Forrest's car pulled up beside him.

Jack! Let's go!

Then Howard was standing beside him, bending, taking the wheel hub in his hands, then with a moan straightening and lifting, the hub rising to the top of the springs, the wheel coming an inch off the ground.

Get it off, Howard breathed.

Jack slipped down next to his brother's feet and worked his hands under the wheel, feeling for the chains. The hot engine smoked, the smell of oil and axle grease filling his head. He found the hooks and slipped them off, inching back out from under the car. When Jack cleared the wheel he slapped at Howard's leg and Howard released the car and it sank back on the road.

Hodges's car crested the hill, another close behind, churning a wake of snow. Jack could see the dark shapes of the drivers hunched over the wheel. They were a hundred yards away and closing fast.

Go, go! Jack yelled to Forrest. We'll catch up!

Forrest nodded and started down the hill, Everett close behind. Howard was rubbing his hands in the snow, his palms sliced open and bloody. He turned to the two cars steaming toward them, then back to his younger brother and waved Jack on.

Be right behind you!

Jack put his car in gear and began down the hill, Forrest and Everett disappearing down the slope. He watched Howard get in his car, Hodges slowing just behind him. A man opened the passenger door and stood on the running board, aiming a pistol. There was a puff of smoke and then a loud *thwack* as the bullet crashed into the back of Jack's car. When Jack looked back he saw Howard grinning at him through the windshield like some kind of lunatic.

Don't do it, Howard. *Don't!*

Howard put his car in reverse and gunned the engine, popped the clutch, and shot backward. Hodges wrenched the wheel to avoid it but Howard turned into him. The man on the running board was aiming another shot, clinging to the swinging door as the car swerved. Howard smashed into Hodges's right front fender, crushing the wheel, the man on the running board flung forward like a rag doll against the open door and then whipped backward into the snow. The second car, brakes locked up, slid into Hodges, pushing the back end of his car into the ditch.

Oh damn, Jack thought, and slowed his car. Hodges struggled with his door, and the driver of the second car, whom Jack could see was another deputy, Hodges's son, staggered out of his car, his hands to his face, blood running through his fingers. Howard tried to pull forward, his tires spinning in the snow. The man who was flung off the running board was on his knees in the snowbank by the ditch, digging through the drifts with his hands. Jefferson Richards.

Then a wrench of metal and Howard's car inched forward, went sideways, then caught and came on up the road. Richards found his pistol and came charging through the knee-deep snow, his face a mask of fury, leveling the pistol at Howard's car. Jack scrunched low in his seat and punched the gas. *Pock. Pock.* Jack gathered speed down the hill, going forty, sixty, the burning smell of brakes. A last look back: Howard floundering in a flurry of white, his car sideways, churning. He will make it, Jack thought. He will make it.

MAGGIE WAS SITTING on the bed in the upstairs room when she heard the cars whining down the hill. She walked barefoot to the window that overlooked the road. The sound grew, the gears changing, then Maggie saw the two cars charging down the road, Forrest and Everett. As they passed, Forrest slowed almost imperceptibly, a slight turn of the head in her direction, then he was gone. A third car, Jack's Dodge, came soon after, the engine racing and Jack hooked over the wheel, his windows open. Then it was quiet. Maggie looked up the road, where it went up and over Grassy Hill. She lit a cigarette and pulled a chair to the window, pulling the heavy drapes close together to cut the draft. Not a sound from either direction. The heavy cloth allowed a diffused rim of winter light that she traced with her hand.

A car came roaring back from the north and pulled into the station lot. Everett parked the Chevrolet, jumped out, ran to his own car, and gunned out of the lot heading south toward Rocky Mount. Then another motor, coming down the mountain, and she couldn't help parting the curtains to look. A 1928 pine-green Ford with Howard at the wheel, the back end crumpled, the rear window shattered, Howard's bulky form filling the car, his face so intent on the road it seemed to Maggie that he was willing the car through the snow toward Maggodee Creek.

After the car disappeared around the bend Maggie went to her room and sat before the mirror, working a comb through her hair, over and over. When the gunshots came floating through the trees

Maggie crawled into the bed, pulling the sheets up to her chin, and closed her eyes.

JACK CAUGHT UP with Forrest and Everett as they slowed before the Maggodee Creek bridge. The thick stands of pine opened up in a rough egg-shaped clearing around the bridge, the hills on either side humped like shoulders. Forrest stopped about thirty yards from the bridge and Everett and Jack pulled up behind. A car was parked blocking the one-lane wooden bridge, Henry Abshire and Charley Rakes standing by the front. Another car behind had two men sitting inside, the engine running. The creek rippled as the dark waters passed over stone, a crust of ice on the edges.

Forrest got out of his car and walked back to Jack, standing by his window.

Howard?

Said he was coming, Jack said. He wrecked Hodges and the other, put them in the ditch.

Did you see him get away?

Last I saw it looked like he was pulling away, Jack said. Richards was there, shooting, but I don't think he got 'im.

Forrest straightened and looked over to Abshire and Rakes. Rakes, leaning on the hood of their car, smiled and gave him a tight little wave. Abshire scowled and looked away.

Can you talk to them? Jack said. Think they'll let us by?

Maybe.

What about Howard?

He'll catch up, Forrest said. Do you have the gun?

Jack grabbed his coat off the seat and pulled the pistol out of the pocket. It was a .38 with a squeeze-handle safety mechanism, a gun Forrest loaned him.

Get out and put your coat on, Forrest said.

Forrest slipped a pistol out of his pocket and held it along his thigh.

Don't do anything, he said, until I say.

As Forrest approached the bridge the other two men exited their cars, one cradling a Thompson across his body, the other holding a shotgun. Jack had never seen them before. Rakes said something to these men and slipped his coat back over his holster and put his hands on his hips. Abshire threw down his cigarette and walked out to meet Forrest. Jack walked up to Everett's window.

Listen, Jack said, if something happens, you turn this car around and get back to the station. Just leave the car there and split. Okay?

Everett nodded, his hands gripping the steering wheel.

ABSHIRE AND FORREST exchanged words, then Abshire turned and walked back to the bridge, shaking his head. Forrest turned and signaled Jack to put his gun away, so Jack put it in his coat pocket, his hand resting on it. Rakes nodded to the two men behind him and came striding across the clearing toward Forrest, walking right past him, heading toward the line of cars. The pistol felt slippery in Jack's hand and he squeezed the handle safety a few times to get the feel. He noticed that his camel-hair coat was smeared wet with wheel grease and road dirt. Where the hell is Howard? Rakes came up and looked in back of Forrest's car, then up to Everett's car.

What you got in there, boy, he said.

Nothin', Jack said. Just some groceries for the station.

Rakes straightened.

Wudn't asking you.

Well, I'm telling you, Jack said, he ain't got nothin'.

That so?

Rakes eyed the lump of blanket in the backseat covering the stack of five-gallon cans.

Whadya know, Rakes said, I guess he don't have anything.

Then he moved on to Jack's car, wiping away the frost on the back window and peering inside. The wide expanse of the small clearing seemed oppressive to Jack, and he squeezed the handle of the pistol and tried to keep his breath. Forrest must have fixed it; they would let them by. Easy, he thought. Rakes won't do anything, not like this.

But you, Rakes said, *you* do, don't you?

Then Rakes turned and walked back across the clearing to his car and sat in the front seat. Abshire came out to talk with Forrest again, and the other two men flanked their car with rifles propped butt-end on their hips. Jack walked up to where Forrest was standing talking with Abshire.

You can let them all through, Forrest was saying, as easy as you can let one.

We'll need to take the other two, Abshire said.

We can't do that, Jack said.

Abshire eyed Jack and tugged his collar up around his ears.

Listen, son, Abshire said, let's make it easy. The one car doesn't have anything, so that one can go. And keep those damn pistols out of sight!

You can't have the other cars, Forrest said.

The worry on his brother's face made Jack nervy and he fingered the pistol in his pocket. The clearing was still and rapidly warming, nearing noon.

Go on over to the cars, Forrest said. Tell Everett head back and go home.

We need all of them, Jack said. They can't take any.

What? Abshire said. We ain't afraid of you, son. You boys gotta take your medicine.

Forrest stepped between them.

Listen, Henry, he said calmly. Somebody is gonna die unless you let us across this bridge.

Don't be a fool, Abshire said.

Forrest turned to Jack.

Git back to the car and tell Everett to get on.

Jack walked back and told Everett to turn around and head back to the station. There goes four hundred dollars, Jack thought, as Everett turned the car around and left the clearing. Where was Howard? If they negotiated something and Howard showed up it could all go to hell. But if things got sticky he would sure like to have Howard at his back.

When Everett was gone Rakes came over and headed for Jack's car while Abshire and Forrest stood by the bridge, talking.

We gonna have to take these cars, Rakes said. You boys can walk on back to the station from here.

As he walked around to the driver's side of Jack's car, Jack ducked through the window and snatched the keys out of the ignition. Rakes whipped out his pistol, covering Jack with it as he came back around the hood of the car to the road.

You're acting might smart, Rakes said.

I reckon, Jack said, I can take the keys out of my own car.

Now, I told you, Rakes said, we gotta have that car.

Jack held the keys in his hand, unsure of what to do. The keys were in his right hand, the same side as the gun in his pocket. He would never be able to draw quickly enough.

Just then Howard came barreling into the clearing, the green Ford fishtailing and overcorrecting, and he slid to a stop a few feet behind Jack's car. Jack had never been so relieved to see his brother in his life. The trunk was stove in and from the stench you could tell that some of the crushed cans were leaking liquor. A swirl of steam rose from the back end of the car. Howard was breathing hard, his eyes mere slits.

Now gimme those damn keys, Rakes said.

I'll offer him a bit more money, Jack thought. The seventy dollars in his front pocket.

Look, Jack said, I gotta little somethin' here for you in my pocket.

He started to reach for it and Rakes cocked the hammer.

Are you reachin' for something, boy?

I got seventy dollars here, Jack said.

I think you reaching for a gun, Rakes said.

Jack saw him close an eye and sight him down the barrel and he raised both of his hands in the air, flinching away at the last moment as Rakes fired.

Wait!

The bullet hit Jack in the side just under the arm. It felt like a hammer blow and twisted his torso around, his feet swiveling in the snow. He never heard the initial pistol report, but rather the continuing echo that sounded like it came from a long way off. He cried out:

Forrest!

Jack fell on his stomach and elbows, his head still up, no real pain but the feeling of warmth under his armpit and spreading into his chest. He could see Forrest start toward him, his arms pumping, Abshire following, his gun out. Forrest charged to him, his teeth set in a grimace, his hand in his pocket rooting for his pistol. Rakes turned, crouching, and shot Forrest at a distance of about twenty yards. But Forrest kept coming, pistol out, and Jack thought, well damned if it all ain't true after all.

Then Rakes went to one knee, stretching out his arm, and shot again, and Forrest suddenly doubled over at the waist, took another few steps, then stumbled down to his knees, his hand clenched at his belly, his head down.

Howard lurched from his car, jacket flying under his arms. Rakes was standing over Forrest, who knelt in the snow with his knees apart, sitting on his heels, hands folded at his gut, motionless.

Oh, yeah, Rakes said, *you that goddamned hard-boiled son of a bitch, ain't you!*

Then he turned and sighted his pistol at Howard, who froze, one hand on the open car door. Rakes cocked the hammer.

Jack wanted to rise but knew that he wouldn't, even if he possessed the strength to, even if he had all the strength of the known world.

Abshire came up and chopped Rakes's arm down just as he shot again at Howard, the round discharging into the snow in a flush of white.

Jack felt a hot spasm down his ribs and across his chest and he rolled to one side. A dark stain was spreading across his jacket and his left arm flopped onto the ground, numb. He stared at his fingers, the dirty sleeve, as if they were things not of himself. Then a shiver went through him and he lay his head back and watched the sky shrink to a pinprick of black.

Chapter 29

JACK'S EYES felt like iron and his mouth was so dry he had a flash of terror: Someone had stuffed him full of clay; he was being drowned like Cricket Pate. He shifted his body and felt his torso encased, something wound around his chest, his hips and buttocks on sheets, the feel of them on the tops of his hands. He was in a bed. The relief brought a rush of sweat to his face. He struggled to open his eyes again. There was a ring of dark shapes around him. Low lamplight, the ripple of white bedding stretched over his body, the peaks of his feet. He wriggled his toes. A dark shape unfolded itself from the corner to his right and loomed over his bed.

Hey there, son.

An unfamiliar voice. A man, wearing a dark three-piece suit. A watch chain dangling from his waist pocket. A tall, hooked form. Jack moved his lips but could not speak, his throat like sawdust. In his gut he felt the seizing, knotting sensation of terror. Where is my father? The man bent from the waist, down over Jack's face. The long fleshy horse face, stubbled chin and dirty collar.

Lookin' good, Floyd Carter said.

Several other men materialized, standing around his bed, men in long coats and wearing hats, their arms folded. One of the men shifted and Jack caught a glimpse of a window; darkness, the glass streaked with rain. What day is it? Floyd Carter bent closer to Jack's ear.

I figured, Carter said, you could use a little visit from the Midnight Coal Company, after all the money we made together, eh?

He grinned, a mouth of yellow horse teeth, then bent to Jack's ear again.

I got a little somethin' for ya, he whispered.

Carter held up a small piece of folded paper in front of Jack's face, waving it back and forth. Then he picked up a book from the bedside table, opened it, contemplated the contents for a moment. Carter chuckled and showed the other men the cover of the book, then held it open and inserted the piece of paper inside.

Your girl brought this in earlier, Carter said, left this here.

He closed the book and showed Jack the cover: Holy Bible.

Bertha was here?

Carter patted the book thoughtfully and rubbed the spine, then placed it back on the table.

Seems like a nice girl, Jack, he said. You oughta marry her once you get up and out of here.

Forrest, Jack croaked.

He's gonna make it, Carter said. Your daddy was here. Him and Mister Lee. Seems they came to an arrangement. Commonwealth attorney's office gonna pay your medical bills, no charges filed. Figured you boys can settle up with Rakes later, eh?

Carter bent close to Jack's ear again.

Listen, he whispered, on that piece of paper is the names of two men. The two men who cut your brother. You give it to 'im yourself, if you like.

Carter straightened up and the men shuffled, arranging themselves.

Take more than a bullet to kill Forrest, you oughta know that by now. You take care now, Jack. Come see us sometime.

The assembled men flowed out of the room and Jack craned his neck, his shoulders swathed in bandages, to look at the bedside table, the Bible lying there, a tip of paper protruding like a bookmark.

———◆◆———

LUCY WAS IN the kitchen, stirring a pot of sugared damson berries. Her cotton shift hung on her shoulders, the bones of her hips visible. She seemed so small, so fragile to Howard that he was afraid she was ill. But she turned to him as he came through the door, a smile of relief on her face, the glow of health on her forehead and neck, and she flung herself into his arms.

Oh, Lord, she said, I'm so glad you're here!

Howard straightened up, leaning back slightly and Lucy's feet came off the floor and she hung there on his broad bulk, her arms around his neck, resting on his chest.

Where's the baby? Howard said into her hair.

Sleeping, Lucy said. Sleeping good. Oh, Howard the last few days she's sleeping good and eatin'. You oughta see her. Everybody all right?

Jack will be good in a few weeks, he said. Forrest was hurt real bad, but he's gonna pull through.

Howard could feel the bones of her back and ribs but the weight was solid, a comfortable density and firmness of bone. He shifted and swung her slightly from side to side, her feet swaying.

I almost lost them, he said. I almost lost them both.

Oh, Howard, it's all gonna be okay.

I went into the ditch down the hill, had to push out. If I hadda been there earlier—

Oh God Howard don't say it. Please don't say it.

His throat knotted and he gasped for air.

You're a good man, Howard, you're a good man.

He knew that he could stand and hold her like this throughout the night if he wished to, such was his strength. Was that enough? Lucy buried her face into his neck.

Don't let me go, Howard said.

I couldn't, Lucy said. You got me.

He gave her a slight squeeze, tempering his strength, and heard the breath come whistling out of her lungs. She nuzzled in his neck, murmuring.

Don't let go, Howard said.

THAT NIGHT Howard lay in the bed in the cabin with Lucy wound around him. The baby lay next to them in her crib, and the dark room was softly patterned with their breathing. Howard fell asleep almost instantly, not having slept in more than two days. He dreamed of a vast, long white road stretching to the horizon. As he adjusted to the light he could see it wasn't a road, rather a river that wound slightly into the dull glow of the sun, everything blinding white and cold. His hands ached and when he held them up they were battered and deeply cut and scabbed on the knuckles. In the distance a figure separated itself from the white, someone standing on the frozen river. Howard walked toward the figure, his footing unsure on the slick ice. The figure began to convulse, bending rapidly. It was Forrest, jerking his body toward the ice. He was attacking the frozen surface with an ax, striking it repeatedly, sending up a shower of ice and spray. Howard tried to yell out to his brother but his voice was lost in some kind of white noise, a solid wave of sound. Forrest brought the ax over his head with two hands, his feet planted wide, hacking away at a spot, moving too rapidly, like he was animated by some strange force. *Forrest,* he called out again, and he could hear the name in his mind but he knew there was no sound. He could see the thin hair on his brother's head, the hawk-like nose, Forrest dressed in his wool shirt and pants, bare-handed, chopping at the ice again and again. No scar, no meandering line under his chin. There was some other movement and looking down Howard could see a dark ripple under the ice, a shadow moving under them, an enormous shape more than fifty feet long. *Forrest! Stop!* he shouted. But his brother only chopped faster.

———◆◆◆———

MAGGIE SHUTTERED the windows and the Blackwater station remained closed for the four weeks Forrest was in the hospital. Everett Dillon came by after a few days and found the door locked. It was morning, the snowfall of the week before now a mottled crust, a border of stained brown along the road. The snow in the lot was still crisp and even, untouched. Everett knocked a few times. The curtain moved upstairs, and he could see her looking out. He looked up to her and pointed to the door, rattled the handle, but Maggie only let the curtain fall and moved away from the window. Standing there quietly in the lot he could hear the faint sound of music coming through the window.

———◆◆◆———

WHEN JACK WOKE one day Bertha was sitting beside his bed, holding the slip of paper with the names on it. She asked, and he told her.

Jack, you can't give this to him. You can't.

Why?

Bertha tucked the paper back into the Bible on her lap, placing both hands over it. She pursed her lips, breathing quickly through her nose.

You know what he'll do, she said.

Jack's rib cage ached so hard it made him squint. It seemed to be dusk, or perhaps morning. The light was uncertain.

Jack? Promise me.

He let his head roll on the pillow toward her. Her face was white and her eyes hard upon him. The window was dark but he could hear the wind buffeting the side of the building. What time is it? he wondered.

You gotta promise me, Bertha said, or so help me you'll never see me again.

AS HE SLEPT FITFULLY over the next few weeks in the hospital Jack had extended vivid dreams of his grandfather. The old man was continually exhorting him on, his beard whipped by wind, eyes flashing, leading him into a deep wood, a shape in the doorway of a barn, waving him across a field of snow.

His grandfather was an industrious man, always working and trying to scrape together a few dollars, but in the end it never amounted to much. Most Bondurant men, including Jack and his brothers, had that strange obsession of the terminally poor; the dreams of wadded sums of cash, of heavy lumps of change in your pocket, the small stacks that speak of little dreams. They banked on the salvation of a few dollars. It meant nothing in the end because it would take far more to ever break out of the tunnel each was tumbled into at birth.

In his crudely lettered last will and testament Jack's grandfather left his son Granville three acres, a pair of worn-out mules, and a black boy named Julius, who had grown and left many years before.

Jack remembered the old man sitting on his bed, whittling away at his figures. The feral look on Forrest's face as he played with them by the creek, hiding them in the woods. After a few months the weather began to work on the pieces, hidden as they were in a hollow log, swelling and distorting the carved features. The wood grew discolored with molds, and fungus split the grains, making the men look as if they were erupting from within. Forrest continued to play with them until they were unrecognizable lumps of rotted wood, having memorized by then who each character was and what role he played. Finally he buried the moldy bits as they came apart in his hands, depleting the ranks over time.

One winter afternoon Jack watched his brother chisel a hole with a stick into the icy ground by Snow Creek. Jack hid among a small bunch of catalpa trees along the creek, his knees damp on the frosty ground, the afternoon chores finished and nearly supper time. When Forrest finished and left, loping back across the field to the house, Jack crept forward and carefully dug up the figure. The final remaining character was an ambitious piece, a man on horseback. Warped and swollen with frost, the man on horseback held out his broad-brimmed hat in his hand as if waving on his men. The other hand held his sword, raised high and straight, ready to strike. His chest was thrown back and he held his head at an unnatural angle, cocked to one side and looking up, as if he were asking for a favor from someone above, the instruments of encouragement and punishment in each hand at the ready.

Jack knelt there in the cold mud for only a few minutes, studying the figure carefully, turning it over in his numb fingers. His body shook violently with the cold and he placed the figure back in the hole and carefully buried him. When he stood he saw Forrest standing at the crest of the hill, several hundred feet away, a slanted silhouette against the indigo sky, watching him. Forrest stood there for several minutes, motionless. Then he turned and walked over the hill into the darkness.

Jack waited a full hour by the creek, teeth chattering, before venturing back to the house. At the supper table Forrest was an impassive specter, and that night Jack begged his mother in tears to be allowed to sleep in their room on the floor so he wouldn't have to sleep in his normal bed with Forrest.

What on earth is wrong with you, son? said Granville.

But his mother finally agreed and wrapped him in blankets on the floor next to their bed.

In the morning Jack woke with a fever and he spent the next week sweating and tearful and his mother fretted over him with hot broth and alcohol rubs. When he was well again he went back to the bed with Forrest. Forrest never spoke of the figures to Jack or anyone, and no one in the family ever mentioned them again.

Chapter 30

1933

A FEW YEARS LATER Forrest was at his sawmill camp in a section of deep wood near Smith Mountain overseeing the loading of a long trailer. The camp sat in a depression among a circular set of ridges, the road a steep switchback. The camp was being run by a man whom Forrest had hired, but Forrest still came by the camp regular, particularly on loading and transport days, although he was withdrawn from the operation in a way that made him a somewhat shadowy presence. A hand would be working a crosscut saw or planing boards and turn to see his angular form standing in the sunlight grove, the stippled scar running across his neck.

A stand of twenty-foot mature oak trunks was cleaned and stacked and strapped for transit, to be pulled out of the hollow with a donkey-engine tractor with track wheels. On the first switchback he walked beside the trailer with some other men to monitor the pitch and roll as the tractor lurched up the hill. The elevation rocked the trailer and on the second turn a sound tore through the air like a herd of wind animals and there was a pause, the logs seeming to vibrate, then they tumbled in that awful slow way off the low side of the trailer.

. . .

MEN WHO saw it said he didn't even make an attempt to get out of the way; rather Forrest flipped his hat aside with a cursory movement and turned to face the rolling tons of wood that came for him.

BUT FORREST was not done. They arrested Whit Boitnott, the same man Forrest had cast out years before from his camp. He was hired the day before by the unknowing manager. Whit cut the main straps along the high side, in full view of some other men, and when taken in he refused to say a thing other than it was an accident. While Forrest lay in the Rocky Mount Hospital for three months encased in plaster the charges against Whit Boitnott were dropped to reckless endangerment and he was sentenced to just three weeks with good behavior, all on the orders of the commonwealth's attorney, Carter Lee.

FORREST LAY like a totem in the hospital bed, wound in plaster from head to toe, eyeholes and two straws in his nose for breathing, iron rods strapped to his limbs, lashed down to prevent shifting or struggling. For the first few weeks Forrest wouldn't say a thing, wouldn't respond to anyone. Maggie was there most often in the evenings, smoking and gazing out the window, blowing long plumes against the glass. During the day she ran the station, with Everett Dillon working the fuel pumps. Forrest was unconscious much of the time, and when awake he lay silent, his gray eyes merely staring at the ceiling, blinking.

One afternoon Bertha and Jack sat quietly in his room, looking out the window at the tall wooded rise of Grassy Hill, Forrest sleeping soundly behind them. Jack's hand was cupped loosely over hers, and he gave her fingers a squeeze occasionally.

It wasn't for nothing, Bertha said. Like the hymns of the next world.

She looked back at Forrest, lying straight out like a dead man, then fixed Jack with her eyes.

In heaven, she said, the afterlife, they'll be singing about this world. That's what my grandfather says. All the stories, all of our lives, will be sung like hymns. That's how we'll remember them. That's why it all means something. The problem is that we have to live in this world first, we have to bear it.

She took up his hand, smiling slightly to herself. At that moment it seemed to Jack that some uncomprehending part of the world had broken open, and his love for her, somehow amplified and deepened by the chain of events, came shining into the room.

ONE EVENING during the second month, Jack was at the hospital just as Maggie was preparing to leave. As he stood in the doorway he saw her run her hands over Forrest's plaster shell of a head, tracing over the lump of his nose, his chin, and down around his neck. She seemed to track the line of his scar with her fingers, moving back and forth as she gazed into his eyes. Jack could see his brother staring back at her, blinking hard. On the bedside table Maggie had placed a picture of the two of them, standing in front of the Blackwater station, Forrest with his hands on his hips, Maggie's face impassive, her mouth a grim line. Next to the picture lay a small lump of moldy wood, a knotted swirl that faintly resembled a figure.

LOOK HERE, Forrest said to Jack one day at the hospital. Something you oughta know.

After two months he was still swathed from head to toe in plaster. The fractures in his skull were healing and soon he would have his face free, but for now he still peered out from the worn eyeholes, rimmed with caked dirt and sweat, his mouth hole a ragged orifice stained with food, drink, and spittle.

Jack was sitting on a chair reading softly from the Bible, something Bertha introduced and Forrest seemed to enjoy, and the two of them had spent hours like this, Jack droning on through the long days and into the night, Forrest staring hard-eyed at the ceiling, the faint rustle of his shifting skin under the plaster. Maggie stayed with him through most nights, running the station during the day with Everett and Jack's help.

Jack set the Bible down in his lap, blinking his eyes from the strain. The bedside lamp was weak and the sky darkening quickly through the windows.

Before Maggie gets here, Forrest said.

His voice was thickened and he worked his cracked lips. Jack bent slightly toward him as he often struggled to speak clearly. He could see some kind of alarming intensity in his brother's eyes.

Should I get someone, Jack said. Are you hurtin'?

Forrest's chapped lips bent ever so slightly at the corners. The squeak of shoes in the hall, and Forrest cut his eyes to the open door, a slot of flat light.

That night at the County Line, Forrest said, it was Maggie that pulled me out.

She was there?

Forrest closed his eyes and squeezed them with some effort and to Jack it seemed like his body was vibrating in the husk of plaster, like some kind of molting insect spinning a new skin.

After they got me down, Forrest said, she was in there, inside the restaurant. I heard her screaming. While I was lying in the lot. I couldn't understand what it was. It didn't make any sense to me.

Forrest opened his eyes and gazed at Jack, his eyes warm and round. A burning clot began to form in Jack's chest. He couldn't imagine the sound. Maggie was not a creature who would scream.

She wouldn't ever tell me, Forrest said, what happened in there while I was lying in the lot, bleeding.

Jack nodded, gripping the Bible in his lap.

When we got to the hospital, Forrest said, I got out and walked in.

Why didn't you just tell 'em?

Forrest let out a dry chuckle that turned into a hacking cough.
When it settled he smiled at the ceiling, pleased with himself.

Hell, Forrest said. I thought I was *dead*.

Well, Jack said. I guess I have something to tell you too.

Chapter 31

SEPTEMBER 1934

IT WAS CLOSE to midnight when the heavy knock came at Jack's door. Bertha was asleep in the bed, the baby dozing by her side, blowing small iridescent bubbles of saliva with his steady breathing. Jack was lying there in the dark, listening to the sound of their lungs filling. The knock was strong, and for a moment Jack remembered the sound of George Brodie's anguished midnight visit. He had wished many times that they had never answered.

He shot up in bed, Bertha clutching his arm.

Lord, Jack!

The baby coughed and whined.

Jack slipped on his trousers. The .22 was on the rack over the fireplace. The creaking of feet on the porch floorboards. The door bolt was sound and Jack stood to the side to catch a peek through the window. A tall figure in a long coat and hat stood facing the closed door. Forrest. Jack lit the oil lamp and opened the door. Behind Forrest, Jack could make out the bulky form of Howard standing in the dark yard.

You were right, Forrest said. We know where they are.

Once the call is answered, Jack thought as he struggled into his coat, it can't ever be made right again.

• • •

IN FORREST'S '32 V8 Ford driving north Howard sighed and took a jar from the floorboard, spun the lid off, and flicked it out the window into the rushing night. He pulled on it a few times, heavy, desperate swallows that brought water to his eyes. A shotgun lay angled across his lap, and on the seat a box of shells. As he drove Forrest took a pistol from under the seat and without looking handed it back to Jack. It was his .38 with the squeeze-grip trigger.

Don't take it out, Forrest said to the windshield, unless you plan on using it. You throw it on someone you best empty it.

Jack slipped the gun into his coat pocket and a surge of bile gripped his chest like a vise. Howard passed back a jar and Jack took a couple big gulps and felt it loosen his chest and bowels. He wiped his forehead on his coat sleeve and the deep smear of sweat surprised him. The car quickly filled with the sour scent of men perspiring. Watching the back of Forrest's head Jack knew that there wasn't anything he could refuse his brother. At the same time, he felt like there needed to be some kind of signal that it was his time. He wasn't ready. The car rattled over the rutted road, the headlights stabbing out trees around the bend. Howard's face was placid, his eyes half closed, and this gave Jack some comfort.

They drove west across the county for nearly an hour and stopped at a filling station on the eastern edge of Franklin County, near Calloway, a place Jack had never been before. Though it was already past midnight there were eight cars parked in the lot and in the upstairs room there was a light shining through thin curtains. Forrest swung the car smartly around to the back of the building with the headlights off.

They could hear music and laughter from the upstairs window. Jack tried to pick out the tune but couldn't place it. In the front passenger seat Howard held the shotgun, one hand around the cold, greasy barrel and the other loosely on the trigger guard, tapping it lightly to the tune. Jack passed the jar back up to him and he took another deep drink before passing it to Forrest.

The dusty shaft of light from the upper window wavered as men passed before it, flashing shapes over the windshield and the trees beyond. Jack felt the sky lift over his head and knew that it was opening up, like a smooth road cut through the mountains, the way easy and straight. Howard seemed to settle in his seat. Forrest watched the door of the station.

JACK THOUGHT of candlelight, the warm stove, his sisters winding his fingers with string, their quiet, secret language. His mother holding him tight while outside in the cold a bonfire blazed. His sisters lying side by side on the floor in a neat row, his mother's face covered with a quilt.

Dragged himself near ten miles through the snow with his throat cut.

Howard was thinking about something Jack said one night around the fire at the lumber camp: *Forrest would never die by another man's hand.* They were drunk and it was late, the deep woods black and open like a field, and sometimes around the small sphere of fire Jack felt like making statements that matched his grand sense of the world.

Forrest thinks, Jack said, that the world is all one thing, but he's wrong.

I've seen it, he said, what lies beneath the earth, and it's a terrible and beautiful thing.

Howard enjoyed listening to him struggle with the words, Jack's eyes laced with such sincerity that it was difficult to look away.

Howard felt a dull ache in his ribs and he shifted in the seat. He thought of Lucy and his daughter, growing and becoming an agile creature in the woods. He would stay away from the card games and put some money away and maybe next year get a job up in Martinsville at the textile plant. Things would change for him. The world outside the window blurred. The car felt like a promontory by which the rest of the hills and trees and clouds passed with terrifying speed.

Howard took another drink, looked through the muddy windshield, and saw the far distance, the land beyond this one, and holding the shotgun across his lap he thought he must feel like the ancient oaks deep in the forest, looking over the canopy into the sun with their toes buried deep into the heart of the earth. It would hold.

AFTER AN HOUR men began to file out of the front of the filling station, some talking and laughing as they went to their cars, others quiet with their hats pulled low and the shuffling gait of men who had lost money. The noise from the upstairs window grew quiet, just the sound of the crackling radio and the occasional grunt of furniture on the floorboards. When only two cars remained in the front lot Forrest nodded to Howard and the three men got out of the car. Howard slipped the shotgun under his long coat and patted his pockets, feeling for the extra shells. Forrest checked the load in his pistol, glancing at the upper window.

You set, Jack? Forrest said through his teeth.

He spun the cylinder of his pistol.

This will be quick, so stay close.

Jack nodded. His heart throbbed in his chest as they rounded the building toward the front.

Howard will go in hard, Forrest whispered. He will take the first man, you come in quick with that pistol out and throw it on the second man good. No mistake, right up against his eyeball, you hear? He moves wrong, you squeeze and keep squeezin'.

Jack put his hand on the slick wooden grip of the pistol in his pocket. Was it too slippery? Could he swing it out and point it true? It was quiet and Jack watched the white space of the open door, the plank stairs going up. His underclothes were soaked through with sweat and his crotch itched with damp heat.

The radio tune wavered in the light wind and for a moment became clear and Jack found it. Bertha played it often at home on the banjolin, singing softly to his son, her voice as true as Sarah Carter's:

The storms are on the ocean
The heavens may cease to be.
This world may lose its motion, love
If I prove false to thee.

His brothers silently mounted the steps of the porch. They stood in the doorway, Howard with the shotgun at his hip pointed up the stairs, ducking his head under to look up, Forrest gazing at Jack with a blank look. Three simple steps but he could not make his feet climb. He was rooted, as if the ground had shifted and pinched his legs in place. Jack knew Forrest was watching him and waiting, and he fumbled with the slippery pistol in his pocket, as if he were looking for something, a flash of light, a remembered song, and he gestured helplessly.

After a moment Forrest flicked his head back toward the car. Howard glanced back, just for a second, then Jack watched his brothers ascend the stairs.

Jack got behind the wheel and took the pistol out of his pocket. The entire weapon was slick with his body grease and he tossed it onto the seat, disgusted. There was a sharp crunching of gravel and Jack saw a man burst out of the front of the station, running from the front door to a car. Jack fumbled for the pistol and pointed it awkwardly through the windshield. The running man had no coat and hat and he didn't look back as he struggled into his car and tried to start it, the starter motor squealing several times; then the car fired up and spun out of the lot into the road and Jack looked back up to the upstairs window. Jack could make out Forrest's voice speaking low and straight and a chair or table was thrown to the ground and the sounds of a quick, desperate struggle. It was quiet again for a few moments and then a powerful, sharp sound that Jack took to be the discharge of a shotgun, but as it echoed out over the lot it was clear it was the high, strangled scream of a man. Jack felt his eyes bulging in his face and he cursed and slapped the wheel.

Good God! he thought. God . . . what is it?

The scream continued on for a full minute, starting higher then dropping and becoming clotted. The sound crowded Jack's mind and he stared through the windshield trying to focus on the red dirt and gravel in the headlights, the tall pines along the road. Howard was stepping off the porch, shotgun in one hand and a small paper sack in the other. He walked to the car and got in the back, setting the sack on the seat beside him, and Jack could see that the sack was wet and stained at the bottom. Howard broke the shotgun and checked the load, then pulled his coat around him and leaned back. Howard's eyes looked bright and watery but his body seemed relaxed and he said nothing.

Forrest walked slowly in front of the headlights and around to the passenger side. Sounds of ragged sobbing rang out across the lot, the awful sound of a grown man weeping. Standing outside of the car Forrest bent down and picked up some dirt and rubbed his hands together quickly, like you might do on a cold morning in the field. He got into the car and nodded to Jack who pulled into the road and headed east, going slowly at first because the night seemed so impossibly dark and the lights of the car a single straw of color. He heard the rattle of Howard opening a jar in the back. The breath of his brothers filled the car and Jack could smell the corn whiskey mixed with another scent, the heady, sweet smell of birthing cattle in a winter barn or the steaming scalding trough when a hog was gutted and lowered. Howard flipped the jar lid out the window and off into the woods and Jack pushed the throttle and drove faster into the dark mountains.

Chapter 32

OCTOBER 12, 1934

GRANVILLE BONDURANT STOOD behind the counter of his store working over the day's receipts. A half-dozen old-timers from Snow Creek loitered about the stove, having a chew and griping about the weather. Granville had swept the floor and covered the flour and grain bins with sackcloth, the stove fire banked to a dull glow. The day had grown cold as evening fell, the ground damp from sporadic rains, and there was talk among the men of an early frost that night. The main topic of discussion was the murder of Deputy Jefferson Richards the night before, shot to death in gruesome fashion on the road near Antioch Brethren Church, just a week before he was due to testify.

Carter Lee cleanin' up the mess, a bearded fellow said, scratching his neck.

Loose ends, said another. Lotta lead for one man.

A car in the lot crunching in the gravel, and Granville raised his head, wiping the receipts with his hand to clear the pencil dust. A moment later a broad man in an overcoat lurched through the lot. The door was flung open, bringing a damp draft whistling along the floor of the shop; the men murmured and looked at Charley Rakes stepping through the doorway. His coat was open at the front and his tie askew, his fedora pulled low. Rakes stopped and surveyed the store quickly before marching up to the stove and throwing back his coat and holding out his hands. He stunk of whiskey and sweat and the old men around the stove hummed and shifted in their slouched poses.

Need a few sticks here, Rakes said. This damn thing is cold!

We shuttin' down, Granville said. Can I get you somethin', son?

Rakes glared at him, his eyes wild under the brim of his hat.

Need fuel.

Pumps're shut down.

Turn 'em on then!

Granville pushed his receipts into a stack on the counter and rested his hands on either side. He looked at Rakes, who swayed slightly, his coat hanging open.

What do you want, Charley?

Rakes looked wildly about, then turned back to Granville. He reached behind his back, pulled a pistol from the waistband of his pants, and pointed it at Granville's chest.

I want you to know something, Rakes said.

He turned and waved his gun around the room.

All of you. All of you need to know something.

Now take it easy, Charley, one of the old men said. We know that things are a bit—

You don't know a damn thing! Rakes roared. Everybody thinks they know somethin' but they don't!

Rakes turned back to Granville, his arm halfway up, the pistol gripped savagely in his hand. He seemed to tire suddenly, his round, red face going slack and he took a step back and wiped his forehead with the sleeve of his coat. A light rain pattered on the roof and window, and the men at the stove shuffled their feet. Rakes hung his head for a moment.

You oughta go home, Charley, Granville said.

Rakes wiped his face and regripped his pistol, bringing his arm up so it pointed at Granville's throat.

Why? You think I oughta be hidin' somewheres, that it?

He turned and addressed the other men.

What about you? he demanded.

The men tucked their chins into their collars and looked to the stove as if it still provided some heat.

Rakes kicked over a stool. Not satisfied with this, he grabbed the rim of a grain barrel and pulled it over. A fog of flour dust quickly rose, billowing like smoke and the men around the stove began to mumble. Rakes looked at his pants, one leg covered in flour, and cursed with a sincere vengeance. The pistol still in his hand he stepped to the counter and seized the receipts and books and swept them all to the floor. Granville stepped back from the counter and stood quietly, his face impassive. Rakes then cleared the rest of the counter, sweeping his arms across and pushing canned goods, chewing gum, tobacco onto the floor with a clatter.

I ain't afraid, Rakes roared at the room. I ain't afraid of got-damned Carter Lee!

He whirled and pointed his gun once more at Granville.

And I ain't afraid of your got-damned no 'count boys, neither!

Rakes was breathing hard and he wiped at his face.

To hell with all you!

He clamped down his hat and waving his hands through the flour-filled air banged through the door. The men coughed and slapped at their coats and pants.

Howard stepped from the storeroom doorway and passed silently through the white cloud. Granville stood behind the counter, his eyes on the floor as his son passed. If the other men in the room saw Howard follow Rakes out, they made no indication.

THE RAIN STOPPED and the skies went black. Later Charley Rakes pulled into the dirt drive of his house. A light was burning in the window of the small cabin and his dogs set to barking in the back. Rakes slammed the car door. He pulled a flat bottle from his coat pocket and took a slug, wiping his mouth and face with his coat sleeve. On one side of the house the hill sloped steeply down into woods, carved at the bottom by a narrow branch of Blackwater Creek. A light flickered along the edge of the woods. Rakes stared hard as it wavered, yellow. A candle burning on the edge of his woods.

Rakes whipped his head around, spinning in place, his house, the car, the woods, his breath steaming around him. He put the bottle in his pocket and pulled out his pistol and walked around the side of the house down the slope to the fence line. He scanned the woods but the darkness was vast and complete, save the small circle of golden light. The candle was set on a fence post, the wax piling around its base. Rakes stood there for a few moments, the pistol stretched out, listening. His dogs picked up his scent and stopped barking. The creek gurgled down below and in the woods was the tick and patter of rainwater. Rakes took out the flat bottle again and pulled the cork out with his teeth. He drained the last of the whiskey, a shudder going through his body, and he glanced around again, the lights of the house, the dark sky, the sloping hill that led around to the back of the house. He chuckled for a moment, then seemed to choke, doubling over, the back of his hand to his mouth. He gagged, spit, and coughed into the wet grass. He heaved the empty bottle into the dark woods.

After a while he leaned forward and blew out the flickering candle. In that last moment of light, before the darkness closed in, he saw Howard rise up out of the trees. He tried to scream but Howard already had him by the throat.

Howard heaved him over the fence and slammed him to the ground, pinning his gun hand under a knee. He kept a hand around Rakes's windpipe and peeled his fingers off the pistol stock and tossed it into the woods. Rakes gurgled and his face went scarlet to purple, clutching Howard's arm, kicking legs in the wet leaves. Howard looked at him for a moment, studying his face, before dragging him down the hill by his neck.

In the tight pit of the valley a three-foot stream ran clear and cold and Howard flung Rakes into the stream on his back. The streambed was a mix of smooth rock and clay, about a foot deep, and Rakes shrieked as his body hit the water, his face going under and then coming up, spitting and gasping. The dogs began howling again and

Rakes looked wildly up at the black shape looming over him. Howard shook his head for a moment, as if clearing some memory, his breath in a steady plume like an engine fire.

Oh, God! Rakes sputtered. Oh, God no please!

Howard straddled Rakes's midsection and using both hands on his neck pushed him under the water. Rakes clawed at Howard's face but Howard simply turned away. His mouth tightened as he watched Rakes's wild eyes and twisting face under the clear water. The dark seemed to close in around him and he felt a sudden blankness fall over him and he raised his head to watch the night move through the trees.

After a moment he hauled Rakes out of the stream by his shirtfront. Rakes sputtered and coughed, clutching at his throat, scrabbling in the muddy leaves. Howard stood and debated kicking the man a few times just for sport, but decided it would be better if he was left unmarked. He reached down and turned Rakes's head to face him. Rakes shuddered and sobbed, his face slick with water, saliva, and snot. He was a bit blue, Howard thought, but he'd be all right.

Remember this, Charley, he said. You hear?

Then Howard started up the hill, leaving Rakes lying by the stream. He turned after a few steps, regarding the huddled man shivering in the wet.

You should know, Howard said, that we had nothin' to do with Jeff Richards. He had plenty of enemies. He done himself in some other way.

The dogs began to howl again as Howard stepped off into the dark.

Chapter 33

JULY 1, 1935

THERE WERE MEN standing everywhere, leaning on long black cars, men on the sidewalks holding their hats and wiping their foreheads in the heat, men on stools along the window of Jess's Lunch, men in the shade of the granite bank building, men in suits and hats lining the steps to the court building, several holding cameras at their sides, assistants with bulky black cases fingering spare flashbulbs in their jacket pockets. The courthouse stood like a sundial in the Harrisonburg town square, the shadow dropping first over the bank opposite, then across to the lunch counter and the Baptist church as the afternoon drew on. Around the courthouse a gentle slope of grass ran to the street, cut by a broad set of bluestone steps. It was a warm July day, the sky traced with clouds, and the Great Franklin County Moonshine Conspiracy Trial was finally over after fifty days, longer than the previous record for Virginia, the 1807 trial of Aaron Burr. On a bench in front of the Methodist church a woman sat with a skinny towheaded boy in a white shirt and dungarees; they huddled together and talked quietly. A policeman sat in a chair by the courthouse door, cap pulled low over his eyes to shield the sun, his pistol dangling off his hip.

There was a palpable shift in the air, a murmur, or perhaps it was imagined, for no real sound came across the square. Yet the men felt that they had heard something from inside the doors. The policeman raised his head, men dropped their cigarettes in the grass, a car door opened. The woman with the little boy remained bent, talking low. Then the courthouse door opened and a man stumbled out into the sunlight. Sherwood Anderson slid a hand through his thinning hair, blinked, then clapped a hat onto his head. He saw the people in the square come to attention for a moment, looking him over, then slumping with disinterest.

It was a distinctly American tragedy, he thought. The trial had crystallized his thoughts on the matter, and the smoky form of an epic story, one that could be read aloud in a cornfield, began to form in his mind. Anderson came down a few steps and, tucking a copy of *The Roanoke Times* under his arm, checked his pocket watch.

Individuality will pass into the smoky realm of history. The day will come, Anderson knew, when we will all become soldiers in the army of the corporate age. When he was a boy there were no autos, planes, radios, chain stores, or great bloated trusts pushing their interests around the world. Men lived free lives then. Anderson tried to describe this in *Perhaps Women,* which was roundly despised even among friends. He was only trying to say that when the world is mechanized something goes out of men, something elemental is lost. The female world, on the other hand, was ascendant: the world of possessions, the material world. The female is at home among these things. Men suffered for a lack of drive, starving for the tactile world. Instead they develop the pathological obsession with obvious power. A real man doesn't need these things, and there are so few real men left. This is why Hemingway is so obsessed with the bloody work of bullfighting, and with killing in general. This is why he felt he must crush his former mentor in the public realm.

Literature is bigger than both of us.

A *groper,* Hemingway called him, a *muddler of words.*

They had that final drink together in Paris, having been there for a month, Hemingway constantly telling everyone that he would come and see Anderson. On the final day, Anderson was in his room, all his bags packed, and there was a knock on the door and there was Hemingway. How about a drink? he said. They went into a small bar across the street and ordered two beers. Hemingway raised his glass.

Well, here's how.

Then he turned away and walked out of the bar.

The constant assertion of masculinity is always the most obvious tell of a fake. You do not constantly assert what you know you have.

I don't give a damn about all this calling a man a groper, a muddler. We are all facing a wall, but I am throwing the words from my heart.

The party at the Greenwich restaurant to celebrate the publication of *Perhaps Women* in 1931, when Faulkner came in, unexpected, and approached somewhat sheepishly. He offered his hand and Anderson took it. Faulkner offered his congratulations. He grinned and pulled at Sherwood's sleeve.

Sherwood, he said, what is the matter? Do you think that I am also a Hemy? You know it isn't true what they say.

They exchanged some pleasant words before Faulkner wandered off to another part of the party. By this time his fame had grown and eventually the crowd siphoned off to Faulkner's side of the room, leaving Anderson sitting alone at a booth, holding his hat. He knew that some might see in his expression the knowing look of a writer who understood well what was occurring, a passing of some kind of torch perhaps, and his tight grin was the look of a content elder literary statesman. He stroked his hat, a large, soft hat that he had recently purchased and never worn, watching the crowd around Faulkner, stroking the large hat in his lap as if it were some kind of animal.

Forty-three years old when *Winesburg* came out. He wanted to retch when he thought of the time spent in the grinding gears of commerce, participating in the great deceit that snapped men between its fingers every day in the new age of American industrialism. He had walked through the streets for years, thinking little of the lives that crouched behind opaque windows, what crabbed forms sat alone in the darkness, and what hungers they fed there. Oh, if only he had seen behind those doors earlier!

And now he had focused so long on the precision of the word, the utterance that was most unfettered by artful manipulation, that the thing had become mere style. Sure, it was *his* style, but the style had become the substance. There was nothing else there. It was over, but he couldn't stop.

THE MAY 24, 1935, *Roanoke Times* headline read: *Woman Pilot of Whiskey Cars Is Placed On Stand*. Willie Carter Sharpe testified on May 23 for a half hour.

"So great was the interest with which her appearance has been awaited that it served to overshadow a full day of varied testimony . . ."

The experience was a disappointing one for most, including Anderson, who saw his hopes of a great mountain heroine die with her appearance on the witness stand.

"Mrs. Carter, whose name became so widely known here in the palmy [*sic*] days of the bootleggers during Prohibition, appeared minus the diamond that once gleamed in her teeth. She was dressed in a white outfit with hat and shoes to match, the dress having brown ruffled sleeves and collar gathered in front with a large cameo pin."

To Anderson she was jowly like a bulldog and crass of language and aspect. The overall impression was more like that of a gorilla in a dress.

THE VERDICT had been read and the trial was finally over. Anderson moved farther down the courthouse steps, snapping a fountain pen into his vest pocket, his brogans scuffing on the limestone block. The policeman looked into the darkened doorway for a moment, then stood back quickly as a crowd of men emerged, flowing out of the courthouse onto the steps and into the lawn, men quickly dispersing across the square as if they had an aversion to any sort of crowd, and each sought out his own space. The men standing around moved to greet some of them, and the men with the cameras raised the heavy contraptions and began to search out the faces of the emerging crowd.

Sherwood Anderson sought out the shade of an old oak tree that grew at the edge of the sidewalk. He loosened his dark tie and watched the other men and some women who walked out of the courthouse. The gentle clatter of voices tumbled out over the square as men and women began to talk to one another. Men shook hands and patted each other on the back, and men in expensive summer wool suits carrying leather-sided briefcases stepped into long cars that idled at the curb. A small cordon of police joked together as they headed across the street to Jess's.

A midnight-blue roadster parked on the curb caught Anderson's attention. A woman was at the wheel; she cut the engine and swung her legs out of the car. Maggie wore a long, shimmering dress of brocade silk, the color of jade, her hair pulled back in a simple knot. Anderson was directly in front of her, but she seemed to look through him, gazing at the courthouse with her gypsy stare.

CARTER LEE WAS acquitted of all charges. Twenty men were convicted, including Sheriff's Deputy Henry Abshire and other bootleggers and moonshiners who participated in the conspiracy. His case was certainly aided by the demise of Jefferson Richards, the acknowledged first lieutenant in the scheme, and the mysterious passing of Charley Rakes from pneumonia. Also a single juror, a man named Marshall, refused to add Carter Lee to the names of the guilty and threatened to hang the jury. The Bondurant brothers were never formally charged; rather they served as material witnesses for the prosecution.

A tall man stepped out of the courthouse and into the sunlight, wearing a thin cotton jacket and dungarees. He had a thick scar that ran across his neck that was clear from forty feet away. He paused, and two other men stepped out into the light and stood at his back. They were both tall, one of them an immense figure whose jacket strained to hold his barrel chest, his tanned neck rolling over his starched collar. The other man was obviously younger, with a red face and hawklike nose.

Sherwood Anderson stepped from the shade of the tree and walked toward the three men.

The younger man thrust his hands in his pockets and smiled at his brothers for a moment before turning and walking toward the woman and the child on the bench. The towheaded boy, all legs and arms in his overalls, ran to him.

Epilogue

THE FOLLOWING YEAR Anderson published his last novel, *Kit Brandon,* the story of a mysterious and beautiful Appalachian woman who loves fine clothes. She works in various mills, hitchhiking around the country, before becoming involved with a bootlegger and becoming a pilot-car driver for a moonshine syndicate. The book had moderate sales and was a critical failure.

On February 28, 1941, Sherwood Anderson and his wife, Eleanor, set sail for a tour of South America. Aboard ship one evening Anderson accidentally swallowed a toothpick while eating an hors d'oeuvre. He developed severe abdominal congestion and peritonitis, and eight days later in a hospital in Panama, Sherwood Anderson was dead.

THE DULING BROTHERS, Hubbard and Paul, heads of the largest West Virginia moonshine syndicate, were eventually convicted for the murder of Jefferson Richards. On the morning of December 23, 1933, Jeff Richards had engaged their brother Frank Duling in a high-speed chase as Frank was hauling a load of Franklin County moonshine to the brothers' West Virginia markets. The chase resulted in the death of Frank Duling, and it was well known that the Dulings sought revenge. This conviction has remained in doubt, particularly after in later years other men claimed responsibility for the death of Richards, including Hallie Bowles, who claimed to several people and in his suicide note that he and another man were paid to commit the murder, presumably at the behest of Carter Lee.

FORREST CONTINUED to run the Blackwater station, with Maggie at the counter and Everett Dillon at the pumps. No one ever saw a display of affection between them. He continued to help his father and brothers with their tobacco crops, and liquor continued to run through his station, though never in the same quantity.

Howard moved to Martinsville and found work in the textile mills there. Throughout the years he kept a still up on Turkeycock, and each summer he and his brothers would gather on the mountain and make a small run. Lucy eventually bore four healthy children.

Emmy Bondurant graduated from high school and moved to New Jersey, where she worked in a typing pool and shared an apartment in Newark with two other women. She eventually married and divorced later in life.

JACK BONDURANT went on to run his father's store and to raise beef cattle and tobacco in Snow Creek. Occasionally he had Forrest over for dinner, and Jack's oldest son always marveled at the lump that developed in Forrest's midsection after he ate, where the food was leaking through the lining of his stomach. The country hack that sewed him up after the shooting neglected to sew up the interior lining of his stomach, and a few minutes after eating, a bulge the size of a grapefruit would push out his shirt at the belly button. The boy would poke the mass with one finger, Forrest grinning even though it clearly pained him greatly.

• • •

ONE EVENING IN 1941, after helping his father with a cattle sale, Forrest was crossing through the bottomland that separated Jack's property from Granville's when he stepped through the icy crust of Snow Creek and was wet through to his armpits in the icy water. He walked up the hill in the dark to Jack's house, arriving late, when everyone was already in bed. He refused Jack's offer of some hot food and drink and dry clothes, electing instead to go to bed in the back room. Forrest said he would be up and out in the morning before they woke. He seemed embarrassed by the whole thing.

In the morning Jack's oldest son, now ten years old, woke with a start. His sisters Lee and Betty Louise and his brother Bobby Joe slept soundlessly. His youngest brother, Granville Thomas Jr., would be born the following year.

The room was cold and black and nothing moved, but the boy could sense that someone or something was down the hall. It was as if there were something pulsing through the walls, a wave of vibrating cold, and he got up without waking his siblings and chucked on his clothes quietly. The back-room door was slightly ajar, the air significantly colder there as it was the room farthest from the stove.

Inside the boy saw a shape lying on the narrow cot in one corner, next to an old pie safe his grandfather had built, and boxes of paintings by his mother, simple oil landscapes. He waited until his eyes adjusted to the light, then moved forward. The boy touched the edge of a boot, hanging over the edge of the cot. It was cold and faintly wet. As the boy stepped closer, treading lightly on the boards so as not to wake the house, Forrest's face came out of the dark, a mask of blue stone, his eyes open, his mouth set in a hard frown, a grimace of inconvenience. His fingers on the sheet, held to his neck, the nails gone purple, covered with a thin sheen of ice.

YEARS LATER, when Maggie passed away, records revealed that she and Forrest had been secretly married for more than ten years.

• • •

THE BOY STOOD in the dark room, the only sound his own breathing and thumping heart. He was frightened and alone. He looked over his shoulder, white-blond hair, widely spaced eyes, the nose of his father and uncles. You could tell by the stretch of his legs that he would be a tall man, as tall as his uncle Howard.

The boy looks over his shoulder at me, at us.

He is scared to move, unsure of what to do.

He is the only one who knows we are here, that we are watching.

This boy is my father, Andrew Jackson Bondurant Jr.

Author's Note

WHEN I WAS YOUNG, a few times a year my family would make the drive down to Snow Creek, four hours from Alexandria, to visit my grandparents. My father's brothers and sisters all lived in the area as well, so the gatherings usually bloomed into full-scale Bondurant family reunions each time we came to visit; all the uncles, aunts, cousins, and others crowding into my grandfather's old farmhouse for giant breakfasts and long, slow talks before the woodstove where little was ever actually said. I spent most of the time wrestling in hay-filled barns with my giant cousins, riding tractors in the early morning along muddy creek beds, and grabbing electric cattle fences because they dared me to. My grandfather died in his late eighties; he had just bought a new truck the day before and was building a new house.

I have many important memories of my time there, and of my grandfather; his quiet, hawklike face, early rides in the pickup to feed the cattle, the staggering stoicism of this man. I also remembered the back utility room where he had a gun rack up on the wall. This wasn't so unusual; in those days in Franklin County shotguns and rifles hung from nearly any flat surface, and in many houses they still do. What struck me about this particular gun rack was the pair of rusty brass knuckles hanging from a nail just below the gun rack. As a young boy the idea of a man putting on the heavy metal implement, purely designed to crush another man's face, was a thrilling prospect and I spent long periods of time gazing at those brass knuckles. To me they represented something remarkably primal, hanging there below the guns, as if to say: *If you are still alive when I run out of bullets I will pull this hunk of metal off the wall and pummel you into unconsciousness.* Back at the dinner table my grandfather's heavy, placid face would take on a whole new light. I was terrified of him and fascinated about the life he had led.

I didn't know of his true past and involvement in the events of the early 1930s until much later. My father didn't even know he had been shot until a few years before my grandfather's death, when as part of his genealogical research he came across a series of newspaper articles documenting the events at Maggodee Creek in December 1930. When asked about the shooting my grandfather merely said: Oh yeah, shot me through here, and raised his shirt to show my father the entry wound under his arm. Not much more was said about it after that, which is the way my father's family communicated about such things.

I must add here that my grandfather, after a few more run-ins with the law, went on to be a respectable, law-abiding, and even revered member of the Snow Creek community for many years until his death. His children and their children, including myself, have all basically faded into the gentle obscurity of decent citizens. It seems that perhaps that part of our blood that prompted such dramatic and dangerous behavior as committed by my grandfather and his brothers in those desperate times, has faded as well.

The basics of this story are drawn from various family stories and anecdotes, newspaper headlines and articles, and court transcripts, particularly from T. Keister Greer's compilation of grand-jury testimony, titled *The Great Moonshine Conspiracy of 1935.* Greer's book also provides testimony from the other major players in the conspiracy, as well as background and biographical information. However, this historical information does not help us fully understand the central players in this story, at least in terms of their situation or what their thoughts were; all involved are now deceased and little record exists. There are no letters, and my grandfather and his brothers did not keep diaries. My task in writing this book was to fill in the blank spaces of the known record. There are the family stories, and for this we must rely on the recollection of relatives, like my father, who was alive during the trial though as a very young boy, as well as other local people and friends who knew my grandfather and these other men. These memories and stories are vague and often specious at best, mixed with several decades of rumor, gossip, and myth. These were people who lived and died in real and dramatic ways, but due to the passage of time and circumstance it is difficult to render their lives with complete accuracy or fidelity to actuality.

In order to get at that truth, I created characters based on these people, some who are combinations of the original figures, some quite close to the historical record as we know it, and others who are almost wholly fabricated. Anyone who is a surviving relative of any of the involved parties should not assume that certain characters in this fictionalization are somehow meant to portray someone distinct. It was not my intent to flatter or slander anyone involved with this tragic story, least of all anyone in my own family. I suppose you can consider this a parallel history. I have imagined a number of things for which there is no record, and I have presumed upon the actual historical figures with the liberty that is granted a novelist. My intention was to reach that truth that lies beyond the poorly recorded and understood world of actualities.

There are the facts: The drought of 1930 was severely damaging to the already poor county, and moonshine activity exploded. The "Bondurant filling station" was known to be a hub for moonshining, drinking, fighting, and general mischief. My grandfather and his brothers Forrest and Howard were known around the county and in the papers as "the Bondurant Boys." My granduncle Forrest Bondurant had his throat cut and somehow survived. He was then gut-shot at Maggodee Creek and later nearly his whole body was crushed by a load of lumber that was dropped on him. He survived all of this, finally succumbing when he fell through the ice in a shallow creek. Maggie was a real woman who stayed with my great-uncle under mysterious circumstances, and their relationship is a matter of family lore. Jack was also shot at Maggodee Creek, and a few years later he

married Bertha Minnix, my grandmother, who was a skilled mandolin player who played on the radio and whose parents were members of the Dunkard Church, or Old German Baptist church as it was
alternately called back then.

We know that the writer Sherwood Anderson did spend some time
in the area seeking out the famous female bootlegger Willie Carter
Sharpe, and he did attend the trial where my grandfather and granduncles testified. He spent several years in the area, working on his
house in Marion and traveling the countryside. Anderson contributed
a story to *Liberty* magazine in 1935 about the "Great Franklin County
Moonshine Conspiracy." His last novel, *Kit Brandon,* is commonly
understood to have been greatly influenced by his experiences in rural
Virginia, the legend of Willie Carter Sharpe, and the Great Moonshine
Conspiracy trial.

The shooting of "the Bondurant Boys" at Maggodee Creek by
Rakes and Abshire is well documented in court transcripts and newspaper articles, as is the horrific murder of Jefferson Richards and the
curious death of Charley Rakes.

Everything else, as Sherwood Anderson would say, is "transmuted
by fancy."

Afterword

ONE OF THE QUESTIONS that readers of *The Wettest County in the World* ask me most often is: "So, have you actually drank moonshine?" When I say that yes, I have, they invariably follow with: "So, what's it like?"

At this point I begin with a few questions of my own. It is a difficult thing to describe, and some knowledge of their past history with alcohol helps me frame my attempts at re-creating the experience. I ask them if they normally drink hard liquor, whiskey in particular, neat or on the rocks. Few people do these days, of course, except yuppie hipsters who haunt bourbon bars (guilty) or the people whose last trip to Europe was in a uniform with a rifle. But if you do, then moonshine whiskey will likely taste quite familiar to you. You may really enjoy it. Warning: Pure corn liquor will smell awful. Don't let that faze you. Get past it and you are due for a treat: a clean, slightly sweet taste, hot on the back of the tongue and throat but smooth and pure tasting, hints of grain and sugar. If you get some good stuff from a guy who knows what he is doing, it is some of the most pure and clean liquor in the world.

On the other hand, if your idea of a "cocktail" involves something other than ice, tonic, or soda; if your martini comes in several dazzling colors; if your drink normally involves a blender, you will likely spit real moonshine out in the sink after a few choking sobs, your eyes blurry with tears. If fact, don't even try it. Trust me. Besides, it would be a waste.

But actual moonshine drinkers aren't necessarily sitting around slugging back white-hot liquor. If you probe the back cupboards of nearly any house in Franklin County, or check in the garage fridge, back behind that bloody hunk of venison, you will likely find a half-gallon mason jar of clear liquid with some kind of cut fruit suspended in it, most often peaches. This is the easiest way to give a bit of flavor to your 'shine and cut the heat a bit. When you have a taste of "peaches," as it is called, make sure you get an actual piece of the fruit and pop that in your mouth for a real surprise. It makes eating the worm in a bottle of tequila (mescal) seem like chewing breath mints.

Most people assume that all moonshine comes in one style, the clear, Everclear-type stuff. There are other types, like something called "crazy apple" which is like an apple brandy. The clear stuff, called "white mule" or "mule" or just "corn" (absolutely nobody calls it "moonshine"—people in the North created that term), is usually either doctored with fruit or mixed with a soft drink. In Franklin the soda of choice seems to be something called Sun Drop, a kind of regional Mountain Dew–type beverage. I've never seen this stuff for sale anywhere else in the world, and I'm sort of convinced that Franklin County moonshine is what keeps that little soft drink company in business.

But I'm afraid, unfortunate reader, that unless you are from Franklin County or related to someone who is, you will likely never be offered a drink of real mountain liquor. You will not see it out at parties. Nobody walks around with a glass of white mule on the rocks at a BBQ. No, it is still consumed the same way it has been for the last century: by men, in dark gravel parking lots or behind the barn, out of the open trunk of someone's Oldsmobile or from behind the seat of a pickup, using paper cups, ice unlikely, but usually a warm bottle of Sun Drop.

The first time I had some corn liquor I was a teenager in a shed with a dozen men in Carhartt coveralls and Philip Morris ball caps, quietly watching a scratchy NASCAR race on a TV from the 1960s. Nothing was ever said, I don't even really know how I *got* there, but at some point a guy handed me a plastic cup (opaque) with what looked like a slice of peach in heavy syrup. I sniffed it. I may have grown up in a prototypical leafy suburb in a major metropolitan area, but I had been around. I'd had a few drinks. So I slugged it back. I remember a guy in the corner, his face obscured by his cap, spat a stream of tobacco juice on the floor and let out a snort. You know that moment, right after the words leave your mouth, right after you swallow, when you swing at a bad pitch, when you wish you could take a decision back?

If you are offered a drink in Franklin, better put on your coat and kiss the wife good-bye, because you are definitely going outside and I'll guarantee a vehicle is involved.

In fact, you will almost never see a man in Franklin County drink *anything* in front of women and children. If you do, it will be in an opaque cup, plastic or paper, and it will remain off the table. I was in Franklin a few years ago for an aunt's birthday party, held in a large barn on my cousin's land. They had several long tables set up, laden with food, at least fifty cousins and friends, and when we sat down to eat, I was the only person there with a can of beer at the table. I wasn't the only one drinking, some of my uncles and cousins were positively ripped, but I was the only one that anybody *saw* drinking. And this is the county that *The New York Times* reported recently produces half a million gallons of illegal liquor a year. You could spend years there and never see it, even as it is all around you.

This strange relationship with liquor was one of the more interesting challenges I had to confront in *The Wettest County in the World*. The novel takes place in the 1920s and '30s, and people in Franklin have been making, selling, and drinking the stuff the same way for a century. It is a kind of secret world, a shadow behind the neatly mowed lawns and shining tobacco greenhouses. The people of Franklin are some of the friendliest people I've ever met, but there are things that they won't talk about and that you will never see. This was the insular world that I tried to project in my novel.

Acknowledgments

I AM INDEBTED TO T. Keister Greer's exhaustive account of the events of the 1935 trial taken from grand-jury testimony, titled *The Great Moonshine Conspiracy of 1935*. His book provided not only an overview of the often complex and confusing conspiracy, but also court transcripts of my grandfather and his brothers. The works of Sherwood Anderson obviously played a large role in my research, particularly *Kit Brandon; Dark Laughter; Winesburg, Ohio;* and his collected memoirs and letters. Probably the best book ever written on the topic of illegal liquor is Jess Carr's *The Second Oldest Profession: An Informal History of Moonshining in America*. Another invaluable resource was the Franklin County Historical Society and all of its generous and helpful volunteers. Their exhibits, photos, and records were a great aid, and I encourage anyone who is interested in this topic to visit this museum, situated in downtown Rocky Mount, the epicenter of the moonshine trade.

I would like to thank all of the early-draft readers of this book, including Seth Tucker, Mike Mannon, and K.S. I would also like to thank the various writers who have assisted me in some way with this, including Tony Early and Margot Livesey.

I would like to thank my agent, Alex Glass of Trident Media Group; my editor, Alexis Gargagliano; and all the fine folks at Scribner who made this process a pleasure.

I thank my family for their continued support and love.

And my wife, Stacy, my dearest friend and companion.

THE WETTEST COUNTY IN THE WORLD

QUESTIONS FOR DISCUSSION

1. Upon the death of his wife, Granville Bondurant says, "All the goodness has gone out of the world." What does he mean by his sentiments? How is each member of the remaining Bondurant family impacted by this death? How do they bear out Granville's sentiments?

2. Discuss the night that Forrest Bondurant's throat was cut at the County Line Restaurant. What do these events and the stories they spawned reveal about Forrest? Maggie? The community?

3. Discuss the symbolic significance of the opening sequence, the sow's slaughter. How does it relate to the novel's major themes?

4. Why do you think Matt Bondurant decided to make Sherwood Anderson, author of *Winesburg, Ohio*, one of the principal characters in the novel? What does Anderson allow the reader to understand about the Bondurants and the larger community in which they live? Discuss the parallels between this novel and Sherwood Anderson's own work.

5. Discuss the female characters in the novel. What is the role women play in this world? What do the women reveal about the men of Franklin County, particularly the three brothers?

6. How do the brothers and the people of Franklin County negotiate and make sense of their lives in relation to the natural world?

7. Jack thought of Howard as "some kind of machine or animal, reacting to the world in an instinctual manner." Why is this line of thought both comforting and frightening to Jack?

8. Explain the sequence of events that precipitates the Great Franklin County Moonshine Conspiracy Trial of 1935. What were the outcomes of the trial for the Bondurants?

9. What parallels does Anderson draw between the Bondurants' struggles and his own literary battles? Do you agree with his assessment? Why or why not?

10. What is the picture of the American psyche and way of life that emerges from Bondurant's story? What are the threats to this way of life? Where do you believe the author's sympathies lie? Where do yours?

Enhance Your Book Club

1. Who is Sherwood Anderson? What does Bondurant intend for us to understand about his inclusion in the novel? Consult www.bartleby.com/156/, which publishes an online version of Anderson's *Winesburg, Ohio*, a group of short stories about small-town life. What do his stories reveal about his point of view on the world? What do their narrative structure, style, and characterization allow us to understand about *The Wettest County in the World*?

2. Immerse yourself in the sounds of the era by purchasing and playing moonshine songs at your book club meeting. These songs tell their own tales of the moonshine lifestyle. You can listen to a sampling of the songs at these websites:

   - www.scopecreep.com/yahoo/2006/09/30/moonshine-songs/(http://new.music.yahoo.com/playlist/AF025089–4181–4C28-AE93-A11B290966A0)
   - www.rhapsody.com/goto?rcid=alb.12063326&variant=play&lsrc=RN_im

3. Want to sample moonshine? You can acquire legal moonshine called Virginia Lightning for your book club meeting by visiting and ordering from www.virginiamoonshine.com/vaLightning.html.

"[An] utterly engaging fable of bootlegging, revenge, and remorse . . . Bondurant will be compared to Cormac McCarthy. It's warranted: Both have a gift for describing brutality so clearly that we see beauty in the honesty."
—MEN'S JOURNAL

BASED ON THE TRUE STORY of Matt Bondurant's grandfather and two granduncles, *The Wettest County in the World* is a gripping tale of brotherhood, greed, and murder. The Bondurant Boys were a notorious gang of roughnecks and moonshiners who ran liquor through Franklin County, Virginia, during Prohibition and in the years after. When Sherwood Anderson, the journalist and author of *Winesburg, Ohio,* was covering a story there he christened it the "wettest county in the world." Anderson finds himself driving along dusty red roads, piecing together the clues linking the brothers to "The Great Franklin County Moonshine Conspiracy," and breaking open the silence that shrouds Franklin County.

In vivid, muscular prose, Matt Bondurant brings these men—their dark deeds, their long silences, their deep desires—to life. His understanding of the passion, violence, and desperation at the center of this world is both heartbreaking and magnificent.

"Bondurant is a nimble writer. . . . [His] prose is lyrical when the whiskey floods in, but also when the blood flows out." —THE NEW YORK TIMES BOOK REVIEW

"You have to go back to William Faulkner's novels about the Snopes clan to find the kind of cold-blooded Southern amorality that drives Matt Bondurant's second novel. . . . Bondurant's prose is thick with the kind of blood-soaked descriptions that would do Cormac McCarthy proud." —WASHINGTON CITY PAPER

"[An] engrossing novel . . . [Bondurant is] wonderful at evoking historical atmosphere—the elaborate stills camouflaged in the woods, the music, the drunken gatherings that explode into shattering violence." —ENTERTAINMENT WEEKLY

FEATURING A NEW AFTERWORD

MATT BONDURANT is the author of three novels, the most recent of which is *The Night Swimmer*. *The Wettest County in the World* (also published as *Lawless*) was a *New York Times Book Review* Editors' Choice and one of the *San Francisco Chronicle*'s 50 Best Books of the Year. His first novel, *The Third Translation*, was an international bestseller, translated into fourteen languages worldwide. He currently teaches literature and writing in the Arts and Humanities graduate program at the University of Texas at Dallas.

© STACY BONDURANT

EBOOK EDITION ALSO AVAILABLE

0110

MEET THE AUTHORS, WATCH VIDEOS AND MORE AT
SimonandSchuster.com
THE SOURCE FOR READING GROUPS

SCRIBNER

COVER DESIGN BY TIMOTHY GOODMAN
COVER PHOTOGRAPH COURTESY OF THE AUTHOR

ISBN 978-1-4   -8   **$15.00 U.S./$19.99 Can.**

51500

PRINTED IN THE U.S.A.

9 7814   1408